As It Was Written

As It Was Written

SUJATHA HAMPTON

Thomas Dunne Books New York
St. Martin's Press

This is a work of fiction. All of the characters, organizations, and events portrayed in this novel are either products of the author's imagination or are used fictitiously.

THOMAS DUNNE BOOKS.
An imprint of St. Martin's Press.

www.thomasdunnebooks.com
www.stmartins.com

Book design by Sarah Maya Gubkin

Library of Congress Cataloging-in-Publication Data

Hampton, Sujatha.
As it was written / Sujatha Hampton.—1st ed.
p. cm.
ISBN 978-0-312-58412-2 (alk. paper)
1. Physicians—Fiction. 2. Daughters—Fiction. 3. Blessing and cursing—Fiction. 4. McLean (Va.)—Fiction. 5. Family secrets—Fiction. 6. Domestic fiction. I. Title.
PS3608.A6963A9 2010
813'.6—dc22

2009040035

First Edition: February 2010

10 9 8 7 6 5 4 3 2 1

For my mother, Chandramathi,
who led me here

I am restless. I am athirst for far-away things.
My soul goes out in a longing to touch the skirt of
the dim distance.
O Great Beyond, O the keen call of thy flute!
I forget, I ever forget, that I have no wings to fly,
That I am bound in this spot evermore.

—RABINDRANATH TAGORE, *The Gardener* (1915)

As It Was Written

Long, Long, Never-ending Life

Gita rose from her table at the Au Bon Pain and carefully wiped away the crumbs. A passing employee murmured a quiet thank-you, to which Gita did not respond with so much as a smile. She did not even raise her eyes. It was much easier to pretend she hadn't heard the woman, and anyway, none of it made any difference. When she opened the door to leave, a breeze caught up in her hair and she turned her cheek to her shoulder to brush back a stray lock. The bony contact hurt her teeth. Her shoulders had grown so skinny they were like shards of broken glass under her tight skin. She turned to look at herself in the restaurant window and she breathed sharp. *My head has grown too large for my body; I look like a bobble-head doll. What will Chetta say?* It was the whole reason for going to the Au Bon Pain. The first full meal she had eaten in several weeks. A whole sandwich, a bag of chips, an apple and some juice. She wondered, staring at her feeble frame, if it would show by the time she saw him tonight.

When she arrived at her office ten minutes later, there was a line of students sitting. Just sitting there and waiting. She stopped midway down the corridor and lowered her head to her chest. She had forgotten about them. She raised her hands to her face and shook her head slowly. The poor students sitting on the ground, awaiting the beginning of office hours, there with their endless, endless queries, their constant failure to understand, their small noses and full lips, their faces blank with the total lack of comprehension, when really, what was it anyhow? English. It was only English. They all spoke it and most had spoken it every day of their lives since they were born, or anyway, close enough.

She took a deep breath and sighed loudly, so loudly that a few students, eyebrows up in alarm, gathered their half-written papers, their thickly packed leather satchels, their discarded sandals, and left, barefoot and trembling, for it was surely better to not understand at all and to put your shoes on out on the street than to sit and . . . *Meet with me? When did I turn into this?* Gita sighed again.

There were a few who remained nonetheless; it was hard for them, hoping they might find her in her glittering goodness, fearing, however, that there was just as much likelihood, more perhaps, that it would be this Dr. Nair they would find, the cold one. They entered her office one at a time and offered their bunko blah-blah-blah, their poorly conceived and even more poorly executed analyses of the something, something that was so dull and so average that she could barely even keep her mind focused while she read whatever paragraphs she read. Not one did she stick with to the end. It went in that difficult-to-witness way: Student hands his best work to professor for preliminary judgment, mostly because student feels the work is so elegantly rendered that professor might just hand over the A right then and there. Student, anticipating this, is sitting in seat opposite professor, containing his pride and waiting for the praise to come. Instead, professor, who is woefully beautiful, so beautiful it takes you fifteen minutes to recover every time you are around her—and her hard heart and her gleaming fury only make her that much more magnetically, frighteningly gorgeous—and instead of the praise he is so sure he deserves, the professor reads what cannot be more than six lines of text; throws the paper down on the desk in an exasperated slam; shakes her head back and forth, which throws her lustrous hair back and forth, further confusing the poor student; and says, "*Mr. Banks.* Mr. Banks? Are you coming here just to waste my time?" She is glaring at the poor student now and seems to be waiting for him to answer, which of course flummoxes him completely. She is staring and staring and staring and there is no way out. The very young Mr. Banks does not know what to say. She throws the paper at his chest and swivels around in her seat to face her desk, which is mountainous with work. She has told them she is writing a book, the story of her family curse. Despite her cruelty, her swift and acid tongue, her disdain, he wishes he could read what she was writing now. She is utterly brilliant in her every move, and sometimes, some sweet sometimes, she is so very gentle, offering tender understandings in such a quiet voice; sometimes her eyes fill with tears from the reading aloud of verse. And she is so woefully beautiful, as well.

He moves out of the office, she calls after him, "Send in the next one." The next one never comes. They listened at the door and when he emerged with his white face and blotchy, reddened eyes, they all got up to leave.

It was as she desired. She orchestrated it thus. She wondered: *When did I lose patience with every aspect of humanity?*

Gita sat in her office listening to the quiet hum of things and the periodic footfall in the corridor. Her door was decidedly closed, and why would anyone enter anymore? She was definitely alone. Her arms ached with the heaviness of their skin and bones and all that infernal blood. She sighed and shook her head; *I am barely worth the effort my body makes to stay alive.* She reached for the folder atop the rightmost heap on her desk. She read from notes for her new book in progress, so many theories to unravel. So many versions of the thing. There were facts that were unchallenged and then details that might change from the telling: the composition of Parameshwaran Namboodiri's paan chew, the identity of the boy who accompanied them back to his house when he stole her away, the exact moment when he decided that he would take her for his own. Some saying it was in the temple, others insisting he had talked of it from an earlier time, that he watched her at a Kathakali festival. Gita sighed, considering the magnitude of the work relative to her waning stores of energy. *Omanakumari had more courage at fourteen than I have at thirty-two.* Courage would be something to have, she has thought it many times. To Gita Nair, it seemed that courage might be the best attribute of humankind. *She was my own great-great-great-grandmother. And I am so weak.* She considered then that should this curse be true, it obviously could not apply to her. *I would hardly be a loss to the world if the old Brahmin's hand came down on me . . . cursing me would be a big, fat waste of time.*

But the writing would wait for no one, and tonight she would face her enormous, gigantic brother. She looked up at the clock and then down at her watch. *In these next hours, let me be fruitful in my writing that I might be stronger for the challenge of defending my skinny, my shockingly skinny body to my* chettan, *whose shouts might crumble my bones through my skin.* And thus fortified for the challenge, Gita picked up the next folder from the pile and began to work.

The Cursed Life of Sreemathi Omanakumari

Kerala, India

1849–1865

By
Gita Nair

Around each of her toes, Omanakumari weaved circlets of slim leaves and she danced them and secretly admired her feet. Nice, but they would be much improved with anklets that jingle-jangled. It was not quite light; the blue was cast with black and wet with all the dew that had not yet settled. She sat quietly in the corner of the veranda, and watched her morning toes, still clean and so dazzling in circlets of leaves. Her mouth poked out with the effort of not smiling out loud. If anyone was looking they would see a pretty, pretty girl with her mouth poked out, smiling with her chin and her cheeks and with her eyebrows. And on her eyebrows, any onlooker's gaze would linger, for they were long and sleek and visible even in the shadowed corner of the veranda.

Omanakumari lifted her eyes from her toes and looked out over the trees at the color of the day. Such promise in the dark blue sky, the first whiff of fire, the first tittery remark of a bird and then another's prompt retort. The receding of the night sounds into the day sounds; such promise there, every morning. Strand by strand she unwove her toes. She stood and cast her greens over the veranda and something flew out from somewhere and rustled the treetops. She inhaled the sour smell of the first things cooking on damp wood far enough away to smell only of smoke and not of food. She heard the woman Anjukutty shout angrily and with malice at a dog that had claimed her space. Water was thrown, it splashed and she heard this too.

Inside her house it was dark and she delighted in the quiet and the solitude of being awake. Karthika was sweeping bent low to the ground. She didn't look up, the misery of her life being equal whether she was alone or watched. Omanakumari entered the cooking space and poured water to her mouth and her mother came in. She was wiping her hands against her hips, drying them. Her hair was not yet tied up, but secured with a strand of itself, behind her neck and loose down her back. She had been milking and she was happy. Milking made Narayanikutty happy. She had a talent for this task and the cows gave and gave to her as they did for no one else. The cows made her special in that *taravad* as none were as gifted at cows as she.

"Did you take bath?" she asked, walking close and holding her daughter's face between her hands.

Omanakumari smiled with her eyebrows and her nostrils. "I am going now."

"What were you doing so far?"

"I was thinking."

"What were you thinking? About how little you do to be of help?"

"Yes, I was thinking just that."

"Mmmm, you are not even clean to be impudent."

"Better to be dirty when being impudent." Omanakumari's mouth trembled in its poked-out position, her eyes twinkled.

"Mmmm, like Anjukutty you will grow, screaming at dogs. That is what happens to impudent girls." Her mother's eyes sparkled too, but she smiled a full open smile that released her daughter's laughter to spill out onto the kitchen floor. It rolled about like marbles that got lost in crevices, never to be seen again.

Omanakumari lifted her mother's hands to her face and rubbed her nose against the skin that was moist and smelled of outside. She inhaled deeply, her morning kiss given with this most loving gesture. *I breathe you, Mother, bless my day.* Narayanikutty bent her face to her daughter's hair and did the same: *I breathe you, child. Go forth with my blessings.*

The alarm on Gita's watch sounded with a pulsing insistence and reluctantly she lifted her head from her pages. It was time to go. A page slipped from under her fingers and slid to the floor underneath her desk. She bent to retrieve it and felt her blouse fluffing and puffing out from her pants, and as she stood up she felt the void around her middle. She was afraid there would be no hiding that, and how to wear a poncho when the weather was so warm? Then suddenly a thought! She brightened: *I will wear a sari, I will wear a puffy, cotton sari!* And with this, Gita gathered her things and hurried to her place to change. Her brother was coming home from Kerala today, and she would put on a puffy sari that would hide the points of her hips, and the bones of her shoulders, and the slightly bluish tint of her arms, and she would arrive to greet him thus camouflaged. And in a puffy cotton sari, hidden behind her five darling and very fat nieces, perhaps she could deflect all scrutiny for one more evening. From her dwindling size. From the secrets of her new book. From the misery of her long, long, never-ending life.

The Journey

Dr. Raman Nair collapsed in his seat, exhausted. His gargantuan carry-on, stuffed with what might be elbows or periscopes or some other pointy and protrusive objects, splayed across the aisle. The thought of cramming this monstrosity under the seat filled him with . . . yes, it was true . . . it filled him with despair. But there would be no point in delaying. One way or another, he would have to manage to get through the twenty-two-hour plane ride home from India. Standing again, he took a deep breath, braced his back and lifted the clanking bag forward. With a heaving push and the full force of his nearly 250-pound body, he squeezed it under the seat. Panting and dabbing the perspiration from his brow, he again fell into his seat. It was a monumental ordeal.

His neighbor chuckled. "My dear sir, what a project your bag, eh?" He reached out a friendly hand and patted Dr. Raman Nair on the shoulder.

Dr. Raman Nair shook his head resignedly and sighed again. In a low and sonorous voice he lamented, "O . . . ooo . . . this bag, I have been carrying it for one thousand miles. It might as well have been on my back. And I might as well have been on foot!"

"Is it heavy?"

"Heavy!! Oh goodness gracious! It weighs like the Himalayas, but has none of their charm or beauty! A bulky madness, a prodigious weight, without even the grace to be pleasing to the eye, or even surely beneficial to the recipient!"

"What is it?"

Dr. Raman Nair sighed a prolonged breath. "Brahmi oil."

"That whole bag has Brahmi oil?"

"And only Brahmi oil."

"What on earth for? That is a lot of Brahmi oil."

"Sixty-eight bottles."

"Sixty-eight bottles of Brahmi oil? What on earth for?!"

"An intractable affliction."

"Yours?"

"My nephew's."

"Why didn't you ship it . . . or check it in?" There was a clinking as the person in front settled into his seat. His neighbor reached down and shook the bag a bit, perhaps to ascertain that indeed there were bottles within.

Dr. Raman Nair paused and measured his words. He dropped his chin to his chest in defeat. "My sister would not allow it." Without letting his neighbor respond, he continued, "Chechi's son, he is very good. He is a very good boy, my nephew, he is a medical resident, Johns Hopkins University, but with a chronic affliction for which he can find no relief. It worsens in the winter." Here he paused again. "Winter will be fast approaching."

Before the plane had even taken off, a small seep sprang in the bottom of this bag. By the time they landed to change planes in London, Dr. Raman Nair and his sympathetic neighbor both felt that simply by having inhaled this ayurvedic remedy for fourteen hours, neither could ever be afflicted by whatever curse plagued Chechi's son so chronically, and even worse in the winter.

As Dr. Raman Nair was crossing the Atlantic on his way home, his illustrious nephew, Manoj, with the chronic problem that worsened in winter, was faced with a dilemma. George needed him to cover call.

Squinting in the bed, bleary-headed with fatigue, what was he to do? Say no? Dive back under the covers and sleep off what had been his own exhausting call night? How could he do that when his friend, his colleague, his countryman even, the good George Thomas, had had his car burgled again in the middle of the night? Again?

"I have no shoes." George sighed.

"No shoes?"

"They were in the car."

"What were you wearing on your feet?"

"It's four A.M. I was barefoot."

Hmm . . . there was no point in pursuing it. Manoj sighed and carefully rubbed his head. "I have to pick my *ammavan* up at Dulles tomorrow. He'll be . . . really, really mad if I am late."

"I'll get there. I just need to call the insurance company. And . . . I need to get some shoes. And then I'll catch the bus in. But I just got paged. I can't . . . you know . . . I don't have any shoes."

He could hear George's deep exhale. *It's true. You can't go to work with no shoes.* Manoj rubbed his hand down his face. "You know what, George?"

"What?"

"You really need to move."

George sighed again. This was most definitely true.

A Fitting Arrival

Dr. Raman Nair stood amid the fray, struggling to remove his suitcases from the circling conveyor belt. He was fatter than normal, swollen from the trip, and his white *kurta pajama* was soaked with the sweat of his efforts. His grip slipped from the handles again and again, and his continual wiping was of no use. One hand would not do, for inside each bag was enough for three more. His *chechi* was an artful packer, and when she removed all the items from his giant duffel to accommodate her son's remedies, she had promised to make it all fit.

The gigantic Dr. Raman Nair, bloated and on edge, couldn't have mistaken his luggage even if it were not labeled so many times with placards covered over with cellophane tape and further ignobly marked by one hundred miles of lime green bungee cords (by his own extremely delightful apple-of-his-eye *chechi*, the root cause of all his frustration), for they matched, man and bags. They were, all three, black and bulging at the seams. In the heady delirium that followed his arrival from such an exhausting journey, even he himself was able to see the resemblance. He looked about in embarrassment.

His slightly askew stance, straddling the sopping Brahmi oil bag to prevent further breakage, was throwing off his balance, and he had already watched his luggage make two or three turns around the belt, when once more he lost hold with his greasy grip and was forced to release at the last minute. Dr. Raman Nair pursed his purple lips and fumed. *A fall onto the conveyor belt holding tight to my Samsonite would be just exactly the thing at this moment. I will lose my steps with my oily sandals, fall on my head here and be flipped and rolled like a* papadam *until I tumble down the chute and am unceremoniously dumped onto a cart on the tarmac and returned to my homeland in the underbelly of a giant 747. Where is Manoj? That boy should be here now waiting for me, ready to be of service, and instead, I arrive, the oily, stinking one, grease on my silk* juba *and every other part of me, private and exposed, and still he is not here.*

He grabbed the blackened-wet handles of his duffel and threw it behind him out of the way. He heard another bottle crack, but what difference did it make at this point? Turning back toward the carousel, he readied himself for the return of his suitcases.

Dr. Raman Nair was somewhat astonished, upon later reflection, to learn that he still had access to his preternatural instincts, because at the moment he turned away from his leaking bag he felt a tingling in his body that seemed to indicate imminent disaster. He actually remembered shuddering. And that was surely at least several seconds before a little boy racing through the airport at full speed, running from the outstretched fist of his brother, hit the Brahmi oil–coated perimeter of his enormous, bulbous, carry-on bag. Even with all he had been through, Dr. Raman Nair never imagined such consequences.

The first boy hit the oily floor with his left foot, skated in arabesque for a graceful moment, his right leg extended behind him, until he struck the bag with his shin and was sent hurtling into the air in a remarkably arced trajectory. Approximately three seconds later, the second boy, who looked exactly like the first boy, followed behind with the same series of missteps.

As one child and then another flew through the air over the upturned heads of hundreds, perhaps thousands, of Indians and the implements of their overseas travel, a general "Ooooooohhh . . . aaaaaaaahhhh" was exhaled by the dazed crowd, who didn't exactly know what this was about. Dr. Raman Nair, on the other hand, was horrified. There was nothing he could do. Despite the fact that he had been tingling with prescience, he was so surprised and taken so unaware that he had not even extended his hand to perhaps stop them preflight. He just watched with the rest as they went up, up, up, and when they fell in a heap atop a providentially placed pile of empty suitcase cartons, he was at their side before they even opened their eyes.

"Oh my God, my goodness. Oh my God. My goodness," he repeated again and again, clutching the two stupefied boys to his enormous chest.

Suddenly, out of nowhere, he was pounced on by a tiny mite of a woman who pounded his substantial back with her fists, her bangles clanking and scraping. "Let them go, let them go," she shouted into his ear. With one hand this lady pounded and with the other she bent back the fingers of Dr. Raman Nair, Ph.D., son of M. T. Pankajakshi, also known as Ammukutty, and Dr. T. Gopal Nair, the first dentist of Kerala. Dr. Nair was, of course, completely shocked. He was already mortified to witness the airborne result of the ill-fated placement of his bag. The whole trip—from Kannur to London to New York to Washington—he had been burdened with this monstrosity of a valise. Four enormous cases of Brahmi oil, the bottles unpacked to fit the duffel, wrapped in sheets of *Manorama* newspaper despite his vociferous complaints about what was sure to be an irritating crinkle and clink as he grunted the bag halfway around the earth, all to no avail. Chechi would not be dissuaded in sending her good boy Manoj (who still had not shown up) this sure cure for his chronic dandruff that was a constant source of discomfort and humiliation and worsened in the winter. He loved his *chechi* so, and she loved her son so, and he loved him too, so he had obediently followed her orders and not checked it and not shipped it and had been alternatively cursing her and apologizing to God and everyone else for the past twenty-four hours. And now, to have reached finally his destination, considering himself, as the saying goes, "home free," only to have slung a pair of small children through the air with the force of a trebuchet all because of this ridiculous boy's dandruff! This was the final injustice! he thought. Until, of course, he was bushwhacked by this ferocious woman who seemed to be the boys' mother.

Thus was the state of affairs when Manoj, who got stuck covering not *one* but *three* emergency surgeries while George went shoe shopping, arrived on the scene panting from the parking lot. His uncle, on the floor clutching two small boys to his chest while a sari-draped lady desperately tried to kill him. Manoj looked down at his watch; he was forty minutes late. He sighed; there would be hell to pay. And then he dove in. He uncoiled the mother from his uncle; he righted the toppled and smothered children and, when he finally extended a now mysteriously greasy hand to his uncle, he was alarmed at the look in his eye. Dr. Raman Nair grabbed Manoj's hand, rose from the ground and stood glowering at him in a purple-faced vex. "Hmph," he muttered.

Manoj stood bewildered. His eyelashes swept up beyond his one long eyebrow; his hair was so black, so shiny, so thick, it looked almost fertile, as though seeds could be germinated simply by burying them in his hair. And of course, it was for this hair that Dr. Raman Nair had traversed the hemisphere so encumbered. Annoyed and aching, he could not help but take a long and silent look at this mass of gleaming blackness that in all likelihood, now that ayurvedic nourishment was imminent, would grow its own brain and vascular system. *The boy will now have nerve cells in there. He will grow unable to have haircuts, he will have to wind it atop his head like a Sartharji and then his mother will regret that she thought this was such a necessary thing.*

"Boy!! Why are you late—you know what trouble you caused? Forcing me to put down that infernal bag of potions!" Dr. Nair smacked Manoj lightly on the head, releasing a shower of dandruff.

"I am sorry, Ammavan, I had some emergencies!" Manoj replied, delicately combing his hair back into place. "What happened?!"

"I'll tell you in the car," and together uncle and nephew quickly escaped the airport.

The Five Fat Daughters of Dr. Raman Nair

When Dr. Nair arrived home after his long ordeal, he was greeted by his five angelic, loving, extremely fat daughters, the very joy of his life; his sister, Gita, who looked like she was hung on a hanger in the hot sun to dry; and also by one somewhat less than angelic, somewhat more than loving, strikingly tall Great Dane, named Taj Mahal because he was huge, white, expensive and very beautiful. Absent from the scene was Dr. Nair's wife, Jaya, the only small thing living in the house. She had dashed to the grocery store to buy whole milk. During her husband's two-month journey, she had immediately switched them to skim. Week after week she guiltily threw away gallons of milk, her children being brainwashed against the skim, until in this last month when she bought only the half gallon, and felt only half as guilty. She had read an article in the newspaper that simply switching to skim milk could reduce ten pounds over the course of a year. As she had only two months, and each of her daughters had at least five times as much to lose, she had gone to more drastic measures: no rice. The rice was a ludicrous proposition, for without it there was nothing to sop up the curry, and of course she had to make rice for her father-in-law, and if there was rice for Muthachan there might be rice for all of them. She made only half cups in saucepans, but by dinnertime, invariably, she would find there was a whole platter on the table, and of that, only half a cup went to Muthachan and the rest disappeared into the bellies of her own jiggling girls. It was the miracle of the rice, making half a cup feed everyone until they could barely rise from the table. They laughed at her consternation, and called her Jesus. In the two months her husband was gone, the girls remained the same and Jaya lost ten pounds; she had refused to eat the rice on principle.

Entering his brightly lit home, Dr. Raman Nair was flooded with satisfaction and happiness. Never before had a trip to Kerala been so difficult. So many problems, so many issues to handle, so much money to be doled out among family, relative strangers, and then to complete strangers as well. Never before had there been such a continuous parade of charities seeking contributions, one person after another with medical needs, children in trouble, houses to be fixed, businesses to be financed. Though this was nothing new, never before had he left feeling that perhaps he was being used, even by some in his own family. And then, looking around at all he had, and at his well-educated, beautiful children; his sister, whose loveliness and intelligence shone even through her bony anger and her deliberately chosen puffy sari; and his nephew, who was such a constant pride despite his dandruff and its resultant impact on his travel, how could he fail to be generous? Loudly, he sighed and sank into a kitchen chair.

In the garage, his dog barked loud and strong because the green bungee cord wrapping the suitcases seemed to herald something that needed attention, and Manoj and Usha, the third daughter, were struggling to get them in the door. Recognizing that another hand would be helpful, Taj was running round and round and between their legs, barking at them, insisting they use his mighty back. Resting the bag on the threshold, Manoj considered it.

From the kitchen and out of sight, Dr. Raman Nair shouted, "Do NOT use my dog to carry the luggage!"

The two humans continued their task. Usha quietly whispered that she would go get a laundry basket from inside and unpack the second suitcase in the garage, when from the kitchen again her father shouted, "Do NOT unpack my suitcase in the garage." As an afterthought he added, "Use your strength!"

The Brahmi oil bag was still in the trunk sitting atop a pilfered white lab coat that Manoj was grateful to have had in his purple Probe.

The verdigris stain would seem like just one more bodily fluid and no one would ever know that his uncle had come ten thousand miles shoving, kicking, and rolling this leaky sack so that he might find some relief. Quietly, Manoj pushed the enormous suitcase with his cousin, who periodically shouted out in irritation, "Dad, why did you put so much tape on this bag? You had a luggage tag, jeez. Does everyone in the world have to know from all angles that this is your bag and not theirs?" She was annoyed by sticky things. The DR. RAMAN NAIR placards were beginning to show the signs of wear and drooped at the edges, exposing their adhesive and the grime that had adhered. "Now everyone in the airport and all the baggage handlers know that 'Dr. Raman Nair lives at 1071 Timber Church Road, McLean, Virginia 22102 USA.'" Her brows were knit with strain and through her grunting effort still she complained, "You know, you don't live here by yourself, you have a houseful of women to protect. Do you honestly think that eight signs would do anything more than your luggage tag to get your bag here safely?"

Manoj crooked his face, knowing fully the handiwork of his mother, who had never gone farther than Bangalore in the bus. He feared his *ammavan* might speak against her, being so tired and frustrated, and the thought of it made Manoj homesick. From nowhere, he caught a whiff of Remalayam, his home.

Sharply from the kitchen, Dr. Raman Nair called again, "I think that I will tape placards on the front door for when the baggage handlers come. They will say in large bold print, 'The third of the lovely daughters of Dr. Raman Nair talks too much and doesn't know when to stop. She can be found directly at the top of the stairs, first door to the right. You may take her if you wish, though I do not advise it.' I will write nine signs, in case eight is not enough."

Manoj smiled with gratitude. He smelled his home with every puff of air exhaled by the suitcase bouncing against his legs and his cousin's chest on its way back across the threshold of 1071 Timber Church Road. Standing them up in the kitchen, Manoj and Usha stood aside bathed in sweat, and the remaining four daughters of Dr. Raman Nair encircled the enormous bags wondering what could possibly be inside.

Sitting at the long table, the luggage safely unloaded, Taj Mahal at his feet, surrounded by his five cherubic daughters; his beautiful, skinny sister; and his brilliant, handsome nephew, all that was missing was his pretty wife and, consequently, a perfect cup of tea, as Gita's never tasted as good. And as always, at just the moment this thought materialized in his mind, his tiny wife returned with proper milk.

"AAAaah-ha, you've come! Then . . . Did you drink tea?" Jaya looked about expectantly at her daughters and sister-in-law.

Dr. Raman Nair was momentarily startled, not by her entrance, but rather by her appearance. "What happened to you?" He stood up from his seat and hobbled over on swollen feet to poke at her sunken cheeks. Her polka-dotted shirt, untucked from too much empty space between her waist and her pants, made her look like a homeless woman and he longed to pull her to him and tuck it in.

Usha, plunked down at the table, raised her head and without thinking exclaimed, "Skim milk." Her sisters looked at one another aghast. Now they would have to endure the . . .

"*Skim milk?*" He looked around the room at all of them. "*Skim milk*? In my house? Skim milk?!!" Dr. Raman Nair wished he weren't so bone tired; still though, one could only be vigorous about skim milk. Jaya looked at her middle daughter with a dark brow. Usha saw the deep sense of betrayal in her mother's lips and wished that she ever thought to just be quiet. As it was too late, she shook it off and considered instead going a different route to reingratiate herself to her mother.

Sitting up and serious, renewed of strength, seemingly by her commitment to the argument she was about to pursue, she began, "We really ought to switch, Dad, all of us, I mean you too. Not only would it be healthier in general, but we really ought to consider the weight-loss benefits." Looking back at her mother, she saw the brow clear and love sparkle in her eyes. Restored, she slumped back down.

"Healthier?" Dr. Raman Nair's voice raised and he put his finger in the air like a torch, which he was wont to do when making an irrefutable point. "What is healthy about skim milk? Is it the calcium? Much research has told us that there are better sources. Instead, eat broccoli and yogurt and you have all the calcium. Is it the reduction of fat? If that is the purpose, why drink skim milk at all? Why not drink water? Is it the vitamin D? We get sufficient vitamin D from sunshine, pure and simple. And if all this is so, and it is, then what is healthier about skim milk?" Dr. Raman Nair rounded the kitchen counter and stood over the table with his finger raised and his eyes pointed at each of them in turn. "One dash in my tea and I should have skim milk? The sight of the blue sheen in my refrigerator makes me lose all appetite."

"Another overlooked weight-loss benefit of skim milk—complete loss of appetite," Usha retorted wryly.

"You shut up, girl; the problem with this one is she never knows when to shut up." Dr. Raman Nair continued, now turning to his suddenly wan and skinny wife, "Is it in this way that I come home from a simple two months' absence to find you nearly wasted away to nothing, a waif, looking like . . . looking like . . . ," he looked furiously around the room, "looking like—*her*!" He stood his full height staring his wife in the eye, pointing a shaking finger at his sister, Gita, who sank inch by inch down her seat. Jaya looked at him and silently pursed her lips, being that it was exactly the way she had lost so much weight. She felt that she did not, however, look *that* bad. "I do not look *that* bad."

"You do. You definitely do." Looking up at the ceiling again, he went on, "Skim milk is a fraud perpetrated on foolish people. It has no nutritional values that outweigh its vile appearance and vomity taste, as does soy, for example." Pointing at them each in turn, he underscored, "*It-has-no-place-in-a-house-full-of-growing-children.*"

Manoj's eyes widened. His *ammavan*'s finger-pointing; the skim-milk diatribe; the irony of his *ammai*'s rapid weight loss, while his cousins crowded every inch of the perimeter of this outsized table—the irony was really too much to resist interjecting with mock horror, "Oh my God, are they still GROWING?" Realizing his mistake too late, and not having any quick recourse of action, being wedged in at the table, tight as a jack under a flat-tired school bus, he winced and braced himself.

When they all five turned at once to glare at him, the combined momentum of their gigantic breasts, each pair bumping the next sister's and then the next, resulted in a g-force that squeezed him from the table and shot him to the floor like a spat watermelon seed. From his new perspective, they looked particularly formidable, especially all together as they were, and he was more than a little afraid that though they were gentle and beautiful, they might decide to sit on him.

With narrowed eyes, Usha looked down from where she sat, the only one who would know, and squarely said, "SHUT up, Dr. Dandruff,

I already looked in that bag you stashed in your trunk. Is all that nasty oil for *our* problem or for *yours*?"

Manoj stroked his hair defensively, but remained quiet under the table, afraid to get up. Gita sank lower and lower and seemed to completely fade away, hidden inside her puffy, cotton sari. Dr. Nair, unsettled when he lost the floor, put both his hands in the air and announced to the general assembly, "Children, stop it, stop it. I am tired. I have had a most vexing trip."

They entered his life one just after the other, like perfectly flowing lines of verse: Veena, Mira, Usha, Dhanya and Shanti, aged twenty-six, twenty-four, twenty-two, seventeen and fifteen, because there was nothing he loved more than the sight of his beloved wife pregnant, with one in her arms, and another wrapped around her leg. Her long, black, lush, wavy hair was ever so much longer, blacker, lusher and wavier when she was carrying one of these gorgeous girls. Only girls could make a beautiful woman even more beautiful, or so the wives' tale told. It was certainly so in Jaya Nair's case.

The five daughters of Dr. Raman Nair were legendary in their domestic abilities, in their precocious talents, in their gracious temperaments, and of course, in their prodigious size. Never had a family of American-born Indian girls been given the same careful guidance with regard to traditional cooking, from shopping for the ingredients, to preparation of the vegetables, to grinding of the spices with a mortar and pestle. If they were together, they could prepare an entire *sadhya* themselves, without the assistance of their mother. For this alone, they were held in high regard by all the friends and colleagues of Dr. Raman Nair. He looked at them always with great pride.

Then these same girls could sing, they could dance, they each played the piano. They studied other things; they liked to study things; they learned things quickly and used the things they learned to learn other things, like learning violin because they played the piano, or learning Italian because they knew French. They taught each other the things they learned, and sometimes Dr. Raman Nair would peep into the room of his youngest daughter, Shanti, to catch her leaned against the shoulder of his oldest daughter, Veena, watching her *chechi* finish a complicated stitch in a hand-knit sweater that later they would present him as a surprise for no reason at all, though it was summer, because the yarn was on sale then, and they were, in addition to all their other qualities, frugal as well.

The beautiful daughters of Dr. Raman Nair laughed all the time and when the doorbell rang, they all went running along with Taj the dog, because they were similarly eager to have one more person around, or three or four, and if there were four, they would immediately call it a party and begin to cook and laugh, and pull out the photo albums that showed the pictures of the last time these four people came to visit, or the first time these people came to visit, and they would feed them with great care, and one would be standing beside to refill the glasses, and another would heap in a bit more fish, or rice, or a small spoonful of mango pickle, and they would chatter just right about current events, or funny stories, and ask just the right number of questions about just the right subjects, with just the right level of curiosity without nosiness, and when these four people left, they would get into their car and sigh and say to each other, "I can't wait until the next time they throw a party." Even if there never had been a party, but simply some saris to pick up, or some check to drop off, or simply stopping by because they were in the neighborhood. Dr. Raman Nair would close the door behind the company and turn back into his house, glowing with great pride.

Everyone in the world loved the daughters of Dr. Raman Nair, and perhaps it was because of this that their enormous, gigantic, astounding size made so little difference to them. They did not seem to be bothered that together they could barely fit in Veena's adorable Audi. When they all took a deep breath and inserted themselves, cushioned against each other and certain that the steel frame of the car would hold them in place until they reached their destination, they didn't even mention the discomfort. And because they could each sew, they looked spectacular always. Their clothes fit to perfection, and their hair was so remarkably lustrous and thick and their faces were, every one of them, absolutely breathtaking, so that really, between their irresistible personalities, their sensational clothes and their supershiny, extra-glossy, curly or wavy or mirror-straight hair, they turned heads everywhere they went.

And because they were so happy, and so bright, and so accomplished, and so beloved, the five fat daughters of Dr. Raman Nair had healthy self-esteem and no body issues. And because they had healthy self-esteem and no body issues, they were accustomed to their fair share of attention from men (though they really didn't pay much heed), because nothing is more attractive in the long run than a woman who feels she is beautiful, especially if she never bothers to think about it at all. And beyond all that, the five fat daughters of Dr. Raman Nair were endowed with the largest, juiciest, roundest and most irresistible pairs of breasts ever seen in the universe. And the five pairs of breasts of Dr. Raman Nair's daughters were a never-ending source of distress among hotel porters, taxi drivers, shoe salesmen, and the diminutive clerks at the India store, who were often forced to share small spaces with these five girls and their ten breasts, crammed in tight, leaning forward, squeezed together. Every once in a while, one of these men would whimper aloud from the strain of reining in his hands and mouth. He would turn in his lips and his eyes would tear up and then he would utter a pitiful whimper and drop his gaze in shame. Being the girls that they were, when this happened, they all gathered in closer to assure he was okay, they felt his head, they held his hands, and they looked deeply into his eyes with theirs, long-lashed and limpid. Every once in a while, one of the whimpering men thus fainted into their formidable chests, never to know that he had been there. When this happened, the girls would lower him gently to the ground, they would loosen his shirt and massage his chest, and once in a while, Veena, Mira, Usha, Dhanya or once even Shanti would have to give him CPR. When the poor man awoke, he would be told by his coworkers that he had been laid down, undressed, massaged and essentially kissed by one of the five fat daughters of Dr. Raman Nair while the others encircled him on their knees, bent forward with concern, hands resting on his thighs or abdomen. When he realized he had slept through it all, he would curse his weak constitution, and wish he had the talent to have faked the whole thing.

Baby George

In Rochester, Minnesota, everyone was freezing much of the year, but some were more freezing than others. In one very lovely neighborhood called Brookstone Lake, on a maple-lined street that was naturally called Maple Street, lived the perpetually freezing Dr. CV Thomas and his frozen wife Elizabeth. These were Baby George's parents.

From October until May for the entire thirty-three years he had lived in the States, CV had awakened every day and uttered the same oath, "Damn, I'm cold." And his wife would get out of bed, squeeze her face in tight and say, "Oh . . . so cold." Then she would make him a cup of tea. In his first letter home to his best friend, Chandrasekar, the physics *sar*, Thomas had written only this:

JANUARY 22, 1965

My dear Chandrasekar,

This place is buried in snow. You may think I am only exaggerating, but I am not. If I had a camera I would take a photo. Right now, there is 1½ meters of snow on the ground and it is steadily snowing. I am so cold I can barely breathe. Luckily, the hostel for Fellows is only a short walk from the hospital. But when my

Elizabeth comes from Kerala, I have to move to the married student hostel and that is quite a long, long walk. Luckily again, she comes only in June.

Your friend,
CV Thomas

One month later, Chandrasekar received another letter:

FEBRUARY 27, 1965

My dear Chandrasekar,

I enjoyed receiving your letter; it is a lonely life here, like a Polar Bear. It is so cold your eyes water like sorrow when you step outside and then before you reach up to wipe the tears away, they have frozen to your face. You may think I am exaggerating, but I am not. In the month since I have arrived I have bought a pair of rubber boots with a lining and a heavy coat. They were very expensive, but necessary. I will buy one for Elizabeth in May when the prices go down. My work is fine. Please send my regards to your mother and father and everyone else.

Your friend,
CV Thomas

Chandrasekar received this letter with some astonishment. What kind of cold was this?

MARCH 11, 1965

My dear CV,

I cannot imagine how cold it must be there. I went to the library and looked up your place, but I could only find information about the Mayo Clinic, and nothing so descriptive about the weather. I am enclosing a card with a colored photograph of the boat races at Alleppey. It looks warm in the picture, so maybe it will help you forget your troubles. I am very eager to hear about your studies and your experience in U.S. Please tell me about all you are doing there! Everyone here sends their regards.

Your friend,
K. O. Chandrasekar

April 15, 1965

My dear Chandrasekar,

Best regards to your family. I received the letter you sent and thank you for the wonderful card that was enclosed. I keep it in the edge of my mirror and it fortifies me for my walk to the hospital. When I think of Kerala I feel a longing in my heart that is difficult to manage. Yesterday there was another snow and the first 100 snows had not melted at all (it is like a world made entirely of snow) and it is very, very cold. And it is so cold that once I come home, I do not feel to go back outside to socialize. I have gone to the hardware store and bought a type of plastic sealant that is called Xcellseal that has decreased the amount of cold that enters my place. And the wife of one of the attending physicians was kind enough to give me some old draperies and I believe that has made a difference. They say it will warm up next month. I am waiting.

Your friend,

CV Thomas

Elizabeth arrived from Kerala in a pink sari that nearly matched the color of her dimpled cheeks. When he saw her nervous face searching the crowd, alone, afraid, he was overcome for many moments, his emotion misting his eyeglasses. When she joined him, they stood staring and grinning shyly. It was like they barely knew one another. It was like they were already very deeply in love. It was a very good beginning.

One year later, CV and Elizabeth gave birth to their first child, Theresa, who was so lovely no one noticed her expression was a bit vacant. Elizabeth was alone with her baby, without a mother or a grandmother, or even a friend to tell her about some baby they had seen somewhere once, who flapped her arms or shrieked like a monkey when the mustard seed popped in hot oil. Theresa, with shining black curls and chubby rosy cheeks, who never seemed to smile and who never cuddled her mother, was too pretty for the doctors to believe a first-time mother's nagging and persistent refrain that something just wasn't right. They told her to make friends with other mothers. They said to lay her fears to rest.

But by two, other children were talking and playing with things and laughing with one another while Theresa, with her eyelashes so long and her lips so red, sat alone in the corner staring blankly at a green plastic shovel, and gently stroking her elbow.

⁂

With great faith, Elizabeth prayed. Nine times a day, for nine days on, and then nine days off, again and again. Without fail. For five years. What to do, then, but adore to distraction the miraculously healthy, too precious to hope for answer to five years of unswerving prayers to St. Jude of Hopeless Cases?

Most holy apostle, St. Jude, faithful servant and friend of Jesus, the Church honors and invokes you universally as the patron of hopeless cases, of things almost despaired of. Pray for me, I am so helpless and alone. Make use I implore you of that particular privilege given to you, to bring visible and speedy help where help is almost despaired of. Come to my assistance in this great need that I may receive the consolation and help of heaven in all my necessities, tribulations and sufferings, particularly that we could have another child most particularly a boy, *that I may praise God with you and all the elect forever.*

I promise, O blessed St. Jude, to be ever mindful of this great favor, to always honor you as my special and powerful patron, and to gratefully encourage devotion to you.

Amen.

And so Baby George was born. He grew up in a weird home, balanced between two women who were relentless in their need for him. Theresa could only be calmed by his presence, and his mother suffered in her love for him. Her every breath rose and fell thinking of how best to please him, to ease his burdens, though he had no burdens at all except them. She followed him around, force-feeding him sweets and fruit. She forbade sports as too dangerous; she sat beside him while he did his homework; she accompanied him to the bathroom when he peed. And yet, George was a very good boy.

For poor CV, George was a true mystery. He was so good, so patient, so accepting of his sister and so gentle with his mother, and never a word of his needs. How had this happened? CV wondered.

"You let him go to sleep by himself, he is not a baby, let him grow up," CV would say every night, standing from his chair and pointing his finger at the two of them heading up the stairs.

"Of course he isn't a baby! We are praying together; you could join us instead of sitting there finding fault. Families pray together." Then she would turn to her son and adoringly ask, "Georgiekutty? Don't you like to pray with Mommy?"

George would look into his mother's besotted gaze and his guilt was too crushing. "Yes, Mom."

"Ha!" Elizabeth would declare, pointing in triumph. They would proceed up the stairs to the bathroom, where she would wait outside the door for him to pee.

It seemed it would always be this way, and that is the thing with life. It is only this way until it is not. On George's fourteenth birthday, his best friend gave him a *Penthouse* magazine. It was an old one he had taken from his father's collection in the closet. The boys sat together looking at every page over and over, crossing and recrossing their legs. Gleefully, George put it in his backpack and boarded the bus quivering with anticipation. With his backpack in his lap, George closed his eyes and saw scenes he had never imagined, titillating him all the way home. Arriving at his bus stop, he blinked several times, and tried hard to compose himself. He was still carrying his backpack in front of him, smiling secretly, when he saw his mother looking out the kitchen window waiting for him to return from school. Like a slap in the face, her eager expression took the wind out of his pubescent sails. He slung his bag over his shoulder and headed up the walk.

Elizabeth and Theresa both rushed him like groupies, kissing and pawing all over his face. CV, who had come home early to celebrate his son's birthday, stood in the doorway and watched the spectacle with a clinical disapproval. He could see the irritation in George's face; certainly Elizabeth should be able to see it as well. George ran upstairs, neglecting to retrieve the backpack his sister had knocked to the floor, saying he needed to go to the bathroom, the only place he could be alone. Elizabeth immediately picked it up and opened it, to see what all homework needed to be done before they could begin the festivities. Taking one look inside, she gasped and fainted, right there in the foyer. Rushing to her side, CV caught a glimpse inside the open bag, which she had dropped in her fall. The magazine was opened to a particular page, the cover bent backward to expose two women with their fingers between each other's legs; one was chewing on the other's breast and that one had her head thrown back in ecstasy. At the moment CV removed the offending periodical from the backpack, George came rushing frantically down the stairs, eyes wide with fright. And there they were face to face, father and son, one smiling vaguely with his eyebrows arched, the other nearly collapsed from terror and mortification. Theresa had wandered away when her brother left the scene, and Elizabeth, thankfully, was still passed out on the floor.

"What is this?" CV asked, calmly and with a slight smile.

"I . . . I mean, it's nothing, well, I didn't buy it, I mean, I didn't even ask to see it or anything, I mean, it's nothing. Well, it was a gag gift, like a birthday gift. I just got it today, I swear to God."

"Don't involve Him; I doubt he had much to do with it." CV was looking through the magazine. It had been a long time since he had seen one of these.

"I really just got it today. I didn't even ask for it or anything. It was a gag . . . but . . ." And then Baby George started to cry, big sobbing tears of humiliation and frustration. He ran back up to his room and threw himself down on his bed, covering his head with his arms.

CV took the magazine and the backpack and headed up the stairs. George's room was spare, no embellishment. He stood in the doorway a moment and watched George heaped on the plain blue bedspread, tormented over being caught with a dirty magazine, and he felt relief, huge relief, and compassion. Then and there, CV decided that things had gotten out of hand, that they had clearly been *long* out of hand. He sat on the edge of the bed and quickly handled the situation with his son.

"Georgie, I understand that you wanted to look at this magazine, that is normal, but you are too young. You are entirely too young to look at this." CV paused and thought. How to put it? How to tell the value of love, the value of women, the value of honor, the time it would take to understand. The value of giving enough time to grow one's self. How to put it to a small boy who was so good and yet so willing to be what others needed him to be. Yet who had now shown him what he had always known must be true, that he too had needs and questions.

He took a deep breath. He continued, "Because women are not like this, and you are not to do things like this with women for a long time, until you are married." George had stopped crying and was listening to his father with his head still buried in his bed. He ached with shame, such deep shame. His father continued behind his back, sitting on the edge of the bed. "I am not angry with you . . . I understand how you feel. I used to feel like that too, all boys do. But your mother saw this and she is going to be very hurt and upset. But I will take care of it. You are never to discuss it with your mother. Do you understand?"

George nodded his head, still turned down in the bed. CV put his hand on his son's back and told him to turn over. George's dark face had hair above the lip. Long, sparse hair was growing on his chin. He had grown and CV hadn't noticed. How did this happen that I don't know my own, my only, son?

"It is not wrong to think about women. But you have to remember that sex is best kept within the bounds of marriage. Otherwise it can be unhealthy, you can get dangerous diseases, and it can, well, it *will* make babies that you do not want. The *babies* can be unhealthy, as well. You can get very dangerous, *very dangerous*, diseases. Very bad things can happen. Do you understand?" George did not reply. It was terribly uncomfortable, and he absolutely understood.

That night, after spending his fourteenth birthday locked in his room, George heard his mother and father arguing. A huge fight that lasted hours and hours and his mother cried and cried and Theresa screamed and screamed and banged her head. But this time CV did not stop. He was steadfast in the face of every retort, every plea, every tantrum, every single tactic she used. And that night, CV won.

So now Elizabeth snuck away from the kitchen every night and stood outside her Georgiekutty's door, pining to kiss him good night again, praying he was not touching himself, hoping he was praying for freedom from temptation, missing him so very much, feeling banished and knowing in her deepest heart that she would only be banished further and further as his life went on.

No Hope for Anyone

In Gita's apartment with the palladium windows, there was no hiding from herself. The windows were floor to ceiling and covered with gauzy nothingness, for she had always liked the light. So had Chris, though her view was nothing like his at Innisfree. Of course, this was only hearsay. She had never seen his view. *I have never seen the view through his windows. In all these years, I have only heard of, and never seen, his view.*

Today, when she sat down at her desk to write, she was distracted by the blue lines in the backs of her hands, and by the scraggly lengths of her untended fingernails. She shook her head slowly to release the constant tension in her neck. *It is from holding up my big bobble head.* It crunched and clicked and yet there was no relief. She stood and took a deep breath. Each time she breathed she was astonished to think how long she was able to survive without doing this, breathing deeply. *No wonder I am unable to move in any direction; I do not breathe.* She thought of her brother's practice of meditation and deep breathing and wondered how she could have grown up in the same place with the same people, albeit so many years later, and not have acquired the same good habit.

She picked up her recorder and her headphones and sat down on the sofa to listen to interviews. In the ancient, toothless, betel-choked and rasping voices, in the cadences of her mother tongue spoken in the old ways, with the colloquialisms of the elderly, she could paint a whole world that was completely separate from any of her present sufferings. And the story they told was so immeasurably more grievous than anything in her own life story that she would have to admit that she had done this to herself. No one had made her do anything. Omanakumari's story had that lesson in it, and in the telling of it, Gita gained perspective. Unfortunately, it was a perspective that lasted only as long as she was working, but still, there was respite from her grief in those moments, and so again, it was time to work. She plugged in her headphones and turned on the tape player and leaned back into her sofa and listened to the crackled voice, coughing and sputtering out the miserable tale of the darling and innocent Omanakumari, daughter of Anandan Nambiar of Chandroth, her own great-great-great-grandmother. And for the few hours after this when she wrote it down, she was okay.

The Cursed Life of Sreemathi Omanakumari

Between Omanakumari's house and the temple there were only leaves. And their trees, their stalks, their bushes, their vines and the paths which they covered so thickly that footfall could never be heard. The sounds were only the whooshes and shivers of these leaves as the breezes passed, as a hand parted them to make way, as a bird alighted or lifted off. Sometimes these birds spoke too, and that sound might be there. And sometimes two boys or three would walk through, and then there would be the sound of boys. It was a quiet walk between the house of Omanakumari and the temple. The day was brightening as she left her home to bathe and it was especially quiet at that early hour of only slate blue. Watching, even intent watching is a silent thing.

Through the leaves, west of this slightly beaten path to the temple, there were eyes peeking through like the birds that also watched and waited for something interesting to drop from a hand, or to be left unattended. Squatting low like a hyena, Parameshwaran Namboodiri caught sight of the girl and blinked once and slow.

As he watched, sweat beaded on his brow. His hand reached for the forward corner of his *mundu*, and he drew up the edge in both hands. He folded it above his knees and retied it around his hips. Omanakumari sang quietly as she walked, a song from her head about butter and being hungry. With his right hand, Parameshwaran Namboodiri took the cloth from his shoulder and mopped his face. She tweeted something like "The butter hangs just above the threshold, when will it be time to come down? The butter hangs in a bag just out of reach, when can I have a lick?" Parameshwaran Namboodiri felt in his heart that he would never hang the butter so high. That he would put that bag on a pulley for when her eyes twinkled. That he would lower it, reach inside, scoop out a palmful for her to lick out of his hand. He imagined just before he lowered the butter how her eyebrows would arch at him, with her face slightly turned down and her mouth in the tiniest coy yearning. He imagined those beautiful eyes, so large and long, turned up to him with gratitude. He imagined what it would be like to be loved by someone so alive as to sing about butter.

He followed her from slightly above, hidden by so many leaves. His heart beat in his plump fingertips. His chest was beating wildly. They walked like that together, one above, one below. One watching, the other singing. One sweating and nervous, growing more entitled with each step; the other simply walking and singing, about butter and the feeling of wanting some.

As Omanakumari arrived at temple, a cool wind blew down from the roof bringing a rain of tiny yellow flowers the size and shape of apostrophes. She stood in the jasmine-scented shower and giggled with her head thrown back, but then nervously she stopped and looked over her shoulder. She thought she felt someone looking . . . but . . . there wasn't anyone there. Still . . . she looked through the trees for little boys, who sometimes came to watch, curious and excited. But she couldn't see anyone, and more important, neither could she hear anyone. Boys were small, but they were loud in their secrets. They tittered and shushed, they pushed and tousled. They amplified the crinkle of leaves with their efforts to be quiet. She continued on her way and began descending the steps toward the temple pool, but just before her head receded from view, she scanned the surrounding trees. She narrowed her eyes and was watchful. Parameshwaran Namboodiri watched her watching. It increased his ardor. She turned back around and her head dipped out of sight.

The stone steps would still be cool. Her toes might curl in surprise. Parameshwaran Namboodiri, who couldn't see her anymore, closed his eyes to imagine her graceful descent. He held the closest thing, which was a small tree with slim silver leaves. Parameshwaran Namboodiri stared at the horizon below which Omanakumari would be stepping into the water and he gathered his vigor. His power began to course and his fist clenched and unclenched on the small branch of the silver-leaf tree until it broke in his hands. The snap turned his head and he saw the delicate wood hanging limply, exposing a greenish pulp. It was such a young tree. He pulled the branch, to put it out of its misery while exhibiting his force to the natural world, but the tiny thing held on with vexing tenacity by threads of light brown bark. Turning back to his silver tree, he peeled the broken limb down the trunk until the bark split and the branch came free in his hand. Holding it at his side, Parameshwaran Namboodiri walked out of the dappled forest and toward the dark temple doorway where, if he were to go all the way through to another door in the back, and if he were to venture out onto a veranda, he might look down the same steps she had just descended and find a girl wrapped in two white cloths just stepping into a green temple pool.

The light was gone in Gita's apartment. She looked up from her pages and felt the dread of what was to come. For her great-great-great-grandmother, and for herself. There was no hope for anyone.

Too Late

There was a night many years, fourteen years, earlier that changed everything. On that night, Chris Jones, beautiful in his sad and aching way, sat in the airport with an old newspaper. His flight had been early and his wife was late and he couldn't find her when he called home. Having already read today's news, he was bored and quiet, and he found that two weeks ago was much like today only then, the sun had shone, and today there was end-of-the-world-as-we-know-it rain and when he looked out, he was not sure if he was upstairs or downstairs for he could see no sky, no ground and no other inhabitants of the earth. He stood up to go buy a book, for the weather was unforgiving and surely his wait would be long. He slung his brown leather satchel over his shoulder and walked, leaning just a bit to the right to balance his stride. When he passed the mirrored walls at the corner, he caught his reflection and surprised himself with his own height. In the Hudson News he stopped at the back wall of books and set down his bag.

To his right, there was a girl, whose face was hidden behind a glinting curtain of hair, draping her shoulder and unfolding over her body. She had tiny hands and wrists and wore a skirt that was made of layers of cloth so that if she spun in a circle, it would rise and show her legs. When she was still, the skirt revealed nothing but slim ankles and small feet. She wore sandals despite the rain, and she had rings on her toes.

Perhaps it was the rings on her toes that made him think of her more than once after he bought his book and left the Hudson News. Also, she had moved the hair from her face to her back with a swing and a twist of her neck. With her shoulder moving forward and back, and without even taking her eyes off the book she was reading, her hair had lifted and flown in formation, like a flock of ravens. When she did this, there was a long white stripe of light. He was dumbstruck and unaware of his staring. With her hair out of the way, she felt him looking at her and lifted her face and caught him. He gulped and swallowed, and she smiled a tiny smile.

Back at the baggage claim, he had nearly forgotten her toes; he read and wished he had a place to lie down. Sitting not too far away, the raven-haired Gita Nair from the Hudson News sundries shop held her book on her lap and watched the man carefully. There was a terrible loneliness in the close line of his lips and the long lean of his torso in an incommodious chair. His clothing looked warm and she felt chilly. Something about his deep chest in his navy blue shirt made her want to put a hand beneath his jacket and her face against his abdomen. She had never known the pull of a man before. His focus on his book, his muscular hands turning pages, his black socks, his black shoes, his large feet, his long legs; she had never known a man to look like he belonged next to her. She did not know what to do about this and she shook her head, agitated.

When she shook her head, there was another flash of light. It happened very often that the gleam in her hair caught people surprised, and they looked up and around as though someone had snapped their picture, while she innocently walked on, oblivious to the stir she had caused. And like them, Chris looked up; she was looking at him. She lowered her head a bit and swallowed, and he smiled a shy smile. He blinked at her very slowly. Gita could feel his agonized containment, and his struggle against a willful, disobedient impulse. She was too young, too utterly without experience, to know the language of a man's face, but something about his quiet looking answered questions she didn't even know she was asking.

Unprecedented in all his thirty-two years, he got up and almost went to her. Almost, for he lost his courage midcourse and instead, threw a piece of the old newspaper he was using as a bookmark in the trash and turned back to his seat. In his sudden jerky movements, in his trying to refold the remaining newspaper, he dropped his book in a goofy, bumbling hurl, and he stared at it for a second or two. Embarrassed, sure she had seen his stupid advance and retreat, his clumsiness, his book on the floor, he had to bend to get it.

Gita Nair was seduced by his reddened face and his fingers sweeping through his auburn hair. When he bent down, she could see his pant leg tighten over his muscular thigh. Muscular hands, muscular legs. He had removed his jacket before rising from his seat, and though she didn't know his intentions to come talk to her, she was further made breathless by his thick back that cut into the shirt when he extended his arm to retrieve the book. Gita Nair had never noticed the individual parts of a man before. She had never noticed that necks could be thick or that forearms could be sinewy, or freckled near the wrists. She never noticed that they had small lines around their eyes, or that their eyebrows were coarser and less committed to an arch than her own. She was altogether pleased to find herself so pulled to this man by his sad, blue eyes and his thick chest. When Chris stood up, he could not resist turning to see if she had seen him drop his book, and the look in her face made his sad heart yearn for her. She smiled again, and he smiled back.

And then, some latent boldness caught her by the scruff of her neck, stood her up and bent her down to gather her things. She walked over, sat next to him, and said, "I am Gita. I watched you throw away your rubbish." And then she bit her lip for it had been such a stupid thing to say.

And yet he smiled and replied, "I'm Chris, and I usually am more graceful when I throw away my rubbish." And then he blushed and continued, "But I am usually not distracted by . . . you." His blush grew so deep, Gita felt she had known him all her life and she reached out and put her hand on his thigh. They stared at each other for one full minute, by the end of which time they were, of course, something well beyond strangers. They talked for one hour, in this way both strange and familiar. They forgot the time, and that her brother was coming, and that his wife was coming, and then they both looked up as if on cue to see a custodian roll a mop and pail out of a closet, pushing the door closed behind him. The door did not latch, but he was gone down the corridor. They looked at each other, held that gaze, and wordlessly walked into the closet and made love standing up. She sat in the palms of his hands with her legs curled around his waist. When they finished, he eased her to the ground and lowered her skirts and righted her blouse. She held his face in her fingers and looked at him silently.

When she came out of the bathroom where she had gone to clean up, her brother was standing there waiting for her, as large as the night sky, and dressed from work, soaking wet, his shirt clinging to his enormous stomach, showing the lines from his undershirt against his dark skin.

"Oh, Chetta, here I am, did you wait for long? I just went to the bathroom." His wetness and shivering made her guilty and her eyebrows closed together; her eyes filled with tears. "Oh, Chetta, you are wet."

Dr. Raman Nair looked at his youngest sister and as always felt a flash of pride and joy. So smart, so pretty, coming up so good, always reading and thinking. He hoped always that his girls would grow up to be as well turned out as his youngest sister. "Gitu, Gitu, oh, but it is a terrible storm, so many accidents and they closed 66 because of an overturned vehicle. I passed the accident scene . . . the car was a burnt crisp. Surely the man driving it is dead. I am so sorry I was late." Seeing her standing there teary with worry made him guilty and uncomfortable, and so it was with great vigor and speed that he picked up her bags and led the way, as he was wont to do. Following her brother, she looked over her shoulder at her closet lover, who was looking at her as though he had been with her for a thousand years and now suddenly she was gone. For a moment, she wondered what she had done, and then, when she walked out of the airport, she wondered what she would do now. He was so far away from her.

Without Gita, the baggage claim, which before had been just a baggage claim, was an empty hull, and he thought of the terrible loneliness, the failures, the pretended happiness that awaited him when Jeri arrived, the same empty life of sad disappointments that they had lived for so many years. He went out to the curb instead to sit under the wide overhang, and he thought about what he had just done. What he did not regret for one moment. Looking out into the crashing rain that misted even in the shelter where he sat, he wished that it had been him coming to the airport to pick up that fresh, beautiful, serious, happy girl with the curtain of hair and the large, long eyes and the lips to feast on, the girl who told him that her name meant "song." He felt that he would marry her tomorrow, that he would move to Princeton, New Jersey, so she could finish her studies, that he would go anywhere she wanted to go, that he would marry her tomorrow. Tomorrow. With her he would try again.

A lone pair of headlights along the arrival road at the airport woke him from his thoughts. The water rose in tall sheets on either side as the tires swam through the rain. It stopped at the curb. It was time to go. He threw his bag in the trunk and came to the driver's side. Jeri jumped into the passenger seat over the gearshift and leaned over for a kiss, but Chris was preoccupied with the weather and tired, she assumed.

"I am so sorry."

"Oh, don't worry about it, the weather, don't worry, I bought a book."

"It wasn't the weather. I had a doctor's appointment today and they were so backed up I got a late start, and then I needed to go back to Innisfree to change clothes before getting on the road."

Chris looked over at her for a moment; so many years of doctor's appointments, anguished rejections, but now? He was shaken. "A doctor's appointment?"

Jeri looked at him quietly, a quick darting look that Chris had seen many times, but that he missed this time with the rain and the darkness. "Just my regular appointment. My physical."

"Don't worry about it, I bought a book." In his mind he wondered if it was only his imagination that Gita smelled like the library . . . as beautiful as she is, he thought, surely she doesn't smell like the library.

Jeri watched his face fade in on itself, and was too tired to fight for conversation. She turned her small eyes to the window and watched the rain rise in wakes from the tires of the cars on the road.

A Good Man, Even Though

The ten minutes that Chris held Gita's entire weight in his hands and around his back was enough to add her to his life's list of loyalties. Her youth and her willingness to see something beyond her reach humbled him, and the only shame he truly felt was that their story began somewhere toward the middle rather than with the care of a slow courtship. There in the airport baggage claim, he didn't tell her he loved her; in fact, it was not love that took him to the closet, but neither was it lust, nor passion, nor chemistry. It was need. He took her in the closet, between the shelves of disinfectant and spare mop heads, because he needed her. But he loved her now, and he had loved her for so many years.

For Gita, it might have been simpler, but probably not. She was never able to articulate what stood her up from her seat, bent her over to get her things, and walked her to his side. What raised her up into his hands to do something she had never done with someone she barely knew. When she was still very young, lying in his arms in a hotel room, afraid of the waning night, she would try to say something because she thought he wanted to know. She thought, in her youth, that he would need to know that he was special and that she followed him into that closet because she was in love with him. But he was so much older than she, and a simple, gentle, and good man, and he always knew she didn't love him then. How could she? She hadn't even known his last name. But she loved him now and she had loved him almost half her life.

But there was in Chris the knowledge of basic truths. A simple man in a complicated life. He was quiet in his faith, and never sure there was only one way to the end. His loyalties extended to those who needed his care, and to those who were constant and abiding. His was an unshakable loyalty formed in a childhood home where someone was always dying, two grandparents in hot, thickly wet rooms, and then his own mother, who struggled to live though he heard his father crying to the Lord to let the poor woman die. His mother tended his grandparents. Then his father tended her. Then, in the end, he tended his father, who turned to drink and never laid a hand on him in anger. He was too loyal to beat his son out of loneliness and an empty home. And Chris, so redheaded and tall, gangly and fast, had long ago turned to baseball and he was loyal to his friends, and to his team, and to his father, who out of love and loyalty never showed up drunk to games, but sometimes drove over the neighbors' trash cans on his way home. When Chris's father drove into the neighborhood rattling a lid behind him or pushing on a child's left-out tricycle, he burned with shame and thought sometimes of never going home, of bunking with a friend whose mother would pity this motherless, redheaded child, cook for him, push his hair out of his face, and tell him he looked like he'd gotten too much sun.

Chris made good friends, who kept a straight face and turned their heads up to the sky to watch the contrails whenever his dad drove into the neighborhood drunk; and then while the clattering of latched-on detritus could still be heard, they started up again, resumed their play, leaving only Chris watching his dad rattle down the road. This was loyalty born in boys who played baseball on the street and in sandlots and in any empty space, but Chris never bunked with any of them, even when the shame was so great. When the car faded over the hill, he picked up his glove and his ball, and he followed behind, righting toppled trash cans, replacing errant lids, because he could not have abandoned his drunken father any more than his father could have abandoned his dying mother. And when his father died while he was still in high school, he was both lonely and free. Nearly every night of the week, one of those neighborhood boys spent the night at his house, and on the nights they didn't, they came and got him, saying their mother saw him today and he looked like he got a little too much sun, she wanted to give him dinner.

But alone, he made choices based on the suggestions of others who seemed to know what to do and so with the help of a concerned guidance counselor and his strong-armed, big-voiced coach, Chris went to college on a baseball scholarship, which didn't mean he was extremely good, but only that his college was inexpensive and his team was also not extremely good. Chris, with his red hair and his gangly height, his quiet watchfulness and his loyalty to his team, did not engage in too many distractions, did not date a lot of girls, and would not expect anyone to think twice about him. He was not melancholy and he was not shy. He was comfortable with what came to him, and he sought out only what he needed and let the rest be as it would be. Sometimes girls, piled up as they were, would watch him and giggle at his attention to the floating of dandelion seeds, the way he would lie on the grass with his head on his bag and watch the movement of the clouds, the way he seemed only too content to read in a warm corner of the library. He had no flash and no zing, but he was tall and played ball. These things were not enough for some girls, but plenty enough for others. And in this way, Jeri emerged from a pile of girls and announced, "I am going to go talk to him."

Jeri stood in Chris's light and when he looked up from his book, she said, "Hi, whatcha reading?" He answered, "Whitman," and she shrugged and sat down. Before he really knew how it happened, they were a couple. He never remembered asking her out. Jeri, who had always been popular in high school, went to college thinking the same rules applied, but her perkiness was not always enough to compete with the beautiful girls that filtered through from the little ponds of home to the big ocean of college. Chris, with his too-red hair and his long, bony chest, had never thought about competition of this sort.

Jeri wasn't bad to have around. She was perky and small and she was always into something, lots of friends and happy times. And she wore T-shirts that made his team think he must be a lucky guy, and which made her seem pretty even though she wasn't. She had one with a pair of lips that said WANNA PET MY and when she walked away you saw a kitten on the back saying, PUSSY? She took Chris's virginity and he was always thankful to her for this. She was always there at the games with signs that read I ♥ CHRIS JONES and cheering with a pile of girls. After practice she would meet him on the field and reach up to push his hair from his face and she would say, "I think you got too much sun," and after the games she rubbed his back, and his shoulders, and even his feet, and she asked him where it hurt and whatever he said, she would rub it or ice it down.

Later, when they both got apartments, she would make him breakfast, and if he came over in the evening, she would make him dinner. If he had friends at his apartment to watch the game, she would arrive with snacks, she would put on a pot of chili, she would feed them, and she would leave. When she walked out the door, all his friends would say she was one hell of a girl. They called her a keeper. And she was there the next day and the next. She was always there. When she made love to him, she surely seemed to mean it when she said, "I love you, Chris." And he said it back because he assumed that must be what he felt. And he did love her; she was a very good friend to him.

Over the years, Jeri knew to hang on. He had made slow changes and they were all for the better. His red hair deepened to auburn and all his freckles faded except a few at his wrist and over the bridge of his nose. These freckles were endearing and boyish, and when he sat on the ground and looked up at her, his crooked smile and those freckles on his nose were exactly what was most beautiful about his face. And then his eyes, which were autumn-sky blue all the way to the edges, no flecks and no dark rims. His body filled out and thickened from baseball; huge shoulders, thick chest, rippling legs that shifted their shadows with every step and above all, a deep back that sent a tremble through her stomach every time he turned around. She thought that with Chris's back, their children would have a chance. His quiet, serious nature graduated him well and earned him an entrance to business school. Jeri loved all the things that Chris represented toward a perfect life, and she was more than willing to do her part.

She imagined four babies like bookends. A boy, two girls, and a baby boy that would come like an accident, toward their older years. The last one would play baseball and charm them in their old age; this one would be the one with the all-blue eyes. She would work until they had their first child, and then together they would realign their priorities to allow her to stay home and take care of the growing family. She imagined her small breasts would grow larger from the pregnancies and that Chris would come home from work and call her a nickname when she was pregnant, like Bundle. "Hey there, Bundle." She imagined that pregnancy would make her beautiful. This was what she thought of when she went for her morning run.

Chris never even proposed, but he was very loyal, and she had been his girlfriend for four years, she had been to every game, even traveled, and she had rubbed his shoulders and his feet and made him breakfast and dinner day after day, and she still noticed if he got too much sun. She wanted to get married, and he didn't *not* want to get married, and so he picked seven boys from his team and he got married the third Saturday in the June after they graduated. They were twenty-two years old and their whole future lay ahead of them.

Quiet Pond

Seven years later, they arrived in Quiet Pond, Virginia, on a Sunday, to heal in a little cottage that looked like the cabin on the Lake Isle of Innisfree, though only Chris could see the possibility of growing nine bean rows there. Jeri didn't read Yeats. And anyway, she wasn't paying attention; she was jelly eyed like his dad, on painkillers that she no longer needed.

Chris had stopped talking much in these last years. He waited outside locked bathroom doors; he steeled himself to endure her pain. Sometimes, out of nowhere, in his office or on the train, he would lift his head and smell a scent from his house and, unable to shake the dread, he would linger a little longer over errands or work.

Their first baby was conceived without trying and died without even making his presence known; he didn't count in Jeri's enumerated list of miscarriages because, thank God, she never knew he was there in her monthly bleeding. There were others flushed out the same way, but after their first year of marriage, they were listed under a different heading: MONTHS I FAILED TO CONCEIVE; this was a much less tearstained list, though it was rumpled and twisted in its own way. This first invisible baby was conceived on their honeymoon on a cruise ship to the British Virgin Islands; Jeri never mentioned to Chris that she had stopped taking the Pill, and she was right in assuming that it would have been fine to him either way. To hear her talk about their life's plan was to build faith in it himself. She uttered her ideas with joyful hand-waving and eyes turned to the windows, imagining the valences and draperies that would best suit a family and its various rooms, a boy, two girls, and then an accidental blue-eyed baby boy who would play baseball.

Chris started to think of them himself, and when sometimes the girls presented as twins, he too thought that yes, they would be adorable in matching Sunday dresses. He finished graduate school and got a good job, and the babies that never came but surely would became more and more of a possibility rather than less and less of one, because now they could afford the draperies and the matching coordinated rugs and bedspreads. And when Chris started his own successful business, sending them all to college at once became easily imagined, and the accidental blue-eyed baby boy might go to college on a scholarship as he had. And when Jeri, with her perky personality and her attention to detail, and her powers of persuasion and her unrivaled confidence, became an award-winning real estate agent, there was nothing missing from the picture but the kids.

When they scraped her out the first time, she had been twenty weeks along, long enough to feel like she was having a baby and long enough to love the baby too. Her breasts were larger, and her hair was glossy for the first time in her life. The added weight padded the knotty humps on her spine and when she walked down the street hand in hand with her tall husband, she could see passersby thinking she was beautiful and that they were a gorgeous couple. She had already named him David, though Chris told her that he thought that was silly because of the singer, and so she never mentioned it anymore, though his name was still going to be David, and then without more than a day or two of cramping, he squeezed and wrung out of her in painful clumps that she didn't know what to do with, but couldn't flush down the toilet. She arrived at the doctor's office with her husband in shock, and her baby in a blue-lidded Tupperware bowl.

Jeri lost a baby in every bathroom in the house. She had gone into preterm labor against the wall of the basement guest room, in the upstairs corridor, and on the carpet of the formal living room, which had to be changed because, though there was no visible stain, Jeri could smell the child when she opened the door. Chris was afraid of every drawer and every closet, which might hold thermometers, or medicines, or herbal treatments, or brochures for classes on conception meditation and "eating to bear fruit." One evening, having left Jeri at the hospital to sleep, he entered his home to find her tiny handprint in blood on the kitchen wall by the phone where she had called 911. He went to the garage to find the paint and, with his trembling hands, fixed the white wall. In the morning when he walked into the kitchen, he saw that by the faint light, and with his mind not at ease, he had painted over the handprint with a patch of banana yellow, the color of the garden bench he had built her for their fifth anniversary. In this house of tears and cursed beginnings, there was grief around every corner.

There was a magic in Quiet Pond that was undeniable, and in retrospect, years and years of retrospect, Chris would always say that the magic of his life, all the unbelievable, unparalleled magic of his life began only once he came here. Even this first journey had been magical; in his life, only Quiet Pond and Gita had ever moved him to action, had ever called him home.

They were things for which he never found alternate explanation. In one afternoon in Quiet Pond in their rental by the lakelike pond, there were these miracles: Jeri showering, dressing, painting her toenails, doing her hair, napping without screaming, without moaning, without even moving. Jeri taking a walk with him around the pond. Holding his hopeful, nervous, unsure, extended hand. Smiling at him when he brought her handfuls of daffodils from the woods. Taking photographs like in all the days of their youth. Wanting to walk to town. Wanting to go to dinner; eating. Watching her eat at the Soaring Quarter, he had to hide his face in his hand so she would not feel self-conscious at his wide-eyed wonderment over her sopping up oil with bread, over the risotto clinging to her lip. One day in Quiet Pond and she ate more than she had in several months together. But then, that Thursday night there had been a miracle of sorts in the Soaring Quarter that had nothing to do with

Jeri. They read poetry there. So in retrospect, years and years of retrospect, Chris knew that Quiet Pond was home when a man stood up and told him so.

At seven o'clock, the lights became dimmer and a very tall man with black hair and an indented chest that made him stoop walked to the front of the room, onto a huge hearth. A crackling fire burned behind him. The room broke out into riots of applause, they shouted, "Felix! Felix!" The atmosphere of the room changed, and Chris sat up in his seat. The dark-haired man turned on the mike and tapped it. It popped and whistled. The man brought out a stool and a small music stand. *Oh, music,* Chris and Jeri both thought. *They play music here at night.*

But it was not music. Chris felt the room swell with patient anticipation and then the dark-haired man spoke.

"Tonight, we have a few old poets and a few new ones, and a few of the old poets are reading some favorites along with some new things. We have five on the list, and a few more have asked to come up if there's time, and I think there might be time for a few extras, right?"

Chris turned to his wife with his eyebrows up in appreciation. He mouthed, *They read poems!* Jeri rolled her eyes and smiled. Chris leaned forward with his elbows on his knees and his face in his hands and listened. They were all remarkably good. And then the last poet of the night read and it was one of the moments, like years later in the airport, that would change his life forever.

At 8:30 a tall, narrow man with silver hair and a face like a statesman came to the hearth, and put his page down on the music stand to raise the mike. "Sandlot," he said, and read with a gravel-deep voice a poem that rushed Chris way back, and threw him out on the fields of his childhood, where he went to play while his house was dying. It was a baseball poem that began thus, *Buddies meet at first light,* and went on: *Ernie Banks says, "Let's play two," Yanks–Indians first from the house that Ruth built* and on, and wonderfully, magically on, so that when the baseball poet closed: *Friends are friends but this is still ball,* Chris stood and cheered, and somehow there were tears in his eyes and a fire in his heart. He had done just that, just what this poem said; he and his friends had played the whole team. He reached over and tapped Jeri awake and held her by the wrist. "That guy, that baseball guy. Let's go talk to him." Jeri shook her head in surprise and cleared her throat. She didn't even know what he was talking about, she hadn't really been paying attention, but she was more herself than she had been in so many years. Down for whatever. And they went. The man's name was Tom.

Chris introduced himself and his wife and sincerely gushed, "You are a great poet."

The man smiled and turned back to his family standing around him, "See? I told you I was a great poet!" Turning back to Chris, he asked, "Yankees?"

Chris smiled humbly. "Orioles." But raising his eyebrows, he added, "But, you know what though? In my year, the Orioles steamrolled through the American League East winning a hundred and eight games to finish fifteen ahead of the Yankees. Three games in a row, one-two-three, against the Twins and . . ." The man's family began a hooting laughter.

Chris blushed and stopped his gloat. "I'm sorry."

The man smiled. "19 . . . 70 then, right?"

"Seventy. Yup, 1970. Tom, you know, I have an old friend, and when my mother died, he used to get up and go play early with me like that. Before anyone else got up. He let me play Cuellar for a year . . . and Buford."

Tom the baseball poet said, "When your mom dies, a friend lets you play who you want to play."

"Well, we played the whole team."

"So did we."

On their walk home, Jeri was quiet and Chris was loose of tongue. He remembered his friends, his family, his mother and how she worried when he came home with a bloody face and a lump on his head. Again and again he said, "I can't believe that there is a place like that, where you can stand up and read your poems and everyone who reads is great and then someone reads a poem like that. About baseball." Chris looked up at the moon. "I tell you, Jeri, I could live here. I could live right here in Quiet Pond. I could live here for the rest of my life." Jeri was not averse. She had nothing at all but him, as he had nothing at all but her.

The next day, they looked around and found that on the shore of that same lake there were lots for sale. Chris picked a perfect spot with the woods to the side, and the daffodils shining within, a wood filled with redbuds and white dogwoods, and he told his wife that they would build a home there "of clay and wattles made" and they would call it Innisfree, which she didn't understand because she didn't read Yeats. Still, in his mind he picked the spot where he would plant his nine bean rows. And then they went back to their town house and put it up for sale, while they built a home in Quiet Pond free from any heartaches and disappointments. Standing in the hallways of his town house, he would close his eyes and he could hear that lapping on the shore and he felt his future in his deep heart's core.

It Turns Downward

In the apartment with the floor-to-ceiling palladium windows, Gita awoke with a start and found her apartment was pitch-black and she was slumped forward like a drunk in a tangle of dirty laundry. Or maybe it was clean. She couldn't tell the difference; it was dark. She licked at her dry mouth, which smacked and stuck, and rose to turn on the lights. She turned them all on, one after another, and soon she stood in the corner squinting from the glare of too much light all at once. *Right now, what is he doing? Is he walking along the shores of Innisfree wondering what I am doing? While I am wondering what he is doing? Yes, exactly. We are being simultaneously pathetic. I am sure of it.*

Pulling her hair over her shoulder, she braided it quickly and walked over to her mess. Her papers had fallen to the floor when she had fallen asleep. *No wonder I fell asleep, it's all downhill from here.* Gita read where she had left off last and continued.

The Cursed Life of Sreemathi Omanakumari

Parameshwaran Namboodiri was already clean and he entered the temple and prayed quickly with his forehead to the damp floor. Rising, he dipped his thumb into the sandalwood paste and drew the cool slick up his brow in a long stripe. The cold of the paste focused the coursing power in the inner corners of his eyes, increasing their acuity. His brain was much invigorated for the task of wooing, and the immediate desire of watching a girl bathe. Outside, behind a wooden pillar carved with phalluses and grateful women, Parameshwaran Namboodiri took his position. Down in the green pool, Omanakumari was alone. Her back was to him and her hair was loosed and blue-black over her shoulders. Parameshwaran Namboodiri drew passion from her glowing shoulders. He was certain she would be his very soon.

His study of her back was minute. How closely must one watch to catch the lengthening of shadows, to note the elongation of the arms between noon and twilight? How acutely aware would a man be if he noted that micromoment when the torso grew the tiniest bit? How much worth must be ascribed to that shadow to measure its change? It was with this searing focus that Parameshwaran Namboodiri noticed how Omanakumari's hair was curling up her back, and that as it dried it pulled upward and upward in a languorous seduction and nearly drove him down the steps and into the water beside her. With each passing moment a lock sprang away from her skin, breaking from its sister hairs and beginning its passage up toward her shoulders and her neck and her fine-boned jaw that receded to her ears like perfectly pieced parts. Parameshwaran Namboodiri moved slightly into the open to see her better as she bent forward to splash her face again, and the sight of her dripping made him shudder. He reached for cover and hid again. Turning his back, he leaned on the column and faced the temple. He closed his eyes and fought to control his heart, which was thudding and emptying his chest of air. The full resources of his lungs were expended in the simple act of staying alive in light of this bathing girl, and he imagined that all he needed to be happy forever was her curling hair spread across a pillow and her naked breasts in his mouth.

Peeking around the pillar, he saw that she had emerged from the pool and was dressing, removing her towels as she went. She took one tendril of hair and gently wrapped the rest with it, securing it slightly, so it would not hang in her face as it dried. She looked back toward the water and threw something. Parameshwaran Namboodiri wondered what it was, because she was fascinating in her every movement. He wondered if she smelled like fresh milk. He imagined that it might be so. Walking back into the temple, he stood in the dark and waited for her to come.

Omanakumari, softly climbing the steps to the temple, was thinking that she was hungry and that she would pray and hurry home and eat. This thought made her climb faster, and when she entered the temple, she was smiling. The wet hair around her temples was curled in wisps that looked like thinking, rather like dreaming. Parameshwaran Namboodiri felt that he might rise off the ground on her cloud of purity and happiness, so large that it filled the temple and made the gods wonder who of their rank must have just entered.

It seemed to Parameshwaran Namboodiri that he had been waiting an eternity for her. It seemed to him that this morning's stalking had gone on for days rather than the perhaps half an hour of pursuit in which he had actually engaged. He was tired. His head was light, his shoulders were aching. His patience had been admirable, and the moment he had imagined at least all this day, and certainly portions of other days as well, for at least one year, and maybe even longer than that—that moment had arrived. He was long ready.

Parameshwaran Namboodiri stepped into a stripe of light painted along the ground and stood there, arms at his sides, towel draped over his shoulders. His hair was tied in a knot and his chest was bare. He had the dwindled frame of an old man with a large paunch like an umbrella and he was smiling. Omanakumari jumped back with a gasp and a squeal and she dropped her cloth but didn't dare to retrieve it. His teeth were pointed and his tongue was squeezed between them like an udder. He had drawn back his lips in a smile that exposed his gums, swollen and red. All her fear was centered in the look of his mouth. The cloud of joy that had changed the air when she entered just as quickly dissipated, and the sudden dankness made Parameshwaran Namboodiri reach for his towel and mop his face.

She backed toward the temple door and Parameshwaran Namboodiri followed her slowly, staying in the column of light. The illumination of him did nothing to improve his aspect. In the light, he appeared like a hairy thing that has been shaved, too pink, too raw, unnaturally naked. Omanakumari stepped backward over the threshold. He noticed that there was the smallest gathering of fat about her middle as she raised her leg. As she stood in the light outside the door, he noticed that nonetheless, her waist was no larger around than the circle of his fingers and thumbs.

"Are you not Omanakumari from Chandroth, daughter of Anandan Nambiar?"

"Yes."

"You are so big now. Such a big girl. I remember when you were so small." Parameshwaran Namboodiri's voice was full of spittle. He cleared his throat, turned his head, and spat. He coughed slightly and exhaled in satisfaction.

Omanakumari looked down and drew her toes in toward her ankles. She stepped one foot on top of the other. She pulled in her chin to her chest. She drew hair from behind her to cover her body, and then clenched her hands tight. She held her clenched hands over her chest and shut her eyes. She receded until there was nothing left that moved.

Parameshwaran Namboodiri stepped boldly toward her and took hold of her hair between a finger and thumb. She turned her throbbing head slightly away. Her wet hair slid between his fingers.

Parameshwaran Namboodiri was enchanted by her reluctance. He was delighted by her modesty. He twisted his fingers around a lock of her hair and with the same hand reached for her chin. He turned her head toward him and looked at her face. Her clenched eyes were brimming and her lips were pursed so tightly that tiny lines were drawn in her baby skin.

Omanakumari was not breathing because she could feel his heat so close, and she dared not open her eyes. Parameshwaran Namboodiri let go of her chin and unwrapped her hair from his fingers. He stood back one step. Omanakumari stood with her hands clenched to her chest, with her hair over her body, with her toes drawn in, one foot atop the other. She remained tucked tight, with her eyes closed, barely breathing, her tears flowing like a rill between her fingers, trickling down her wrists.

Parameshwaran Namboodiri watched for a moment longer. He drew his towel over his chest and his arms, which were sweating profusely. Looking at Omanakumari trembling before him, he was unnerved by the intrusive realization that to this child, he looked loose and gray. That he was spotted and yellow. That she would be repulsed by him. That she had not a single desire for him, though he was overturned and hypnotized by the thought of her. He found that his tenderness was suddenly roiled with resentment. He looked at her, still standing there with her eyes clamped shut, and realized that she didn't open them because he revolted her. Parameshwaran Namboodiri turned back toward the temple and stepped inside.

"Eh? Omanakumari?"

Omanakumari was silent and did not move at all, but for the thorough trembling.

"I say, Omanakumari? Do you hear me?"

"Ah," she replied as she heard the dangerous insistence in his voice.

"I will be coming."

With this, Parameshwaran Namboodiri turned his back on the trembling girl and walked away. Soon after, Omanakumari also left the temple, but as it was she forgot to pray. It seems that God never forgave her.

Innisfree

Innisfree was built with two glass walls that were joined with a seam in the corner. The broad floor planks in this most special room facing the pond were nearly a foot wide; he had scoured the famous New England restoration houses for salvaged colonial flooring because not in two hundred years had Americans built homes with floorboards like these. He finished the planks himself, and in the round and round scrubbing, he nearly finished off his shoulder as well. He never again threw a baseball with comfort. But even playing baseball could not compare with the satisfaction of knowing the gleaming floor was his own to take pride in; and baseball was better for watching these days anyway. Jeri picked flowing fabrics for curtains that would have cascaded over the floor in a pooled drape, and in the second major decision of his life, he said, "*No, these windows will remain uncovered.*" She said, "*But the furniture will fade.*" "*Buy white furniture,*" he replied.

Jeri bought sofas upholstered in cloudy tufts, and tables of blond wood or glass. Chris built in bookcases around a fireplace that he kept blazing from October to March. He chopped wood in a clearing behind his house, and his back grew even broader and deeper and on his shoulders, a few freckles returned.

Peeking from the hallway, Jeri watched how still and content he was, roaring fire behind his back, looking out the windows, book in his lap, feet up, relaxed, at home. Her smallest jealousies churned in her stomach and itched in her skin, but she could not name them clearly. This was their house, not his alone. He was at home in his own house, how else should he feel . . . and it was her house too . . . yet her skin always itched when she saw him look so happy. Tired of herself and her petty and unspeakable irritations, she thought to take a different outlook as she was predisposed to be perky, though her life made her terribly depressed. The wooden floors and the pastoral views, the handmade bookshelves and the fire blazing with wood chopped by his own deep back and thick arms made Chris virile in his abilities, manly and territorial; and putting a better face on things, Jeri thought that perhaps here, they might be able to conceive a child. But of course, the problem had never been with him, but with her, and even Innisfree, with its nine bean rows on the western side, could not bring her closer to her animal nature where she might be more fertile and strong.

She began again, without knowing it was happening, to take her temperature maniacally, to insist on his eating potent things like soybeans and raw spinach; she removed the meat from their diets, and she stopped running and took up cycling, concerned about the jarring up and down. Chris opened a drawer where he kept the Scripto lighter he used for the grill, and found another list of failed months to conceive, and the same old list of baby names that was worn illegible in the places where he knew Luca, Gia, Jared, and Molly had been. He caught himself feeling irked that she hadn't marked through Gia before it faded away. Years ago, he had told her that Gia Jones was a name for a porn star. *Who cares*, he thought, *why do I care about that?* He exhaled with exasperation over his pointless annoyance.

He helplessly let her fade farther and farther away. Their home meant not *nothing* to her, but so much less than it did to him. She had been a little put out with Innisfree. She said it sounded like a bed-and-breakfast, "Inn Is Free." He read her the poem and still, she could not see. She said, "The Irish poet? I thought you were English and German." She said, "I don't like poetry." He closed his eyes and winced; she saw it and said, "Oh boy, so now you're a big poet? You don't talk much to be a big poet." Sometimes, these days, she was mean and her words bit down hard. Being the man that he was, he never even thought of comebacks and retorts. He just got quieter, and he often walked in the woods.

One day, while walking in the wood around his home, he was suddenly aware of a rare satisfaction and happiness. A home by the pond, perfect in every board and beam; he could not look at Innisfree without a clutch in his heart. Struck by a sudden urge to finally name something that existed, he walked up to the middle of a flower bed and pushed in with his shoe the place where he would name his home. He went inside and drew his idea; he thought it looked very good.

It was a day for walking and thus he made his way into town and asked shopkeeper after shopkeeper where to find a good man for the task of making him a sign. Silas, with swooping hair that shone like white silk, who said he went to school in the hills a hundred years ago, who bragged of having whittled the face of Teddy Roosevelt somewhere in the Cumberland Plateau, sat waiting for someone to ask him to carve something. Chris asked Silas to make him a sign for his house and pulled out his drawing.

"Innisfree. Pretty name." And then the old man looked out his shop window and said, "'I will arise now and go to Innisfree.'" Chris walked away knowing his sign would be better than he could have imagined it. In two weeks, he walked back into town and brought home his better-than-perfect sign. When Jeri arrived from her new real estate job, she saw him out there with a posthole digger and a bag of cement. She said, "Don't I get a say in the name?" And he said she had never mentioned any thoughts about it. In the evening, over dinner, she blinked once and said she thought they ought to call it something that everyone would understand, like . . . Lakeview, or Lakeside. He rolled his eyes. She welled up and quietly said, "I am sorry I'm not the big *poet* you are." Chris simply stared. She continued, "I can't get all excited about the house when there is no family to live in it." She stood up from the table and threw down her napkin and walked away. She slammed a door and Chris heard it lock and for the first time, he did not follow, perhaps because for the first time, he realized that she did not consider him family. It was a slight chink in his sense of loyalty, so small he barely perceived it.

Chris tried to talk, but as the years passed, she seemed to want nothing but his sperm. She grew obsessive in her focus on the calendar and marked the passage of time with insane rituals and off-hand humming that could not be interrupted, lest she have to start over again from the beginning. She watched the phases of the moon, and she adjusted her caloric intake accordingly. On the new moon she fasted. On the full moon she ate only beans. Chris was dutiful on his end and performed on command, but because she was not to be touched after intercourse, and she was not to achieve orgasm except at the waxing or waning gibbous, and he was to ejaculate as close to the vaginal opening as possible, their sex became a complex and clinical function, and Jeri was unsympathetic if he forgot the rules. When it was not the right time to conceive, he was to sleep in the other room. He was not allowed to masturbate. Sometimes he watched late-night TV, and the blue on his face was as sad and lonely as it ever was on anyone's face seen alone at that hour of the night watching infomercials and the four-hundredth repetition of the story of Jesus Christ. He tried hard to love her even when it was clear that through the pain, she had lost everything she ever had for him.

But then one May she conceived. They did not even note it with more than a quiet blink and bowed heads over supper. Whenever she conceived and missed a period, she was touchy and teary. This time, she still watched the moon. She still hummed her tunes. He still did not interrupt her, and of course there was no sex. And then they passed the twenty-two-week mark where they had been disappointed before, and this they acknowledged with bitten lips and quiet blinking when the doctor told them it was a boy. And then they reached the thirty-two-week point, where the doctor told them that a baby born now would almost always survive, especially one with a heartbeat like his, and with his healthy size and perfectly normal development. And then they reached thirty-six weeks, and without writing it down, they named him Jack, a name that had never been on a list. And then, while Jeri was at home writing thank-you cards for gifts she was given at a shower the day before, she began to bleed. Chris, who was home just in case, raced her to the hospital, where in the covered drive-up of the emergency room, she abrupted and gave birth to a perfectly formed, completely dead, nine-pound baby boy. The doctor called it a neonatal catastrophe. They scraped her clean and took her uterus and thus relieved them both of the only purpose of their lives together.

The Joy and Despair of All Real Things

Sometimes in the coming of dawn, Chris could not help but watch Gita's face change with the shifting shadows and the rising light. He woke too early to awaken her, though their minutes were precious and few, and really, he was perfectly satisfied to lie still and simply watch. If she slept too long after 7 A.M., he would nudge her with his shoulders and his chest. If she continued to sleep, he would sidle in close so she could feel him erect with whatever skin was exposed, her fingers lying out by her knees, her buttocks thrust back in her bending slumber. When she awoke this way, it was always with a grateful smile and closed eyes. She would reach for him and open her legs. She never kissed before brushing her teeth, so she loved him with everything but her lips.

Once, he dined with colleagues on Main Street in Charlottesville, and through the window he spotted an art store where he returned the following day to buy himself paints, a sketch pad and set of good brushes. In his hotel room that evening, Chris tried to paint Gita as she looked at the various points of the morning. When he slept that night, he dreamed she bought him a kitten. When he woke up, he painted her at noon with the cat in her lap. He hadn't known he could paint.

Sometimes she didn't open her eyes until their lovemaking was well under way, and then she was shocked at how handsome and strong and in love he looked on top of her. When she finally opened her eyes,

Chris, who focused on every shifting shadow that indicated pleasure or satisfaction; Chris, who would turn a fraction of an inch to the left or right to see a certain clench in her jaw or flare of the nostril, would momentarily stop midthrust, overcome with the look in her face. The way Chris looked at Gita made her sure and strong; the way she looked at him made him humble, happy and very weak. He sometimes felt that he could not live without her. She had barely lived without him, so she really didn't know. When they found each other, he was thirty-two and she was eighteen. In those days, Chris could feel his cells sloughing and being reborn, he was aware of the movement of cilia and the growing of his hair. In those days, Chris could see the movement of the sun, and he could see the rivers of the moon. He knew that, should he try to sing, he would have perfect pitch. Alive.

From the Journal of Gita Nair

OCTOBER 13, 1985

I have nothing that I want more than this. I fear nothing more than I fear this.

Gita too grew poetic and romantic, and sat dreamily watching dandelion seeds. She too curled rhymes over her tongue and read Gitanjali that she might offer him slips of paper with one phrase or two that would sing in his heart as he drove from her Princeton apartment or a nearby New Jersey hotel room to Innisfree, perfect in every board and beam, except that now when he sat in his tufted chair, he imagined she was sitting on the small sofa across from him, her legs curled up tight, her hair over her shoulder, twirling it with a finger, reading a book.

Once, while she was still at Princeton, before she moved on to the next thing and then the next, he lay beside her in that early morning way of not moving, and he watched her face in the cool, blue light. Her hair was thrown behind her on the pillow and her face was too flawless to be real, but every so often she twitched or turned in her sleep. In that moment, when she was only eighteen, he decided that he would figure it out. Alive was worth something. Alive didn't mean that he would leave Jeri helpless. He would figure it out. In that moment, he felt the peace of having made up his mind and he awaited her awakening. When it became 7 A.M. and she was still asleep, he drew in close and curled his arm over her shoulder and around her back. She was small, but in a very different way, and Jeri and he had never done this. Jeri was too perky to lie still and sleep long, unless she was trying to conceive or recovering from the aftermath of conception. He had never held a naked woman in languid peace. He had never felt the way a naked woman in languid peace could open across a bed with just her legs and the flow of her hair. He had never seen how a naked woman in languid peace could draw a man's breath from his chest just by finally opening her sleepy, satisfied eyes, and when he discovered this, he was lost. Chris could hold Gita's warm, soft body for hours without moving. This languid peace was so enchanting that he could be held in check, waiting until 7 A.M. to move in for her. The morning that he made up his mind, he held Gita longer, and woke her with his erection on her tight, girlish tummy. Chris held his breath until a smile spread across her face. She slid her hand under his body and he lifted up to allow her to hold him close. With her eyes closed and her face in his neck she pulled him on top of her and spread her legs. She was always wet for him.

This morning, he loved her for over an hour and when, perhaps a third of the way through, Gita opened her eyes, they immediately filled with tears of love because the look in his face was new and powerful and deep with devotion. She was utterly safe and she loved him with every bit of her soul. At that moment, she knew she would never love anyone but Chris Jones. She was only eighteen. Chris stopped midthrust and his eyes welled in response to hers. A tear dropped on her breast and he leaned down and licked it off and when he put her breast in his mouth, she shuddered and held him tighter.

When they were finished, she closed her eyes once more and put her left leg over his and was nearly asleep again, because he was stroking long across her chest, back and forth, back and forth, and every so often, he would stroke through her hair right at the temple. It was deep pleasure. She was nearly gone in the quiet morning when he asked, "Gita?"

"Mmm?"

"Are you sleeping?"

"Mm-mm."

"Gita?" She inhaled and exhaled in response. He felt it in the rising of her chest and yet he could not hold off. "Do you love me?"

"Mmmm." Which of course he already knew.

"Gita?"

Rousing herself to his rare insistence on anything for himself, she opened her eyes and smiled at him with her closed mouth and dreamy, love-drunk eyes. "Gita," he repeated.

"Yes, my love?"

He turned over to face her directly and then said he would love her for the rest of her life, that he couldn't imagine living without her, and then he said that he would figure it out. And suddenly from nowhere, he tasted a sick vomit because when the words left his mouth he remembered promising Jeri in that last hospital room after they lost Jack that they would be okay and that together they would figure it out. Suddenly from nowhere he could smell the sweat from the underside of Jeri's hair when he held her up to vomit into a kidney-shaped pan entirely too small. She probably didn't remember his promise, her heart being utterly broken. Realizing then that he had thought this thought, of her perhaps not remembering that he had promised to figure it out with her because at the time she had been too sick with grief, he panged in his heart over his poor, tiny wife who worried over the humps in her gnarled back and felt like an ugly, useless and empty husk. His stomach knotted. But then he noticed that while his mind and heart flashed to a guilty space, Gita, the love of his soul and his life, flashed fear across her face that he had never seen before. Did he miss something in his momentary shift of focus? She did something he did not expect in light of his offer to be there forever and to figure it out; she turned her back and began to cry in a bad way.

This was not the love crying she sometimes let loose when they said good-bye. That crying made him stronger for the road, because he loved her more than he could easily bear and he needed to know that she loved him that same way. Her turned back twisted from his touch; she recoiled. She stood up and walked to the bathroom door with a panicked tripping. She locked it. He rose and stood outside. He called her and begged her to come out, something he had never done outside a locked bathroom door. He was nearly driven mad in her ten minutes of sobbing behind that locked door. As quickly as his life's obligations had flashed before him, all memory of them was lost in the realization that it was not all up to him, though he had never considered this before.

When she emerged she was still whimpering, for she was only eighteen and so desperate as well, so in love. She crawled under the covers and buried her head in the pillow. When he tried to touch her, when he called her name with rising frustration and terrifying fear of losing her, she reached out a long brown arm and felt along the bed for more pillows to stack against the first. She was holed up and crying, "Noooo . . . nooooo . . . nooooo." Chris held his face in his hands and beat his forehead against his palms. He did not hide a moment of his agony, for he had put his entire faith in love in this girl. He did not believe it could be true that she did not want him as he wanted her. He did not believe it, for when she looked at him, he could see the pulse in her neck quicken, and she held his face for hours at a time, stroking it and counting his freckles. She had told him all her stories while she held his face in her hands. She had whispered that she loved him into his hair and then she decided to also whisper it into his belly button because it occurred to her that perhaps then her words would rest closer to his soul.

"My soul is in my stomach?"

"No, but your umbilicus was your first connection to life and love."

This had made sense to him. Before he left her to drive back to Quiet Pond, he had knelt down, lifted her blouse and whispered the same into her belly button. She was his perfect love. And now she wailed no. He beat himself at the chest and drove blackened marks into his eyes with his balled-up fists.

Finally, she came up and slumped against her pile of pillows, exhausted and all cried out. He was staring at her through the mirror on the dresser; he too was all cried out, and perhaps it was his sudden silence that silenced her and brought her from her cave. When she appeared, he knew that it was not lack of love that drove her to the bathroom or locked him out, that buried her under cover, because she looked up at him with terrible tragedy. She was too young to see it any other way; he was not quite old enough to have a calmer perspective.

They stared at each other with fear and quiet and Gita whispered, "Are you asking me to marry you?"

Chris hesitated, not knowing the right answer, surprised by her horrible reaction, assaulted by both his own guilt and his terrible panic at the thought that something was going wrong, so wrong. He took a deep breath and too loudly shouted, "I am married now. I was saying I don't want to live without you. That I would figure it out."

"Figure it out?"

Gita did not drop his gaze and suddenly he thought she looked nearly as old as he, wise and composed, and very sad and resigned. He felt he had lost her already. "It is a lot to figure out, but . . ."

"You mean with your wife?"

Again with her composure, her composure, where was this coming from and where was his gentle girl? What was this grownness, this composure, this composure after such an outrageous, tormenting cry? He felt her intellectualizing, her scrutiny over something he could not see. He slammed his hands against the dresser top behind him. He rattled the mirror. The wilder he got, the calmer she spoke. She was horse whispering, betraying him with her too-great containment and her questions.

"Yes, with my wife, with my marriage." He felt a rising curse, a need to shout at her and beg.

"You mean to marry me?" Gita's eyes focused hard and narrowed just a bit, not angrily. She analyzed his reactions with microscopic attention. He wondered, could she see that the moment he proposed to figure it out, his heart had questioned the rectitude of this decision? That his sense of loyalty had rebelled?

He stood still and stared at her. His face blanched and reddened at once. "Well." Chris felt he was taking too long to answer. He was thinking too hard. He did mean to marry Gita; he said what he had said so that he could marry Gita. His head dropped a fraction of an inch. He worried that she would read something into his movements, into so much time passing without speaking his mind. He realized that he had not yet answered. He worried that his answer was now too late. Gulping from the effort of so much metacognition, he replied, "Yes!"

Looking away, breaking her gaze for the first time and without even a second's thought, she said, "I can't marry you." She lifted her finger to her mouth and bit it hard enough to stop her tears.

Her cold response, her quickness, the apparent ease with which she denied his only semiuttered proposal cut him to the bone and he shivered with anger and hurt. "You mean because I am married?" This being the only answer he could allow.

"Well, yes." There was more, he knew, but he didn't want to hear it.

"I told you, I will get divorced. We can't get married until I am divorced."

Gita looked back at him with her finger still in her mouth. It was no use now; she pulled it out and the tears rolled like she had pulled the only plug from the dam. "Well, no." Again, she looked away.

"What?" The strength to stand was leaving him.

"My brother. My family. My father. My mother is . . . I can't."

"What?"

"I can't marry you."

"What?"

"I am Indian!" She said this and looked at him as though he should understand. Her eyebrows were up. Her mouth was severe.

"What are you doing with me?" He threw it at her like an accusation.

The tone of his voice made her angry and she threw it back at him with her young might. Righteous, she shouted, "You can't marry me either!"

"I can get divorced."

"You never mentioned that."

Chris stared at her in disbelief, and he sneered the first sneer of his life. "What? What are you doing, then? What are you doing with me? What? Are you in this because you *like* having affairs with married men?" Her eyes filled with tears and she gasped. He had bludgeoned her, and he felt the force ricocheting through his arms, worse than chopping wood. She stood up, naked and beautiful. She looked at him with long trails of tears and she slowly raised her arms to cover her bare breasts. She reached down and pulled a sheet from the bed, and wrapping herself as she walked, she went to gather her things.

He ran to her and knelt at her feet. "Sorry, sorry." He held her around her knees, forcing her still. His face pressed into her stomach, but her shame was too great now to stay, he having named it for her. She tried to push him off, but he was too strong and she was too weak. Finally, she dropped her hands to the sides and whimpered in a plea,

"Chris, please. Let me go." His complete shame and his fear of making it worse loosened his grasp from her legs. He sat on the bed while she packed her bag, dressed without even showering, and left without saying a word. He sat on the bed without moving, for fear that if he left, she might return; if he showered, he would not hear her knock, he would not hear the phone. Finally, when the day had turned to blackest night, he rose to bathe. She had left a bar of soap, which he used, and on the long drive back to Innisfree, he inhaled her with every breath and cursed himself, that his loyalty had left him when he needed it most.

Absurd and Atrocious Moments

Gita stood at her apartment window staring down at ongoing life below. When she thought back to those days she wondered how she ever had the strength to leave him. *Was I so much stronger then?* For now, even breathing serrated her lungs. She tapped on the window and drew a letter "G" in her breath. She inhaled and winced. *Why didn't I marry him then?* She puffed in disgust. *Because I am a coward. I am no better now than I was then; fourteen years has improved me not one bit.* Gita looked down at her spent, thinning fingernails. She shook her head and sighed at her worthlessness. *Just right. A great-great-great-grand*mother *like* her, *and of course I would be suffused with the spirit of my great-great-great-grand*father.

Gita shuddered. His paan spittle alone was enough to be ashamed of. Another shiver down her arms; she flexed her fingers. Walking to the couch with one of her short-lived, disgust-induced spurts of energy, Gita sank into the same laundry she had sat on, slept on, and picked through for weeks. Wincing again with her deep breath, she reached for her notebook and pen, and began to write the absurd and atrocious moments that brought Parameshwaran Namboodiri to Omanakumari's door. If she could not seem to avoid *being* like him, she would at least make sure everyone knew just how awful they both were.

The Cursed Life of Sreemathi Omanakumari

Parameshwaran Namboodiri entered his house and was momentarily blinded by the shift from sunlight to darkness. He stood still with one hand on the wall while tiny blue and red spots exploded in his eyes. Gayatri averted her eyes from his struggle because the sight of her husband blinking with his lips parted, the sound of his fearful breathing, his bad smell, made her feel like pushing him down, and knowing she couldn't do such a thing made her doubly resentful. Gaining his equilibrium, Parameshwaran Namboodiri moved toward his dining room and sat down in a wordless thump. He began to eat, though his mind was a few hours ahead, on the task to be accomplished. Gayatri went back and forth, bringing and taking food. Distracted from his thoughts by her movement, Parameshwaran Namboodiri looked up and watched her. She was more distasteful to him than he had remembered, more distasteful to him than she had been earlier that day. Compared with Omanakumari. Parameshwaran Namboodiri felt himself warm at the thought of her, and a girl as supple as she would surely bear boys. This useless one here, four girls. All the others as well, girls. He stood at the head of a long, disappointing line of girls who had two things in common: ears that stuck out to the sides like an elephant and a father who didn't give a damn about them. As he saw it right now, none of these women from his long, long history had been as supple, as lush, and as sure to bear a boy as Omanakumari.

Parameshwaran Namboodiri belched loudly and smacked his lips. Gayatri heard him from outside and came back quickly to remove his leavings.

Watching her work, Parameshwaran Namboodiri was suddenly struck with the great injustice of his life. "Eh, *eddi*? Why didn't you have boys?"

Gayatri shot her eyes his way and said nothing. She placed a cup of water near him and quietly squatted down to clear his place. Parameshwaran Namboodiri, with rare presence, noticed that she had a rather heavy growth of hair along her jawline and on her chin. Her hair had gone streaked with white and with the dark blackness of the undercoat, she looked like a skunk. Inside, he felt good at this thought. It loosened him to notice that this silent, moving thing that had been present for so many years in one way or another was so funny-looking. He didn't remember ever thinking of her before, but they had been married for too long to keep looking at someone. He reached up and pinched her arm hard on the back where it was fat and laughed when she dropped her bundle, splattering the ground with bits of rice and curry.

"O!" Gayatri reached to rub her arm and thus smeared herself with the garbage.

Parameshwaran Namboodiri chuckled as he watched the show. He found that his spirit was lifting. He was smiling a monstrous, red, gaping smile as his wife squatted down again to pick up the trash; the slightest exhalation of glee came forth like a whistle through his nose. Belching again loudly, he pushed his wife slightly with his toe, rocking her off balance; she tipped onto her hip and again dropped what she had retrieved. She looked at the ground and counted some small black spots the size of peppercorns. At the sight of her lying there waiting for his next whim, staring at the ground without a single thought in her empty head, Parameshwaran Namboodiri felt so lighthearted that he spoke to her. "Hehe, you know . . . you look like a skunk." He smirked and showed his red-stained gums. He rose up from the ground and walked out of the room. She could hear him chuckling as he walked out of the house.

Gayatri also rose up from the ground with the folded leaf on which he had been fed, his empty water glass. She went into the kitchen and out the back door. Throwing her bundle into the woods, she wondered if anyone had ever told him what he looked like. . . .

With a mouthful of paan spittle, even innocent people will look like the devil. Parameshwaran Namboodiri, chewing his paan, was even more like the devil because he was not at all innocent. And because his face was twisted into a sneer at the thought of claiming his right over Omanakumari's shoulders and the rest of her, he was ever the more diabolical looking. The blood-colored paan trickle was seeping from the corners of his mouth and dripping onto his chest, where it mixed with his perspiration to create the appearance of gaping wounds about his torso. Every so many steps he took the towel from his shoulder and mopped his face and neck and chest and made the whole situation worse. This was due to his horrible hyperhidrosis combined with too much saliva. He was unaware of the spectacle he made.

When he arrived at the clothing shop, he was a most miserable sight. The sensitive shopkeeper who sold him the lady's white *mundu* couldn't help but feel terribly sorry for the poor woman who would soon be asked to be this man's bride. The simple quality of the cloth the man had purchased told the shopkeeper that she would be one of many and not his equal, and the age of the man who had purchased it told him that she would probably be the last. He would die on top of her.

The shopkeeper wrapped his package, tied it securely, and sent up a prayer as he fastened the knot that the girl for whom this *mundu* was intended might be strong of heart and placid of spirit. Handing it over was difficult, and the shopkeeper found himself unable to let it go. Letting go of this cloth would bring her that much closer to her doom. As many steps away from this shop as the cloth went, so many steps closer it was to her. He felt a terrible tug to save her.

Parameshwaran Namboodiri could see a touched gleam in the eye of this shopkeeper and it gave him a shudder and annoyed him. He snatched his parcel, and turned from the counter. "Crazy, are you??" Parameshwaran Namboodiri shouted as he left the shop.

The shopkeeper leaned forward to see him swaggering away and felt a mist come over his eyes. This had never happened to him before.

Parameshwaran Namboodiri took his parcel and continued up the street. The day was large about him and the street seemed thicker with people. Also, it seemed that many eyes were upon him and he thought that it must show, his impending good fortune. Again, the image of Omanakumari bending low to the water, the tiniest droplets visible and lost in her curls upon curls. The whole thing magnified in his mind as though he had been standing right at her side. As though he were bathing her himself, close enough to smell her wetness. He could feel his mouth beginning to overflow and he was unable to slurp before a slim flow of pink saliva dripped onto his wrapped package. Before his eyes, the drop spread and the edges grew red. Being that the wrapping was simply a piece of brown paper tied with a string, Parameshwaran Namboodiri's heart leapt at the thought that his betel stain might have reached the wedding clothing he was about to offer the girl, and he struggled to remove the string to check. Standing in the road, streaked with reddish stripes, trailing long strings of red paan spit, struggling to remove the paper from his package, Parameshwaran Namboodiri became more and more of a spectacle, and he drew pity from some passersby who didn't know him and thought he might be dotty. The more he struggled, the sweatier he got, and before he was even aware of his perspiration emergency, he noticed that his hands were causing similar spreading stains on the parcel and that now the paper looked thin and dark and yet the twine used to tie the package was not to be undone without a knife. Parameshwaran Namboodiri didn't have a knife.

Frustrated, he wrapped his parcel in his towel, which was a light pink shade by now and as wet as his *mundu*, and toddled back to the clothing shop. Parameshwaran Namboodiri appeared to toddle when he walked quickly. He had noted this before, that his respectability was much diminished by a speedy gait, and he therefore rarely walked fast, but a failure to get the paper off the *mundu* in time could result in having to purchase another *mundu*, and Parameshwaran Namboodiri was not one for extra and unnecessary spending. Gasping for breath, he arrived at the counter, removed his towel and threw the parcel down.

The gentle shopkeeper stood staring at the beastly little man with his eyes so wide that Parameshwaran Namboodiri felt too watched to turn and spit. His mouth was overflowing. He brought the towel up, and released a small flood. It seemed that this final effluent strained the last fiber of that cloth, which was now drenched beyond use. The shopkeeper's eyes dropped to see a shining silvery thread of something flowing steadily from the bottom of the disgusting man's rag onto the ground. His stomach flipped and he again felt a pang of pain.

"You boy, take that string from the package, I think you have sold me a stained garment." Parameshwaran Namboodiri stood smugly. His chest hairs, which had earlier looked like a broom down his stomach, were arranged in a paisley pattern that seemed thoughtfully distributed over his entire torso. If he were to have turned, the shopkeeper would have seen that the same design adorned his back as well. The longer the shopkeeper looked at Parameshwaran Namboodiri's chest-hair pattern, the less like paisleys they looked and instead he saw a definitive face in there; it was a man's face and it seemed to be wearing a hat. Parameshwaran Namboodiri was unsettled by the shopkeeper's silence and staring. "Hey, crazy boy, did you hear me? I say, you sold me a stained garment."

The shopkeeper, being infused with honest spirit, saw the return of the *mundu* as portentous, and he could not see it as anything less than a sign from God. As he realized this, a beatific smile passed over his lovely face, and Parameshwaran Namboodiri was now unequivocally convinced that the shopkeeper was unfit. Nonetheless, he needed the *mundu*. "What are you going to do about this?" Parameshwaran Namboodiri was now sweating with no towel and the rivers flowing off his arms and chest made the earth beneath his feet dark and muddy.

Turning away, the shopkeeper cut the strings and removed the cloth from within. It was unstained, as white and perfect as when he had sold it.

He turned back to Parameshwaran Namboodiri and said, "One moment please, let me get another." Going to the corner of his stall where he kept his gods and where he prayed, he offered up the cloth and bent his head low. "Please protect the girl who gets this *mundu*; she has only You."

Satisfied, he turned back, rewrapped the cloth in several layers of paper, and then several layers more. He tied it with a string and then made a little handle from more string. He asked Parameshwaran Namboodiri to wait one moment and found a long stick and he tied the package to the end of the stick. The gentle, kind, resourceful shopkeeper now handed the package on a stick to his grotesque customer and told him to hold it far from his body. Parameshwaran Namboodiri humphed and muttered about putting up with the insane. Taking the stick, he turned and walked, trailing sweat that poured off his skin and squirted from between his toes, glowing pink from heat and effort, shifting the pattern of his body hair from one recognizable image to another. And in this absurdly atrocious way, holding a package that hung from a stick far from his body, he arrived at the home of Omanakumari.

Lying back against the laundry, Gita put down her notebook and considered the journey to here. Somehow, even with this miserable ancestor, she herself had been given perfect love. She remembered how way back then, Chris had gone to the ends of the earth to bring her back to him. Madison County. When she closed her eyes, she could still see a purple envelope in the box.

A Gentler Courtship

Chris took a P.O. box in Madison County because Gita would not answer the telephone. Quiet Pond was his home and the town was too small. He even knew the postmaster; his name was Ed Rimes.

Chris stood in the rain in a dingy strip mall in front of the Pro-Tan Sun Spa in Criglersville with the dead telephone in his hand. Alison the roommate said to him, "Look . . . just . . . just leave her alone." He had driven forty miles for an anonymous pay phone. When it became clear that it was hopeless, he took to calling from Quiet Pond, because it didn't take more than thirty seconds to know she would not talk to him. People saw him out there by the Smallmart and Cerises et Surprises, but as grace would have it, not the same people more than once. He gave up calling when her roommate said, "Look, all I can say is that you disgust me."

When he called, Gita left the room. She stood outside the door until Alison dismissed him, then she ran to the bathroom and pretended she'd been there all the time. Alison came to retrieve her and said, "He is such a loser." *He is not*, Gita knew. When Gita heard Alison tell him he disgusted her, she could see his face pale and torn, and she wanted to run to the phone and throw Alison out, to lock the door and sob into the line, "Come get me, please come here and get me." But she couldn't do it. Her shame was too heavy to put down, and she still could not marry him.

At night, sure he would call the next day as he had the last, she tried to imagine it. She pictured bringing him home to her brother's house. All the girls would stand around with their mouths open and their eyes frightened and darting, flitting here and there, distracting everyone with their size and eager displays of brilliance and achievement. All their nervous laughter, and Chettan growing purpler and purpler. Shanti running to him and putting up her face to be kissed, climbing in his lap because she was afraid of the tension she could not understand. Finally, he would stand straight up, Shanti would tumble to the floor and rub her head, and he would bellow aloud, "*Chris, do you realize my sister's tender age? Is this some archaic idea of an ancient and obsolete India? Do you realize that Malayalees are a very educated people? One hundred percent literacy! Do you realize we are a matriarchal society? Do you realize how hard my sister studied to come here on a scholarship to study at such a prestigious university as Princeton? Chris, where did* you *go to school?*"

Chechi would wildly offer tea, even if they had not yet eaten. Even if they were in the middle of eating. Even if they were already drinking tea . . . Worse, what if Chettan left the room. What if he came back and continued, "*Did you know that my sister has plans to do Ph.D.? Chris? We are a family of Ph.D.s. Do YOU have a Ph.D.?*"

Still worse, what if he actually asked the question and Chris answered, "*Yes, I am recently divorced, I am going through a divorce . . . ten years . . . no children . . . we tried. . . .*" And her brother then?

"*A divorced man? Nearly twice your age who cannot bear children?*" And Gita with . . . "*It was her. . . . She could not bear children. . . .*"

"*He abandoned her when he found she was barren? Monster. Chris . . . he is a Christian? Does he know you are not a Christian? Were you planning to convert and dunk yourself in a baptismal font and then to go out and proselytize all over the world? Will your children be named Bobby and that kind of name and then they will go to church too? Where did you find this person? How did this happen?*"

"*I don't know. . . . You were late, and I found him in the bookstore.*"

She stopped writing in her journal, because her words were gone. She studied and found the opposite of peace. With a frenzy she could not control, she studied and filled up her empty moments. She waited for his call, which she would not take, but which she needed to keep herself alive. She took furious notes and highlighted, waiting for the phone to ring, which told her she was not alone. And then he stopped calling.

"Hey?! Gita, Chris didn't call today!" Alison stood by the blue phone and smiled stupidly and her foolish, stupid, gaping mouth looked like a black disease hole and her stupid teeth looked so stupid and small. *You told him he disgusted you. I knew that. I knew that would be the thing. You stupid, foolish, ugly and terrible person.*

Gita's face crumpled despite her awesome pride. She took to frightening grooming, like French braiding her hair from the crown to the ends and tucking the tail in tight to her scalp. This way she removed it from view and turned into a skinny-headed, large-nosed girl with eyes as wide as a starving animal. She wore gray hooded sweatshirts that zipped up the front and gray baggy sweatpants that turned her androgynous and invisible. Her face turned gray before Alison's eyes.

The phone did not ring for two weeks and Gita's schoolbooks were untouched. She stopped going to class. At night, she curled into a ball, wrapped around her pillow, with her hair still tucked under, and she imagined he was there behind her, watching her sleep. She went deep inside. When she awoke, it was always before dawn and her head throbbed from her braided hair. When she could not stand the pain, she silently arose and went to the bathroom and let it down. It uncoiled in ringlets though it was really as straight as a pane of glass. She stood in the hot stream of the shower and cried. While her hair was still wet, she braided it again. She wore the same clothes every day and she slept in a long-sleeved T-shirt he had pulled from his bag one day when she was cold. It was blue and it said RAGGED MOUNTAIN RUNNING SHOP, CHARLOTTESVILLE, VIRGINIA.

In her gray hooded sweatshirt and pants, Gita returned to her room from a walk to nowhere, under bare boughs and a sky exactly the color of his eyes, and she stopped to check her mail as she did every day, because nearly twice a week there was a letter from home, because her parents wrote her regularly and they sent her all the news. Who went to the hospital, and who had sugar, and who had pressure and who married a girl from another place, and who could not get married because her horoscope was bad; it was all so much more important now that the phone had stopped ringing. But today, in the small box she could see, even by the waning light, a purple envelope and she knew it was not from home. And it was addressed to her and the return was a P.O. box in Madison, Virginia.

Gita, the song of my heart, please forgive my cruel words that were uttered at the thought of your not wanting me as much as I want you. You are nothing less than the angel of my life. Mea culpa, mea culpa, mea maxima culpa. I see you as nothing but pure, I took you to this, tragic lies and misspent life. I know I was your first love, and I know you want me to be your only and last love. I know this, I do not believe what I myself said on that terrible day and I only want you. I don't care how. I don't care in what way, but I cannot live any longer imagining you behind every tree in the woods, rising up from the water in the pond; my life without you is haunted with ghosts. Please do not stop loving me. Please do not leave me alone. I cannot live without you.

She sank to the floor and cried.

Chris, clean but deathly pale, made his daily drive to Madison. Opening his always-empty P.O. box for the fourteenth time (that he had no choice but to check though its emptiness was so painful), he saw that inside was a two-inch-by-two-inch envelope of palest pink. At the sight of it, he broke down and sobbed. It took him nearly two full minutes to steady his fingers to handle such a tiny note.

Chris, you are my life's beloved and I will never stop loving you. Do not call. I am learning to lay down my shame, so I can stand up under it all, for I too cannot live without you. Write to me.

He wrote.

You are always beautiful.

This much he said with certainty and a sure hand. Chris struggled over the next sentence because he wanted it to be perfect and he had never wanted anything as much as he wanted her. The last time he had spoken to her, he hadn't thought of how his words might be received. What he said, which seemed so simple and so clear, had ruined him. Perhaps rather than speaking of what he wanted, he need only speak of what he felt. Perhaps rather than speak of what he felt, he should speak of what he did. Perhaps a little of both would come out perfect. He continued,

I swim in the pond because it is clean and numbingly cold and under the water I am free to remember every beautiful thing about you, knowing that though I am lost in reverie, I am alone in my imaginings. . . .

What if what he did and how he felt rang maudlin? What if he bored her with his yearnings and need? It was his need, no, that drove her away? Or was it his boorishness and his accusations? Perhaps a little of both . . . then through the open car window blew fresh late fall air and the scent of something sweet and suddenly he thought that what he really wanted was to woo her in that first-falling-in-love way, rather than in that mop-closet way. What he really wanted was to win her with his charm and keep her with his true love and abiding devotion, the way he might have in better circumstances. Chris imagined what it might be that drew women to men; he considered what it was that drew men to women. He thought of what might be received as both deep love and healthy contrition. He thought of what to say that would sound sincere and yet poetic, assertive yet not haughty. He thought of how to write a love letter, and then he resumed,

. . . alone, but for a pair of sister mermaids. On land I am that man with unfocused eyes and a taut and empty face. Who, but you, knows why? But I am in love, and so I should be excused. Underwater I am free to cry, and underwater there are only mermaids to bear witness to my terrible shame at having hurt you, and my great pain at

having lost you. Gita, do not fret in petty jealousies over my swimming naked with mermaids, for mermaids hold no appeal to me who has found the most beautiful girl in the world and the best, and the sweetest and the very most pure of heart and soul. I adore you. Write to me.

Gita took down her braid and washed her clothes. She laughed and skipped to the post office and when her hair glinted, people again turned to see if someone had taken their picture. She went to class and lied and said her mother was dying, and was excused from absences. Her mother really was dying. This was true. Failing would only kill her faster, she justified.

Gita Nair, Princeton University, Rockefeller College, 403 Witherspoon Hall, Princeton, NJ 08544. He wrote it with patience and slowly because he had not made love to her in so very long. He smothered the envelope with kisses and he rubbed it on his chest after he addressed it. He lingered in the car to tend to his odd rituals of correspondence in private and then, shyly, he wrote to her that he did this. She wrote back to rub his envelopes on his belly button and she told him she would do the same. After many weeks of writing, he asked her to rub her letters over her breasts and she wrote that she would. Knowing where her letters had been, he grew hard at the sound of his key turning in his mailbox lock. She wrote that she had written him a poem, but that it was silly and long. *It is too rhymey-rhymey*, she worried. *I prefer rhymey-rhymey*, he had replied. *It is too long*, she worried. *I read Whitman*, he replied. *Is it as long as Whitman? No, but neither is it as good. This is yet to be seen, but then, Whitman didn't write a poem for* me *and that alone makes anything you write, rhymey-rhymey and long, better than anything he wrote, except "Body Electric." Nothing you write will be as good as "Body Electric."* He inserted the *ha ha*, for they were still courting, treading gently. It took several letters, and finally she sent him her rhymey-rhymey, too-long poem that she called "A Thousand Years Ago on the Day of Boat Races," and when he got it he sat in the car and read it straightaway, and when he was done he wrote her on the back of the take-out menu from Shin-Xo Fortune Garden that he was coming to get her and he wrote that he would never betray her again. He made an envelope from a folded piece of paper and return address labels and before he dropped it in the box he had a thought, and on the back he wrote,

> *We were together a thousand years ago and we will be together a thousand years from now.*

Kissing it top to bottom, left to right, he dropped it in the slot and left. Chris arrived home with screeching tires and he leapt out without removing his key from the ignition. Jeri was not there and so it was easier when he wrote her a note saying that there was an emergency in Trenton with the Santorini project and that he would call her that evening. He packed his bag and left immediately because Gita had sent him a rhymey-rhymey, too-long poem and he knew she had forgiven herself and forgiven him. She was asking him to come back and get her. And so he went. He would never again ask her for more than she was able to give, and he would take everything she offered.

Such a Good Boy

When George left home for college, he never looked back. He was still a dutiful son, and he was still a good boy. A *good* boy. He never forgot the afternoon of his fourteenth birthday when his father had been so understanding. *The diseases, the babies.* The image was never far off. But the world was full of beautiful, incredibly willing women. They waited around outside the medical school at Harvard. Boston women, looking to improve their lot in life. They came to socials, wearing halter tops and no bras. In Baltimore too they were everywhere. George would go to a party and some girl who smelled so delicious his eyes would get dreamy when she leaned in would whisper she had a secret. And when he leaned over to listen, she would lick his earlobe and show him just the tips of her white, white teeth. Women biting their bottom lips and bending to pick things up right in front of him. Women calling him at all hours of the night, inviting him over; some so forward they offered no pretext—no busted pipe, no jar to open, no leftovers, just sex. Hyped-up sex—"I'll blow your mind, George." "I'm a ballerina, George." "George? My roommate thinks you're really cute . . . and so do I."

So he prayed, he ran, he worked out with weights, he studied, but mostly he masturbated. And with each passing year, the women in his fantasies, who began like those two in the picture of the one chewing the other's nipple, became more and more and more buxom, until he had to imagine the woman on top, because her breasts were too big for him to mount her.

Many times he considered calling his mother and giving her the go-ahead to find him a bride. He really needed to get married. But he was still a resident, and he didn't have time to go through the motions of finding a wife, especially when all he really wanted to do was have sex. But he couldn't have one without the other. After he masturbated, his sense came back, and he realized that he could wait until he found the right woman himself or until he finished his program. But then, the next day would come and there they'd be, long-limbed, shiny-haired, shiny-mouthed, top-heavy girls licking their lips, standing too close to ask him the time.

One Saturday morning before rounds, he went for a long run around the campus and there were just too many of them, sweaty, their bras unable to keep all the play out of their bouncing boobs, and George ran home, went immediately to the telephone and was prepared to bite the bullet and tell his mother to find him a woman. But the conversation went a different way. If only Elizabeth had picked up the phone instead of CV. If only she had been there to hear her desperately horny son say, "Mom, I'm ready, find me a wife." But Elizabeth was not home—she had gone to the market, it being Saturday morning—and CV was there, and he had something else to say to his son.

"AH-ha, you called! I was just going to call you!" CV said. George could hear his smile on the other end, like he really had been just holding the phone ready to call when it rang. That was always an interesting feeling.

"Hi, Dad." George wanted to ask for his mother, but his father sounded so happy to hear from him.

"I wanted to ask you something. Are you free next weekend?" CV sounded hopeful.

George felt a sudden shiver. How should he answer? He had the next weekend off, but he absolutely could not go back to visit, he needed the rest.

CV felt his son's hesitation. "Don't worry, I don't want you to come home, although we always miss you. You know we can't travel because of Theresa. You should come home sometimes."

"I have next weekend off, why?"

"Well, do you remember my friend Chandrasekar from Kalliassery? The physics *sar*?"

"Does he have a big scar on his face?"

"Yes, that's him; well, his son is visiting the States. His name is Govind, you never saw him. He is a younger boy. Maybe only twelve or thirteen? He has won a prestigious writing award. A scholarship to do some semesters' study here."

George felt the shiver return. What was this going to be about? Was this Govind going to have to stay in his place?

"Yeah?" George hoped his irritation was translating loud and clear for his dad.

"He is visiting the States for one year. He will be staying there in Virginia someplace close to Washington. He is a good boy, everyone says so. Anyway, I want you to meet him for Onam Sadhya at one friend's house, you may not remember him. He was that one: Palakat Unni's Ammai's sister-in-law's brother. Do you remember that Palakat Unni? He is the man with that one tooth that comes straight forward from his lips? Do you remember?"

George sat down and put his head on the table. "No. No, Dad. I don't remember Palakat Unni with the tooth that comes straight out of his head."

"Anyway. It was a very strange thing. Especially since really . . . you know this one friend, his father was a dentist. Anyway . . . I want you to take this boy, Govind, to see the sights in Washington, D.C."

"Dad, I don't live in Washington. I live in Baltimore. It is not close. It is not easy. In fact, it is a pain in the ass." George immediately regretted his choice of words. Guilt, creeping guilt. "Even if he is a good boy."

CV, always gentle, waited for a minute. Quietly, he finished his thought.

"I know it is so hard for you, but his father is my friend; perhaps my best friend in the world. When I came to this country, he sent me a photo of the boat races in Alleppey in Kerala because I was so lonely. It was cold. So, so cold. It was so cold I often awoke wondering if I had died. You may think I am exaggerating, but I am not. He knew the picture would make me feel less homesick, warmer. I was alone here, you know. Without your mother." CV's voice sounded gentle. George, of course, knew the story.

Alpha and Omega

In the year of their new beginning, Gita loved Chris with great care and a gentle touch. Never again, she promised herself, would he endure another humiliation at the hands of some know-nothing roommate. Never again would she fail him by sharing their dark secrets. She would be alone but for him and it seemed not even a sacrifice. She took an apartment; she paid for it with two jobs; she never regretted it, even in the times when he was not there. She studied very hard.

How starved he was for her generous affection, for her naked hanging over his shoulder while he read the paper, for her naked walking about for no reason at all, for her open nakedness that told him she was at ease and completely at home with him, the only love of her life. For his part, Chris would have lain down and died for her, but then she would be alone. So instead he watched over her like a guardian angel, and held nothing back but the maudlin insecurities that plagued him, despite his faith in her constant and abiding love. In secret, he padded her bank account because she worked two jobs to keep an apartment where she could hang over his shoulder naked while he read the paper. When he visited, he went grocery shopping, saying that he had a taste for . . . rice, yogurt, tea, crackers, breakfast cereal, milk. He bought fish and shrimp and put it in the freezer, and by dinnertime he would say,

"You know what? I feel like having . . ." so that he could take her out to eat and leave all that food for the times she was alone. She made tea by the potful and studied very hard.

When she showered, sometimes she called him, "Chris!" and he would answer from the living room where he might be watering plants, or reading a book, or fixing the VCR she always managed to break. "Can you hear me?" she would say because she couldn't hear him. So he would come to the door and repeat, "Yes?" with a smile in his voice because she was so delicious to call for him from the shower, unable to wait, her thoughts burbling out, joyfully squeezing the drops of time they had together.

"I just thought of something!" she would say.

"What?"

"Would you like to have sushi tonight?" from the doorway; through the shower curtain he imagined her eyebrows up and hopeful, her mouth in a small o.

"I wouldn't mind at all, would you like to have sushi tonight?"

"Yes."

"Well, then let's have sushi tonight."

"Chris?"

"Yes?"

"Do you want to take a shower with me?"

And inside the shower she would talk about this and that and they would rotate around and around so that they both stayed warm, and when she was outside the stream, he would pull her close to him and hug her to keep her as snug as one can be when standing wet outside the stream, and when he was outside the stream she would soap up his chest and his back and sometimes, if he was willing to kneel down, she would shampoo his hair. He was always demonstrably appreciative. When they kissed in the shower, her lips felt swollen on his tongue.

In the unendurable moments, Gita arose from her beautiful bed tufted with silken covers and consumed her lonely mind with study. Sometimes she closed her eyes and imagined how much more of a penance it would be if only she had a kerosene lamp to study by, if only her eyesight were being steadily ruined by squinting in dim light, if only it were too cold or too hot. Ferocious study became the recourse against loneliness and resentment for loving another woman's husband, and for committing to a life that could never be fulfilled in the normal ways. And thus, when she left Princeton, she did so with distinction, despite being desperately and irrevocably in love. It was the love, the need to be carefree when Chris came to stay, that pushed her to extremes during his absence. It was the love, the need to be distracted when she looked out the windows at couples holding hands and kissing under trees in the broad daylight, that kept her from daydreaming, and earned her recognition after recognition. She became a wunderkind, a superstar, a prodigy.

The summer after she graduated, Gita went home to Kerala where there was not even the privacy to receive a letter and where all her post was carried into town and looked over by her uncle on his way to work. It was a very lonely summer, and she wrote her love notes in a journal that she marked like it was her schoolwork. In this way, it escaped the scrutiny of so many people who were curious at how America was treating this prodigal daughter who came home looking dangerously alive, powerful, vibrant and almost caustically independent.

Her mother had been dying for a decade, and out of decency, she waited until her daughter arrived and settled in before she left forever. And yet, it was not grief that contorted Gita's face in angry lines and twists of restraint, but rather the resentment of her circumstances and frustration over the inability to write a letter or make a phone call to Chris. A mighty loneliness for him welled up in her heart and rose through her body and cut so hard into her face that she came back from India with a crease between her eyes that never went away. She burned with the need to escape.

When her mother finally died, her father lost his grip on his mind, which he only held on to in order to make decisions regarding his wife's care. That task completed, and left alone after so many years together, Gita's father walked in circles, because going straight led nowhere, he said. He screamed when the fishmonger's bell rang and he ran outside with a stick to beat him, "HE IS THE BELL RINGER OF BELL

RINGERS. THEY ARE ORGANIZED, AND THEY WERE HERE YESTERDAY TO TAKE MY FOOT!" The fishmonger would jump from his bike and run to the gate shouting for someone to come take this crazy old man inside. Her father, his white hair rising and falling with his own shifts in energy, would wildly look around for understanding, and when his eyes rested on Gita, his youngest child, he told her, "Ammu, Ammukutty, where were you when I called you, where were you? You were not there, and now you have to go inside and take that bundle to give to the man so he will leave my foot. Good girl, now go then." And Gita would swallow her face into her cheeks to keep from crying because Ammu was her mother, and she would go inside and bundle a bundle of rags and leaves and hand them to the man with some money, for no reason but to spare her father's feelings, and to hush the fishmonger who nonetheless went to his next house and announced that old Dentist Nair whose wife just died has lost his mind. Gita would hold her shrunken father's hand and walk him inside, telling him that when the bell rang tomorrow to come get her because the bell ringer had no use for her small, girlish feet and she would quickly be able to get rid of him. Her father nodded at this wisdom but the next day came hurtling out of the house when the fishmonger's bell rang, screaming, "HE IS THE BELL RINGER OF BELL RINGERS. THEY ARE ORGANIZED, AND THEY WERE HERE YESTERDAY TO TAKE MY FOOT!" That afternoon, Gita heard some tender whispering and shushing and she followed it to find her father eating butter out of the palm of his hand and talking to the picture of his wife. "Ammukutty, you want some more butter?" And he took a smear with his finger and put it on her mouth. The framed photograph was greasy from top to bottom, the heat having melted Ammu's uneaten mouthfuls so they dripped down her entire glass-covered body. Gita stood in the corridor and watched with her lip between her teeth and her father looked up at her and said, "You? What is your name?"

Gita said, "It's me, Achan, Gita."

"Aaaa-ha . . . Gita, Gita, Gita, could you get some more butter for us?"

With tears in her eyes, finally feeling the loss of her mother, shot through by the sudden loss of her father, unable to even weigh the missing of her lover, ashamed at herself and yet unwilling to change a single thing in her illicit life, Gita called her brother and broke down.

"I am coming day after tomorrow," he said more quietly than she had ever heard him speak. "I will bring you both home."

Dr. Raman Nair arrived without any fanfare in a hired car he got at the airport. He brought only one suitcase, and in it there was nothing but enough. He entered his home and, with everyone otherwise occupied, unaware that he had arrived, he cried all alone in the front room. Gita heard his muffled sobbing and quietly went to him. She held him around his enormous left arm.

In her notebook she wrote to Chris:

> *My brother arrived today and he is as wretched as a good man who has lost his mother should be. I awaken in the nights and I am so afraid, it is like I am a small child who has lost her parents in a tragic accident. How can this be when I am so grown, and I have been away for so long, and I have a brother such as this who loves me like a daughter? I am not alone, and yet, I awaken in the nights and I feel that I am asleep atop a heap of garbage or in a doorway, hoarding my belongings—my one red glass bangle that no longer fits and a pile of mismatched playing cards—under my head in a bundle of ragged cloth. I feel destitute and I don't know why. I need you more than I can say.*

Dr. Raman Nair expedited the paperwork, bought his father a ticket, and brought them both home to his house in McLean, Virginia, at the end of the summer. Gita sedated her father for travel, and watched his sleeping face, peaceful and sad. Dr. Raman Nair barely spoke. When he looked over at his sister stroking his father's lank cheek and shining hair, he had to turn to the window because his tears knew no check, and it was a long flight.

From Heathrow, Gita escaped to the bathroom and called Chris collect. She prayed he would answer, and when the operator asked him, "Will you accept a call from 'Sanker deMan'" Chris heard his code and was at Dulles airport at 5 P.M. the following day. Jeri said, "Pretty short notice for a trip, don't you think?" It was the first time she had ever questioned his odd comings and goings. He turned red and gave her a kiss on the forehead. "It's only for the day. I'll be home by evening." She looked at him with narrow lips and swallowed.

From behind a pillar in the baggage claim, Chris kept his eye on the door and when they emerged his stomach shot up through his head, re-entered his body and crashed to his toes. He nearly lost his footing, and he knew again that he was in love.

She came into view holding the hand of an old, old man who could have been her grandfather. Behind them her brother carried a few totes. It was the first and only time in his life that Dr. Raman Nair followed. They were soon swarmed by a rotund tumble of girls with wet hair and soaked shirts, for it was raining again at Dulles airport. Gita felt Chris and looked up. He saw her face crumple and she dropped her head to her chest. That she was so moved quelled his fear that she had forgotten him. Despite her loyal commitment and so many private "ceremonies" of her own design—before fire, knee-deep in water, facing the sunrise in the east, and then the sunset in the west, and once, in a show of adoration and faith that would have quieted the doubts of Thomas, she smeared him with a mixture of ground cloves and the mud from the shores of Innisfree and recited from Gitanjali; she cried, it was the offering of herself—despite all this, he was still never fully confident that she could love him so much because she was so beautiful and bright, so glorious and amazing, so young, so bold and so completely unmarried. And he was just simply a man.

Gita said something to the group, took a bag from her brother and walked toward the bathroom and Chris made his way in that direction, but when she was only feet from out of sight, from nowhere the smallest one of these chubby girls called out, "Ammai, Ammai, wait, wait for me, I need to go too." Gita looked back at Shanti, and then up at Chris, who stopped midstride, unsure what to do. In the moment the two locked eyes, Gita mouthed to him, *I love you.* And then Shanti caught up and grabbed her hand and pulled her along.

It was a long trip back to Innisfree, and from the pond road he could see his home, this evening ablaze with lights on the other side of the water. Inside, Jeri had a committee over to plan some event he would not attend. He came in and moved quietly to her side, and when she looked up, he leaned down and gave her a kiss on the cheek. His eye lingered on her face longer than normal because it was troubled and sad. He wanted to say, "What's wrong," but he himself was so troubled and sad that he could not muster enough energy to ask her. In their lingering gaze, he imagined what a fine mother she might have been, what a fine person she was, so strong and resilient, how abominable it was of him to betray her, his lifelong friend, and then of course, he also knew he would never give up the love he had found so unexpectedly four years earlier. In the mirror behind Jeri's back he imagined his own guilty reflection and so he kept his eyes focused on his wife, who looked up at him longingly and full of loss. The ladies assembled around the table and milling around the room watched the two of them gazing at each other with such focus and sighed, wishing their husbands were just like Chris.

"You inspire me to great things," Chris announced as he returned home from the grocery, with an armload of daisies from Nasir's.

"Really?"

"I love the way you talk."

"I talk just like you, but with a better vocabulary."

"This may be generally true; however, my love," here he finally took her in his arms and kissed her, interrupting himself, "when you say 'really' it comes out, 'rree-uh-li' and when you say 'vocabulary' it comes out 'wo-caah-boo-luhry.' It makes you sound educated."

"I am educated."

"Yes, but even if you weren't, if you talked like that, everyone would think you were."

"If I wasn't educated, I would not talk like this."

"You are just being difficult," Chris replied with a smile, pulling her back to her enormous tufted bed covered in a huge hand-printed cotton bedspread. Elephants, flowers, peacocks . . . elephants, flowers, peacocks.

From the Journal of Gita Nair

SEPTEMBER 8, 1990

This love is a burden on my soul.

There were too many years to count and so many of them so good, so why then, she wondered, was it so very bad now? How long was the journey to here?

❧

"I'm reminded of you whenever the wind blows. Even a breeze touches me like your fingertips when I'm alone and away from you."

"Well, that's your choice, isn't it?" Gita would reply, extricating herself from his grasp with cruel abruptness.

"What is my choice?" Chris would ask, his face pale with the sinking knowledge that she would not belong to him his whole life.

"*What was your choice?* What could I possibly be talking about, Chris? What choice could I *possibly* be talking about?" Gita would scream, her long hair would pitch back and forth behind her as she stormed around the room making a furious show of straightening his things. *His Fortune* magazine, *his* bowl of pretzels, *his* jacket left on the chair instead of hung in the closet.

"Gita . . . Gita please!" Chris would stand and walk behind her, which only infuriated her further.

"Get out of my way. I don't need this kind of thing." Gita would then slam out of her apartment, leaving her lover standing alone, shaken and blotched with fear and hurt.

Gita would walk around the block, once, twice, a few more times. These days the walk did little to calm her. It did little to bring her remorse for her behavior. It did little to remind her of her old love for Chris. Gita's walks after these outbursts felt like sitting still and stretching a rubber band in front of her face, each time a little farther and tighter, anxiety mounting with the certainty that the next stretch or the next or the next would be the one that snapped back the band and smacked her across the cheek.

❧

At the GWU English department's happy hour at Sequoia, Gita sits like a stupid and looks left and right without moving her head. She had said yes after so many years of saying no; she has thought maybe she needs to make new friends. Maybe it is time to meet *other* people. But she has grown bizarre from solitude. Man after man approaches, each not at all dissuaded by the outright, blank rejection of the one who came before him. They come and stand beside her; some lean forward and whisper in her ear; she says nothing to any of them. She stares. She looks at them without opening her mouth and she stares. Her blinks come only one per minute and they are mesmerizing. The men cannot leave, and she cannot speak. It is beyond strange to deal with her. Again, her colleagues stop asking her to join them. Again, she doesn't even notice.

The department held her in the highest regard for her work ethic and for her beauty that, despite her eccentricities, made her work popular worldwide. Two novels along with everything else? And still, she was so young. They considered her an odd case, a rarity in their academic world, and they wanted to keep her close; they had already granted her tenure. Sabbatical was what was needed. She needed to write another book, she knew, because she would never leave Chris, and she needed to go back to the ferocious focus to survive the loneliness. She would never leave him, for his love was now the only connection she had to being alive. She punished him for it with ruthless hatred, which was not the opposite of love, but rather its very worst manifestation. Sometimes she looked out the window at the passing-by cars and the happy people with families and lives and she hated him to death.

"You are a brooding girl. This is why you don't get married," Chechi said, looking at Gita's serious face. "There is nothing happening to be unhappy about, and you are sitting at the table with everyone, and there is no reason to be unhappy and still you are brooding there."

"You leave her alone," Usha piped in. She stood behind her *ammai* in a show of solidarity.

"You shut up, girl, and don't mind our business," her mother shouted at her daughter. Turning back to Gita, she continued, "When did this happen to you? I remember you for your whole life and when did you become so miserable? As if you weren't so blessed."

Gita felt herself begin to shrink and, despite her reputation to let loose in angry tirades, she was still unable to talk back to her family. It was true, what her *chechi* said. When did she become so miserable?

"If you would only smile and look happy with happy eyebrows then we could find you a husband," Chechi went on. "So good-looking, such a waste to make ugly faces."

"I don't want a husband."

"Happy eyebrows?" Usha, unable to be quiet, interjected with a naughty turn of her lips.

Jaya shot her a furious look and raised her voice. "You shut up, girl." Facing Gita again, she rejoined, "Don't you want a husband?"

"No."

"Why not, how can you have kids?"

Usha moved beyond the reach of the spoon her mother was using to gesticulate and interrupted again, "You don't need a husband to have kids."

Lunging forward quick as light, Jaya hit her once across the arm and once back again, a one-two slap with spoon. "You shut up, girl." Usha screwed up her face and, rubbing her arm, stomped away.

Gita put her head in her hands and remained perfectly silent and still until they all forgot about her and went about their business. Shanti, her sweetie, sat next to her and put her darling head against her shoulder. When everyone else was gone, she whispered into her *ammai*'s ear, "We can live together, and we will neither one of us get married. We will be old spinster ladies together."

Gita turned her head and looked deeply into the child's eyes, so close to hers and full of love. *I might have had a daughter by now.*

❧

"I take a handkerchief from your drawer when I leave here and I keep it in my breast pocket, so I can take it out and smell your scent . . . sandalwood. When I close my eyes, I can feel you near me."

"But I am not near you, am I? I am never near you for long, am I?" Gita would look at him deeply, something between anger and hurt dwelling in her dangerous black eyes.

Chris would look at her a bit too long and his face would begin to blotch because he didn't know how to respond. He would blink, and open and shut his lips, and lick them nervously, and she would look at this and misread his meaning. *Why doesn't he say it? Why doesn't he tell me he wants to marry me, be with me forever? Why won't he say, "I am never leaving you again"?*

He then would watch the dangerous look in those eyes change to teary frustration and think that he had said too much instead of too little and would say nothing. And then Gita would turn him to ashes with a white-hot stare, whirl away, and storm out of her apartment and around and around the block, gaining no peace, leaving him alone and unsure of whether to stay or go. His gorgeousness had long ago withered in her presence.

Many years ago, she had lain quiet and sated in his arms. Absently stroking the curly hairs on his chest, she asked, "If we had a child, what would you want to name it?"

Chris turned red and his eyes smarted and stung. He was afraid to answer and he remained quiet for too long. In his mind he blurted out a thousand names, none of which he had considered before. Brilliant, resplendent names, names of kings and names of goddesses, the muses, the fabulous characters in fabulous books. If he shouted out Scheherazade, would she laugh out loud? Surely she would, no? Scheherazade Jones was a preposterous name, but who cares? Who cares? *If I got to have a baby with you, I would give her six names in a row, and I would call her one each day of the week and on Sunday I would call her all six. If it were a boy, I would call him Chris, because you love my name.* In his mind, he answered, but out loud he said nothing at all.

She raised herself onto an elbow and looked him straight in the eye and a slow tear fell down his cheek. With her long first finger, she pushed it away and said, "Chris?"

He turned from her and wiped his eyes on the back of his hand. Finally, he answered, "Don't ask me questions you don't want the answers to."

She never asked him again.

Between the Dupont Circle Metro station and 1616 Q Street, N.W., was a flower shop. Nasir's Fresh Flowers. Over the years, Chris must have bought entire fields of flowers there. To see the glimmering spark on

Gita's face, he would stand in the rain and select flowers one by one, though Nasir always had bunches already wrapped. Like the kerosene lamps of her imagination, the individual choosing of flowers in the rain was some measure of misguided penance. He felt better if he arrived wet, and she appreciated it for what it was, homage to love, penance for love. She would take him in her arms, unwrap him from his cold clothing, and hold him until they were one again.

But now, standing on the sidewalk facing the shop, Chris hesitated to buy flowers. They seemed to strike her as a foolish gesture these days. He would arrive with a bouquet he had chosen bloom by bloom as he always did, and she would greet him with a roll of her eyes. She would throw them on the table and stare at him. And why was it that he could not feel that she didn't appreciate them, but rather that she wanted something else? And yet she rejected everything he offered. Even his love was refused, and he began to perch on the side of the bed, afraid of touching her accidentally, afraid then to sleep. If he reached out for her, lay a hand on her hip, she would pick it up and throw it off. It had been happening for months.

"Do you no longer love me?" he asked, afraid, whispering, terrified of the answer.

"Of course I love you, of course I love you. How dare you ask me if I love you? I have given you everything. I have given you my entire life. Everything. How dare you ask me that question?" And she would get up and storm off. Sometimes she would leave in her pajamas, and then he would sit up and watch out the window, afraid to leave lest she come home, afraid to stay lest she come home, afraid of what might be happening to such a beautiful girl in the city, angry, in pajamas, in the middle of the night.

Gita, angry, in pajamas, prowled the city in the middle of the night. There was no more inside her but the instinct to stay alive. She sat down on a bench under a streetlight and pulled her legs in tight to her chest. Perhaps she fell asleep. Before dawn she was roused by the smell of the person beside her, where there had been no one before. She looked up. It was a woman, toothless and abject, looking her straight in the eye.

"Whachyoo doin' here?"

Gita was suddenly afraid. She stood up and turned to go, but the woman reached out and took hold of her wrist. The woman was holding on so tight, and looking at her so hard, that Gita began to shake; she pulled back, but the woman held fast.

"God is tryin' to tell you somethin'." And then she let go and turned her head back into her bag.

Gita turned away and walked home, still trembling. *Enough. Enough. This is enough. I am . . . I cannot. Enough.* It was the end. There would be no more. It was over. When she arrived home, he was gone, and there was a note on the table.

You are the love of my life. I will die loving you.
Chris

Gita read the note many times, tore it to shreds, lay down right where she was and fell asleep.

Something to Do

Two days later, Gita boarded a plane to Kerala. She took two weeks of sick leave; who could fail to believe she was sick? She looked like a vampire.

"Chetta, I am going home for two weeks."

"WHAT? What do you mean, you are going home? Why are you going home on such short notice? Why are you doing such a thing? So expensive, why are you going now, in the middle of the semester? *What do you mean?* Is there something wrong . . . with you?"

Gita stared at him without speaking. She began to shake slightly; she held her hands tightly under the tablecloth. Jaya sat nearby and watched them both, silently. The girls listened from the top of the stairs, drawn from their beds by their father's booming shouts.

"I have to go home. I need to do some research for a book I am writing, and I need to do it now. Emergency."

"Emergency? What book? What book is such an emergency that you can't wait a few months until semester is over? What research cannot be at least begun from here?"

"I need to talk to people. The old people. In our family." Gita pulled in her breath and waited with her eyes open on his face. His glower grew darker. Jaya gasped quickly but said nothing.

"Why?"

Gita sat and blinked quietly. Her cheeks pulled in a loud smack when she opened her mouth to lick her dry lips. "I need to know some things to write this story."

"What story is it that you are writing that needs the old people's memories?"

Again, she said nothing for a long time. They stared at each other. "Our story, Chetta. Omanakumari, the Brahmin, Parameshwaran Namboodiri."

Jaya gasped. It was a terrible sound full of anguish and fear. "No." She got up and pointed in Gita's face. "No. You cannot tell that story. You cannot bring it over here from over there. You cannot. You leave it where it is." She began to cry. "Do you not see who is in this house? Five girls, Gita. There are five girls here, Gita! No. You leave that story where it is over there. We came all the way here and left it there, and now you are going to go back and bring it here?"

Dr. Raman Nair was silent. It was ridiculous when she spoke her superstitions out loud. Preposterous, really. Jaya, speaking as though she was making sense when she sounded so ridiculous. He could say nothing. Until she spoke, he had been thinking quite the same way, but to hear it . . . it was . . . ridiculous.

But they were all going senile now, they were all old enough not to worry about her anymore. They were so old that their talk was like a bacchanalian revelry. They would talk now about their orgasms, about the size of their long-dead husbands' penises. They would tell you how their daughter-in-law, who might be your mother or your aunt, would never give them enough oil for their hair, or how they stole money from the box, not for spending, but just to watch her go mad in the searching, searching. It was what happened with very old people. They were less protective of the secrets. And anyway, it was a novel. Mixed and muddled, truth and lies, made for a better story.

Two weeks. And when she came home, she prayed, she would be over it, it would be gone from her heart, this glittering, raw pain. And she would have a story to write. She would have something to do. Just something to do. Anything. Something. Anything to do but lick and paw at her glittering, raw pain.

Gita Nair Continues Her Story

The Cursed Life of Sreemathi Omanakumari

Omanakumari stood on her veranda looking out into the twilight and wished she could more comfortably sit down. Her feet were swollen so large that sitting was even worse; lying, even with her giant feet elevated, was unbearable because she could not breathe. Standing still was no better because within a few minutes, her feet would become so heavy that to take her first step required a heaving exertion that taxed her weary heart. Walking was the only thing to do, and how many miles could she walk in a day?

And when she walked, she was called to from every corner to go home, to sit down, to lie down, to be still. And walking alone in the morning, in the forest, no longer brought solace for she cursed the forest with an angry heart, for sheltering Parameshwaran Namboodiri that day so many months ago, when he watched her and later took her for his own.

But anyway, best to move, she thought. And she heaved around and walked back through her home, past the kitchen and the dining space, through the corridor and out the door without anyone seeing her to tell her to come in and sit down. These days, the only thing she was expected to do was to sit down and eat. It could have afforded her many minutes to dream, but she was spent of dreams and there seemed no reason to think about many things at all.

She turned out of her house and walked to the south and through the forest for a moment, where it very soon opened into a field that was broad and full of the last light of the day. The long grasses picked up the evening breeze and gave Omanakumari a few moments of conscious pause, to feel the cool air and to see the calm and open space. She had changed so terribly over this last year. Her smile that was always overflowing her face had receded entirely and these days, she looked terribly ill. And though she was so big with her child, the rest of her had shrunken to wisps. Her neck was too long and coiled with the strain of her shoulders to support her enormous abdomen. Her arms were as thin as stalks and her back was so weak that every lump of her spine and each cut of her ribs was as evident as the hopelessness of her situation. The light turned slightly bluer and she moved on.

Before long, she felt a grave thirst and her baby began a wild and horrible dance that squeezed her back and made her cry out, and then, just as suddenly, her belly became as hard as a stone, and in this periodic tightening Omanakumari always found it even more difficult to breathe. From a nearby house, an old lady came out to see who was crying. This old woman was called Amma, or mother, simply because she was older than everyone, and black enough to have given birth to the earth itself. Despite being indisputably the oldest person anyone had ever known, she had amazing hearing and could walk a hundred miles in a day, they said. She knew everything, also, and her age was so advanced that she had divine insight to the future, which, she said, was nothing but the past repeated over and again. Seeing this small girl afflicted with a gigantic pregnancy, Amma went back into her house and brought a cup of water and a stick to walk with and then she scooted up the path with the frightening shimmy-hop of one who was almost old enough to fly, but somewhat too old to walk. It was nonetheless an amazingly quick gait, and she arrived at Omanakumari much faster than if Omanakumari had tried to come to her.

"O," she said, supporting the pregnant girl on her shoulder and lowering her to the ground. "You are enormous." Omanakumari gratefully drank down the water and silently wished for more. "I know, but if you want more, you will have to get up and come to my house because I cannot be expected to carry more than a cane and a cup. I am very old."

Omanakumari smiled weakly and blinked her eyes to indicate her respect. Amma read her mind then too. "Ah, little girl, don't worry about these silly things. You are thirsty, you wish for more water. You are pregnant, you wish you were not."

Omanakumari's eyes widened and in a frightened hush she whispered, "It's not that way."

"Mmm." Amma held the girl against her thigh until her breathing returned to normal. She kept her old grizzled hand on her abdomen until she felt it surrender to the pressure she placed there, and when the spasm was over, she sat Omanakumari upon the ground and told her to use the stick. "Raise yourself onto your knees and by then I will be standing and then you put one hand on my shoulder, and push up using the stick. Understand?"

With that, Amma stood up, and standing, she was exactly the same height as Omanakumari on her knees. "I think when I was young like you, I was tall."

"Mmm," Omanakumari replied. She had taken hold of Amma's shoulder and was pulling herself up.

"Really, I think I was tall."

"Oh, Amma, yes, you were surely very tall." Omanakumari smiled for the first time in over a year.

"Everyone here used to say that I had a very fine figure and my hair was this long." She indicated the backs of her knees with her hand, which looked like a leather sandal.

Omanakumari smiled again. She had emptied her mind of internal talk but her eyes flickered and sparked because Amma was nearly bald and lank as a rope.

"Really," Amma insisted, shimmy-hopping alongside the girl, who was perhaps three times her size.

"Oh, Amma, I can see how long your hair was and how tall you were and how fine your figure was just by looking at you now." Omanakumari's eyes sparkled so brightly that Amma too sparkled to herself. They were nearing Amma's small house, and Omanakumari's thirst began to rise just knowing the well was close by.

"I think you are joking with me, little girl." Amma pulled Omanakumari up the step and arranged her in a cloth hammock of a chair that gave the child the first comfort she had felt in many months. Drinking down several cups of water from the deep well, Omanakumari felt light and refreshed and, looking deeply into Amma's gray eyes, she lay her head back and fell asleep. She dreamed that she was digging for something she had buried, but that she didn't remember where. Her mother and her father were watching from the front steps of her house and they had no advice to offer though she asked them many times, and with this frustration, Omanakumari woke up.

When she opened her eyes, it was darkest night, lit with a full moon. Amma was still there, sitting on a small stool, resting her chin on the rail that enclosed her porch. She was so black and so small that with her feet dangling far above the ground and her hairs standing on top of her head, she looked more like a monkey than a person.

Amma turned her head to Omanakumari and said, "Hmmm. You think so?"

Omanakumari was not sure what she had been thinking. She felt frustrated and hot and jittery in her body. Her baby was swimming so fast that its elbows and feet could be seen through her skin. Amma, seeing her belly dance, hopped from her stool and came close. Placing both her palms on Omanakumari's middle and feeling this way and that, she sighed deeply and shook her head.

"What?"

"What have they told you?" Amma's gray eyes were now bent close to her belly and she seemed to be able to see inside. She continued to shake her head. "Did they tell you anything?"

"What is Amma saying?" Omanakumari asked her. She looked down as well, but all she saw was her brown belly, with a long black stripe cleaving her in half. She was so large that her skin had stretched to its maximum and was run this way and that with red-scarred attempts to enlarge further.

"Hmmm . . ."

"What?"

"*Mole* . . ."

Omanakumari's heart began to beat faster at whatever news this old lady found too disturbing to tell her, having seen all the miseries since the beginning of the world.

"It's two."

"Two?"

"Twins."

"Twins . . . ?"

Omanakumari put her hands on her belly and felt around. The baby's elbow or knee or foot poked out at her rib and she pushed it back and it popped out on the other side. She pushed in again, and a distinguishable hand punched her from the inside, low toward her hip.

"That one is the boy." Amma pointed at the fist.

"A boy?"

"And a girl."

"A boy and a girl?" Suddenly, Omanakumari felt a sick bile in her throat and she struggled to get up from her seat. Unable to hoist her weight, and Amma unable to lift her, Omanakumari leaned her head to the side and vomited onto the porch. Breathing hard, Omanakumari wiped her mouth on her clothing and whimpered, "O, Amma, I will clean it!"

"*Mole* doesn't have to worry on that, just rest there." She patted her belly and the babies came up to Amma's hand as though she were offering sweets. One and then the other in swimming circles.

From far away, Narayanikutty could see a lantern glowing in front of a house edging the field. As she came closer, Omanakumari knew it was her mother by the swinging of her hair and her gait so familiar. With great difficulty and the use of the stick, she rose to meet her on the porch.

"Ah . . . she is with Amma." Narayanikutty felt relief in the quieting of her pulse. She held out her arm and grasped the girl's elbow with her hand. Since before nightfall, she had walked here and searched there and grown frantic without showing it on her face, without lengthening her stride or speeding her step, that no one might know her child had disappeared in the night, as big as an elephant and as wan as an orphan.

Amma made an earthy sound, like the moving of mountains, and looked out into the night. "She was falling down there." She smacked her mouth a few times and Narayanikutty looked at her intensely. "Then I brought her here, and she fell asleep."

Narayanikutty stood on the porch and for the first time in her life was irritated by the movement of moths around the fire. The flitting shadows they cast flickered too quickly over her daughter's face, changing her second by second. They gave the mother no peace in recognition. How could the child be bright as a star and a moment later as dark as death? Not equipped to change the world or even the curse of the evening, Narayanikutty sucked her teeth in an echo of Amma's gum-smacking resignation and she too chose to look out into the night.

They stood in this way for so long that Omanakumari's feet began to hurt again and, using her stick, she oomphed herself back into the chair that gave such comfort. The comfort made her sigh so deep she coughed. This cough, like all coughs, made her abdomen so hard her toes curled up, and her neck curled down. And then the pain was so intense it removed her from her mind. For a few minutes, Omanakumari was seized tight and unaware of her pain.

Narayanikutty, gripped with panic, dropped to her knees and pleaded, "*Mole, mol!*" As though desperately calling her would act as protection.

Amma, knowing all things, thrust her hips and legs forward in her walking way and laid on her planished hands. She groaned like the piling of the earth into mountains, which was her way of breathing, and this sound and this touch soothed the babies, who went back to sleep.

"They are so restless there, these days . . ." Amma kept her hands on Omanakumari's belly, the way a mother does to assure the babies are deep, and she continued her mountainous groaning, and with each exhalation she pushed out her purple lips and her face went flat with the collapsing of her cheeks and her forehead into a single plane of near-archaeological senescence. Her appearance of being so old as to be nearly reborn gave Narayanikutty faith.

Watching as Amma laid hands on the child, she could hear her question rise in that calm and peaceful place. "Hmmm . . . she has always been restless, always walking, walking and smiling loudly . . ." Narayanniamma smiled herself remembering her daughter as a child, running too much and being so happy. "You think this baby will be that way too then, Amma?"

"Hmmm . . . perhaps the girl . . ."

And in that moment the mother knew it was two and she knew one was a boy, and what this meant was too enormous a thought for such a simple slice of the hushed and gentle night.

Gita Nair looked up, for her phone was ringing. Again. She put down her papers, leaned her body over to the right and, clenching her pen in her hand, fell asleep.

Invitations

Jaya Nair looked out the window to check if the flag was down, and seeing that it was, she went to get the mail. The days at the end of the summer aggravated her allergies that still, after almost thirty years in this country, had not yet abated. She spent as little time as possible outside. It seemed a grievous trick to live peacefully for so many years without as much as a cold, and to move to a new place halfway around the earth to settle down forever only to find that just living there made you sick. She had grown up infested with worms and never been sick, and now? A hacking cough and merciless sneezing that made her wish she were dead, if not for all the work that would pile up in her absence waiting for her reincarnation. *With my luck, I will return to exactly the same life.*

When her allergies acted up, Jaya was as miserable as her sister-in-law, and every bit as unreasonable. She was unable to see it. These days, however, there were drugs. The children insisted that she try them out, but she had a certain aversion to the idea of pharmaceuticals, though Usha claimed that she refused to take them because she wanted to make everyone miserable right along with her. But then, Usha was argumentative and disrespectful with her marijuana T-shirts and loose hair, so what did she know. Sometimes Jaya looked at the small squirt bottle of relief and was tempted to try it out, but there was something empowering in so much suffering. It was like walking on your knees on rocks, or self-flagellation. It might be purifying. She had used the spray when they had company coming, and it did help quite a bit, but she didn't see any reason to use it for every day. Just special occasions. She was afraid of becoming dependent, and she thought that was very sensible.

Inside the mailbox, she caught the bright blue corner of an aerogramme and her heart fluttered because still, after so many years, she missed her home and her people. Pulling it free, she read that it was from her college friend and roommate Premala, and she felt light as she extracted all the catalogs and bills and rushed back to her house to open her letter. Going to the office to get the letter opener, she thought, as she always did when a missive from this group came, of the particular excursion they took when they were so young to Kanyakumari, the temple and the beach. The times of their lives. Each of these ladies, now with children and living all over the world, thought of this trip, or the one to the hill station in Utti, or the time they were in a production in fancy dress and Chandri played the man because she was so tall. And each of this far-flung sisterhood smiled and ran for the letter opener, regardless of whether the kettle was whistling, or the husband was calling, or the children were asking for food. She ripped it clean and sat down, glad for Muthachan's tendency to sleep in the day, glad for the quiet in the house.

When Dr. Raman Nair came home, he was in a jovial mood because the air was getting cooler in the evening, and the autumn was such a joy to anticipate. He loved the change of seasons, and because he was so satisfied with his life in all its blessings, he never felt that pang of sadness that struck at those with longings at these times of year. He was a man of no regrets and so he entered the house with a whoop and cupped the face of his enormous horse of a dog and shouted out, "Taj! It is almost autumn! I believe you will grow one more foot this year! You are a dog to be proud of!" Taj nodded his head and stood on his hind legs to give his master a kiss. They danced. Dr. Raman Nair called to his wife, "Jaya!! Come see me dance with my dog!" And she did come, and the girls who were home came too, and Usha took a picture because it was a fine thing to see their father dancing with the dog, and they knew that it would be a wonderful night.

Over a sumptuous *biriyani* dinner that Jaya made for no special reason other than that they all loved *biriyani*, and she had gotten a letter that made her happy despite her sneezes, Jaya told Dr. Raman Nair that Premala had written a letter today.

"Ah, Premala, Premala. How is Krishankutty? How are they?"

"Oh, it's all very good. Gopi is in London on assignment and then Krishankutty has been doing better, he is able to see almost clearly after surgery."

"Who is there now?"

"His mother is there, but she is okay. Just diabetes and she doesn't do enough exercise. They have a lady who comes to help when she is at work."

"That is good."

"True. Anyway, she is fine. She asked me to look up a boy who has come here. One friend of hers has a boy."

"Which boy?"

"I know her, actually, I know her, but only a little bit."

"You know the boy?"

"No, the mother."

"Ah, the mother."

"Anyway, do you remember there was that one M. K. Panniker in Pallakat who had that one sister who was an albino and she got her hair dyed and then she married that other Menon one who was the *sar* at UC College in Malayalam along with that M. G. Sarngadharan Nayar?"

"You're kidding, right?" Usha interjected. "'An albino who married that other one?' You're kidding, right?" The girls were all laughing and Muthachan, who had been sitting calmly, was beginning to get agitated. He was sometimes more uncomfortable when they all laughed, because in his poor eyes they looked like they were coming apart, like it was an earthquake, the trembling, the shaking, it made him feel like he should take cover. Shanti got up and went behind him. She leaned over his shoulder and kissed his sunken cheek. She picked a toasted cashew off of his plate and put it in his mouth. He looked up at her and smiled and pinched her nose. They all breathed deeper and let their mother finish.

"Oh yes, oh yes, that is a true story. She was white as a ghost. Really.

She was. And she had pink eyes like a rabbit and of course it was a terrible tragedy, but then she grew up and she had such a beautiful body shape and her hair, even though it was yellowish, was so thick and lustrous. Really. And then they came with these other technologies, you know? And so they got her black contact lenses and they dyed her hair and then she could get married! I mean, her hair did not come really black, but it was dark and she had a good body shape and when they did all those cosmetic touch-ups she was really so pretty and so she could get married! It was a miracle."

"Did they ever disclose the horrific truth?" Usha mocked. "I mean about the miracles?" The smirk went unnoticed by her gentle mother alive in the story.

"Oh, well, yes, of course, they had to tell that truth, but it was okay. They were very good people, the Menons. You remember them, right?" she added to her husband. "Anyway, they have kids now and none of them has that problem." Jaya smiled and nodded. It seemed everyone was enjoying the *biriyani*.

"OH, for heaven's sake." Dr. Raman Nair threw his fork down on the plate. "What about the boy and his mother?"

"OH, oh," she glared at Usha, "you see what you did? You interrupt me and then I lose my thoughts . . . where was I?"

Dr. Raman Nair raised his voice and answered, "The albino who married the Menon who taught in Malayalam with M. G. Sarngadharan Nayar at UC." He exhaled sharply.

"Oh yes, yes. Anyway, that M. K. Panniker has a first cousin Sridevi, she is married to Chandrasekar the physics *sar*, and their boy, Sridevi and Chandrasekar's boy, he is here in the States. His name is Govind. I am going to call him to come for Onam. Always the more the merrier for Onam."

❧

It had not worked out the way Gita planned. She returned in two weeks with the full tragedy of the family's curse, but her pain had only grown more raw and more glittering. She was in no way weaned from him. Over these last months, Chris had called hundreds and hundreds of times. Of late, he said nothing, a long silence and then he cried and cried. It was nearly intolerable, and yet it was a just penance for her to have to hear what she had done to such a good man as this. He was a far better person than she. He always called from pay phones. There was no way to call back.

She had left for Kerala without saying good-bye. She had left without telling him where she was going. He called in those first days with such fear and panic in his voice. He pleaded with her to just let him know she was alive. "You walked out in the middle of the night and I haven't heard from you since. Please. Gita . . . please." He was a far better person than she. When she returned, she listened and listened curled in a ball on her bed. Unable to part with a single message, she called the phone company and increased the size of her voice-mail box. As the days passed, her strength waned from the listening. Again, her skin turned gray. Her lips turned black. Her hair came out in her fingers. It was far worse than the first time she had left him so many, so many, so many years ago. She stopped eating and her hips grew so pointed it hurt her to lie on her side. At night, she got in bed without washing her face or brushing her teeth and she called her voice mail. She listened to his messages all night. In the morning, she got out of bed and without bathing went to work. Everyone noticed. When the semester ended, they called her into their office; they accepted her proposal for sabbatical. Suddenly, she had nowhere to go, and in her state of mind, again . . . nothing to do.

Chris went to his P.O. box and found she had written him a line.

Do not come for me. Please, do not come for me.

When he came for her, he discovered that she had put a bolt above her knob. He did not have that key. He sat on the floor outside the door until he drew the attention of the watchman, who came up and told him he had to leave. He sat in his car outside her apartment until he thought he would be better off dead. He considered driving into a bus, but then what would she do and who would she have? Instead, he drove home. Innisfree felt like a haunted house. He could not sleep and he started at every creak in the floorboards, every chirp of life in the woods. All the comforts of his home scared him to death. He sent her a note.

> *If you leave me, you will leave me shattered and destroyed. But even if you leave me, I will never leave you and your heart will always, always have a home with me. If you must leave me now, then one day, please Gita, one day, come back.*

She cried until her face hurt so much that she could not even touch it with cold water, and she lay down on the bathroom floor and fell asleep.

She was awakened on a late July night by the phone ringing and it was an odd hour, or so it felt, because she slept so often and yet was always tired. Coming out of the bathroom, she saw that it was only 9 P.M., and when she checked the voice mail, it was her brother and not Chris. It was a discomfort, though Chris's messages tore and scarred. Her brother calling meant it was not Chris. She had to call back for he had been calling for a few days now, saying he had not heard from her and to call him. *Onam is Saturday.* She hadn't even remembered. Soon, he would come looking for her, certainly if he didn't hear from her for Onam, and even *she* was appalled by the catastrophe of her living environment and her personal hygiene. Considering the state of their father, she feared he would put her on medication as prophylaxis against dementia, or have her subjected to tests. As it was, they already found her a complicated and difficult person.

"AH-ha, there you are!"

"Hi, Chettan."

"Are you screening your calls these days? Are you so busy you can't find time to call home? What is the problem there?"

"Hi."

"Mmm. Anyway, we want you to come on Saturday."

"Chettan . . . I don't know . . ."

"What do you mean you don't know? It is Onam." Dr. Raman Nair paused with a flutter in his chest that he was not accustomed to feeling. It was dreadful. "Do you want me to come get you?"

"No, no, it's not anything."

"You did not see us in so many days. You know that Dhanya is going to college in only a few weeks and still you are not coming here?" Again, he felt that dreadful feeling. "*It is Onam.*"

"No, no, it's not that, it's just . . ."

"I will be there to pick you up at—"

"No, no, I will be there; I'll be there at five." Shamed, Gita looked at her chewed fingernails. "It is Onam. I just forgot it was Onam. I have been so busy."

She forgot it was Onam? "Okay then, I will see you on Saturday. Come on Friday if you want. There will be the Suprabhatam in the morning. You like that."

"I'll see you on Saturday, Chettan." Gita hung up the phone and sat in the dim light. She went to the bathroom and looked in the mirror and gasped. She bathed and washed her hair and then made a small meal of cheese and crackers. If she had to be there on Saturday evening, she had better start preparing now. Her appearance, as it was, would frighten them even more than if she didn't show up at all.

Baby George had a dream in his Spartan campus apartment that he was a baby again. He was awakened in the middle of the night by the sound of his own crying; he was drenched. His chest hurt and his throat. He sat up and waited for his heart to settle its frantic beating, to recover from a peaceful sleep shattered by noise and sudden pain in the body. He had dreamed that he was watching while his mother killed the neighborhood with a flaming wooden stick. She held him on one hip and they ran from house to house while she set fire to everything in her path. He tried to make her stop, but she said it was all for the best.

It was a very strange dream, and his mother was always very cordial to the neighbors. He turned and looked at the clock. Two o'clock. He had to leave for work in a couple of hours and so he lay back down on his pillow, and then, because it was wet, he switched it with the other one. Comfortable now, he immediately fell asleep. It is the habit of doctors to sleep despite bad dreams.

When he awoke, it was dark, as always, and he was a little groggy, as always. He showered and then he felt better. He left his dream behind in the night, because it was not the first time his mother had plagued him with internal conflicts that manifested in odd places. He still could stand no clutter and he always had ten pencils in a case in his bag. His toilet paper unrolled over the top and he could not bear excessive preening and neither, slovenliness. In general, his compulsions were private and minor. But certainly his mother had some ownership for his bare walls and his alphabetized bookshelves.

After eating a breakfast of two boiled eggs, one piece of link sausage and one sausage patty, and a bowl of Rice Krispies, as he always did, he washed his dishes and put them away, brushed his teeth, put on his scrubs and left, locking the door behind him, and then checking a few more times to see if it was locked. This was just to be sure. He liked to be sure, if it was possible. Why fight it? But then, George was no stranger to chaos either, and he dealt with it like a man.

When he got to his car, he noticed that it was tilting a little oddly, and then when he got closer his heart sank in that familiar way. He saw that both tires on the left side were slashed and flattened. The windows were also smashed and his stereo was stolen, likewise his compact disc case, a jacket and his current pair of running shoes. Baby George shouted a curse at the sky, "NOT AGAIN!!!" and then he caught the bus that stopped up the street, because, despite the violation, he had to round. On the way he called the police, he told them his car was broken into, "AGAIN!" and no, he couldn't meet them in the parking lot, because he had to round. He told them to go check it out if they could, and to page him. "They stole my stereo, a disc holder with all my CDs, a jacket and a really new pair of shoes. Here's my pager number." At his first break, he called the insurance company. He was paged during that call and he answered it using another line. A resident walked in and laughed, "Working two phones today, George?"

"Somebody broke into my fucking car."

"Again?"

George looked up with a dark face.

"That sucks."

Indeed it sucked. And then the insurance company said it would take them a while to get him into a rental for some reason he did not understand and didn't have time to pursue in between patients, while answering pages. It had something to do with its being a Friday afternoon.

"So if your car gets broken into on a Friday afternoon you can't get a rental until the following week?"

"Yes, sir; if your car had been stolen, we could have you in a rental today. In fact, we would actually bring the car to your residence. But, you see, you are not technically without transportation."

"My car is practically standing on its side. The tires are slashed."

"Oh, well, sir, if you would like, we would be happy to give you the number for your local Triple A. Are you a member of Triple A?"

"Yes, I have Triple A, but why would I need Triple A?"

"Well, to change your tires for you, sir! Or to give you a tow. They are very helpful. Have you ever had a chance to use Triple A?"

"The windows are smashed to smithereens! It's completely undriveable!"

"But sir, you said the car starts fine."

There was no use in continuing. Anyway, his pager went off.

The following day was Saturday and he didn't need to be into work until later, which was good because his night was again plagued with bad dreams and this time whenever he woke up, he would remember that his car had been broken into and that it was still out there in the parking lot and that he would have to deal with that and it was a terrible waste of a free morning. There was no ease in falling back to sleep. When he finally woke up, he was exhausted, miserable and in terrible need of a long run. He was agitated in mind, body and spirit, and he was horny as hell. *I need to fuck something.* Even though he never had, it was the kind of morning that let him know if only he could fuck something, everything would seem much, much more manageable. He had his prerun breakfast of just a small cup of coffee and half a banana and set off on the road. He ran for two hours and still when he came home he was in much worse shape than when he started, and he called his mother to tell her to find him a wife to fuck, or really to marry was what he was going to say, but instead his father answered and told him a long story and asked for a favor and said, "I was alone here, you know. Without your mother."

And so suddenly he needed to borrow a car and make a trip next week to Northern Virginia to take a little boy sightseeing. He looked out his window and there in a glittering sea of shattered glass sat his crooked car looking like a piece of modern art or an example to wayward teens.

He closed the blinds and stripped naked as he walked to the shower. *Something's got to give.*

For a few days, George arrived at the hospital soaked with sweat at 4:30 A.M., raced up the stairs to shower in the residents' locker room and, after many hours, sometimes caught the bus back to his apartment. More often, he just slung on a backpack and ran back home the same way he had come. In a week, he was leaner and his eyes gleamed with feral wariness. Manoj, pulling out of the parking lot at midnight, saw his friend as he turned up McElderry, running fast and nervous like he had just stolen someone's watch. *Again!?* He pulled alongside and rolled down the window. "Again?"

George, frustrated with humanity that shouted from windows, left trash and effluent on the streets of Baltimore and sometimes grabbed at his backpack, jumped in. "Yes. I'm waiting for the rental."

"Really, George. You need to move. But in the meantime, you need a ride to work tomorrow?"

George turned to look at Manoj and felt less angry at the world than he had a moment earlier.

The next morning, Manoj, feeling that George was angry at the world, invited him to go to his uncle's house for Onam celebration on Saturday. "He would be happy if you would come. For sure." They arrived at the hospital and before he left him at the elevator Manoj said, "Page me when you are ready to go home."

George was very grateful and that evening at six, he paged him, and when Manoj was finished at seven, they met outside.

Walking to the car, Manoj touched his hair and pulled his lab coat up on his shoulders. His dandruff was much improved, he thought, but when he was busy looking at the road, he did not like the thought of George pitying his snowy shoulders. When they got in the car, Manoj repeated his morning's invitation to Onam Sadhya at Ammavan's house. "I will call him when I get home and let them know you are coming. Then you can come if you decide to without feeling like they didn't know. They would be very happy if you came."

The invitation reminded George of his predicament. How was he going to get to his dad's friend's house on Saturday for Onam to see Govind? Just remembering it made him even angrier with the world and he glowered and hit the dash. Manoj looked over because he loved his purple Probe. "Don't hit my car." Then he smiled. "I love my car."

"Sorry." George, being who he was, reached back out and smoothed over where he hit and, silly as it might have been, Manoj felt better.

"I'd love to go with you but I can't, I've already got an Onam invitation. Not that I want to go. I have to figure out how to get to D.C. for this Onam dinner at one of my dad's friends' somebody's place in McLean. He has a son visiting from Kerala who won this award for this story he wrote or something and they're going to be at this guy's house and my dad wants me to go see him and take him around, and of course my car is destroyed. I can't bail. I'm hoping the rental comes through, or I might just have to rent a car myself for the weekend." George sighed and looked out at the ugly street. "I'm screwed if I do it myself. They will never reimburse me. They want me to call Triple A."

"You are going to Onam at a man's house in McLean who is having a boy from Kerala who won an award for writing a story?"

Just then, they pulled into the parking lot of George's apartment complex and shining like a black eye in the lot was his jacked-up car which, in the intervening minutes between the break-in a few days back and this morning, had had the steering wheel stolen and the tires on the right side stripped off. He shuddered when he saw it.

"They want you to call Triple A for that?" Manoj stared with his hand on his cheek.

"Yes . . . yes they do."

"Okay, that doesn't make any sense." Manoj sat looking at the car.

"Ya . . . and they won't get me a rental till . . . I don't know. And I am screwed this weekend."

Manoj turned and smiled broad and slow. "No, my friend, in that sense you are not screwed, for the weekend anyway. Because the house you need to visit on Saturday is none other than the house of Dr. Raman

Nair, my *ammavan*, host of the Onam Sadhya and of the award-winning boy from Kalliassery, P. M. Govind, the teller of tales." Manoj bowed down low, and in the mock tipping of his hat knocked his hand against his hair, which showered the black steering wheel of his beautiful Ford Probe with dandruff that did not go unnoticed by George, who didn't care because he couldn't quite believe the serendipity involved in all of this and wondered then if something might be about to change in his luck.

❧

Om.

Before the golden glint breaks through the morning, let us feel the perfection of another risen day.

Om.

It is day, isn't it, even before we see the shine? While the first fog is still settled deep in the hollows and even hovers higher amid the trees against a tame gray sky, it is still morning, isn't it?

Om.

Thank you for this day. Another year passed for me, my Lord. I am very thankful for all these people and all these things You have given me and for another year. You know this, isn't it?

Om.

❧

On the mornings of birthdays, Dr. Raman Nair woke his household with the blessings of the Suprabhatam played loud and clear over his booming stereo system.

Om.
Good morning.

How good it made them feel, and sometimes they wondered why they didn't do it every day, though perhaps not so early. But by the following day, so many hours from the dawn of the prior day, they no longer remembered how good it felt to be awakened by Sri Subbulakshmi's clear recitations of the morning blessings, and no one even noticed what they were missing until another person's birthday morning, when again they wondered why they didn't do this every day. It was a sad oversight.

In some sense, then, they were lucky that there were so many of them in the house, for they did hear the blessings eight times a year. And sometimes if he could, Manoj spent the night on his birthday eve, because there was a joy that lasted in the birthday Suprabhatam. In the old days, Gita had come to stay as well.

So the girls learned from their very first year that there was something wonderfully special about a birthday. They learned to be contemplative and also thankful for one more year lived well and in earnest. Dr. Raman Nair was a man without regrets. He loved the marking and celebrating of the journey. And then, of course, he was born on the luckiest and most auspicious day of the year, Onam, and so it always seemed to him that the whole world was celebrating his birthday with dances and song, and the most important feast of the year. Really, the only feast of the year, the harvest, the time of great abundance, and how else could he have grown up but to believe that the entire host of blessings were his to partake of, and he did so without regrets.

Jaya taught her girls to make petal patterns on the front porch for Onam just like they did at home. They used dyed carnations because other flowers were so expensive. When his first baby was only two and his second baby was barely born, he came home from work on his birthday and found all three of them, Jaya, Veena and Mira on the porch making diamonds within circles and petals within these, and wearing fine clothing and awaiting his return. Inside, there was a feast of outrageous abundance. On Dr. Raman Nair's birthday, Jaya put the Suprabhatam on the stereo and turned it up and woke the household. For these reasons and many others, he cherished her like the sunrise. The first thing he did on the morning of his birthday was to bathe and pray, the latter being a habit about which he was somewhat less punctilious than the former.

Om.

It was another glory of glories, holy of holies, and he was one year older and *thank you, thank you for every blessing, and please, please continue to watch these precious people around me. I cannot be happy without their happiness. And please watch my sister, Gita. She is sad and lonely and angry, and she is such a wonderful girl. Guide her to seek peace. And thank you.*

Om.

In the home of Dr. Raman Nair, the first chords of the Suprabhatam ring out. The girls open their eyes to the gray glow and the good-morning blessings. Dr. Raman Nair, awake since long before dawn, quietly lies still as his tiny, little wife stealthily sneaks from under the covers and exits the room. He squirms in anticipation and waits, holding his breath, until finally the perfect first chord, and then the first om. Inhaling the tranquility, he holds it for a dizzying moment and then he exhales, repeating: *om.* He turns to his side, carefully touches his right foot first to the floor and stands.

Around the house, the girls lie in their beds looking up at the ceiling. They are quiet and contemplative, though it is not their birthday. No one speaks. They turn to their sides, carefully touch their right feet first to the floor and stand. Wrapping themselves in their robes, they come down the stairs smiling at one another and touching each other with sisterly affection and loving silence. It has been an auspicious awakening on Onam morning in the home of Dr. Raman Nair.

While these girls helped their mother with a beautiful birthday breakfast, their father showered and prayed and when he entered the room, it was to the resounding and joyful greetings of his daughters, his wife, his dog and even of his momentarily lucid father who extolled too loudly, "AHA, MY SON. MY SON. RAMU! A GREAT AND FIRST-RATE SON, AS STRONG AS AN OX, AS BRILLIANT AS THE STARS! IS IT YOUR BIRTHDAY AGAIN? HOW OLD YOU MUST BE!!" Muthachan tickled under his son's chin and poked his enormous stomach with his stick. "YOU HAVE BECOME VERY FAT, RAMU!! IS IT YOUR BIRTHDAY AGAIN?" Muthachan laughed and laughed and then sat down at the table and said that his tea was cold. The girls also laughed because when Muthachan was in a good spirit and aware of things, it was such a good omen for the day.

There is joy in the preparation of meaningful celebrations. Dr. Raman Nair subscribed to the school of clap twice and "make it so" and thus his daughters learned very early how to make drudgery feel like a party, how to work twice as hard for half as long, and most important they learned the time-warping powers of a well-told story.

The first time we went to India, we were standing in the airport and it was so hot we were covered with flies and I was so afraid one was going to land on my eyeballs and lay eggs.

What did you do?

Mommy made me jump up and down so they wouldn't land on me, and it worked, but she never said that they wouldn't lay eggs. I kept asking her, "Mommy, will they lay eggs on my eyeballs?" and she kept saying, "Just keep jumping."

What did you do?

I kept jumping!

When we first moved into this house, do you remember, we used to swing from the vines in the backyard. Do you remember the time that Mira got a splinter in her hand that was as long as her finger?

OH, but do you remember the time that Usha stepped on the cocktail toothpick and Daddy and Babu Uncle had to do emergency surgery on the basement bed?

They did emergency surgery on me too, outside on the deck.

I remember that. I remember that. You were shrieking and everyone in the neighborhood came running. They said it was a screech owl. . . .

Remember the owl on the deck? Did you know their feathers muffle the sound of their flight so they can better stalk their prey?

Did I ever tell you about that person who lived down the road from Gauri Ammai who was stalking Paru Chechi and Deepti Chechi?

Oh THAT is a scary story. Listen . . .

The girls together were a monumental force. There was nothing they could not do together, and very little they chose to do alone, and their

Onam Sadhya preparation and the preparation of the house for sleepover company was that kind of happy bustle that makes men crave home and family, and makes women feel that life is complete and satisfying. They cooked together, and they cleaned together, and they laughed and told stories as they went, and when Manoj and his friend from Johns Hopkins arrived a little early, they were already done with their major tasks. They were bathed and dressed and still busy with the final touches that made things look effortlessly perfect. They themselves looked effortlessly perfect. Veena, Mira, Usha, Dhanya, and Shanti, each and every one looked effortlessly perfect.

George awoke with a tickle in his throat that he thought might be a late summer cold. Because he had promised to be ready by noon, he ran a faster pace and was home twenty minutes earlier than usual. This allowed him to make the homeopathic remedy of honey and lemon, which he sipped off a spoon. Holding his tongue out to catch the sweet drizzle made him feel like a child and so he smiled and got somewhat excited as children do when there is a party to go to. He went to shower in a scalding stream, for he had issues with the heat of water that flowed over his body. It seemed cleaner if it was hotter, and so he was nearly boiled every time he washed. It was true, however, that he always appeared a little cleaner than other people, and today when he emerged from his bathing and dressing, he was a singular sight. He was as handsome as he had ever been in his life. When he opened the door for Manoj, his friend said, "Hey, you look wonderful." George looked at him, and laughed. What a thing to say. But then, George thought, why not? And he looked Manoj up and down and replied, "You know what, Manoj? You look wonderful too." Manoj smiled and compulsively smoothed down his hair. George picked up his overnight bag because they were staying through Sunday and they walked down to the parking lot together.

"Your car was gone."

"Yeah, they came for it yesterday, finally."

"When do you get your rental?"

"According to them, I already got it last week."

"Of course."

"Of course."

Manoj slapped his friend gently on the back. "Well, tonight there will be *payasam*."

"*Semiya* or the brown kind?"

"Both."

They both climbed into the Probe and set off on the journey to Onam Sadhya at Dr. Raman Nair's house.

On the same Saturday morning, Jeri awoke before the sunrise. When Chris, who had never fallen asleep, rose from the bed just after dawn, he found her. Standing at the window. Standing at the window, staring at the pond. When she heard the slight brush of his hand against the wall, or was it his leg against a chair, she turned away and went back to their room without a word. She locked the door. He sat down on a white tufted chair and buried his head in his hands.

Back at the home of Dr. Raman Nair, Shanti and Taj, with the knack for hearing cars before they arrived, walked out to the driveway to await their company. From the sound of the dog, Shanti knew it was not her mother and father, who had gone out to get some extra naans from the Aarathi Restaurant, for Taj had let out a wonderful leaping bark that caused him to rear up like a horse, and this particular display he usually saved for guests. Inside, Muthachan heard the warning of Taj Mahal and stood up frantically, dropping his belt to check for the presence of his foot, which he never found when he was afraid, though it was always there at the end of his leg, covered with a warm woolen sock. When the dog barked, Muthachan sensed the coming of thieves and then when he looked down he found that they had already come and stolen his foot and God only knew what else. Sometimes he paced with anxiety. Dhanya, hearing the dog bark, went to the back room to check her grandfather, who would be rising in panic.

"Muthachan, I found your foot in the kitchen, you should be very careful not to leave it lying around!" She bent down to his feet, removed his socks and rubbed both feet tenderly. She replaced the socks and put his shoes on for him, and then she bowed her head. He touched it with both his open hands. Before she left, she threaded his belt and buckled it. He stood like a child with his arms outstretched.

Manoj and George pulled into the driveway at exactly 3 P.M. and George drew back in his seat. Together, Shanti and Taj Mahal looked like an Amazon warrior princess and her trusty steed.

"What is that?"

"It is my cousin Shanti, and their dog, Taj Mahal."

"That's a dog?"

Manoj just nodded.

"Wow."

Shanti held tight to Taj's leash and it was only her extreme weight that allowed her to hold the joyful beast in check. His low-throated bark of happiness sounded like the start of an airplane engine and George stood behind his opened door, unsure whether to come forward.

"He's harmless," Shanti offered with a smile, but her body flexed with exertion; the strain in her sweet voice, her near-horizontal position, left George speechless though he was not afraid of dogs, and he considered asking Manoj if he would mind bringing the *payasam* out to the car.

"Keep him in the garage!" Manoj shouted. "You have people coming here, and this dog is like a—"

"Horse!" George yelled from the car.

"Bigger, like a—"

"Mythical horse!"

"Yes, this dog is like a mythical horse!"

"He's going, he's going. We were just coming to see who it was. He's going to the garage when everyone gets here."

"*We* are here."

"You are not everyone."

"We are not *no one* either!"

Shanti stuck out her tongue at Manoj and called out to George, "Hi, I am Shanti and this is Taj Mahal!" She wound the leash one more time around her wrists and leaned back another few degrees and yelled, "Don't worry, I've got him. And he doesn't bite, he only licks and jumps. But don't worry, I've got him." She smiled and George from behind the car door smiled back and, despite the size of the dog, felt completely safe with the promise of this beautiful young girl who was exactly right in every feature. He thought he may never have seen such a lovely face.

"Hi, I'm George."

"Come on in through the garage. You and Chettan have to do the ice." Turning to her cousin, she added, "Chechi said."

"Where is it?" Manoj took their bags from the car, one over each shoulder.

"I think in the cooler in the basement, or in the basement freezer."

He turned to George and said, "Come inside." As they walked into the garage, Manoj whispered, "Don't be a fool, it is true that he only licks and jumps but one lick will soak you head to toe like you jumped into an ocean and one jump will throw you back and pull you under like a riptide. I tell you that being assaulted by that dog is like being hit by a tsunami and they all think this is just very cute. I am warning you in advance. Watch for the dog."

George looked back. Shanti and Taj were in the driveway dancing some sort of a waltz and Shanti was singing for their accompaniment. He made note to watch for the dog.

Manoj and George went in, took off their shoes in the mudroom and entered the kitchen. It smelled like good food and George felt a hopeful sort of feeling that comes from the scent of deeply familiar places and things. The hope lighting his eyes made his handsome face even more charming.

There in the home of Dr. Raman Nair he was suddenly swarmed by a fast-moving and happy gathering of girls who were graceful in their introductions, if not wholly single-minded. They came carrying platters and pots, vases and bunches of flowers, and one held the hand of a bent and confused old man who was made more nervous by the energy around him. Quickly, they introduced themselves and George did the same, but they didn't linger around him. One of them with a long tousle of curly hair pulled back in a waist-long ponytail that swung when she walked and grazed her enormous behind sat him down and said, "Here you go, sit here for a moment, what would you like to drink?" And before he knew what was happening, another one with more excellent long hair and a similarly enormous behind brought him a chilled glass and a bottle of beer and threw her hair over her shoulder, leaving George a little nervous too, though he didn't know why. The girls were spectacularly beautiful, and so gigantic that he didn't quite know what to make of it. The regal dog of mythical proportions, the beautiful girls of mythical proportions. He sat there looking around dumbly, doing and saying nothing. They were dressed in wonderful colors and their clothing both clung and flowed; he looked this way and that and felt like he was floating in the air.

Amid all the confusion, one of these girls felt they were being offhand with a new guest, perhaps because he came with Manoj Chettan, perhaps because he looked like he belonged though they didn't know him. She paused from her preparation of cilantro for sauces and wiped her hands on a clean kitchen towel. With the grace of an eldest daughter whose mother is absent, she approached carefully on the right, and laid a hand on this man's shoulder. He looked up and exhaled. She wore a dizzying pink blouse with a swivel line in the fabric that made George feel like he was falling. She bent forward and took hold of his beer bottle and with the softest voice he had ever heard she said, "Let me open that for you." George inhaled and closed his eyes. She smelled clean and green, and when she tossed her hair over her shoulder it glided across his face and it smelled like a lemon-lime Life Saver. With pure-hearted need, he opened his mouth just slightly and caught a tendril as it passed over his lips; he shuddered deep in his heart. When he opened his eyes, she was pouring his beer. *If I dropped to my knees right now and held your full hips in my hands and rested my head against your stomach, would you think I was strange?*

He put a hand on her wrist and kept his fingers there until she put the bottle down on the table and the blush rose to her round, brown cheeks. In his quiet studying of her face, he fell in love at first sight, and because he was quiet and still, Veena could spend a full and necessary minute to notice what was singular and perfect about his angular jaw and his light brown eyes and his small, straight nose and most of all, the look of appreciation that he seemed to already have for her, simply for opening his beer. She stared deep with her eyes two shades darker than his.

Manoj and Mira, coming up from the gathering of ice, caught the two of them paused in time, staring, with his fingers on her still wrist. They shot each other a look.

"Isn't he a Catholic?" Mira whispers.

"He is . . ."

A Propitious Alignment of Stars

Jaya gathered her girls around her like cuddling into the covers or like leaning into fragrant flowers. The girls followed her like ducks and they stood so close that the long hair of one twined with the long hair of the next, and the long hair of them all rested on Jaya's forearms and over her shoulders. When she sat down, sometimes one or another would stand behind her and absently pluck gray hairs from her head, for she had very few. Usha, argumentative and disobedient and loyal and very kind, massaged her between the scapula where she became sore from so much cooking and caring for such a large and boisterous family.

"When you make mango pulisherry, there is a trick that will make yours the very best one." When the girls were very young and still so impressed with the alchemy of the kitchen, Jaya drew them in because they wanted to be near her, and she wanted them near her. She never shooed them or said they were underfoot, and so they all learned to cook just like their mother, though perhaps with more attention to recipes and of course to presentation. Veena always put sauces and pickles in wee, pretty pots with wee, pretty spoons and the other sisters also had learned that a plain bowl of yogurt became a tantalizing delicacy if trimmed with cucumber florets; a simple ginger ale and sherbet punch would be the talk of the evening if there were lotuses made of oranges floating in the froth.

The girls were patient and attentive to the minute steps needed to create artful food. The habit of storytelling while working extended to the kitchen, which was perhaps its most delightful venue, with the warm steam and aromas of the meal to come. And endless gardens of marzipan vegetables can be dyed and formed when listening to the story of the time Papuappan fell in love with Leela the servant girl who was low caste but so beautiful and how they met in secret in the night and took the bus to Bangalore and got married and then how his father had chased them down and nearly killed him with his bare hands. By the time they arrived at the end of the story where the father turned his back on them even when they arrived destitute with his only grandchild, a boy who was very beautiful and very fair, there would be perfect rows of almond-flavored tomatoes, cucumbers, pumpkins, squash and beans, overflowing with leafy vines, growing on hand-rolled trellises, all resting on a crushed-Oreo loam. Standing around their autumn-vegetable-garden-cake masterpiece, the five fat daughters of Dr. Raman Nair would be in tears at the injustice of it all.

"When you cook, you must feel full of love and happiness," Jaya intoned. "There is great power in your food." The girls gathered in closer because there was a story in the pause and the rhythm of the spoon in the pot.

"One time I was very angry with your father because Muthachan had hit me on my head with his stick and made my eyes goggle, and instead of telling Muthachan not to hit me, your father told me not to make Muthachan angry. That night, I made a beef curry and a beans curry and they both tasted the same. How does that happen? I will tell you." Jaya put her spoon into the pot and tasted her fish. Smiling, she shook her head. "It is perfect, very good. Not too sour." Looking from one to the other, she continued, "How does it happen? It happens like this. There is a taste to every emotion, and the most terrible taste is the one that comes in the food when you are resentful, and the next bad taste is the taste of angry food. That day, I was resentful and I was angry both. Together, they were absorbed into the food. They were so strong they completely overcame the taste of both beef and beans and both curries tasted like anger and resentment." The girls all looked at her with awe.

"You may think that this could not be true, but that night, your father ate the food and he didn't say anything, though all of you were complaining. You may not remember; you were younger. Anyway, your father ate the whole thing without saying any bad thing about the food, and it was very bad-tasting. And at the end of the dinner when I was washing the dishes, he came to the kitchen and he said, 'Achan is so sick, I can't say anything to him now, he won't even remember what happened.' And this was true, I knew that, and I didn't make any interruptions. And then your father said, 'But the next time he hits you, I will take his stick right then and tell him not to hit you.' And he has always done that from then on." The girls, dumbstruck at their father's near apology, looked back and forth at each other. *From the taste of anger and resentment?* It was astonishing.

"That is the power." Jaya raised her eyebrows at them and they each looked up at her from the close perimeter of her body and nodded.

This was a lesson they never forgot. Sometimes the sisters found that if they felt a deep and just sadness, their food would pique a grain in the heart that scraped and shredded, and the table would bend with tears. This sad food would be so achingly delicious that, despite the flowing pain, everyone would reach for more and more. At the end of such a meal, they sat spent, exhausted, cleansed and lighter in their sufferings. Those were necessary meals. Sometimes Dhanya, the seer of the sisters, would feel that it was time for such a catharsis, and she would tell a story she had saved for the moment of need, and the other sisters and their compassionate little mother would sob into the rising steam of the kitchen and that night they would be purged of their latent grief.

For Onam Sadhya and the birthday celebration of Dr. Raman Nair, these girls and their mother entered the kitchen in a carnival of good spirit. They danced and they sang and they did impressions of each other doing embarrassing and ridiculous things. They told jokes and funny stories like when their father overheard his grandmother praying and so he hid behind a trunk and pretended to be God and she believed him and began to cry and complain about her daughter-in-law. And the one where he was supposed to walk his little sister to school on the first day and instead how he had ditched her and jumped on a passing friend's bicycle and she got lost and finally ended up back home, and how Muthachan had come to school and pulled him out of class and whipped him with a switch he pulled from a tree right there in the schoolyard.

How could she get lost? She was the stupid one to get lost, she had been to the school so many times. I didn't leave her more than fifty feet from school and she ends up back where she began. If I had left her one hundred feet, where then? Coimbature? Allahabad? Babylon?

It was Mira who did the best impression of their father. Sometimes Shanti wet her pants.

That Saturday, when they cooked for their father's birthday, the Onam meal, the five fat daughters of Dr. Raman Nair and their tiny, little mother were decided in their happiness. Without an ambivalent emotion, without a contrary word, without a tear shed from anything but excessive laughter, the feast they prepared was magic.

They ate in scatters around all available tables and in chairs turned toward each other with plates held on their laps. Dr. and Mrs. Kauffman, the guardians of young Govind, were stuffed such that both leaned back in their chairs with their eyes nearly closed. Govind, so far from home for the first time in his life, ate joyfully, joyfully, a grateful gleam in his eyes. *Subhiksham.* Cornucopia, abundance, copious abundance, the sense that the table might bow with the weight of so much food. *Subhiksham.* The hallmark of a proper *Malayalee sadhya.*

George sat on the floor with Manoj, Usha and Mira and talked about something or other while he watched Veena sit with one group and rise and move on to another. He hadn't said more than five words to Govind, who frankly didn't care, so happy was he with the food. George was there for Veena . . . she had her mother's grace in entertaining, a perfect timing in refilling an empty plate or bringing more water and *papadam.*

George ate quickly to draw her to him, he emptied his glass almost as soon as it was filled, but he was sitting with two other daughters of Dr. Raman Nair, and they all knew to fill an empty glass and to bring more food and *papadam*; Usha and Mira rose with alacrity and wondered where he put it all. Veena came by only once and stood between her sister and her cousin and placed a gentle hand on each of their shoulders and said to George, "Is everything good? Do you need anything?" And damned if his plate and his glass were not just refilled. He looked down and then back up and he said nothing. He just smiled with his mouth open. Manoj looked at George and shook his head. *This will not be good.*

Veena smiled quietly and blinked her eyes very slowly. She squeezed Mira's shoulder and said to her, "If he needs anything, take care, okay?" As she walked away, Veena felt his eyes on her shoulders and her hair, and she spent the evening blushing and suppressing a woozy elation. After twenty-three plastic cupfuls of water, and the original beer he had nursed to keep her fingerprints close to his lips, George inquired with urgency as to the whereabouts of the bathroom.

Gita, hiding behind her niece and her father, found herself without cover when Dhanya took Muthachan to wash his hands. "Don't worry, Ammai, you finish. I will wash him," she said. Gita's plate was still full. She hadn't touched a thing. From corners far and near, her brother and sister-in-law watched her rearrange her rice, and shuttle her curries with the concave scoop of her *papadam*. Jaya and Dr. Raman Nair exchanged glances and busied themselves with the feeding of the nearest person to distract deep worries brought on by any unexplained failure to eat. She had given an explanation; they just didn't believe it.

"I am not feeling well."

"You will feel better after you eat."

"No, I know I will not be able to eat. I have not been feeling well."

"Nonsense. You will feel better after you eat. How long since you ate anyway? You look like a starving urchin, your eyes are sticking out of your head; you look like dead fish." Her brother took a plate and piled on more food than Gita had eaten in a month. Then he sent her to finish it off. "Finish it off. Your bones are protruding from your neck like you are swallowing ladders. Your clavicles are like fence posts. You look like you are hung on a hanger."

Still, Gita's plate was full. Looking down at her cold food, her eyes began to sting. One or two teary drops fell into the spicy curry flowing down her mountain of rice, and her heart began to thud because there was no way to dump her plate and there was no way to eat it. Even in her sadness, it struck her as terribly foolish. *This is the reason I will be miserable forever. Because I am a stupid, scared little girl in an intelligent, bold woman's costume. If I had any sense at all, I would simply get up and throw this plate in the trash and when they started with their raised eyebrows, and their insults, and their admonitions, I would simply say, "I told you I am not feeling well and that I don't want to eat. If you insist on piling my plate when I tell you that I cannot eat it, then you should not be surprised if I throw it away." And when they started with their comments about how I am skinny and sickly, I would simply say, "Yes, it is true, I have lost a lot of weight. I will take care when I am feeling better to be sure to gain it all back." I would simply say this and enjoy the gathering. If I had any sense, I would simply say, "I am in love with a wonderful man and we would like to get married." And when they started with their doomsday predictions, I would simply say, "Well, I certainly have a better outlook on the future, but anyway, I am quite grown up now, and I think I will take my chances." If I had any sense or any courage or anything of any value inside me, that is what I would do. I would certainly start with the disposal of this plate on my lap.* Gita sighed a deep and woeful sigh and made two smaller hillocks of her mountain of rice.

At this very moment, under the same propitious alignment of stars that was being celebrated in the home of Dr. Raman Nair, Chris, unaware of the occasion, lay back on the white sofa at Innisfree and focused on the work of a woodpecker in a nearby tree in the woods. He heard it before he saw it, and in an automatic reflex born of grief, he followed it with his eyes without moving a muscle in his body.

Jeri, suddenly his greatest mystery, appeared and disappeared with papers, and projects, the business of her life and theirs. Every now and then, she stood still with the phone to her ear and watched him while she talked. He put his hands over his eyes, and the darkness behind his lids exploded with orange bursts; if the pressure made him blind, he would not be surprised, and he might welcome the respite from such a pathetic helplessness. The real helplessness of exploded eyeballs would be a distraction from such dishonorable self-pity.

Jeri came into the room dressed and with a briefcase, and said she had to run out and show a house. She said she would be back shortly and she would bring home dinner. Chris uncovered his eyes. She came slowly into focus, wearing a smart blue suit that made her teeth very white and her skin too orange. They stared each other down and Jeri didn't say a word, though she knew he was suffering and furthermore that he was quiet. He swallowed; she cleared her throat. For no reason, she nodded her head. It seemed some sort of check without a mate. *Finish me off,* he thought.

Two days was enough. He sat up with a crushing headache that forced his eyes closed and into the blackness he turned his palms upward and said, "Jeri." He opened his eyes with a look of supplication. She turned her head to the side and put her hand on her forehead. They made a sad tableau.

She spoke so quietly he leaned forward to hear. "This is all I have," she said.

He stood up. Jeri thought he looked a foot taller, though the tremble in his lips and the terrified blanching of his skin made him humble. This way, he was beautiful even in her hurt eyes. She might even understand it, but still. He came toward her and she held up her hand and turned her face again. "This is all I have, Chris. This has to be enough; this is all there is." Without looking at him, she walked out the door.

Alone now, Chris was again stunned and still. There seemed no good direction to go, and where courage would lead him, honor would not follow. The absence of honor drained his courage to act, and loyalty belonged in every camp. He was only one man; he looked back to his sofa and felt if he lay back down, he might never rise again. Instead, he turned to his study and sat down at his desk.

Back at the house of Dr. Raman Nair, Veena with her caring and watchful soul relieved her *ammai* of her plate. When she placed her gentle, long hand on the rim, Gita looked up and chirped with suppressed gratitude. Veena shushed her gently and smiled with her mouth closed and her eyes tender. She was now in love with the length of George's torso, and the shine of his hair, and her heart (grown so large in the few hours she had known him) could feel the terrible suffering of her beautiful and unstoppable *ammai.* Veena, a woman in love with the veins in George's hands, and the shape of his fingernails, and his white, square teeth, knew that Ammai's chewed lips and dark patches came from passionate love, or the death of it. She circled the room and discreetly piled plates on top of Ammai's and threw the whole mess in a giant garden trash bag in the mudroom. There would have to be time later to hold her tight around her tiny waist and stroke her bony back but right now, they had to cut the cake and have tea. She went back to Ammai, lifted her from her seat, and led her to the hallway. "Go upstairs to our bathroom and quickly wash your face. In the medicine cabinet, use the lotion that has the green cap. It will make you look like you had a nap." Gita stood there holding Veena's hand without moving. Veena looked around, fearful of drawing attention and unwilling to leave Ammai alone this way. Dhanya, who saw everything, came to them, took her *ammai*'s hand and led her upstairs. George, who watched everything, caught Veena's eye when she turned back to the room. He tilted his head to the side and Veena lowered her eyes to the floor. It was the moment she knew he would always take care of her.

Around an enormous cake the girls had decorated to look like the Kerala paddy fields surrounded by palm trees that swayed and tipped when he blew out the candles with monsoon force, the family and friends of Dr. Raman Nair gathered in tight and shouted out excellent suggestions for wishes, to which Dr. Raman Nair replied again and again, "No thank you, my wish is much better!" Everyone laughed and agreed aloud, "Yes, I am sure it is!"

With so many people around the table, and so much happy noise, George very cautiously made his way inch by inch behind the row of sisters. The overflow of one filled in the grooves and curves of the next and they were squeezed in so tight that not a chink of light broke through. It was, therefore, without attracting any attention that George stealthily approached Veena and parted her granite-black and gleaming sheet of hair with his left palm sliding up her spine. When he arrived at the place where he could feel her beating heart through her back, he spread his hand open and tangled his fingers deep in her hair. Together they stood quiet amid a cacophony of blowing noisemakers. It was a joyful moment in time.

Cozy, cozy, they sat in a huge circle, cake plates on their laps, teacups on saucers carefully placed between their feet, or beside their hips on the floor. Even the Kauffmans and Govind unwound in that sublime relaxation that comes from knowing there was nowhere to go tonight, that when the evening ended, someone would lead you to a comfy corner where you would unwind and fall fast asleep from a long drive, a delicious meal, easy conversation, and the effort of being on one's best behavior, all in a home warmed by numerous, delightfully large people.

"Ah, a stupendous evening." Dr. Raman Nair looked about at the gathering and nodded his head with approval. "This has been my best birthday thus far for my entire life!"

"Daddy, you say that every single year," Shanti said in her quiet and happy way.

"Ah, but every year it is so. Every year, I find that I am more satisfied with my birthday celebrations. Every year, it is a miracle that I have managed to become so much happier. Every year, I am so grateful."

"Every year, you say that too."

"Should I not say this, my children? If I am thankful and appreciative is it so bad to tell you so?"

"Mmm, you know," Jaya turned and addressed Dr. Kauffman and his wife, "we are always cautious to draw too much attention to our blessings." She looked over at Govind, who nodded wisely, for what she said was true.

Usha interjected here, "They draw flaws on babies." Jaya looked at Usha with her lips pursed.

"What? They do!" Usha answered.

"Why do you say it like that?" Looking at her company, she continued, "She doesn't need to say it like that, she is a very difficult person."

"What? They do!"

"*Mindathadee*!" Jaya warned in Malayalam, feeling that perhaps saying 'Shut up, you stupid girl' would not be well received by Mrs. Kauffman. Turning back, she continued, "It is true that we make a small black mark on a child's face with a black eye pencil. It is to ward off the evil eye." She glared at Usha. "It is obvious that the mark on your face was too small."

Dr. Raman Nair rose from his seat and pointed his finger in the air. "The problem is that in this country, everyone feels it is necessary to tell how beautiful the child is."

Before he could go on, Jaya continued, "Oh, so beautiful, your baby is so pretty, your baby is so smart, your baby has such good hair." Indicating her daughters spread around the room with her hand, Jaya went on, "As you can see, they are all very beautiful girls. And when they were young, they were not so fat."

"MOM!" Usha shouted.

"What? You were not!"

"You don't need to say it like that." Turning to the company, Usha added, "She is a very difficult person."

"What? You were not!" Jaya shook her head and continued, "Anyway, these girls, everyone was always telling me they were so beautiful. I used to put big marks on them, then it stopped. Instead, they would wonder, 'What is that mark on that child?' That is a much safer question." Turning to Gita, she pointed her finger. "This one, this one here, she was a real problem. But we were back home then, when she was so small. You can't tell now because she is wasting away from her hard work and inconsequential worries, but she is a very beautiful lady." She turned and shook her head at Gita and announced for the group, "She is very much younger than my husband, though they are sister and brother, and she was only a small girl when we got married, but we were back home then and there people know how to talk to a child. So even though she was so beautiful, people usually didn't say anything too much about it. But sometimes it could cause a terrible problem. Especially in my husband's family. Strange things happen sometimes." Dr. Raman Nair bristled at her superstition. She was in the mood to talk, and he sensed a story, as did the girls, who nestled in close to one another.

"When she was a very small girl—how old, Ramu, how old do you think?"

"When what?"

"You know when that Sukumaran's cousin who came from Luknow where he was studying and he made those words and then Muthammai did all the *pujas* with the bananas?"

"Ah . . . maybe she was only . . . three?"

"No, she could not have been three, I was there."

"You were not there, it was before you. I was not even there."

"No, I was there, I remember, there was that other one, that . . . Trichur Venugopal with the lumps all over his neck who was there for *ayurvedam* and he stayed in the house."

"Trichur Venugopal? He was not the one with the lumps, he was the one with gout and he couldn't walk without severe pain; the other one . . . that Alangad Venugopal, he had the lumps, but he did not come until later. You only heard the story and now you think you were there."

"I can see it in my mind."

"That is called hallucinating," Usha interjected.

"Shut up, you stupid girl," Jaya shot back.

Gita shrunk low and counted the curtain rings and then the swirls of icing on her uneaten cake. Shanti, who sat beside her, put a hand on her knee and squeezed and then rested her head on her *ammai*'s shoulder. The sharpness poked at her jaw and Shanti raised her head and stared at Ammai's face with a concern she had never felt. Gita, feeling the loss of warmth, turned and met Shanti's eyes and smiled a wan and empty smile. Taking her hand, she pressed Shanti's face back into her shoulder and, loving her as she did, Shanti steeled herself to the prodding bones pushing into her cheek.

"Anyway, one man lived near there who had a cousin doing studies in Lucknow, and he came home to visit and he was there for over a month. One time Gita was walking down the small road there in the village and when she came around the corner, this man from Lucknow came from the bushes and stood there in front of her." Jaya looked around the room and all eyes were on her. Mrs. Kauffman sat up in her seat. Govind, the teller of tales, cocked his head to the side to listen better, and the girls, who had never heard this story, huddled closer and closer. Again, Shanti, sensing the danger, sat up and looked at her *ammai*, whose face had become attentive. Dr. Raman Nair sat still and uncomfortable; the story was terrible and he always felt such rage to hear it told, and to know that he was not there to do better damage, because he would not have cared about Purushu's feelings. What would make Jaya tell this story now, with all these strangers? Sitting across the room from one another, Veena and George each longed to listen to this mothertale snuggled together, with intermittent kisses. Every few seconds, one would look up to find the other already staring and they would smile and look away. Each of the sisters noticed once or twice, and Dhanya caught each and every stolen glimpse.

"Anyway, that Lucknow cousin began to talk some nasty things, and the reason we know this is not because Gita told, she was so small, but because right behind her was coming her Muthammai, which was her father's oldest sister who has long ago passed away. Her husband was killed in Delhi in an accident on a bus and she went crazy after that, and then she died from craziness." Jaya paused and took a sip of her tea, which had become cool. "That cousin, he was a dirty, drunken man with filthy habits, like they say he used to just clear his nose on the street while he was talking to people. And he used filthy, dirty language, and the man who lived there—what was his name, Ramu?"

"Purushu." There was something in this story; there was something that made Gita, and her brother also, very perplexed and absorbed, though they were not sure why. Neither seemed able to reach out and make her stop talking.

"Yes, Purushu, he was very ashamed of him all the time and he dreaded his visits, and after what that Lucknow cousin did, he was always very deferential to Ramu's family." She nodded her head and the room nodded back.

"Well, Muthammai had sent Gita ahead because she forgot the *appams* she had made to take to the other house, and so she was right behind when she came around the same corner and found the Lucknow cousin was kissing her cheeks and tickling her and petting her hair and telling her she was so beautiful he was going to marry her and that he was going to wait for her every day!" Everyone gasped and made terrible sounds and looked at Gita, who turned red with shame and forgotten memories. "There may have been other things."

"Enough, enough!" Dr. Raman Nair said.

"Yes, yes, I am telling this story only because nothing happened!" Jaya looked at Dr. and Mrs. Kauffman. "Muthammai had an umbrella in her hand, she always walked with one in the sun and she took it and she beat that Lucknow cousin until he was lying in the street. He was very drunk, she said, and he fell right down. She said she wanted to take the point and poke out his eyes for saying such things to a child, but she didn't because she didn't want to bring further shame on Purushu, and so she just turned around with Gita and came home and then they did so many *pujas*. *Puja*, *puja*, *puja* to rid her of this disgusting man's filthy thoughts." Jaya saw the confusion and said to Dr. and Mrs. Kauffman, "*Pujas* are prayer ceremonies." Turning back to everyone, she finished with, "Anyway, it was discovered that on that day she was not wearing any marks on her face." Jaya looked up, into her husband's eyes. Dr. Raman Nair's face widened with disbelief that she would say these things to strangers. The girls looked about in confusion, but Jaya offered no more. Jaya looked back at Gita and added, "They never made that mistake again, did they?"

Gita looked at her *chechi*, who never meant any harm, and she paused a long, tense minute. The daughters of Dr. Raman Nair felt some knowledge they had missed, a story they did not know, and then Gita answered in a thoughtful way, "I never knew why they always did that to my face. Why they kept me inside. Why they were forever administering such strange, arcane *pujas*." Gita stopped and thought on it for a minute. *An entire lifetime spent afraid of imaginary maybes and ancient history, a cousin from Lucknow and forever branded in kohl?* Suddenly, it was more absurd than even she, the queen of absurd, could tolerate. She sat up and Shanti straightened off her shoulder and looked at her with a question on her brow. Gita looked up and then she stood. "I must go now."

Oh, how the alarms rang around the house. The protests, the shouting. Her brother alone, a full ten minutes of diatribe.

To Gita: "What?! In the middle of the night? Only crazy people leave their homes in the middle of the night." And to Usha when she rightly pointed out, "Dad, it's only eight o'clock—"

"Shut up, you stupid girl!"

To Jaya: "You see? You see? With your stories and bad memories and evil portents? Driving sane people from their homes and making them behave crazy!" And when Jaya rightly defended, "She was crazy before I said anything at all! Don't blame me for making her crazy!"

"Shut up, you also!"

It was very bad. And in the middle of the whole thing, without offering an explanation at all, Gita left.

When she got home, she sat on her bed and called her voice mail. She listened to every message, and then she deleted it. There would be no more of this. With a decided action, she stood up fast, turning left and right. Her hair swung behind her like in prior, happier days, and she moved with a little more conviction. An idea was coming to her now; there would be no more of this. Gita ran fast to a small chest she hid in her closet and locked with a key. She opened it up and removed a box from whence she pulled a stack of love notes and poems collected over all her loving years. She sat on her bed and turned on the light and read the ones she remembered best, and then found some that she had long ago forgotten, and in this self-administered *puja*, she became honest and truthful again. It took her two hours to read enough to recognize the integrity of her life, the joy and despair of all real things. She was edified in knowing that the place she had chosen for her soul was real. There would be no more of this. *I will arise and go now, and go to Innisfree,/And a small cabin build there, of clay and wattles made;/Nine bean rows will I have there, a hive for the honey bee.*

There would be no more of this. She packed an overnight bag and returned to her brother's house, where in the morning, she would hear the blessings of the Suprabhatam and would begin the journey home.

❧

Under the same stars that were so propitiously aligned, Chris sat at his desk alone in his house with the box pulled from inside his closet where it never used to be. Without worry, he sat on the floor and dumped the whole thing out to look at. It was the first time Jeri had left the house since Thursday when he had come home to find her just like this, sitting amid his years of love notes and poems, her face so twisted with pain that it was as though he had walked into a hospital room again to find her crushed by the deepest blows. He had nearly passed out with the sight.

He opened letter after letter and read the ones he remembered the best and found some he had forgotten, and in this self-administered penance, he was left with no peace and no solace and no clear direction. Gita's love bled and glittered on every page. That love, those joys and this despair from the loss of her were the only things that were real. And yet, she had not removed a thing. Jeri left it all to him and he could see her face and he could hear her, "*This is all I have.*"

Onam night, long after the party was over, Dhanya could feel in her sensitive bones that the whole house was asleep, but she was a harder one to go down. She closed her eyes and listened to the night sounds, which were more numerous than easy sleepers knew. This evening, there was a catfight, and it was only her tremendous natural self-possession that kept her in her bed rather than racing out the door to rescue what a lesser young lady would think were shrieking, abandoned babies; the second-to-last daughter of Dr. Raman Nair was the most poised of the line. *Perhaps if I predict which noises I will hear in the next minute, by the time the minute has passed, I will be fast asleep.* And so began the nighttime games that she always played when she could not sleep. But in fact, this game was a poor choice, for at the end of ten minutes, which felt like only one, she was more alert and hearing more noises than she had when she began.

Dhanya turned her head to the other bed in the room, where Shanti was sleeping, though she had offered to take the floor. *Dhanya Chechi, you make the floor as comfortable as the bed.* And this was true. Her pallets were only surpassed by Veena's, who made a bed on the floor feel like silken clouds. (In the basement, Baby George lay awake on just such a majestic divan, which Veena had created from layers of comforters and cotton sheets that were washed with such care as to feel like silk but less hot, and which were then pulled so tight as not to leave a crease, and then all placed on what had originally been a slim Army cot as austere as anything George owned. When she led him to the cot, he looked at her and thought, *How do you already know?* When she then transformed the cot into a luxurious and decadent sleeping place, he thought, *Perhaps this is complete happiness versus just life.*)

Outside the room, there was a slow creak and then a pause. She turned her head toward the chink of black space under the door and watched and listened as the floor creaked and then went silent, again and again. Though the door was closed, she could see her sister Veena creeping in the hall on her way to the basement where Dhanya knew she would head when the house fell asleep, because she could smell the shocking desire in the steam rising from her *chechi*'s body all night. The shadow under the door blackened as Veena passed. Dhanya inhaled and she could still smell it, cilantro and soap and that other thing that would make her eldest sister get up from her bed and risk sneaking down the stairs of a house where nearly every corner held a sleeping person, or someone just hoping for sleep. Dhanya closed her eyes, and in the same rhythmic creak and silence, creak and silence, she counted the number of steps away her sister was from her beloved. Before Veena even arrived at the basement cot, Dhanya was fast asleep, Veena's secrets safe in her quiet, watching, patient and poised heart.

When she opened the basement door, Veena was pleased at the smell of laundry and felt less guilt at putting this man, whose jaw was perfectly chiseled into his neck and whose bare feet were as perfect as his hands, in the basement. A man who was so ideally formed should have a room on a high floor. At the top of the stairs, closing the door behind her, Veena closed her eyes and imagined that one day, they would build a home and she would insist on a turret with a tin roof, and a bed that she would decorate like he was a maharaja rather than her simple husband, and when it rained, she would lead him up there and play king and concubine to the dulcimer twinkle of rain on the roof, and she would feel that finally he was sleeping in a bed high enough to make up for their first time together having been underground. She gently walked down the stairs.

George—hoping that her having placed her hand on his face when she rose from making his bed, and smiling without saying anything, and lowering her eyes and raising them filled with tears, and walking away with her hand on her heart, all meant that she might come back down to see him this night—was lying awake, calmed by the rhythms of the washer and dryer that these efficient daughters had loaded immediately at the end of the party. When he heard her footfall on the creaky stairs, his heart jumped and his stomach twisted in joy and madness. He sat up and lay back down and sat up again, and for the first time in his life, wondered how he looked and whether or not he had time to replace the T-shirt he had taken off, more out of the habit of sleeping bare-chested than out of any kind of plan to make love.

When she turned the corner to the room where George was sitting up, the moon shone through the small window in the top of the wall and lit a silver white line over his left arm and his hair, and the shadows made him seem broader than he was. In this most flattering moonlight, he might also have looked handsomer than he really was to someone who didn't love him as Veena already did. To her, he became more handsome every day, and when he was an old man and his hair turned completely white and his long legs were skinny and covered with veins, she still raised her face to him for kisses, and carried a camera to capture him on film.

They looked at each other for minutes and minutes because suddenly there was that question of what it meant to have fallen in love like this, and of course, there was suddenly a worse question, *perhaps I love you, but you do not love me?* and *does this count for enough?*

George turned his lithe body from his cot and stood up, and he was taller than she even remembered because without his shirt his torso, which she had imagined all evening, was longer and stronger and his stomach was muscled, more so in the moonlight, and he was wearing a pair of shorts that showed that his legs were longer too. Veena felt a gulp in her throat and an awareness of her size and a deep-enough love to put self-consciousness aside to open her arms and her eyes wide and invite him to touch all over her mountainous body for the rest of his life. And when she lowered her head for just a moment, George read, *If you should so wish.*

And he so wished. He wanted her so much, the huge bulging parts of her that swelled and heaved with her pleasure in him; her sentient, deep black eyes and the eyelashes that tangled in the tousles of her gleaming hair; her red mouth that was always open and searching for him in the darkness. And because when he held her and felt the whole of her up and down there was no end to his desire; and because when he turned her over to see and feel everything he could not see from the front, the fairy moonlight highlighted her mounded back and her round, enormous buttocks and the strong line of muscle in her calves and her hamstrings; and because when he lay back from her, he was exhausted and alive, he knew that there was enough of this woman to please him forever and ever, and there was enough of her to explore and fall in love with anew for the rest of his life.

❧

Veena, mindful of shaming something and someone she would need for the rest of her life, kissed her beloved's face long before dawn to awaken him from his blissful sleep. He had nestled into her naked breasts and pressed down the flesh to allow for breathing, and when Veena wiggled just a bit to reach his broad and perfect forehead for kissing, the shake in her bosom aroused his newly ignited desire. Having started so late in his life, George would take her nearly every day of their life together, and she learned that if she was tired, or unwell, not to shimmy or shake because then he could not help but climb her like his own personal Rupal Face.

She shushed him and whispered, "It is too close to dawn. Ammai asked for Suprabhatam, and Daddy might decide to play it at daybreak."

"There's company," George moaned into her neck.

"I know. He might not. But she hasn't been doing well. He might be afraid. He might just do it to be sure she is awake and happy."

"Veena." George, pulling up from her warm body onto his elbow, was suddenly serious and Veena knew he loved her and that he would tell her so this minute. Her hands came to her cheeks and she was quiet and still. He looked at her, up and down, and he ran his free hand over her and, stopping on her belly, he said, "I love you."

She took her hands from her own cheeks and placed them on his and said, "I love you too." She pulled him on top of her and made love to him once more, and though they were novice and afraid of the coming dawn, they climaxed together and in this bit of passionate luck, they felt they were practically engaged. She rose from the cot, crept to her room and collapsed into bed. This time, Dhanya in the other room was peacefully asleep, but Mira, Veena's roommate, sighed with relief, having spent the last several hours wondering how long she should wait before risking the complete, but necessary, humiliation of going down into the basement to retrieve her sister before the first om of the Suprabhatam woke the house.

Moving On

In the morning, Gita grabbed her nephew by the elbow, sloshing his half-drunk tea, and pushed him out the door to help her move. They returned in the late afternoon to the home of Dr. Raman Nair in a small U-Haul truck filled with necessities and a few priceless pieces of furniture with which she would never part. The rest she arranged tastefully in her small but adorable apartment with an exposed brick wall and all palladium windows. She would list it as a furnished sublet at a reasonable price and it would go in days. Gita was moving on.

When they arrived, there was no one to hold the dog, for the whole house had gone sightseeing in Washington, except Muthachan and Jaya, both of whom were occupied, for Jaya was trying to give Muthachan a haircut and a shave so he would look handsome and clean by the time everyone returned. It was a most unfortunate timing for arrival.

Gita and Manoj opened the garage door, and there he was, already reared back, smiling, panting, one bark for hello and up he stood, taller than even Manoj, arms spread wide. They held their arms out and yelled, "Nooooooooo!!" But he held nothing back. His love was absolute. They were sucked into dog kisses that almost vacuumed their heads. They were enveloped in a humid miasma of gleeful dog breath. They were pummeled with dog fists, they were mauled with dog love, they were knocked to their haunches, and when the great Taj Mahal looked down at them both curled into balls offering nothing but possum play, he whined and cried a little, and when poking them in the shoulders did nothing but make them curl tighter, he humphed and went to the driveway and looked right and left. These were not his favorite ones.

Oh, but inside, the timing was perhaps more unfortunate, for when the barking of Taj Mahal rose to frantic, howling joy, Muthachan lost all composure, and no amount of shushing and petting could convince him that Jaya was not there to cut his throat. She barely escaped, slamming the door behind her. As the latch clicked, the bowl of water she used to wet her comb crashed against the door and a second later all the water from that bowl splashed against the door with a gusting whoosh like wind in the leaves. It would be a staggering mess. Sighing, she thought to look at the bright side; she had managed to flee with both the clippers and the razor. She locked the door from the outside. Every time she was forced to do it, she shuddered and looked up to God for understanding, *He might kill me accidentally, Lord; then what could I do?*

Coming out to the front room, she found Manoj and Gita sprawled on the kitchen floor, sopping wet from head to toe, their hair shellacked with a dreadful dog-drool pomade. Jaya pursed her lips. "The dog was in the garage."

Gita and Manoj exchanged a look and said nothing. Jaya continued.

"Because you two came through the garage even though that was where the dog was staying while we have all the company," she paused and stared at them both with disapproval, "I was nearly killed by *your* father and *your* grandfather." Holding up the clippers and the razor, she bent forward so they could see them better. "*These* would have been the implements of my murder." She walked into the kitchen and placed the weapons on the counter. Taking the key from around her neck, she turned back and pointed at them both still lying there wet and exhausted. "Take this key and after you take bath, you go there both of you and see what mess he has made. He threw a bowl at me!" She held the key out on an extended arm and waited.

Gita and Manoj wearily turned to face her, and when it became very apparent that she would not put the key back round her neck, or even down on the counter next to the implements of attempted murder, they got to their feet and Manoj pocketed the key.

"You two be quick, and don't use too much water, because when they come back from the sightseeing they will all smell like outside and might want to take bath." As Gita and Manoj slowly walked away Jaya called out, "But wash well, and your hair, you both stink." And when they were well out of sight and halfway up the stairs they paused when she added, "Hurry up, they will be back soon."

The key in the lock made a click that buckled both Manoj and Gita, who were not sure what would lie on the other side of Muthachan's door; once already today they had been brutally surprised, and they felt the need to exercise prudence in entering. Standing in the hallway outside, they cracked the door and peered in, Manoj's head on top, Gita's below, like children, or parents, or spies.

In the dark room they could see that he was peacefully asleep. Taking a deep breath, they entered and flipped on the night-light, though it was still daylight outside. The shades were drawn to distract Muthachan from the windows, which he had not yet thought to climb out of, though it was always a frightening possibility. In the dim light, the room seemed dingy and frightening . . . the wet floor, the cast-off bowl. Gita whispered, "We should turn on the big light, this is very scary like this." Manoj just looked at her and she understood that, no, she really did not want to awaken her father with a cheery light.

"I can't see properly," she said instead, looking around. There was a bowl on the floor and by the gloomy luminescence of the night-light, the silver and black hairs that clung to the door and the wall seemed to glow. There was a wet shadow drying in the shape of a monster, and she felt that this must be scrubbed off first before her father woke up. "The shape of the water on the wall will scare him."

"The shape of the water on the wall?"

"Yes, it looks like a monster."

Manoj looked and tilted his head, and all he saw was wetness. The longer he looked, the more it looked like the letter "P." "It looks like a letter 'P.'"

Gita went to the closet and took a white towel; wetting it in the bathroom, she began to wash the wall, and then the door. Manoj took another towel and dried the floor. Like this, they worked in silence and soon they heard the sound of the family and friends returned from their sightseeing. Finishing their work, they surveyed the clean room and left Muthachan snoring peacefully in his bed. He was as harmless as a baby and nearly as small. Leaning over his little face, Gita kissed her father so gently that he did not even change his breathing. Pushing back his wildly half-cut hair, she sighed. *He used to tower and roar.*

In the living room, they were all returned from the best day ever; it had even happened that in the middle of the natural history museum, Veena and George managed to break away for eight unnoticed minutes and, in the little theater that showed a movie on a never-ending loop of the mummification process and artifacts found in ancient Egyptian tombs, he held one hand behind her head and with the other he embraced her. Someplace deep within, she remembered the Song of Solomon and thought, *I am my beloved's and he is mine.*

When the group returned, the house was ablaze with lights and before he threw open the garage door, Dr. Raman Nair faced his family and their new friends, the Kauffmans and little Govind, and put his hand high in the air. In his joyfully booming voice he shouted, "Behold, the great Taj Mahal, who will greet us with a fanfare fit for kings and queens, who will dance to show his joy, who will bark to announce our arrival for those near and far. In tiny seaports in distant harbors, in villages, in jungles a thousand miles from here, people will turn their ears to the sky and whisper, 'What is that barking? Who has come that is so beloved as to earn such a deep and resounding welcome!'" Bending low and throwing up the garage door, they saw him and gasped in wonder. The great Taj Mahal was already standing and at the sight of his master, he began to leap on his hind legs and with his front paws he clapped. His bark was so loud and so happy that the whole assembly of people bent double with laughter. They were safe, for Dr. Raman Nair had joined his dog and the two of them were nearly matched for size and joy, and the great Taj Mahal had no interest in anyone but him. They watched, they laughed, and they felt that the day could not be any more wonderful than this.

When Muthachan threatened her life, Jaya remained jumpy for many hours, not from fear, but from abandonment. Simply the forgetting of her name made her so sad; he was the only father she had ever known, and once he had loved her like his own born child. Deflated and lonely, she felt the need to have everyone gathered in tight, so when Manoj and Gita emerged, she sent them to the basement to bring up the long table. They all washed and changed and settled around two tables laid side by side with Indian tablecloths of colorful hand-printed cotton.

Tonight they ate fried fish, and leftovers, and fresh *papadams*, and George sat with his back to his beloved and felt the tingle of her presence behind him. Many times he forgot to swallow for wondering where exactly her hands were right now, or what exactly she was looking at right now, and every rise of laughter sent a pulse that shot below his belly button and made him shudder. If anyone was looking, they would think the poor boy had a tic. Sometimes, with his mouth full of rice, he leaned way back to hear what she was saying with her low, melodic voice.

It was quiet, the peaceful murmur of the asking and answering of unnecessary questions, the hum of after dinner. And thus they sat, lifting their now-warm *payasams* to their lips for another sip, when suddenly there was a crashing of glass, like an entire china cabinet knocked to the floor. Jaya, the only one who felt it coming in her bones, stood first and raced to the hallway, where she was met with the swinging stick of her father-in-law, half shaved, with his hair standing in spikes on one side and loose down his neck on the other. With his cane in one hand and his other hand thrown wildly to the side, with his maniac eyes, and his bared, shining gums, he looked like John Brown at Harper's Ferry and the Kauffmans had no doubt that they were about to be killed. They looked at one another, thankful that their last day had been so wonderful.

Glaring at Jaya and swinging his stick to catch her in the head, he shouted, "GET AWAY FROM ME YOU VILLAINAOUS SURGEON, YOU DEVIL'S BARBER! DON'T YOU COME NEAR ME ANYMORE WITH YOUR TORTURE AND IDEAS!"

"Achan, Achan, what are you talking about? Achan, stop swinging that cane!" cried Dr. Raman Nair as he carefully approached his father. The rest of the girls and Manoj and Gita also rose to surround the old man, who now swung at them all.

"YOU WOULD TAKE HER SIDE AGAINST ME? WHO ARE ALL OF YOU THAT HAVE SET MY OWN SON AGAINST ME? DO YOU SEE ME? DO YOU SEE MY FACE? IT IS HALF EATEN AWAY, AND I CAN FIND NO PEACE." Taking his cane and turning quickly, he pointed it at Jaya and raised his voice further, "THAT WOMAN HAS SET SOME CURSE ON MY FACE, I WILL DIE CLAWING MY SKIN FROM MY BONES LIKE A LEPER. SHE HAS NO SHAME, NO RESPECT FOR A WEAK OLD MAN!!"

Veena, standing next to her mother, reached in quickly and grabbed the stick from her grandfather, who gasped and covered his mouth with his hand. He pointed at her and shook and sputtered. Shaking in his whole body he shouted, "IT IS YOU. IT IS YOU!" The whole group held its breath and Muthachan continued, "I SAW YOU! I SAW YOU IN THE NIGHT, CREEPING, CREEPING, AND DON'T YOU DENY IT!"

Veena felt the blood slip from her body and she nearly fell down. Dhanya and Mira both nearly fainted as well. George got to his feet from the table where he had remained, unsure of what to do, his heart thumping in the bridge of his nose. He took a step forward, for if the old man were to take a swing at Veena, he would have to take him in his arms and carry him out bodily, and hell be damned, he would deal with her father later. Inching closer, he realized the truth of his feeling. *Veena, I would marry you tomorrow.*

Muthachan stood there madly tossing about his half-shorn hair, flattening his toothless mouth with every sputter and sigh.

"I SAW YOU," he shouted again. Veena felt her head begin to swim. George took another step forward and then another. Mira, Dhanya and even Manoj cringed. "SNEAKING AWAY WITH MY FOOT." He turned his trembling finger down to his feet and his eyes filled with indignant tears. Pouting and weak, he took a deep breath and shouted again, "YOU ALL THINK YOU CAN JUST PUT ME TO SLEEP AND THEN THAT IS THAT. AAAA-HAAA, I STAY AWAKE. I PRETEND!! I WATCHED YOU, SNEAKING DOWN THOSE STEPS WITH MY FOOT!! AND NOW YOU TAKE MY STICK?

YOU ARE A HEARTLESS THIEF." Here, he turned toward the basement door and pointed with his trembling hand. "YESTERDAY . . . YESTERDAY . . . HOW COULD I FOLLOW YOU WITHOUT MY FOOT? HOW CAN I WALK DOWN THOSE STEPS ON THIS PATHETIC ROTTING STUMP?" He pointed down to his two healthy feet, shaking his finger for emphasis. "OHHHHH, A CUNNING GIRL YOU ARE. TAKING MY FOOT AND NOW MY STICK TO ASSURE I CANNOT FOLLOW YOU IN YOUR EVIL DEEDS!" Veena, Mira, Dhanya, Manoj and George took a collective sigh of relief.

By this time, George was standing behind Veena, quiet and waiting for Muthachan to raise his hand against her. As Muthachan declared her a cunning girl of evil deeds, George took his final step forward. Muthachan raised his teary, frightened and angry face to see who had moved and his eyes lit with a bare recognition. Exhaling in triumph, he cried, "I KNOW YOU!!" Redirecting his finger at George. "WERE YOU INVOLVED? SPEAK UP, BOY. WHO ARE YOU AND WHY ARE YOU IN MY HOUSE? ARE YOU INVOLVED IN THE STEALING OF MY FOOT? I KNOW YOU. . . . I . . . HAVE . . . SEEEEEN . . . YOU . . ." Muthachan's finger was bobbing up and down slowly while he stared hard at George, trying to remember. In his quiet distraction, he became tamer and Dr. Raman Nair gathered him up in his large, strong arms. Gita shushed him and petted his half-shorn hair and together, they guided him back down the hall.

In a final show of defiance he cried out over his shoulder, "ARE YOU TWO IN CAHOOTS? BONNIE AND CLYDE, YOU WILL BE FOUND OUT. . . . BRIIIING BAAAAACK MY FOOOOOT!" The door closed and that was the end of that. While Veena and George trembled with relief, and the rest of the group debriefed the incident, Jaya stared down the hallway knowing it was all her fault. In her distraction and self-pity, she had neglected to feed him on time. He was always this way if he became hungry. A tear fell down her cheek that she had forced him to make a spectacle in front of company; she was very ashamed. Returning to the table, she fixed him a plate of rice and yogurt and carefully picked the bones from two very small pieces of fried fish.

Ready

From the Journal of Gita Nair

August 15, 1999

Last night I dreamed I kissed Chris upside down in the flickering light of candles. While I slept, I thought I was awake and when I awoke I thought I was asleep because the light was gone and the room was black. There were mobiles in the style of Calder that hung too close to our heads. They were black and red. They swung in the breeze, but we were inside . . . what breeze? When I dream, I am always with him.

Om.

On the day Gita left for Quiet Pond, Dr. Raman Nair rose early in the gray before dawn. When the morning broke free, he hit the button and the house was slowly filled with blessings of Suprabhatam. It was not merely that his sister seemed to be opening a bizarre, inexplicable new chapter of her life (which surely would require some spiritual guidance and blessing) but mostly because his second-to-last daughter was leaving today for college. Dhanya was moving on.

Om.

While the house stirred, awash in the gentle beginnings of the music, Dr. Raman Nair entered the tiny *puja* room, a closet in his office filled with necessary deities and lamps, but only rarely used. He prayed on his own birthday; and when they were young, on his children's birthdays; and every year on his mother's death anniversary; but always, always, always, on the day they left his home for college. He never prayed more fervently than he did on that day. This morning, Dr. Raman Nair entered his *puja* room and when he finally emerged, the sky was bright, the Suprabhatam had long ago finished its preprogrammed ten loops, and the day had already begun. There was a wonderful bustle in the air, and his heart squeezed tight in his chest. Entering the kitchen that tinkled with glad laughter, he held tight to tears that welled beneath his lids. Jaya looked up from the counter where she prepared the *doshamav*, and between them they shared the look of pride and fear that is the parent's seal on this letting-go day heavy with promise. Dhanya glowed and buzzed, and her older sisters saw this marked change in their contained and diffident baby sister and knew that she was more sanguine, more hopeful, and more excited than she had ever been before. Shanti, knowing that within a few hours her closest friend, her roommate and the one to whom she was the sole baby sister, would leave forever, sat in a chair and picked at the crumble atop her coffee cake. Her sisters saw this marked change in their happy and silly baby sister and knew that she was sadder, emptier, and lonelier than she had ever been before. They walked past her and snuggled her head against their immense chests one after another while they loaded the table with a breakfast fit for kings.

Gita, nibbling from others' plates, watched them all and poured glass after glass of juice. When the table was laid, she kneeled beside her favorite and whispered in her ear, "In only two years, you go too. Imagine your mother and father when you and Dhanya both are no longer here." Shanti lifted her head and caught her father's silence and mother's tight face. Looking back at her *ammai*, she set in a small smile and stood up. "Mommy, today you come and sit. I will do that." She took her mother's place at the stove and by the time they were all settled over breakfast, she had made twenty-five hot *doshas* and her father and mother smiled and nodded in praise, for her *doshas* were perfectly round in shape.

Breakfast finished, Gita readies herself and looks in the mirror. She has magically gained ten wonderful pounds overnight. She is nearly as perfect as she ever was. She smiles, she flashes, she kisses, she hugs. Gita takes her own green Volvo and a suitcase packed for a week. The rest she would retrieve later, for who knew where she would stay except that it would be within a few miles of Chris; the town is very small.

Her brother is terribly afraid. Where is this place? Quiet Pond? Why is she going there? Sabbatical? To write her book? Why not write it here, in her apartment? In his house? Why go to someplace she has never been, where she has no home and knows no one? Why? Her story is, of course, utterly unbelievable, but what else was there to know? Nothing. He is too afraid to ask.

Final preparations began the moment Gita drove away. Standing in the driveway and waving good-bye, Dhanya resumed the mental rummaging and counting she had begun in the early gray light before the Suprabhatam, and only paused during breakfast because her baby sister had looked so sad. That morning, suddenly gripped in a panic, she turned her body out of bed at the very first ringing om, touched her right foot to the floor and raced down the stairs to ascertain that yes, they had not forgotten to put the new iron in the pile for school. Racing back up the stairs, she threw herself into bed before Shanti could awaken so she would not feel twice abandoned this day. Breathing hard and smiling in her covers, Dhanya thought about the iron she had chosen for herself, with the wrinkle-release steam feature plus the water spray.

"This is better than our iron!" Dr. Raman Nair had exclaimed.

"And, kind sir, how is it that *you* would know?" Jaya replied.

"AAH-ha, a very funny girl you are, very funny. A really witty girl!" Dr. Raman Nair had tilted his head side to side with a big grin. Turning to Dhanya, he said, "When you have doubts in chemistry and maths, you ask your iron, and I think if you push this button here," indicating the wrinkle release, "the answer will come out through these holes." He reached up and pinched her cheek and pulled her hair and they all laughed and Veena ironed a tablecloth, just to see how it worked. It was an excellent iron.

Gita Nair in Quiet Pond

Gita arrived at the Stone House Inn in the twilight hour. She had called ahead and indeed they had room for her. The proprietress spoke slow and serious, for which Gita was grateful. She had been afraid of the small-town bed-and-breakfast. She had little patience for frivolity and little skill in the art of conversation, but there were no other options: this bed-and-breakfast or that bed-and-breakfast. Or cottages for rent by the pond. She had been afraid of ending up next door to Innisfree.

When she pulled up to the curb, the door opened. A woman stood in the doorway with two children. Her hair was long, dark brown to her waist. Her eyes were so green Gita could see them from the street. She waved and smiled. She looked so very young to have children as old as this. She looked not much older than Gita herself. *I might have had children by now.*

Gita took her one bag from the trunk and walked up the path. On either side were outlandishly overgrown and massively flowering bushes and trees. She had never seen such a garden in all her life. The outrageous pungency of the flowers nearly knocked her off her feet. A jasmine bush crept over the path and blocked her passage. From the door, the woman called out, "Just step around it, don't worry about the lawn. I like to keep it wild."

Gita reached the front door. "It is an exceptional yard."

"Thank you. I like to keep it wild." She put out her hand. "My name is Penelope."

"Gita. I called earlier."

"I know. These are my children. Jack and Kate."

Jack is staring at Gita with his eyes wide and unblinking. He is dumbstruck. He is unable to move. He is unwilling to speak. He fears his voice will come out in squeaks and hoots. His sister rolls her eyes. They are very close. Shyly, she bats her eyes. She is nine years old, and she knows she should do better, but she relies on Jack to speak first. He has let her down this time, but she forgives him. They are very close. Gita goes inside with them and is unaware that her arrival has been noted.

❧

Del Musik sat up straight in his tall stool to see out the window of his basement office. Next door, the Stone House Inn perched high and bright, the perfect foil for what it really was, a den of iniquity. Surely this was true. He opened his Book to a fresh page.

AUGUST 15, 1999(A)

Today another succubus has arrived in Quiet Pond.

Dhanya Nair at the University of Virginia

From the Journal of Dhanya Nair

AUGUST 17, 1999

Ammai bought me this journal to take to college. She says that I should record all my thoughts and feelings. This is a project I wish I had more practice in, because then, perhaps, I would be more facile at distilling it down . . . maybe this space is meant for undistilled thoughts? Maybe it is meant to engender those moments of catharsis that will help me grow.

Well, in any event, here we go. Everyone has left. I am alone in my room in Lile. My roommate is named Clara Tarakova and she looks like a ballerina. She has gone to the Wal-Mart with her parents because she forgot her toothpaste and shampoo and stuff. When she arrived everyone was in the room, and there was no room for her family to get in. A little embarrassing. We brought two cars, everyone came. Clara also has only sisters. Two of them. They all look like ballerinas. I will sign off now because some of my other suitemates are going down to walk around. Everyone seems very nice. Clara is exceptionally nice. More later.

From the Journal of Dhanya Nair

August 17, 1999

Clara's family just left, she's gone to take a shower. Before they went, they took a picture of the two of us. We look like Saturn and Mimas. She's using it as desktop wallpaper. Ugh.

From the Journal of Dhanya Nair

August 18, 1999

Tonight we all walked up O-Hill because there was to be a "cross-shaped alignment of stars" and they opened the observatory for new first-years. The moon was spectacular. It was huge and low, and we stayed long enough to watch it rise. I turned to Clara to say that the moon was amazing and she kept looking at me and smiling and then she poked Amanda from New York and said, "Look at Dhanya in the moonlight, isn't she so beautiful." Clara looks like a fairy princess and she thinks I am beautiful. Imagine that.

Finally the End

At the same moment Gita pulled in front of the Stone House Inn, Chris pulled in front of her apartment in D.C. He was going one more time to knock on her door. He wondered how long he would continue to make this journey. He longed for the sight of her face.

As always, even knowing she would not be home, Chris stopped at Nasir's for flowers. When she was never there, he left them by the door. When Gita finally arrived home, she would find them, wilted and tragic, like tokens left for the famous dead. Truly though, one cannot stop one's loving heart from loving if there are dying flowers by the door. Those days, Gita took ten minutes to find her keys and ten more to turn the lock.

This time, his hand shook so hard that he bent stems and sent showers of petals to the hose-wet sidewalk under his feet. He had picked through the gerbera daisies like a mother looking through a crowd for her own lost child, fingering each one for the barest moment before pushing it aside and frantically grasping the next as though he sought recognition.

With his armful of flowers, Chris arrived at Gita's Washington apartment and knocked on the door. When no one answered, he put his key in the lock, though he already knew that even if it turned, he would not be able to get in, but this time, the dead bolt was not set, and the door opened with a hollow, empty whine.

Inside, an uninhabited echo chilled his heart as the discovery of the dead bolt had done so many weeks before. Chris put his flowers down on the table that sat with four chairs around it and made up as if for dinner, like in a department-store display, yet the refrigerator was empty. Walking through, he discovered that their place was thus full of irony after irony: a bed that was made up on top, but which had no sheets, and had newspaper-stuffed trash bags for pillows; a bathroom with towels set out, but with no soap and no toothbrush; a small, retro watering can sitting beside silk flowers set in clear gelatin. He sat on the edge of the sheetless, trash-bagged bed and wept.

As the night crept in, Chris chose to lie down there, for she was clearly gone and not coming back, and he was crushed and tired. Their bed, which had been warm, was an inhospitable platform, and as he reclined on the left side as he always had, there was a moment's panic of lying back into an open coffin or being lowered into a tomb. He ran his fingers through his hair and shook it off. He looked out the window and there was the blinking streetlight outside. It had been blinking for many months. Months and months. Gita had grown accustomed to the flashing; he had not. Watching the streetlight on this terrible night, he considered the number of times that she tacitly told him to take her away and he had not heeded or even noticed what she meant. And now, here he was alone in the bed-without-sheets, resting on stuffed trash bags, watching the streetlight that represented just one more way in which he proved his lack of courage to his one true love.

"God, that light is annoying."

"You get used to it. They'll get around to it eventually."

"I don't know how you get used to something like that. It's so distracting."

"Well, I guess you would have to be here for a while to get used to it, right?"

He had blotched in the blinking light, but she had already turned her back. *Was it then that I might have said, "That's it, I am marrying you, and you are not going to say no, and I don't give a damn what you tell your brother"?*

It occurred to him, as he lay there awake, alone and afraid, that he never really saw it coming. He was a sap, a huge sap. He was perpetually surprised by the turn of his life, by the effect of his words, by his own reactions. He never looked to the endgame. His whole life to date had been a series of moves with no endgame. He should have won by now. But then, not one of them had game, did they? They were like three kings on a board, moving around one another, one tiny useless space at a time. Only Gita had the courage to finally declare a draw and to just . . . leave.

The blinking streetlight went out for a while, setting free the splendor of the enormous full moon and giving Chris some clarity in his terrible pain. As the moon rose into the wee hours of the night, he leaned his head to catch it perched so high, and he felt his life in ferocious frankness. Things had happened in his life. Things had happened, yet nothing happened. Even when it seemed his wife had stripped all his pieces off the board, she still did not end the game. They were still avoiding checkmate. Even when she gathered all his pieces and lined them up for all to see, she still never won the game, and he never forfeited. Around and around they went.

Chris fell asleep and the streetlight again began blinking, disturbing his dreams. There were voices, but no faces, and he was too hot and then too cold. Somewhere deep in his mind, he heard his own voice shouting out, "COURAGE! COURAGE! COURAGE!" And somewhere still deeper in his mind he agreed that the time had come to take courage.

Tests of Courage

Morning came. Veena awoke, and in a defiant show of her own strength and power, she opened the bedroom window. Sensing contravention from all the way down the hall, Usha arrived at the door and opened it without knocking. Seeing her sister with her face pressed against the slightly torn screen of the open window, she whistled low and long.

"Death wish?"

Veena, despite her impulsive and valiant boldness, was frightened by the thrown-open door and her heart fluttered in her stomach. Turning back to the window, she tried to resume her courageous stance. *I am just breathing fresh air. It isn't a big deal.*

"I am just breathing the fresh air. It isn't a big deal."

"I am in full agreement, Chech, I am in full agreement. It should not be a big deal." Pulling the door closed as she backed out, Usha leaned forward and whispered, "But since it *is* a big deal, I'll just close the door."

In her bedroom, Jaya was, for some reason she couldn't quite place, in a turbulent state of nerves. She hadn't slept a wink and her skin felt dry and itchy, though the morning was already warm. She had the prescience of orphans, knowing when dangers lurked. Her eyes darted back and forth and her mouth was slightly dry. Something was changing in this house and it was not for the better. As she dressed in her itchy clothes and applied lotion to her dry hands, suddenly she began a fit of sneezing that threw her tiny body around the bathroom and gave her a vicious stomach cramp. Her husband was singing so loudly that she wanted to scale the shower door, throw in an enormous fishing net, capture him like a flailing trevally and throw him back to the Great Barrier Reef. She growled.

Exiting her room, she suddenly felt a slight shift in the barometric pressure of the hallway. She stood still and was abruptly racked with another bout of high-pressure sneezes for which she grasped the banister to keep standing. Between sneezes, she stood still and sensed the air. Usha, bopping down the corridor to the rhythm of her mother's sneezes, saw her concentration and considered what interference to run, but Jaya noticed the very slightest alarm on her face. *Something is wrong.*

"Hey, Mom. What's shakin'? Let's go eat!" Usha took her mother's arm gently and tried to pull her down the stairs but something in her daughter's friendly greeting alerted Jaya's antennae.

"YOU? You are never so cheerful first thing in the morning. What is going on here? I can feel it in the air." Jaya looked around; she really could feel it in the air, but she didn't know what it was. Something had her ready like a mother bear; her instincts alerted, like an animal of the deep, dark woods.

"What are you talking about? Let's go eat." Usha took her mother's elbow again. "I'll make us eggs before I go to work. I don't have to be in until nine."

Shrugging her off, Jaya went down the hallway and opened doors to find her girls in various states of readiness. Scowling, she moved on. When she reached the last room she put her hand on the knob and sneezed so hard she banged her head against the door. Opening it and rubbing her head, she found her eldest daughter standing guiltily before an *open window*, which exposed a slightly torn screen. Jaya felt she could see the pollen entering through that rip in nefarious, yellow whorls.

Face-to-face with her angry mother, Veena took a different tack, feeling it was time to test her courage first with small things. She attempted a daring smile but what came off on her unpracticed face looked more like shifty.

Her sly smile sent chills down Jaya's back.

"*What* is this?" Jaya stood in the doorway and pointed at the window. Her angry calm brought all the sisters, who stood behind their mother and gasped, one after another, when they saw the open window and the look of immovable certainty on their *chechi*'s face.

Looking from her mother to the place she pointed, Veena stared at the window behind her for a moment or two to gather her courage and to fix her face, and then she pointed behind her, and in a calm but determined voice she replied, "What, this? That's just the window."

The sisters ruffled and cringed; they dropped their faces into their hands and then raised them; together and one by one they shook their heads behind their mother's back with their faces aflame. *Stop stop, please stop, have you lost your MIND?!*

Usha wondered for the first time in her life, *Is that how I sound?*

Jaya stood perfectly still. *What is happening that she would do this? Is it she that I feel deep in here?* Weak from her sleepless night and the grim company of her unspeakable fears, she trembled from her head to her toes; her tight black bun lost its hold from the shaking, and down tumbled her long hair and it trembled too, and then she began to cry. She seized each of these girls in her arms and held them as though they were all leaving forever after this one, last, precious embrace. The girls were shocked and frightened, for they hadn't tried to open a window in too many years to remember if it went this badly the last time as well.

Sobbing and not bothering to gather herself before speaking, Jaya stood at the door and faced her eldest child. Gulping down her sobs, she lurched out, "I-will-be-snee-zing-all-day." And then she pushed them all aside, ran back down the hallway, slammed the door to her room and collapsed into bed in her itchy clothes. Overwhelmed and exhausted, she slept for several hours.

Veena stood at the open window with her mouth agog, facing her sisters. They stared at each other stupefied and abashed, and then they all came to help her push down the sash, which stuck, for it had not been opened in almost twenty years.

❧

Morning came. Gita walked down the stairs to the kitchen where Penelope had laid the table for breakfast. She was the only guest in the house. Penelope was at the stove and turned to greet Gita with a big smile.

"Oh, good! You're up. Let me call the kids and we can eat breakfast." She went to the porch door and called and in a minute they were there, hurtling into the kitchen one behind the other, but at the sight of Gita at the table, Jack stopped short and Kate crashed into his back. She backed away rubbing her nose; her brother stuck in place, staring.

"Good morning," Gita offers quietly.

"Good morning," Kate whispers, taking her seat.

Penelope waits for a proper second or two . . . "Jack?" Nothing.

"Jack?" A slight rise toward the end this time.

He turns to her and blinks. He turns away again and sits at the table. He still has not spoken. Kate buries her head in her plate. They all choose to ignore it.

"Well, Gita, what would you like to do today?" Penelope asks over her coffee. *She really is impossibly beautiful*, Gita thinks. Jack stares at Gita. He is thinking the same thing.

"My first order of business is to look for a place to live . . . more permanently." A happy rush filled her stomach.

"Well, then. That's easy. Kate honey, could you go get Mrs. Jones's number from the file."

Gita's happy rush suddenly dropped and pooled in her knees. "Um. Mrs. Jones?"

"Jeri Jones. The real estate agent."

"There's only one?"

Penelope smiled and shrugged. "Small town."

"555-3214." Jack sat straight up in his seat. They all looked at him strangely. He reddened deeply. "Mrs. Jones's number."

Kate returned with a small piece of paper. "555-3214." She handed the paper to her mother and sat back down. They all turned again to Jack, aflame at the head of the table.

"It's on lots of signs around town." His whisper is light and shy; he sparkles. Again, Gita rushes in her stomach at the thought of a new life.

I could have had a boy like this. Penelope reaches for the phone and makes a call. "Jeri? Penelope. I have a guest staying with me. She needs to find a house."

From the Journal of Dhanya Nair

August 23,1999

Well, as always, morning came! Today is the first day of class and it's a bright day and no rain, which is a plus. I have Arabic, Western Civilization, and Women in Literature which ought to be fun. Today is a much better day than tomorrow will be. (Chem., Calc II, and Arabic drill). But tonight is the real test of courage. I'm taking a dance class with Clara at the gym. It meets tonight. Three times a week.

!!!!

She said I don't need to wear a leotard and that it doesn't matter that I've never taken a dance class. She begged and well, I told myself, the worst thing is that everyone else might look like Clara Ballerina, the best thing is that I really like hanging out with Clara Ballerina and it's good exercise. She said I don't have to wear a leotard. I figure, I'll give it a try.

Morning came. Chris awoke in the ersatz love nest to a terrible crinkling behind his head. Groggy and disoriented, he reached back, felt the stuffed trash bags, and remembered where he was. Throwing off the covers, he sat up fully dressed and looked around. The bright morning light made the apartment even more distasteful and the abandonment more grievous. Anger pounded in his ears. It was time to go, and though he didn't know what the hell had happened here, there was no one to ask anymore. It was all over.

Chris got up and carefully folded the covers over to make up the bed but the trash-bag pillows, so perfectly plumped, had never been tied and their filling spilled out onto the floor. This had been a terrible mistake. Staying here the night; he was weak with it. He bent down to pick up the mess, and there, with what was mostly newspaper, were several pages of a story. Something she must have started after she left him. He had never seen it before. He sat down on the edge of the bed and read what there was to read. Which he discovered was not nearly enough.

The Cursed Life of Sreemathi Omanakumari

She Comes Home from Amma's

While the ladies fawned and ministered, there was a deep anger brewing at the home of Omanakumari. Parameshwaran Namboodiri, unaccustomed to waiting, desirous of sleep, and chilled in the humid night air, rose from the woven seat he had been offered and paced in a furious rectangle. Her father watched nervously and as his helplessness grew, he counted the steps in various ways: the number to, the number across, the number back, and the number fro; the number in total, and the difference in sums. When he lost count, he looked down at his toes, and when his nervousness mounted again, he counted the steps in a rhythm of five steps to a count.

"Mmmm," Parameshwaran Namboodiri would grunt at unequal intervals in his pacing. These articulations were so full of mean disapproval that Omanakumari's father would immediately look down at his toes. Parameshwaran Namboodiri seemed unaware of anyone else's presence and uninterested in what anyone else might say. For this, the child's father was grateful, for what was there to say when your child has disappeared after dark, and when your wife has followed her and failed to return? The moon rose higher and higher and the absence of the women made it a blacker night.

If not for righteous indignation, Parameshwaran Namboodiri would have stomped off long ago, but that he should come for a visit at this hour to find his girl gone *somewhere*, full as a seeping thundercloud, probably dragging her chin to broadcast her misery . . . it made him feel badly used. This girl was almost more trouble than she was worth, he thought. That she was almost immediately pregnant reduced his willingness to tolerate her impudence, for pregnancy did not sit well on her. She had darkened in splotches, and along her belly was a demarcation that seemed drawn from the inside with the end of a burning stick. It cleaved her in half, and neither half was willing to be near him. To his touch, this dark, dark line moved and shook and curved before his disgusted eyes. Whatever was in there was preternaturally aware of his nastiness and perhaps of his odor, for it bucked and heaved and she often vomited in his presence. He had lost his desire for her long ago.

Without warning, Parameshwaran Namboodiri raised his head and spat. He took his towel down from his shoulder and wiped his mouth and then his chest, which again was sweating with the exertion of his pacing. Looking up into the trees, Parameshwaran Namboodiri missed everything. The silvery glow of the moonlight in the palms; the variegated greenness; the wild, wide leaves waving like the ocean, their murmured shush that, multiplied one million times in just the courtyard of Omanakumari, was also oceanic in magnitude and rhythm. It was all lost on him, and all he could see when he looked up was that it was late, and his anger surged again.

From away, Omanakumari's father looked up as well, and saw all the miracles that he had seen every night of his life, the minute shaving of each night's moon, its utter disappearance, and day by day, its shy return to grace. To notice this was an evening prayer, an obeisance given in concert with his fairy-born daughter nearly every night of her life. She too looked up and saw everything. The sadness in the pit of the father had never left him since he had allowed the child to be stolen by this ugly and horrible man. Again, what to do? It was the way things were, he knew. And now she never came out with him, she just stayed away. And he never knew what she thought, and if she ever smiled, he never saw it. He raised his towel from his shoulder and wiped his face as well.

When he raised his eyes from the cloth, he saw two shadows far in the distance and he felt them deep in the bone. A sudden fear raised the hair on his arms. Looking then at Parameshwaran Namboodiri, who was glaring at the sky without seeing the moon, he thought hard to spare his child and his wife the fundamental injustice of coming home to trouble.

"*Thirumeni*?"

The old man did not move at all, and had the moon been made of weaker stuff, it would have squeezed to a dry rind and hung limply in the sky, waiting to fall like rotten fruit under the intense, focused glare of Parameshwaran Namboodiri.

"*Thirumeni*?" Anandan Nambiar called again and waited to be heard.

Looking to the left, he could see his family approaching closer, and though they moved so slowly as to stop time, he was afraid.

At that moment, Parameshwaran Namboodiri was imagining a terrible scolding for the girl. He even slapped her face. In his mind, she did not look up at him insolently, narrowing her eyes as she often did, forcing him to beat her again. In his mind, she was humbled and brought to her knees and she looked down crying and held his legs. Her enormous belly was nowhere in this fantasy and she was the beautiful girl he had loved so much. From this scolding, she finally came to see him as the loving master he was, and she finally loved him back. The thought brought a small smile to the old man's lips. Seeing him like this, Anandan Nambiar shivered, but looking left and seeing them more clearly now, he was urgent in his final address. Raising his voice and speaking with too great an authority, he called, "*Thirumeni!*"

Shaken abruptly from his reverie, Parameshwaran Namboodiri was irritated and angry. Looking about, he realized that the truth was that the stupid child had run away because she hated him so, and that she had turned ugly before his eyes and before he had really had a chance to get his fill of her, and that standing in front of him was the stupid child's father looking too proud and talking too loudly. He squinted and spat again.

"Mmmm," he muttered. "You are calling *thirumeni* like you forgot what it means. Shouting at me like a temple elephant trainer? What am I, a temple elephant? Am I a temple elephant that you should call me so loudly, and yet address me with respect?"

Anandan stared at his toes.

"Instead of staring at the ground, as useless as a dry cow that shits rocks, why don't you go find that girl and bring her here?" Parameshwaran Namboodiri swatted his back with his towel, once to the left, once to the right. The mosquitoes were making a meal of him, and his profuse sweating was bringing biting flies and gnats. To Anandan Nambiar he seemed to be nearly swarmed with a black cloud of insects whose wings, though microscopic, still managed to catch the shimmery moonlight. Parameshwaran Namboodiri was phosphorescent with bugs, and this gave Anandan Nambiar a thought.

"*Thirumeni*, in the back beside the well, there is a bucket of *aaryaveppu* water that Narayanikutty prepares every day for the mosquitoes. They can be very bad here in the night."

"Mmm . . . *aaryaveppu*. Mmm." Parameshwaran Namboodiri considered that a neem bath would suit him well as he waited for that stupid girl, for he would not leave until he had beaten her once or twice. Pregnant or not. He didn't ask for this pregnancy, and now he was standing here being eaten alive and she was about somewhere with her sullen face and striped belly.

"Shall I take you there; it is beside the well in a large bucket. There is only one bucket that will be full at this time. It is very clear. You can take this torch." Holding it out to Parameshwaran Namboodiri, Anadan Nambiar looked down at his toes and quietly hoped.

Parameshwaran Namboodiri, aggravated beyond reason by everything around him, humphed. Twisting his mouth and furrowing his brow, he turned toward the back of the house and stomped off without the light. As he turned the corner, Anandan heard him mutter, "As though the moonlight were not so bright as to invade my peace of mind let alone light my way a few steps, he offers me a torch to manage while I douse myself against his mosquitoes. Idiot."

Just as he was out of sight, the girl and her mother walked up the path. The child was moving so slowly it was painful to watch. She was exhausted to the point of fainting and frightfully pale. Her father, relieved to have removed the immediate threat of Parameshwaran Namboodiri, was now more alarmed than ever. Why did she look like this? Why did she seem so changed from when he saw her last? Looking at his wife, he realized that whatever made him scared was more than he could imagine.

"What? What is this? Why is she like this?" Anandan Nambiar whispered frantically.

Narayanikutty closed her eyes and shook her head quickly, silently telling him to let her get the child to bed. She opened her eyes and looked at him long. In her deep and silent face he read, *Let me put her to rest and I will tell you everything and we will make a plan.*

He released her arm, which he was holding too hard in his fear, and watched them move inch by inch toward the door. Looking to the back and counting the minutes that had passed since Parameshwaran Namboodiri went to bathe, he wished these slow-moving ladies wings, or that they might rise on the night's breeze and blow into the house and out of sight. But before they were two full strides away, Omanakumari was again seized with a paralyzing contraction that bent her double and made her whistle in pain. Anandan Nambiar bounded forward. Struggling to keep her upright, he stared wildly between his wife and his daughter and forgot all about the back of the house where one naked old man was trying to dry himself with a wet towel, muttering under his breath about the kind of girl who runs away in the night, and that he had no way of knowing that this child was his, considering that she had such unruly behaviors, and that certainly, then, they should not expect that he would give them even one piece of clothing for this bastard child of some cowherd or fisherman's helper. Behind the house, Parameshwaran Namboodiri said, "Humph," and kicked over the bucket of *aaryaveppu* water on his way back to wait for that slut of a girl.

As Omanakumari's spasm released, she slumped to the ground with grave fatigue and her father saw at that moment all the women and girls who died from this misery of giving birth, and he saw at that moment that his girl might become one of them. For the first time he realized that there might be no way to protect her from what fate was hers. She lay on the ground with her head in her mother's lap, drenched in sweat. Her hair was curled around her face and in spite of its paleness and its loss of faith, she still seemed so like a child to him.

"What is wrong with her?"

Narayanikutty's lips began to move before any sound came out. Like she was testing how her words might be heard if she were to voice them in various ways. . . . "She was with Amma." With that, she pulled her lips in, to keep them still, for they seemed only partially willing to oblige.

"With Amma?" The woman's age made her naturally a being to avoid in good times and to seek in bad, like a sacred burial ground or an arcane text of mysterious magic, and it was terrifying to consider what she might have seen in the barely grown body of his child.

"Yes, by the field, at her house."

"Did she go there for something?"

"This happened while she was walking." Narayanikutty looked down at her daughter. "Amma found her and took her home."

They were quiet for a moment while Anandan Nambiar waited for more but Narayanikutty was still staring with her lips turned in.

"What did Amma say?"

Narayanikutty didn't say anything. Her silence was as horrible as anything Anandan had ever heard. He imagined a monster, twisted and with horns, writhing about inside his child. The longer Narayanikutty remained silent and looked at him, the longer its horns grew, and then it grew claws; soon he imagined it chewing through her abdomen to be released, and when he finally saw his daughter shredded, with her eyes open in horror and death, he shouted out, "Tell me, woman, what did Amma say?" His voice trembled in fear.

"She said it is twins."

"Twins?"

"Yes, twins."

Anandan Nambiar knew that it didn't stop with twins, though that was bad enough. They killed their mothers all the time, every day. Every day there was a mother dead bearing twins. And if not the mother, one of the twins, or both. Never did all of them live. It was the way things were. Finally, he asked, "What is wrong with them?"

Narayanikutty looked up at her husband and her eyes welled with tears. She blinked, and as they came gushing down her cheeks, she shouted out, "One of them, this one here," she pointed as Omanakumari's abdomen jerked in a spot around her rib, "that one, is a boy." Her sob caught in her throat and she coughed.

The gasp behind them made them forget their thoughts, and Anandan Nambiar crushed inside when he realized what he had forgotten about the man in the back. Narayanikutty turned quickly with the shame of being seen this way, crying on the ground, holding their concubine daughter great with child in the deepest night. She didn't even know who had seen her, and still the shame was great.

Parameshwaran Namboodiri stood damp with sweat and neem, smiling so wide he lost his spit, and right then and there he jumped up on one foot and then the other, kicking his legs out before him, jigging like a lunatic, cackling like a hyena. Seeing him this way, Narayanikutty's body went cold. Before Anandan Nambiar had fully acknowledged what he already knew, the old man said it clear.

"Eh, you there, Nambiar." Parameshwaran Namboodiri ambled up slow as a cat and just as sly. He stood and watched the three with amusement, and then with a feeling in his heart he could barely identify. It was a clarity of joy that he hadn't known existed.

Anandan Nambiar looked up and said nothing. The two stood like that for a moment or two, the one defeated, the other full of glee.

Smiling, Parameshwaran Namboodiri wiped at his chest and his arms slowly. He turned his head to the side, spat, and said, "Tomorrow, I will come to get that girl and we will go to my place and stay."

Anandan Nambiar, helpless and searching for words, implored, "But the baby, it should be coming very soon. Don't you think it's best to wait until after?" He looked at the old man's face, searching for the tiniest shadow of care. But without a moment's hesitation, Parameshwaran Namboodiri countered.

"Wait until after? You can't even watch this girl for one night without her wandering off with my son? If you can't watch her properly, that is *my* son there for me to look after."

The father lamely tried again, "But tomorrow is so soon. Do you think it is safe to go now? She can't walk so far . . . with her things . . ." The last words came out in a whisper.

Parameshwaran Namboodiri turned his head and spat. Wiping his chest again, he offered with a sneer, "I live close. I'll bring my nephew to carry her things." He was done. He looked down on Omanakumari one more time and chuckled quietly. "When the time comes, I will bring her back here." Tossing his towel over his shoulder, he walked away. At the end of the walk, he called back, "Tomorrow," and then stepped onto the road.

In the quiet left behind when Parameshwaran Namboodiri departed, Narayanikutty looked at her husband and he whispered, "Tomorrow. He is coming tomorrow to take her there."

"But the baby is coming any day."

"He is taking her with him."

"But the baby is due any day."

"Babies."

"They are due any day."

"He lives close."

"He will not let her come home."

"He will."

"He will not let her stay." To this, Anandan Nambiar was quiet.

Without opening her eyes, she heard it all. Omanakumari steeled herself for the worst fate she could imagine. Within her, the babies could taste their mother's desperation and her resolve. They swum around, splashing water, and sputtering on the wake. When she opened her eyes, they were clear and bright. Her face was rosy, and her lips were suddenly moist. She poked out her mouth in an expression they had not seen in so long that both her father and her mother felt it in their deepest souls.

Omanakumari, knowing everything, smiled and said she was feeling much better. Seeing her smile made her parents cry outright, for the poor thing didn't know what was about to happen and she had emerged so refreshed from her faint. Omanakumari, knowing everything, smiled wider and looked clear of spirit. She held them both, and they hugged her tightly, sobbing all the while because the poor thing didn't know anything and she was suddenly happy at the worst time yet. And Omanakumari, knowing everything, held them closer and whispered that she was fine, just fine, everything was going to be just fine.

A fear grew in Chris's heart. What was she telling him? What was she telling him that he did not already know?

Seeing Home

Mechanical deliverance took Chris home to Innisfree. *I built my home with my own two hands. I laid the cornerstone with my own two hands. I sanded my floor; I stained it with my own two hands. I built its cabinetry with my own two hands. When I named her Innisfree, I did it with conviction.* In this way, Chris ministered to himself, pushed down the fear of what Gita might have been telling him in her story and drove without thinking, without noticing the signs and without any awareness of who or what shared the road with him. A woman turned out of the abandoned Fauquier Motel driveway directly into his path without an inch to spare, but it was neither Chris's nor this woman's time to die, for without seeing her, he chose this moment to change lanes. In that second, her hair turned completely gray and Chris was a mile closer to home.

When he turned onto the long pond road, he stopped his car far away to look at his house, *which I built with my own two hands*, and the late morning sunshine gleamed off the two clear walls that were joined with a seam in the center. The light caught the pond first and then ricocheted up with double its usual intensity. Innisfree shone so bright that Chris squinted and searched for the outline of the house. It seemed to be sitting inside a star.

He resumed his drive and all the while round the long pond road, he kept his eye on his house, for it was beautiful from all angles. As his position shifted, he noted the absolute lines of the eaves, the chimney, the porch rails; the harmonious blending of the gardens with the woods and the gray with the white and then with the black; the synchrony of the leaves waving in the trees with the fluttering of the flag that hung from the pole in the yard. *If this is all I have, it is not nothing.*

Taking his bag over his shoulder, he stood up and checked his appearance in the car window. He ran his fingers through his hair and willed a normal expression to his face. Turning a guilty eye to the house, he shook his head with the worthlessness of that null act. *I spent the night on trash-bag pillows. I did not eat. I have not bathed. I was alone. I was alone. I was abjectly alone.* But did it matter anymore how he came home, what state he was in? Was there anything believable in any of it? Certainly not. *She read things that tell her I am in love and that I will always be in love; she read things that tell her my absences are absences of the heart, and of the soul, and of the body. She read things, and though all I have now is Innisfree and the key to an empty apartment, when I am not in the bed beside her, I will always be hot in her mind, wrapped around another woman, kissing her mouth to draw my own breath from her body. What need is there to check my appearance in the mirror?* Mussing his hair in defeat, Chris walked into the house.

As he entered, Jeri turned from the hallway dressed in a wonderful straight skirt and a crisp white blouse with long sleeves and French cuffs. Her hair was drawn back in a twist, which made her look sophisticated, but older. The whole effect was clean and ready, and very well put together. In a word, Jeri was on her way to sell someone a house, and for sure, when she was dressed this way there was no way she could lose the deal.

She looked very, very thin, Chris thought, and he wasn't sure if it was simply his proving himself a disloyal and terrible husband that had saddened away her appetite, or her skirt, which was navy blue, extremely straight and tight against her extremely straight and tight hips. Jeri walked toward him with a tiny stride. Her heels were very high as well. The whole effect was powerful, efficient and very, very thin.

"Hi," she said not unkindly, but in a thin voice to match her outfit. She looked at him with slow blinks, and then entered the kitchen to get her briefcase.

"Hi, Jeri." Chris walked toward her and stood beside her, because he was in the habit of giving her a kiss when he returned, even after all these many years of deceit. But these days, when he came home from the visits to the dead-bolted apartment that he could not bear to give up, despite having been found out by his wife and abandoned by his lover, he did not know what to do. He left saying he had to travel for work; he returned with a briefcase and a weary expression, just as he always had for so many years. But now he stood beside her knowing he was a fool and she was not. He stood there until she just walked away. This time, she was rifling through her briefcase and checking her listings.

"Going to work?"

"Yes," Jeri said absently, arranging her things. "Penelope called. She has a guest staying with her who needs a place to rent. She is thinking about moving here. She wants the option to buy." She looked up at Chris. "Do you remember when I sold Penelope her house?"

Chris reached up and pushed a stray piece of his wife's hair back against her head. "A lock came loose. . . . Yes, I remember when you sold that house. We celebrated with ice cream."

"I didn't even have to work for that one. She was standing in front of it, and she called and bought it that day."

"Right . . . so you brought home ice cream."

"I wonder why you remember that."

"I don't know . . . maybe because you don't usually."

"Celebrate?"

"Bring home ice cream."

Jeri fiddled around a little more in her bag. "Or celebrate, I suppose." She looked up at him and managed a crunched smile. "I'll be home."

"I'll be here."

Jeri picked up her things and walked out the door. Chris went to the kitchen window and watched her drive away down the long pond road.

Jeri had a strategy, because she was brilliant and efficient at this, and though it may have seemed wise to show the best house first, she had learned long ago that showing the worst house first made the best house seem perfect, but showing the best house first made its imperfections large and worrisome. Jeri had already picked out the house this new client was going to want. She always left a little room, however, for a quirky client with a special idea. When she pulled up, the kids were waiting on the porch.

"Hello, Mrs. Jones," they called.

Jeri turned around and waved hello. "Hi!"

"Are you going to take Gita to find a house today?" Kate ran down to meet her on the street. Jack ran behind her. He needed to keep close tabs on this one. He wanted to deliver Gita's newspaper and mow her lawn. He wanted to know where she was so he could offer before someone else thought to do these things. He would proofread her new book. He would sharpen her pencils and deliver . . . her newspaper.

"Is that her name? That's pretty."

"*She's* pretty," Jack whispered. No one heard, and still, he blushed.

They walk up to the house and Kate opens the door and calls inside. In a moment, Penelope comes out wearing a warm smile. She welcomes Jeri in, but a gentle breeze blows and stirs up the scent of some delectable flower in the yard. Speechless, Jeri turns to find the source.

"It's the gardenia," Penelope informs her; she points to a glossy and colossal bush covered in white flowers. Jeri is entranced.

"Gardenia? How do you get it to grow . . . so big?" she asks, astonished. She turns back to Penelope, who has stepped out onto the porch, and is astonished anew. Penelope stands a full head taller than Jeri and her brown hair is the color of loamy earth. Her eyes are green and a thousand times more so reflecting the light from so many leaves in the gardens around her. She wears shorts and a green tank top and this too makes her eyes greener. Jeri gulps and feels very, very thin. Looking down, she assesses in a moment that her shoes are too high, her skirt is too straight, her hair is too tight, and her blouse is too fussy. When she looks up, the cruel joke continues for Gita has stepped out onto the porch, and in a moment no one would ever forget, she is swarmed by a hundred butterflies that find sunny spaces to touch her and rest in the dappled light that filters through the thousand trees in the yard and illumines her body like stars. Covered in butterflies with red and blue markings, Gita throws back her head and laughs, holding her arms out from her sides. Against her black hair, the slowly fanning wings look like tiny fairies offering kisses and laying down their pretty blankets to take a nap. Watching her stretched limbs nesting one hundred butterflies, Jeri remembers something she has read somewhere before, *Your arms long like branches twined with mine brown like branches.* Something disquiets in her heart.

In the next moment, another puff of gardenia air lifts the butterflies just as suddenly as they had landed. Gita, unsure if they are gone from her body, for they were so light and ephemeral, keeps her arms outstretched and looks left and right, up and down. She giggles and looks at them all with her eyes so bright. Jack is utterly lost in her beauty.

Jeri, always ready with multiple courses of action, takes a few moments to regain her sensibilities and is struck with a wonderful thought. She shifts not to plan B, but to plan . . . G. It comes like a vision, Jeri blinks and there it is: the perfect answer. This woman who drew butterflies with her *arms brown like branches* would buy that house where the scent of honeysuckle was so intoxicating that breathing in too deep would bring you to your knees, where in the chinks between the gray boards, under and over the aged and leaking shingles, around and around the broken and warped spindles of the porch rail, tangled ten thousand creeping yellow roses. A house only a wizard or a kook or an extreme carpenter would buy. A house only a counterfeiter or a runaway or a hunted coca lord would hide in. A house with nothing but leaks, and drafts and problems, but also covered over in ten thousand creeping yellow roses.

This woman would buy that house that Jeri had not been able to sell for over ten years, despite all her best-designed suits and most inspired pitches. A smile spreads over her face and Jeri nods and laughs. *Today, I will bring home ice cream.*

Del Musik was stunned. It took him a full minute to blink himself back from his utter astonishment. His hand was trembling as he opened his Book.

From the Book of Injustices

AUGUST 18,1999(D)

Her power extends beyond humanity; she calls to the fauna, to the insects. They bow before her. The boy stammering and goggling, the butterflies stunned, genuflecting. There are billions of them.

❧

At sunset, Chris saw the glint of Jeri's car catching the last remnants of sun on the long pond road. He laid down the paper on the tiny rocking chair that swayed beside his. It was a baby-doll rocker that caught every gasp of breeze like a gale. If Chris exhaled too hard in frustration over wasteful foreign wars, or complicated tax codes or an unexpected flat tire, Jeri's tiny rocking chair heaved and bucked like an angry pony. The minute weight of the *Quiet Pond Chronicle* resting unbalanced, too close to the front, threatened to tip the chair off the step. He had made this also, *with his own two hands*, for she was a tiny thing herself. He had measured her legs and her straight and narrow hips, and her rocker on the porch fit her more perfectly than anything else she owned. He had always cared for her, even though.

Jeri emerged from her car and held a pint of ice cream high in the air, and in her other hand, a bottle of champagne. "Celebration," she called out simply.

"You sold the house!" Chris smiled and stepped down to greet her, to take her ice cream or her champagne, or even just her briefcase, whichever she would allow. She was talking, and she was happy. He leaned down and kissed her flushed cheek, but right then there was a smash and they both turned before either could feel uncomfortable at so rash a gesture. As the late summer twilight settled and brought that sudden insurgence of cooled air, the fitful rocking chair, teetering under the feather weight of the *Quiet Pond Chronicle*, leapt over the edge of the porch and toppled to the ground.

"My chair!" Jeri dropped her ice cream and the champagne and ran to save this beloved gift from her lost and profligate husband, who before chasing after her, swooped low to catch both the bottle and the carton before either hit the ground, and still managed to reach the chair before her because his shoes were not too high and his skirt was not too tight. Heart pounding and exhilarated, champagne and ice cream neatly tucked at his side, hands already examining the fallen rocking chair, which miraculously had not even a hair splinter, he looked up at his wife who finally arrived and couldn't help but think, "*Yeeeerrrrrout!*" It was like a double play with only the two of them; for a moment, he was back in the sandlot.

"It didn't break at all!"

"You're kidding!" She ran her hands over every familiar rut and groove and even checked the bottom of the rockers, and it seemed that, though the chair had landed so hard, it had not sustained a scratch. Jeri's eyes filled, and she sat on her rocker on the flagstone walk and cried thankful tears. "We have two things to celebrate! I'm glad I brought champagne!"

"So you sold Penelope's friend a house?" Chris stood behind her on the steps and they both looked out at the calm silver pond.

"Not just *a* house, I sold her the unsellable house."

"The unsellable house? You mean the cottage covered in roses?" Chris looked down on the top of Jeri's head.

"That's right."

"Wow, how did you do *that*?"

Jeri closed her eyes and saw Gita stopped in her tracks as they passed the mailbox post overgrown in clematis and the house came into sight. The wind had picked up, and suddenly they were lost in a cloud of honeysuckle that had cut off her practiced spiel. She didn't say a word; she didn't show the house; Gita walked through it herself; Jeri stood at the door, lost in her own inexplicable tears. It had been too much for her; she had to wait for Gita outside. The cottage covered in yellow roses had literally sold itself. Looking far out over the pond, she replied, "I guess it was my lucky day. I should have bought donuts too." Looking back at him, she added, "And a chocolate fountain."

Chris chuckled. "Hmmm. I might have caught the donuts and dropped the champagne." Jeri laughed and Chris forgot his terrible loneliness for that moment because they had been friends since they were so young and there was some comfort in sharing laughter with a lifelong friend, even though.

Jeri stood up and straightened her skirt. She rocked her chair to and fro in an offhand and satisfied way. Looking up at Chris, she sighed and prepared to go in. "I'm going to go inside and change and we can have dinner." Jeri turned and as she walked toward the house she added, "After we celebrate, I'll run some paperwork back out to Gita. I want to handle the sale before she realizes that the wind never stops blowing through that house."

Chris stopped his breathing and felt his stomach jump and plummet. Thankfully, Jeri was already walking up the steps as his face splotched every shade of white and red. He cheeped like a baby bird, "What?" Clearing his throat quickly, he took another shot, for she hadn't heard his freakish murmuring. "You've got to take the paperwork out to *whom*?"

Jeri stopped and looked up, standing still. Chris thought it might be time to sit down. He nearly took a seat in that dollhouse furniture, when she turned back to him and pointed, "Chris, there's a bees' nest there." She looked back up at the frame.

She failed to notice the beads of sweat on his forehead or his hair that stood on end. Importantly, she added, "It's huge. I think it might be hornets."

Chris used this unexpected digression to bring the blood back to his heart and to redistribute it more evenly. His pulse slowed with the relative inconsequence of hornets. "Hornets. I'll go get the spray." Chris swallowed and attempted a little laugh. He coughed, but Jeri didn't notice his breathing difficulty.

She reached down and unstrapped her shoes. She took another look up at the bees' nest, and turned back to the house to change her clothes.

"Jeri," Chris called out, "you didn't answer the question. You're going to take paperwork to *whom*?" His pulse revved and he closed his eyes. He tried to take a discreet and deep breath.

"Gita. Gita Nair. The girl who bought the house. Penelope's guest. She's Indian."

With that, Jeri walked into the house and closed the door behind her. Chris stopped breathing and when he finally took a gasp of air and blew it out in an awestruck blast, the miniature rocking chair drew back and then tumbled forward. It landed with a crack that sounded like a ball on a wooden bat. This time, Chris just stood there, staring at the door, unable to make the last catch of the night.

And Everyone Fell Asleep

Gita sits up in her makeshift bed, inhales and wearily lies back down. *Even in the half-moon gray of night, honeysuckle trickles in my blood.* She finds no sleep, though she is not trying very hard. She sits up again and rubs her shiny shins. She turns her body and sits to the side. Her makeshift bed, low to the ground, no box spring, no bounce; she extends her legs and they stretch over the floor; she feels that her space is not primitive, but austere and perfect. She inhales again and knows it is time to write. *My book will write itself in this honeysuckle house.*

She rises in the dark and lights candles, which are her only source of light. Her power is not yet on. She finds that by candlelight she is more courageous, and less needy of appliances and electricity. She writes with a pen on paper. It takes time. Every word lingers in her mind for seconds. By the time she writes them down, she loves them more having owned them longer. By candlelight, her words look more beautiful. By candlelight, she finds that she is more beautiful too.

At least in her mirror . . . her mirror, however, is more beautiful in the daylight. She walks toward it and fingers the frame that Chris had carved with interlocking "Cs" and "Gs" that together look like swirling clouds or frantic seas. In the dark, this just looks like texture; the drama is lost. He had painted it blue, gold and black, and distressed it with a wire brush and a torn piece of denim. He had ripped the pocket off a pair of jeans. When he wore those cockeyed jeans, the love surged in her neck and made her hair stand on end. In the half-moon gray of night, but lit with candleglow, there is hope on her face; *there will be peace in this life and great love that is mine and permanent.* This she knows. *But tonight, I will write something. If I write something, then tomorrow Chris will find me. If tomorrow Chris finds me, then the next day we will think together. But right now, I will write something. By the time I finish this book, we will . . .*

She ties her hair back and she crosses her legs in the small chair. She takes up her pen and opens her chest, throws her shoulders back, looks up at the ceiling and inhales a yogic breath that sends her mind reeling. She looks down at her half-written page and continues.

The Cursed Life of Sreemathi Omanakumari

Omanakumari looked out from her veranda and the night illumined under her gentle gaze. The morning approached slowly and gave her time to notice, and to think, and to love this view she had seen so many days. Reaching over the edge, her fingers extended to feel the air of her home for the last time. She had taken on a different aspect, the furthest she had ever been from resigned, and the closest she had ever been to sublime. How was it that she felt this way, so calm, so resolved and so full of grace?

The black night turned to indigo as it always did and Omanakumari waited for enough light to take her last walk around her home. And when at last the morning's clouds could be seen in the brightening gray, she turned from the veranda and entered her house. She inhaled deeply and the smell of her home filled her blood, strengthening her as she walked past the kitchen and down the passage, past the dining hall and toward the courtyard. No one else was awake in the home of Omanakumari.

She walked the perimeter with her fingers stretched out; eyes closed, inhaling deeply, she sensed the corners and the edges and the curves in her path. Her babies extended their fingers too, stretching and stretching; they yearned for what they might never see that linked their mother to what was beautiful in the world. They already knew this was home.

Omanakumari opened her eyes when she reached a bend in the path on the eastern quadrant of their land. The morning was dimly blue and by this much light she could see the difference in the trees and plants. She stepped off the path, and her babies held their breath. Her enormous belly caught on all the leaves and within a few moments, the front of her clothing was soaked through. She plucked and pushed her way forward, leaving behind her a trail of flattened grass and broken twigs, tossed-back leaves and petals from her hand.

Near a pile of wood that was stacked for no reason, Omanakumari stopped before a huge bush covered in seeds and spiked green tufts. Tasting their mother's fear, the babies knocked and she hushed them with her hand. They knocked again. "Hush," she said aloud. She patted her stomach and rubbed them. Inside, they opened their eyes and kicked one another; what to do? What to do? In the secret language of twins they kicked and punched each other; they screamed their alarm. Spinning and spinning, they saw that there was certainly no way out.

Pushing with both hands, Omanakumari stared down on them and held their invisible gaze. "Hush."

Looking up into her pooled eyes, they knew that there was nothing left to do. Blinking and confused, the brother raised his hands to the clear sac that separated him from his sister and she placed her palms against his. Holding hands like this, they quieted still as death. Satisfied with their complicit silence, Omanakumari regained her focus.

Brushing through the leaves, she heard the pop of exploding seed pods and, with her thin arm, she covered her belly to protect her babies, who looked at each other and closed their eyes against this fundamental irony. She found a long spike covered inches over with shiny green pods and gently, so as not to expel the seeds, she plucked it bare and put the stash inside her blouse. With a wan smile, Omanakumari turned back down the path and headed home to pack a bundle to take to her new home.

Back at the house it was as silent as her womb. It was darker than it had ever been; the babies noted this too and the quiet and the strange light made one fall asleep only to be nudged awake by the other to keep sentinel.

Neither wanted to be alone when it happened. Their fear kept them awake; their fear put them to sleep.

Narayanikutty was making some food for the journey, though it was only less than a mile, and her father was absent, walking, walking somewhere with his hands clasped behind his back. When the girl entered the kitchen, her mother looked up and her eyes were hard and glassy. She had no more to spare, and her idle hands worked her dough into balls and then crushed the balls into clumps and began again. Omanakumari looked at this and smiled.

"Is that for eating or for playing ball?" she asked with her mouth poked out.

Narayanikutty looked down into the mess she had in hand and blinked. Raising her eyes, she held her daughter's gaze for several moments. Looking back down, she quietly said, "Go get your things. He will be here shortly."

Omanakumari stood and looked intensely at her mother. Her hair was long and tied behind her neck with a piece of itself. Her eyebrows were furrowed in a painful crease. Her hands worked and worked and there were lines of muscle in her forearms that showed slightly with each push and pull. The flesh around her middle trembled as she kneaded, and her neck was long and slim. Her lips were turned in to keep from crying and her nose was very long. She was a splendid mother. Omanakumari thought that a few more times as she turned away toward her room. She was a splendid mother.

In her room, Omanakumari gathered a few things into a small bundle that she could carry by herself. Her babies looked around at the spare space and didn't feel any loss for leaving it; it was not like the veranda, or the face of their grandmother. Looking about quietly, Omanakumari reached into her blouse and pulled out the seeds she had collected and, counting as she went, she chewed and swallowed ten. The remaining five she wrapped in a small cloth and put back in her blouse just in case, and then Omanakumari lay back on the bed to rest. Her babies lay down with her and without meaning to, they all fell asleep.

Gita blinks in the candlelight. She yawns and lowers her head to the table. *Tomorrow, I will find Chris and I will ask him. I will ask him. I will ask him.* And then she too falls asleep.

Western Civilization

"On an intellectual level, anyway, it is clear that Christianity marked a revolution of thought. A revolution . . . an evolution, in effect—of mankind. From the creature he was before to a higher-order being, able to become more . . . to *transcend*." Russell Worthy turned to the blackboard and wrote TRANSCEND. He turned back, still holding a long stick of chalk that he spun between his fingers with distracted dexterity. He was good with his fingers. He scanned the tops of heads, all he saw some days, the tops of heads.

He turned to the right and walked to the edge of the stage. His chalk, spinning at his side, created a ripple in his forearm and periodically he would toss his chalk up absently, catch it in his other hand and resume his spinning. He continued.

"This must be understood. It *must* be understood. It was Christianity"—here he paused at the blackboard and wrote CHRISTIANITY—"not rational philosophy, that shooed away the swarm of greater and lesser gods and goddesses, the blood sacrifices, the self-immolation, the worship of passing objects. It was Christianity"—he added another underscore on the board—"that freed man from desperately seeking solace in magic, in fortune-telling, in divination."

Dr. Worthy turned to pace the left side of the stage. The crease in his pant leg cracked and whipped with his sure stride; his sweater clutched his chest and the round balls of his shoulders bulged with each twirl of his chalk. Bowing as he walked with his neck bent down deep and his eyes closed, he displayed to any who might lift their heads that he, for one, was deep with gratitude for the deliverance achieved through the ongoing development of Western civilization. In this poised attitude, he prepared to give his next line, and as he breathed deep from the diaphragm, he heard a little laugh. Less than a laugh, more of a jocular exhalation of air. Very subtle, and it was remarkable that he heard it at all, because it was a large auditorium designed to amplify those on stage and muffle those below. He looked up and saw tops of heads and more tops of heads and then, shining toward the middle, one girl with her hand over her mouth, staring him dead in the eye. He dropped his chalk.

The unfamiliar sound came as a shock. In a bleary half-conscious murmuring, the tops of heads began to recede, revealing a sea of blank faces. They had been ready for his next words. He looked down; his chalk was in jagged-edged pieces and chalk chips spread about the floor. He walked to the front of the stage and pointed at the perpetrator. He smiled. When he smiled he sometimes dropped his chin and tilted his head; this made his black hair fall forward in its forefront wave. When he blinked, his curly lock touched his eyelid and so he raised his hand and pushed his hair back from his face. He was never more captivating than when he looked this way.

"I'm sure you wouldn't mind telling the rest of us what you found so funny?"

Dhanya looked left and right. People were looking at her expectantly. She sat up straighter and pointed a finger at herself, raising her eyebrows.

"Yes, you. You clearly found something amusing and I am asking you if you could share it with us." Russell Worthy noticed that this young woman had exceptional eyebrows.

"Um, I didn't mean to be so loud. I'm sorry." In her short life, Dhanya had already discovered the power of a well-timed and sincere apology.

"Yes, yes. I'm sure you are, but still. I'd like to know, if you don't mind." Russell Worthy walked slightly to the left and took a seat on a tall stool. As he did this, he placed one foot on the ground and one foot on the bottom rung. He ran his fingers through his hair. Silent moments passed between them. The class chose to look at Dhanya, for she shimmered with an electrified embarrassment that was thrilling to see; the spectacle of her immense discomfort held their attention until Dr. Worthy cleared his throat with some tacit admonishment. When they had shifted their focus to him, he raised his legs and placed both feet in the top rung of the stool; then he very slowly leaned forward and rested both forearms on his knees. The class gasped as one. He looked like he had all day.

Dhanya looked up, she looked down, she blushed into her chest and seeing her blushing chest, she raised her hand to her breasts to cover their blush. She doodled, she poked holes in her paper and minutes ticked by, but Dr. Russell Worthy did not mind all eyes on him. His class forgot what the question was, so entrancing were his rippling forearms. Dhanya looked down at her empty notebook. She preferred to listen to the gasps than to see what drew them, for it might be her silence, her size, her breasts, her blush or perhaps her insolent chortle that had started the whole thing, so little did she realize that she and Dr. Worthy were the only ones who had heard her laugh. She lifted her eyes and met his, and then raising her voice to be heard from below, she plainly stated, "Dr. Worthy, on the blackboard, it says, '*Transcend Christianity.*' I mean, effectively, that is what it says . . . considering your lecture, you know, lesser gods, shooing them away and all, it just struck me as ironic." She paused. "That's all." Dhanya looked down at her notebook because her breasts were so hot she felt the perspiration between them running like a river down her shirt. She feared that if this went on much longer, when she rose, her pants would showcase the sweat-stained V of her pubis and the enormous O of her behind. With this thought, her eyes began to well. She doodled TRANSCEND CHRISTIANITY.

Russell Worthy looked behind him and then back at Dhanya. She had remarkably long eyebrows and excellent cleavage. Excellent cleavage . . . red with heat, the wetness of her embarrassment rising on their fat humps that showed through the top of her blouse. When he saw her self-conscious covering of these humps with her hand, all the while unable to meet his eye, he felt some measure of vindication for the publicly broken chalk.

He waited for her to look up, and when she nervously did, he could see her glistening tears and he was perfectly pleased with her contrition. He replied, "True that, true that. It is perhaps the best example of irony I've seen all month." He smiled with his eyebrows raised. "Come see me after class, though." He ran his fingers through his black curls.

Dhanya felt a little uptake of breath. She looked down at her notebook and wrote, AFTER CLASS WITH DR. WORTHY.

After class, Dhanya walked up onto the stage toward Dr. Russell Worthy. She wore her humblest face. Her eyebrows arced up to make her eyes huge with innocence; her pretty lips were drawn into a tight, straight line. She hadn't meant to laugh and make him drop his chalk.

He was studying the roster and once she had stood there an appropriate number of minutes waiting silently, he looked up and directly into her shirt. He clenched his jaw. "Who are you?" He spoke in a low, distracted voice, running his pen down the roster, looking, looking.

"I'm right there." Dhanya reached over his roster and pointed out her name, "Dhanya Nair."

"Tanya?"

"Dhanya, the 'Dh' are together, sort of hard, see?" She stepped in closer and pointed to the 'Dh,' "**Dh**anya, **Dh**anya." Dhanya looked up. "**Dh**anya." She noticed that though she had stepped forward, Dr. Worthy had not stepped back. She blushed, for she was standing not one foot away.

"That is an interesting name. You're Indian?"

Dhanya nodded her head and stepped back a little bit.

"Watch the edge." Dr. Worthy calmly raised his finger and pointed at the edge of his stage. "It's safer in closer."

Dhanya nodded and moved a step in. Her skin was hot with confusion.

"Dhanya, you're a very bright girl." He narrowed his eyes at her and tilted his head. He looked at her hard and continued, "Every year, I like to offer exceptionally bright students the opportunity to join an informal discussion group."

"Informal discussion group?"

Dr. Worthy nodded. "It's a mixed group. Different classes, different-year students, but the purpose of the group is to apply the content of your coursework to the current world condition in various areas of life and thought. Social status, international affairs, living conditions, tendencies toward bellicosity, et cetera."

"Is it a class?"

"It's informal, no credit, though it is possible to earn independent study through special projects. I think you would make a fine addition to the group."

"When does it meet?"

"Different times."

"I . . . take a dance class."

Dr. Worthy smiled and Dhanya blushed harder. *I take a dance class, ugh.*

"I'm sure you would be able to do both. You don't have to come every time."

"I . . ." Something twinkled in Dhanya, *an exceptional student, a bright student, an exceptionally bright student . . . an invitation . . .*

"I'll tell you what, on Saturday, we are having a little back-to-school party. It's at a restaurant on the Downtown Mall. Why don't you come join us?" Dr. Worthy looked down at his roster and waited.

Dhanya felt a very slight disappointment wash over her, for it sounded fun, like a salon or something. She was intrigued with the idea of an intellectual discussion in a party atmosphere. But . . . it was far to go without a car or a regular university bus route. "Oh . . . oh, well, you know. I don't have a car. I'm first year. And I don't know if . . . maybe I'll just wait until they meet on grounds." Dhanya looked up, hoping the invitation to join was not contingent upon making this party.

Dr. Worthy smiled generously and put his hand on her shoulder. "Oh, that's not a problem. I'd be happy to give you a ride. In fact, it's probably better that way." He closed his eyes and opened them, and Dhanya saw that they were closed longer than a blink. She felt a meaning in the length of his blink. She blinked back, but quickly. *Is there meaning in the length of my blink?*

"I can get you a little early and I can introduce the concepts we plan to cover. Over dinner. Lay the groundwork for you. You'll be more comfortable when everyone else arrives." He smiled and squeezed her shoulder again.

Dhanya too narrowed her eyes slightly in her thinking way, in her noticing way, and it was lost on Dr. Worthy who gripped the great flesh of her body and lost focus. Dhanya, who saw everything, left the auditorium with knowledge she chose to ignore, for reasons she couldn't fathom.

That evening, Dhanya crossed her legs in pink, plaid pajama pants. Her wet hair darkened her matching pink top for she had removed her towel too soon due to a slight headache that grew worse with the balancing of the turban atop her head. Her journal sat open on her lap. Her pen dotted her page, but not a word. That evening?

From the Journal of Dhanya Nair

August 23, 1999

[Doodles, only doodles.]

The next morning she began to eat only when there was great nausea upon her, and then she ate only enough for it to pass. She had an opal dress in which she felt as diaphanous as an angel's wing, as lovely as its angel. And to wear this dress, she had not eaten a bite of food all day. She had drunk only in dropper sips at great intervals. When she emerged from the room with her hair brushed to a heavy black silk, in her shimmering opal dress, her friends ogled and clapped.

She arrived at the restaurant with her professor, and when they were led to a tiny table in the corner, Dhanya could not actually say she was surprised (though she was disoriented, alarmed, alert, and very confused) that there didn't seem to be room in this candlelit corner for anyone but them.

"Where is everyone?"

"Oh, they'll be here."

And later in the evening,

"Shouldn't they be here by now?"

"They should, shouldn't they? I guess they are on their way . . ."

And still later,

"Are you sure we are in the right place?"

"I don't know . . . perhaps I did get the venue wrong. Anyway. This is nice isn't it?"

And throughout, Dhanya sat perfectly still eyeing her full water glass. She was terribly thirsty. Russell Worthy, on the other hand, was on his sixth, maybe seventh refill of water. Plus, he had ordered a bottle of something he kept calling Bordeaux Cuvee Madame, which he assured her went perfectly with the lamb he had ordered them. In the mirror behind Dhanya, Dr. Worthy noticed that he was glowing and that his lips glistened, yet in a manly way. He took another sip of water.

The server appeared, and as he approached the table Dhanya thought she noticed his attitude, even his posture, change. With every step he took, he lowered his head and became more obsequious so that by the time he arrived, he was a fawning maid of a man. Dr. Worthy, though he had a near-equal vantage through the mirror to Dhanya's back, was focused entirely on himself. He found that his right eye seemed slightly smaller than his left today, though usually it seemed the opposite, and he was considering excusing himself to check this out further in the men's room so he failed to see that his waiter had bent and swiveled himself into something perfectly suited for the highest tip to be afforded at this table.

"Monsieur, your wine." He poured a small sip for Dr. Worthy, who tasted it and closed his eyes with an appreciative nod and small grunts.

"Inspired, inspired." Dr. Worthy leaned back and allowed the server to pour him a full glass. When this server turned to Dhanya, he was momentarily stopped by her very clear lack of age. He paused briefly, swallowed and poured her glass, for he worked for tips. Dhanya, who always watched and saw, caught the nearly imperceptible break in his practiced rhythm. She lacked not only the age, but also the interest to enjoy this very impressive bottle of Bordeaux Cuvee Madame. To her inexperienced ear, it sounded like a potion for fat prostitutes, and she was uncomfortable enough as it was. She looked up at the server and smiled a quiet smile, her natural face. He felt a pained attachment to her, for in the natural face of Dhanya Nair there was a lovely grace. And though later that night the server considered scouting out the home of Dr. Russell Worthy, and stealing her away like a knight in shining armor, at the moment that he poured the wine and absorbed her angel face, the waiter of a thousand faces said, "Please enjoy, mademoiselle." He turned back to Dr. Worthy and with a small bow said, "Monsieur." And then he was gone.

Dr. Worthy raised the glass to his nose, his inhale dramatic and full through his shoulders. Coming to rest where he began, he announced, "So clean . . . the apricot so . . . pronounced." He looked at her and narrowed his eyes very slightly. Dhanya felt a rush through her neck . . . fear . . . disorientation. At moments, he looked . . . *wicked.* Wasn't this evening supposed to be altogether different? She looked toward the front, but no one was coming. *There are no other students. There is no salon. I am here with my professor. Alone.*

He inhaled again. She watched him in her watching way. With his eyelids barely touching, and his face turned up to the ceiling, he continued, "Dhanya, the nose. The nose is exceptional." He opened his eyes and stared at her with an intoxicated look. Her hair gleamed as richly as his and they were outstanding together in the mirror behind Dhanya's head, which covered her vast chub and showed only the onyx shine of her thick, black hair. *Her hair goes perfectly with my face.*

"Taste." Dr. Worthy leaned forward and held his glass to Dhanya's pretty lips. He looked in the mirror and it was a touching and romantic scene, he the doting and generous lover, she the grateful and besotted maiden. But shifting back to her he noted that she hadn't taken her grateful sip. She had leaned back instead. He felt heat in his face, and he checked the mirror and saw that his color had risen slightly in his cheeks, and though it made him only more attractive, he was nonetheless irked at her having seen his shock and weakness in such an angry blush.

"I am offering you the first sip!" Dr. Russell Worthy could not sit back with his glass rejected, and so he stayed there, his arm extended, his glass extended, leaning farther and farther in as subtle a reach as he could manage, all the while smiling his most winning smile. He dropped his chin and tilted his head; he allowed his black hair to fall forward in its forefront wave. He blinked, and when his curly lock touched his eyelid, he raised his free hand and pushed his hair back from his face. Dhanya fought a tremble that threatened to rise all the way from her knees to the top of her head; she was so uncomfortable.

"Taste it," Dr. Worthy repeated, with his smiling voice, his smiling face.

"Dr. Worthy."

"Yes, Dhanya?"

"Dr. Worthy, I . . ."

"What is it, Dhanya."

"I am . . . my birthday is in December and . . . then I'll be . . . eighteen years old. And . . ."

". . . and?" Her wide-eyed and vapid look made her seem suddenly only fifteen years old rather than seventeen, and for a split second he felt he might look like a fool to other patrons, who he was certain were all looking at him. He cast a quick glance around.

Pausing and hesitating, feeling really dumb, Dhanya quietly reminded him in her honest sort of way, "It's illegal for me to drink."

He snorted and raised his eyebrows. "Are you serious? Arbitrary. When I was your age, Dhanya, the drinking age was eighteen."

"I also don't drink."

"On principle?" This was even more amusing. Her innocent admissions of purity and moral uprightness made him clench his jaw for her.

"I don't like to drink. The taste."

Dr. Worthy sat back. His smile melted from his lips. His blue eyes iced over. His lips drew into a narrow line; he hissed, "What exactly is it you do not like to drink?" He inhaled deeply. "You mean you don't like that rum-and-Coke, baby-boilermaker, cheap-beer shit they serve at frat houses on Rugby Road? Is that what you mean?" Dr. Worthy could feel his hand begin to throb in the fingers. He ached to crush his glass.

"Dr. Worthy," Dhanya sputtered, afraid.

"You mean the rum and Kool-Aid, the body shots, the Jell-O shots? Is that what you don't like to drink?" He worked his lips with the effort to remain seated.

"Um . . ." Dhanya's confusion registered in a high blush that caught Dr. Worthy's eye. He softened and spoke more gently.

"Dhanya, this is a Cuvee Madame."

Dhanya looked down at the bread and the water. She was terribly thirsty and terribly hungry and she hadn't eaten for two days for this party, to wear this dress, and instead . . . she looked down farther. The wood floor was so polished that she could see the reflection of all the candles in the room. In the drone, she heard Dr. Worthy talking about the wine and she was so thirsty. *How did this happen?*

Looking back up at Dr. Worthy still going on about the Cuvee Madame, Dhanya was jarred by the realization that she was not nearly as surprised as she even pretended she was, and that she didn't know what this said about her.

Dr. Worthy, having decided to forgive her, went on and on. "I had one once, it was extraordinary. Sweet, rich, concentrated . . . layers upon layers. I tasted vanilla custard, pineapple." Dr. Worthy leaned up again and held out the glass to her. With another smile, he poked at her lips with it. "It had a finish that lasted over a minute . . ."

Dhanya caught a glint of the deep gold wine in the candlelight and in her thirst she imagined it might taste like ambrosia. She was suddenly too tired to keep on. She was suddenly delirious with hunger and thirst. She opened her mouth, and in his most tender gesture, Dr. Russell Worthy tipped up his glass. She gulped it like water; her eager swallows clenched his jaws; his jaws were aching from so much nearly constant clenching. He pulled the glass away before she finished it off and Dhanya followed it with a thirsty leaning forward of her head. Again, he clenched his jaw and took the last sip for himself.

Dhanya felt that alcohol made her body smaller and her hair longer. So long she might be sitting on it as she seated herself in Dr. Worthy's tiny car. It was such a tiny car, and she thought it was blue, or it might be white or silver. But, she thought, color aside, I am too big for this car. She had never felt so big in her life, even drunk. *Maybe I am not drunk. Maybe if I were more drunk I would be smaller.* Dhanya craved another drink.

As Russell Worthy walked around the back of the car, Dhanya reached for the door handle. She just needed one more drink so she could fit in the car. It was dark and the leather on the door was so thin she could feel the metal underneath. She groped and groped along the armrest for the handle. *Oh God, I am trapped in Dr. Worthy's car, and I am stuck in Dr. Worthy's car. I am trapped, stuck in Dr. Worthy's car, too big to get in and too stuck to get out and I can't find the door handle anyway. What kind of car is this that has no door handle? How did I get in the car, is the only door handle on the outside? If I reach over the door, would I be able to find the door handle?*

"Dhanya?"

"Umm, yes, Dr. Worthy?" Dhanya quietly groped the door; the place the window would come out of . . . *Maybe this car doesn't have windows? Maybe they didn't have windows on this kind of car back then. Maybe because there is no top, there are no windows? Maybe you are supposed to hop into this car. How did I get in the car?* Her chest was heaving and her prickly, cold skin paled. In her mind, Dhanya counted therapeutically. The number of chairs around her table at home—eight; the number of bottles on her sink back home—six, if you counted the vase. The number of sisters she had whose names ended with "a"—three. *If I reach over this door, I might find the outside handle.* Dhanya focused on this but her arm didn't seem to have the strength to get up over that infernal window void. She groped quietly and looked down toward her feet.

"What are you doing?" Russell Worthy was standing outside the car looking down on her. She was looking for something on the door but she wasn't looking at the door, she was looking at her feet. *Her feet are pretty, but they are big. She needs to do her toenails at least.* Russell had noted all through dinner the absence of fingernail polish on this girl. *She has such nice fingernails,* he thought. *Her hands aren't bad. A little hairy, perhaps . . . I wouldn't even notice if she had her nails painted. And she ought to grow them too. They are too short.* Russell Worthy liked his women polished and with long girlthings. Long hair, long eyelashes, long eyebrows, and long fingernails. Naked, he thought, this girl's hair trailing down my body . . . Russell Worthy shuddered and rolled his head around his shoulders. He was suddenly stretchy. Dhanya made a quiet whimpering sound and Russell noted that she was still running her hand along the door. "Dhanya, I asked you a question."

"Huh?" Dhanya was now squirming away from the door against which she was rather tightly wedged in to see if perhaps her body was hiding the door handle all along. She had gathered her hair behind her head and twirled it into a rope mane and thrown it over her left shoulder to better her visibility. She was somewhat aware that Dr. Worthy was standing there, but it was critically important that she be released from the automobile to just run in for another quick drink, and of course Dr. Worthy could see the practical necessity of her line of thinking. Couldn't he see how she was struggling to be comfortable in the car? She didn't remember having this problem on the way in. It was probably the lamb that had caused some measure of bloat, and she wished again that she had just stuck to nothing. Her dress was too tight, and she could feel it sticking to the seat, further impeding her from moving enough away from the door to be able to properly see the prospect of a handle.

He suddenly considered that being drunk might make this girl surly, foolish and messy. He wondered if he had a bag in the trunk. What if she threw up? *If I go inside to get a bag from the restaurant, she might just fall asleep. If she falls asleep, can I just drop her off at her dorm?* Russell Worthy considered for the first time the possibility that this girl might not be as circumspect as it seemed was her nature. She might be a catastrophic disaster of a girl. However, from his vantage point standing over her outside the car, he could see down her opal-colored dress that had been iridescent all night, swirling around like a hologram. Russell Worthy considered his options. Narrowing his eyes, he reconsidered his position. The shine from the overhead streetlight squeezing in through his lids split Dhanya in two and gave her a bit of a halo. This, plus two bottles of Cuvee Madame and a few gin and tonics suddenly made it clear that she was quite a bit more than breasts and eyebrows, she was moldable and virginal and as yet unformed. He imagined reading to her from his book in progress, how her eyebrows would arch at him, with her face slightly turned down. How her beautiful mouth would poke out. He imagined those inky brown eyes, so large and long, turned up to him with gratitude. He imagined being loved by this girl who didn't know, who was immense and yet seemed paradoxically small.

Russell went back around the car and opened the door. "Are you trying to get out, honey?" Russell Worthy squatted down on the sidewalk and looked at Dhanya's face. She sat there looking at her knees and her hands on her lap, and she put the tip of one finger in her mouth and concentrated on the slight pain that dug at her nail as she bit down. Russell reached out and put his left hand against the back of her head and stroked down the length of her hair. He put his fingers into its depths and scrunched at it to satisfy his craving to squeeze. Her hair was deeper than any he had ever touched. It seemed to go on and on and it was cool and dry and smooth and fathomless. Dhanya whimpered again.

"Why are you trying to get out?" This time, he lifted his hand from her hair and stroked the backside of his fingers along her right cheek. This action made Dhanya sink her head down lower and close her eyes.

Dragging on his first cigarette in two whole days, the waiter of a thousand faces stood under a streetlight on East Market and watched the tiny Triumph bobble and sway with the rocking of that angel-faced girl trying to get out. He blew smoke through his nostrils and the burn gave him great courage. Dr. Russell Worthy had left an excessive tip, which he pushed into this faceless waiter's breast pocket with a word of advice, "Here you go, buddy, you did a nice job. Don't drink it all tonight." Then he turned back and extracted his wobbly date from the table. She could not hold her head quite straight.

There was no longer any need for alter ego. He himself was angry, misunderstood and in need of unconditional love, but that girl's stunned eyes and bumbling struggle dug in his hard heart. She was irrevocably drunk, and he had let it happen. Two bottles of wine, Cosmopolitans that she thought were cranberry juice, four Kahlua Creams that she kept calling "more dessert!" And he had kept it coming even though in all these years he had never seen an angel-faced girl. Again, he resolved to stop smoking. He took a deep drag and swaggered toward them in his real gait, dangerous, alluring, lithe, low-hipped. He stood above the squatting Dr. Worthy and tapped his shoulder. Dr. Worthy looked up in surprise; he no longer even recognized this person who had served him all night.

"Can I help you? We are in the middle of a private conversation."

The waiter of a thousand faces opened his mouth and let out the plume of cigarette smoke, which wafted down all over Dr. Worthy when he rumbled, "I believe she is trying to get out of the car."

"Our waiter," Dhanya said, looking up. The waiter of a thousand faces looked at her and was as close to pristine love as he had ever felt. He thought at that moment that if only he could get her out of that car and into his own, that he would take care of her and cherish her for life, that he would go back to school and quit smoking for sure. That he would reconnect with his family and marry her, that he would love her unconditionally, and he realized that in this way, he would also be granted her unconditional love. All this came clear in her limpid look of desperation. He looked back at Dr. Russell Worthy and resisted the urge to knock him to the sidewalk and kick his head.

"Our waiter?" Dr. Russell Worthy looked from Dhanya back up to the suddenly handsome and powerful waiter he had barely noticed before, and he wanted to drive away or call for the police. He looked about for assistance. "Look here," he continued. "We are in the middle of a private conversation."

"I believe the young, the *very* young, lady is trying to get out of the car." He reached for Dhanya's hand and took it out of Dr. Worthy's. Dhanya looked back and forth between them and began to panic.

"Hey!" Dr. Worthy tried to snatch it back, but the waiter shot him a tired look and with his free hand, put his cigarette back in his mouth and hung it there. Dr. Russell Worthy felt that riling jealousy that made him list his degrees and cite his publications.

"I don't fit in the car," she burbled, and the waiter of a thousand faces held her hand and she struggled to set her feet right. To get out, to stay in, either way, her feet seemed disobedient.

Dr. Worthy stood to his feet and found he was nearly as tall as this man, and he reached down, pushed Dhanya's dress into the car and slammed the door shut against her leg. She winced in pain, drew her hand back from the waiter and covered her mouth to keep from howling, for she was private in her hurts and disappointments, in her embarrassments and shames. This, however, was too much, and she leaned her head back on the headrest, closed her eyes and, without another word to either of them, fell asleep.

Dr. Russell Worthy, his heart beating fast in his chest, turned to the waiter of a thousand faces and said, "I'm going to have you fired."

The waiter looked down at the sleeping girl and then back at Dr. Worthy. "Or maybe I'm gonna have *you* fired."

They stood there looking at one another; in the darkness, the waiter's eyes glowed like a cat. Dr. Russell Worthy tingled with fear and righteous indignation. He looked down at Dhanya asleep in the car and chose to be done. He turned away. Without looking back he circled his car, got in and sped off into the night. The wind whipped his face, and Dhanya's hair stretched and smacked against him; the former strengthened his resolve and the latter . . . sometimes when her hair flew across his face, he held it there and inhaled, and sometimes he chewed it, and all the while she slept.

Dhanya perched on the edge of the bed like something rough caught on a snag. She was lying on her side with her left arm wrapped over her chest, the hand holding the ball of her right shoulder. Her right arm wrapped over this and clung to her left shoulder. She was hugging herself. She was asleep. Her legs were lined up one on top of the other. She was as straight as such a curvy figure might be, stuck to the edge of the bed like lint.

Standing at the foot of the bed, Russell listened to her breathing and concentrated on her sound. She had a tweeting breathing. It whistled without being a snore, and it was endearing in the way of a child's sleep noises. He had not slept afterward. This was his habit, not to be lulled by sex. He was deeply invigorated, rather. But she had reacted strangely. Without a word, silently looking at him and concentrating. Memorizing? Or, it seemed, outside herself. Drunk? Certainly pliable, he wouldn't deny that, certainly pliable, and perhaps a girl such as this would have been less so without drink. But nonetheless, astounding maturity in the face of it all. Astounding. He watched her and felt something like respect, because it could have been such an ordeal.

Russell Worthy's bedroom was upstairs in a two-story townhome in Ednam where the windows were strategically placed to catch every drop of the very best ambient light. At the hour when Dhanya crossed the threshold of this bedroom, the blinds were up and the moon was high and round, and perhaps it was this full moon that pushed her to her extremes. Perhaps it was the lamb, setting the precedent for setting precedents. Moonlight poured through the window and all the wood in the room glowed. Everything masculine and wooden, and a white bedspread that, in the incandescence, looked like the seat at the right hand of God. Wide, and white and safe. She was so tired, so blessedly tired, and here was the bed of all beds in the room of all rooms. She forgot she wasn't alone. She moaned softly at the sight of this sanctuary. It had been such a terrible evening. How she had gotten to this wonderful place was a mystery to her, but thank God Clara was not here. This was definitely not home, for sure. Tomorrow she would face Clara, admit that things had gone woefully wrong. That she had gotten drunk, she thought. That she had not said a word all evening, really. That he had just talked and talked about stuff she didn't care about like jazz and wine and religion in the context of hierarchy or something like that, but by that time she had really tuned out. She didn't know what she was thinking catching a ride with him, but then, she didn't think it was a "date date" but just a something else that wasn't a date but kind of exciting. But it seemed, by the way he was trying so hard and spending money, that it was a date. Dhanya had never been on one, of course. Being the daughter of Dr. Raman Nair meant no dates until you were out of sight. And she had only been out of sight for a little while. No time to date. She was not up to speed on the way these things worked, but she thought that she would have had more of a say in it all. Anyway, it was over now, and she could finally go to sleep.

Dhanya reached behind her neck to undo her buttons. It was awkward; she usually had sisters to help. She usually wasn't drunk. Earlier she had had her new roommate. Now she was stuck again. She got the top one, and reached for the next, but it wasn't as easy. It was in that too-high, too-low place, and her arms were so tired. She reached around her waist and decided to go from the bottom, but that too only got her one more button. She counted the buttons to steady herself. She had made the dress, and as she recalled there were twenty buttons. She had only ten more. She tried to pull it up over her head, but that was a ridiculous idea.

Russell Worthy had followed Dhanya up the stairs. He directed her to walk to the room directly at the top, straight ahead. He stood behind her in the doorway as she had walked into the room and moaned at the sight of the giant bed. It was a beautiful bed. Her reaction was so generous, so grateful. He felt himself impressed at her ingenuous appreciation of the moment. Guilelessly, she began to undress herself. Her fingers were unsteady along that line of buttons. She was trying so hard. Russell's jaw tightened. He walked close behind her and put his hands on her back. At the touch of his fingers, Dhanya jumped and lurched forward. She spun around and breathed his name in surprise, "Dr. Worthy?" She was trembling. Russell registered in his saliva the mildest distaste.

"Let me help you." He put his hands back on her shoulders until she stopped shaking, and held her face in the moonlight. He allowed his gaze to relax her. He was like a medium, a hypnotist in this light. Dhanya felt herself go slack. The first day for first-years, in the amphitheater at the university, there was a hypnotist. He did a performance for all of them. She had gone with her suitemates; she sat with Clara. The people on stage looked at this man and then their bodies went slack. Dhanya felt that slackness and wondered whether Dr. Worthy had been there that night too.

He watched her and listened to her now, tweeting and so dark in this hour's light. She was barely visible but for the bulk of her shape in the sheets, and the flow of dark hair spread like unraveled ribbons across the white expanse of pillows. She was utterly self-possessed, perched there on the edge of the bed. The covers were gathered across her breasts, under her crossed arms. Her hair extended neatly away from her face and the moonglow caught her left cheekbone. She was perfectly beautiful if entirely too big. Russell tugged the sheets slightly at the bottom of the bed. He wanted to make her move a little bit. He wanted to see her loosen her hold on herself. Nothing. He pulled a little more steadily, he felt her grip the sheets with her hands. He felt her resist, but she did not awaken. Russell's teeth tightened twice. He pulled more steadily. As the sheets slithered down her body revealing her broad nakedness, Dhanya, in her sleep, lowered her crossed arms and brought the covers back up. Her hands were now clenched tightly on the fabric, and her tweeting was replaced with a gasping whinny that sounded like a foundering horse.

A Terrible Morning

Dhanya approached walking more carefully after her night with Dr. Worthy. She felt altered in some vaguely perceptible way and thought it might be possible that her right leg had grown shorter, for her gait seemed gimpy and her hips out of alignment. Her sudden self-consciousness with regard to her stride made her shifty as well. She looked about constantly as she walked, and her eyes darted from face to face. When looking at a particular face, like in conversation with friends, her eyes darted from feature to feature. Her nervousness made her companions shudder when she left the room.

Nervousness flowed the way ease had before. The fourth of the five daughters of Dr. Raman Nair rarely thought about how she appeared to others because with such commanding sisters, the attention was rarely on her. She and Shanti had always been left to be as they were: young, serene, sweet, and very beautiful. And of course, she didn't know she was beautiful because she just didn't think about it much. She did know that her sisters were beautiful and fat. She knew that her mother and Gita Ammai were beautiful and slim. She was probably aware that she came from gorgeous stock that came in various sizes, and that it was unlikely that she was unattractive. If anyone had asked, she would have described herself the way she would have described any of her sisters, but modesty would have held back words belying how great she saw their loveliness, and love would have held back words describing their size, if not her own. She might have said, because she had a yen for telling things just so, "*I am the color of toasted cinnamon sticks, my eyes are the color of wet black earth. They are very big and I have long eyelashes that tangle when I sleep. My eyebrows are also long. And I have long hair that is straight and hangs like a black cloak covering my back.*" Because her incomplete description would have made her feel like a liar, she might have added, "*My feet are smaller than you might imagine, considering . . .* " Her inability to accept a compliment might have made her include, "*My mouth is too big,*" though it wasn't, and, "*When I lie down, I imagine that my face probably looks like the topography of Afghanistan, where God went to put his rocks.*" She wouldn't even be sure what this meant, but it would likely draw a chuckle and turn people toward other topics.

This new attention from Dr. Worthy made her unsure of everything she had never considered before. Like her attractiveness, her ability to turn the conversation away from herself toward things less personal, the power of a sincere and heartfelt apology in securing her forgiveness. What she was now was unclear. Those other people sitting under trees reading books, eating in groups on steps of old buildings, gathering at the bus stop; were they all looking at her? How could she know? What if they were? Would that mean that someone might notice her gimpy walk and the cum still dripping down her leg even though it had been days since she had been with Dr. Worthy?

Cum dripping down her leg had been her constant reminder of things she often, but not always, wanted to forget. She would feel a horrified panic and rush to a bathroom stall in a public place and lift her skirt, a wad of bunched-up toilet paper ready to swab. But there was nothing there, four days and sixteen showers later. What she was sensing was a mystery to her, but that first sensation of standing up, there in the morning of Dr. Russell Worthy's light lovely bedroom, made her so afraid. First, mortified thinking her period had come, at this worst possible time in this broad, white bed, in this room where the sun streamed in with the insistence of searchlights, she reached down and found that whatever it was, it was not blood. She shook bodily at the thought of what he might have punctured inside her as she quietly left the bed and searched for the bathroom in this strange space. She opened two closets and peeked through the hall while this cold seepage dripped down her leg, perhaps leaking her plasma, or her interstitial fluid. She found that tears were leaking too. Her fear made her face collapse as she struggled to be quiet, not to wake him. What would he say if he knew he had hurt her during all that sex? What would she do if she had to go to the doctor, if she had to go to the hospital, if they told her father? Down there ached terribly, and she could not close her legs when she walked. She moved with a bandy-legged tiptoe that advertised her shame. Her cellular drip was dotting the clean white carpet of her professor who slept on his back with his arms across his chest like a vampire, though he was so spectacularly handsome asleep that Dhanya couldn't help but wonder what he had ever seen in her to make him want to bring her back to this temple of indulgence and coax her legs open. Suddenly, she realized that this might be the leftover cum that she had felt on her thighs afterward. She hadn't thought of that. Maybe it just pooled in her horizontal vagina waiting for verticality. She always thought that it all went all the way in for use in possible fertilization. . . . Oh God. She shook her head hard to free this new panic. That was one she wasn't equipped to face in this state, naked with the bandy-legged drips.

She found another door in the bedroom that she had missed in her earlier search and entered the bathroom, which was immaculate. She squatted over the toilet and held a giant bunched-up wad between her legs. There was a closet in there that might hold the towels, where she might find a washcloth, but she was afraid to go opening things. Dr. Worthy seemed like the kind who didn't like others to touch his stuff. All his toiletries were in matching sage glass bottles with pewter tops; they were from the same company. Bazhescu. They had simple printed labels and there was no seep over the lids. She marveled at the order here. She thought she had never seen a bottle of shampoo without long black hairs trapped under the cap, sitting in a sticky, little mess of desiccated goo. His towels were white as well, and each had an embroidered monogram, RTW.

Dhanya waddled off the toilet and removed the tissues. She stood there for a moment, testing her dryness. Determining that it was safe, she tossed the wad into the bowl, peed, and flushed.

As she stood at the sink examining the bottles and wondering where the plain old hand soap was, she was slowly aware that the regular sound of swirling and swallowing that defined the successful flush was absent and that in its place was the ominous swelling and exhaling of pending overflow. Cringing, she looked over and more hot tears fried in her nose and above her cheekbones. As if the embarrassments of the last night weren't enough, the "I'm not old enough to drink, Dr. Worthy"; "I don't like lamb, Dr. Worthy"; the nearly putting the tiny car in reverse with her hip spillage on the gearshift; the mountainous, fat nakedness on which there had been some peri-coital commentary that had jarred her out of her drunk and made her long for cover; as if all this humiliation plus awakening thinking she was leaking spleen or something, and jiggle-joggling about looking for a bathroom, bowed out and bouncing like a porno hippo; as if all this weren't enough . . . now this. The final proof that her life was only going to get worse from here on out. The density and size of her cum-tissue ball had apparently been enough to clog the toilet, causing the whole morning piss/unraveling, shredded cum-tissue ball solution to come surging to the surface, threatening the greatest humiliation of Dhanya's life.

Still naked and bowlegged, swinging hair blocking her view, giant breasts further impeding quick action, Dhanya searched everywhere for a plunger, but of course this was a bathroom too elegant for exposed utilitarian devices. The prospects were grim; the water continued to rise. She was stunningly exasperated with the search. What kind of a person was this man? Where could it be? Every bathroom in her house except Muthachan's had its own plunger sitting right there next to the toilet on a plastic grocery bag. The scrub brush was on the other side. This bathroom had neither. Even with the mounting panic, the coming doom, Dhanya still felt afraid of what the absence of the basics spoke of the man. She could understand the plunger, but no scrub brush? Too dirty? Yet, amid all the jars, nothing that was obviously hand soap? More irony, she thought as she gave up the search. The yellow muck slowly reached the edge and gushed forth like a vengeful rapids.

Dhanya's heart surrendered. There was nothing left to save of her pride or her sense of control. She was simply a lost cause, standing in a puddle of cold, diluted piss . . . and cum. Yes, the morning after somehow or other losing her virginity, this is where she found herself: naked in a splendid bathroom, standing somewhat squatty, in a puddle of cold, diluted piss and cum.

The Onset of Hope

Veena and George sit together on the small balcony of his Baltimore apartment. She has fixed up two chairs and a small table. She has painted a broken stool and put it in the corner, and on this she has placed an overflowing plant that trails over the sides; this plant is called verbena, she told him with a kiss as she placed their drinks on their little table. Under the stool she has put two ceramic turtles she found in her closet at home. This time, when she went to water their verbena she noticed he had painted long black eyelashes on the smaller of the turtles. She laughs, but she may have misunderstood for she and George both have long eyelashes, so she asks with a grin, "What's this?"

He circles her waist from behind and announces with pride in workmanship, "She is you, he is me. We live under the verbena." She turns her face to kiss his shoulder and feels so happy that he sees her as the smaller of the turtles.

She has made it very homey out there. They hold hands and she holds a book on her lap and reads. George watches the sunset and thinks about rounds in the morning.

"Are you hungry yet?" she asks him, looking up from the book.

"A little bit." He answers without looking at her for his gaze has gotten stuck on the waning pink line of the horizon.

She stares at him for a while and smiles because he is stuck on the horizon. She can't help but think about walking on the beach with him. *Maybe on our honeymoon.* This thought is unsettling, and she buries it away. She looks back at her book and lets go of his hand to turn the page.

At the absence of her fingers, he turns to look at her and he smiles because she is stuck in her book, and he can't help but think about curling up in bed with her. She will always read in bed. "Do you always read in bed?"

She looks up and stares him right in the eye. "Yes, I always read to sleep. It is my favorite time of the day. Those minutes I read before sleep." She stares at him as he reclasps her fingers in his. He is smiling tenderly.

"Will this bother you? The light, I mean?" She is hopeful and kind. She imagines that it might be possible to retrain herself to sleep without reading . . . the way people whose arms are blown off learn to eat with their feet.

George smiles at her with all his teeth and his eyes bright with love. "Yes, it might bother me sometimes, but I'll get used to it."

She shines with gratitude. "I will get a small book light."

"Or maybe I'll just start reading at night too."

"Thank you, George."

They squeeze their hands and George looks back out at the horizon and Veena resumes her reading just where she left off.

She came here because she is ready. She is ready. . . . Chris sits on his porch in the half-moon gray of night and watches the churning lake. Inside, Jeri is asleep with her covers lax. She is innocent and good, but he will leave her. This much he knows. *I am ready too.* He lowers his face into his hands and sits in the quiet by his lake and he listens. *I do not need to be here to have my peace.* Chris sits on his porch in the half-moon gray of night and says good-bye to his home. He will leave tomorrow and he is hopeful and consoled. *I hear it in my deep heart's core.*

Efficient and Dependable

Gita rose at eight and found that her plumbing was old and not always efficient or dependable. When she inhaled the thickly perfumed air though, she had excellent perspective on such things as the efficiency and dependability of plumbing. *It is fixable; I have money I have never spent on anything of any value. My beautiful home that I will share with my beloved if it suits him to share it with me is of value. My plumbing is fixable.*

None of it mattered in this powerful air. Gita sat down to write without bathing, and without eating a bite. *I have written through much worse.* The end was near and it was not a pretty sight. She inhaled again and steeled herself to continue.

THE CURSED LIFE OF SREEMATHI OMANAKUMARI

It was a peaceful nap. Omanakumari slept a deep and dreamless sleep, and when her mother came to get her, she opened her eyes and smiled like a child. Standing at the side of the bed, Narayanikutty looked down and with her voice breaking announced, "Come. He is here."

Helping the girl to rise, Narayanikutty's heart thudded in her face. When the child was standing she held her shoulders and looked at her. Omanakumari held her mother's face and said, "Amma, I am going now."

Narayanikutty's tears were unstoppable. "You will be back soon. He said he will send you back for the birth."

Omanakumari looked at her mother. She smiled and nodded her head. Narayanikutty nodded back. She nodded and wiped her nose and her face with her *mundu*. Nodding and gasping for breath, she escorted her daughter out of the house. Outside, her father was standing awkwardly with Parameshwaran Namboodiri and his nephew. Looking up and seeing his daughter on the step, ready to leave, her father said, "Should I come soon to get her for the birth?" His quiet desperation was so evident that the nephew of Parameshwaran Namboodiri turned his head in pity. It was so evident that Omanakumari wavered in her resolve.

Parameshwaran Namboodiri saw her standing there big with his son and he sneered. "I'll send her back." At the sound of his voice, the nephew of Parameshwaran Namboodiri felt his stomach coil in embarrassment. "Go get her down," he said. His nephew lowered his eyes and walked toward the girl. Looking up, he stood silently, grieving for the child. Looking straight ahead and holding her mother's hand, she walked down the steps and said, "It is only a small bundle and I can carry it myself." With this, she turned to her mother and smiled with wet eyes. She lowered her enormous body to the ground and touched her mother's feet. The nephew of Parameshwaran Namboodiri turned his back to the whole scene, for the sound of the mother's grief brought an unbearable anguish.

Narayanikutty touched her daughter's head in blessing and raised her to her feet and Omanakumari walked quietly to her father. She smiled again and longed to hold his tired face, but she would not do so in front of Parameshwaran Namboodiri. She again lowered herself to the ground, her father's hand wrapped around her arm. As he touched her head in blessing, his pain grew too much to control and he bent down with racked sobs to kiss her head and hold her one more time. The intensity of the father's anguish was more than the nephew could take and he himself bent his head in sorrow.

"Enough, enough, enough." Parameshwaran Namboodiri's patience was worn thin. "We will go." Indicating her bundle with his head, he turned and began to walk away. His nephew walked over and lifted Omanakumari's bundle from her, and sensing his need to do the only thing in his power to help her, she did not protest. She turned once more and surveyed the only home she had ever known and smiled. Looking at her parents, her smile broadened and she poked out her lips. "I am going now, and I will be seeing you soon." Omanakumari turned to walk away. She did not turn back when she heard her mother's wailing.

For a while, the three walked without speaking. The pace was difficult for the girl to manage with her size, her swollen feet and the increasing pain in her abdomen. Parameshwaran Namboodiri, eager to be home and settled, walked faster than normal. The nephew, afraid to leave her behind, and yet too ashamed to walk too close, hovered somewhat in the middle, turning forward and back and checking both the girl and his uncle for direction on which way to go.

"Boy!" his uncle shouted.

Running forward, the nephew answered, "Yes, Uncle."

"What is happening back there?"

"She is walking." The nephew looked back and saw that Omanakumari was now hunched over double but that she kept walking inch by inch. "She is in pain."

"What kind of pain?"

The nephew paused and looked again. He didn't know what kind of pain. "Maybe the baby."

"I want her to get home."

Looking back, the nephew saw that the girl had stopped entirely and was doubled over. "I think she is vomiting." Parameshwaran Namboodiri stopped in his tracks and hesitated to look back because he was nauseated by watching other people vomit and he didn't feel so well today to begin with. He was perspiring profusely and the heat was rising with the coming of noon. "It is important to get home before noon. The sun will only make me feel worse." He paused and considered what to do. "Go and ask her what you have to do for her to get home. Tell her you want to get home before noon and that she can't stop and vomit anymore. Tell her I feel like vomiting too, and that if noon comes and we are still out here on the road, we will both want to vomit more." The nephew looked at his uncle and then at the ground. Turning, he ran quickly to the girl and the closer he got, the worse off she seemed.

Omanakumari had dropped to her hands and knees and she was

perspiring terribly. Her lips were turning dark and she was vomiting and retching between spasms. Dropping down to see her clearly, the nephew of Parameshwaran Namboodiri saw that something was terribly wrong beyond the obvious horror of going with this man to live in his house and bear his children. Her eyes were rolling back in her head. Frantic, knowing that his uncle would not care to do the right thing, the nephew faltered before calling him.

Through her dying, she sensed that this was an understanding man; Omanakumari said, "Home," and then collapsed on the ground. On the back of her *mundu* the nephew of Parameshwaran Namboodiri saw a creeping stain of blood and excrement and in his life's most courageous act, he gathered the girl up in his arms. She was heavy and soiled and as he raised her onto his shoulder, he could feel her babies kicking him in the side. He raised her off her feet and ran in the direction he had come, leaving his uncle behind. She waved like a rag doll, and her illness was so great that she trailed droplets of herself behind them.

Still facing forward, Parameshwaran Namboodiri called over his shoulder without looking, "Boy! Is she coming?" In the silence that followed, a cold shiver passed over him and carefully, he turned around, afraid of what he might see. But there was nothing but the dirt road and all the trees that lined it. Grabbing his towel off his shoulder, he gave himself a quick drying and then Parameshwaran Namboodiri toddled quickly the way he had come, calling out, "Boy! . . . Boy!!"

Gita's stomach rumbled and for the first time in so many months, she was deeply aware of her hunger. She smiled. This must be a very good sign. She inhaled again and felt the giddy promise of the day. Putting down her pen and notebook, she went to her kitchen that was got up with funny old boards and open cabinets that filled and refilled with dust and she tried to make eggs and toast on the stove. Her kitchen appliances as well were neither efficient nor dependable, and beyond that, there was no power. But she was above irritation in her newly claimed life. She smiled at her pearly egg whites, pooling and sliding quietly without a crackle in her still-cold pan, and thought back. *When I was a small child, my mother cooked over a fire for the electric current was neither efficient nor dependable, but a homemade fire under an enormous pot was age-*

old and constant. I know how to cook that way. If my eggs are not made to my satisfaction, I will dig a pit in the back and pull wood from my woods and build a wonderful fire and I will take a big copper pot and I will boil them. I know how to cook over a fire. Anyway, my appliances and my kitchen are also fixable. Her eggs were going nowhere. She buttered her cold bread and ate it on the steps of her porch.

Looking out, Gita could see (and she had noticed this before) that the trees and the plants all grew before her eyes. She thought it was just the delirium of the honeysuckle that made it seem this way, but it was not. The day before she had found a small sailboat buried in the woods and dragged it to the front with a plan to paint it yellow and blue and use it as a planter in a garden, and after lugging it so far, she was tired and took a seat on this same porch step, and by the time she got there and turned around, there were tendrils of vine and a flowering creeper already inside the boat. She was not afraid of ferocious fecundity, for she was a Malayalee, and in Kerala, where one drops a mango seed he can return three days later to pick fruit from the tree. She felt this as another marker of home. She chewed her soft, buttery bread. It crumbled in her hand and she shook the crumbs to the ground. Instantly, she watched her crumbs swarm with thousands of ants. *I am home.*

When she looked up, she saw Jack from the Stone House Inn running up the path with an enormous bag held in front of him. It did not slow his pace; he ran like the messenger of the gods, shining hair, fleet of foot, golden brown. Gita felt the grip in her heart that sometimes happened when she saw small children waving and dancing like sunflowers. She stood up and greeted him with a shout of his name and his smile glowed through the paper of his bag; oh, he was so happy to see her.

"Watch for the honeysuckle wind!" Gita called out, but before her words arrived, he stood before her, unaltered, bright-eyed, impervious.

"What?" Jack panted, his hair slicked at the brow, sheen across his nose. He had run the whole way.

"The wind, didn't you smell the wind?"

Jack smiled and looked at her with his boy's passionate heart. "You mean the honeysuckle?"

"Yes, it brings me to my knees."

"Yeah, Mom and Kate too. Me, I don't mind it. It makes me run faster, actually. And I don't have so many predicaments when I am out here. I ought to only play here, actually."

"Predicaments?"

"Yeah, you know . . . predicaments."

Gita took his bag and raised her eyebrows for more. When her left eyebrow went up, Jack's heart fluttered. When her right eyebrow went up, he caught his breath. He continued.

"You know, like . . . things falling, me falling, cars, bicycles, drains, wells, rocks, rivers, boats, rooftops, electricity." Jack paused to take the juice Gita offered. He thought for a while. "Hitchhiking, bees, ovens, fire, trees, bicycles—"

"You said bicycles already." Gita grinned.

"Unicycles . . . pogo sticks, hula hoops—"

"Hula hoops? What could go wrong with a hula hoop?"

"Well, I cut a slit in a hula hoop, and I threaded a piece of tarp through it and I climbed into a tree as high as I could get, and I jumped out and hoped that the tarp would open like a parachute, but there was a problem."

"The parachute didn't open?"

"Well, the parachute opened, but I got caught in one of the lower branches—well, the hula hoop got caught in one of the lower branches—and I was way out in the woods because I didn't want to get in trouble, you know?"

"Oh, yes. I know."

"But the other problem is that I forgot to sort of strap myself in."

"So you were hanging from the hula hoop?! In the tree?"

"Not all the way in the tree, was the problem. Like . . . I was dangling."

"Oh my God, Jack, if you had strapped yourself in, you might have broken your neck or cracked a rib."

"That's what they say."

"So what happened?"

"Well, like I was saying. I was just dangling there, and I was too afraid, you know, to scream much, plus it was really exhausting, you know?"

"I can't imagine."

Jack stood staring dumbly and then turning away when the blush rose to his hairline. He glimpsed at her through the corner of his eye; she was looking through his bag and uttering words of thanks he should convey to his mother. He didn't know if he should stay or go, stay or go. Suddenly, Gita looked up with a start. "Jack! I wonder if you could do me a favor."

He turned to her with his heart beating in his chest. A favor? *What favor? What favor? What favor?*

"Would you paint my sailboat?"

Jack smiled and stared at her. "Paint your sailboat?" He stood up, shook his head to restore his sense, took the money and the list she held out for him and ran to the hardware store to purchase sandpaper, brushes and a gallon each of any blue and yellow he thought she would find pretty.

"There's no rush, Jack," she called after him.

But he raced away regardless. He was so thrilled with his project, he didn't even say hi to Mr. Jones, whom he met on the road about a mile up from the path to the house covered over in yellow roses.

"Hi, Jack." Mr. Jones shouted out.

But Jack didn't hear him. In his mind, he was imagining the giddy smile on Gita's face when he removed her blindfold to reveal a sailboat, perfectly yellow and perfectly blue.

A Measly Penance

Outside the cottage covered in roses, Chris put his hand on her cheek and they stood like that so long a tendril of clematis wrapped itself through his shoelace. He broke their gaze only when it began to curl up his ankle; the tickle made him look down. When he looked down, she twined her slim brown fingers into his hair. His heart skipped a beat and he stood still again, this time remembering the astonishing delicacy of her ankles and her perfect little feet. She leaned forward and took his face in her two hands and pressed her palms to his lips one after the other. He kissed them with his eyes closed, kissing, kissing, whatever she gave him to kiss. She put her fingers on his eyelids and willed him to open his eyes and look at her again, and after so much more silent and heavy gazing, she quietly went to her knees and unwrapped that vigorous clematis as it climbed his calf. As she stood, she grasped his legs and his hips and laid her flat palm against his stomach; she reached around him and dug her fingers into his deep back. *He is as he was. He is he.*

Into her tiny, ringless hand she took his hand twice as large, and she led him to the cottage covered over in roses, but then the wind blew. The wind blew, and when the wind blew, the honeysuckle buckled him before she had even turned around. He was down and reeling. She brought his head to her stomach and held him there. She shushed him and she stroked his hair.

"You wear no bangles," he whispers into her blouse, for she always had. He used to hear her tendering in the jangle at her wrists as she loved him with her body, any part, as she wandered to and fro in their shared spaces, as she plunked into his lap, as she wrote, and always so near and common when she stroked his hair, which she was wont to do.

"I took them all off. My jewelry. I took it all off."

"Why?"

Gita stops and thinks. She hasn't given it any thought until this moment. "The sound, it interrupted my thinking. The effort seemed . . ." She looks away into the trees; she doesn't have any words except "worthless," *the effort seemed worthless if* . . . She takes his face back in her hands. "I took the jewelry off. It was my measly penance."

He reaches up with a smile and strokes her cheek. "Very measly."

She looks at him, sorry, deeply sorry. What else to say? *Have I said it yet? I have not even said it yet.* Gita's mouth is true and contrite; it is the bending of a mouth that is working hard not to cry. Her voice quavers, her lips tremble; she is so very sorry. "I am very sorry, Chris. I am very sorry."

His face is weary and alive. He strokes her face with simple and unabashed gratitude. He strokes her, and in his long and familiar caresses, Gita knows she is forgiven.

"Chris?"

He shifts his eyes from her cheeks and her hair to her eyes and he rests his fingers still and quiet against her neck.

"Chris?" Gita inhales and when she breathes out it is with choked and sputtering sobs, for she is unsure of his answer, she is unsure how she will be heard, she is afraid, though she knows him thoroughly. Her brow is furrowed with anxiety and she holds his broad shoulders in her tiny hands; they lay on top, unable to span, like the hands of a child. He stares at her blank with love, there is nothing but love, he does not even ache for her aching, for she is full of truth and acceptance and there is nothing for her to fear. This he knows, for he himself is not afraid of what she will say, so long have they suffered from their failures of integrity. She has nothing to fear. He puts his hands to her face to calm her.

"You have nothing to fear," he whispers.

She cannot stop crying. “Please, Chris, please will you please live with me,” she chokes and sputters, she gasps and her body shakes with the power of telling the truth, “in . . . an honorable life.”

He grins at her and squeezes her face, he rubs her cheeks with his powerful thumbs. “Gita Nair, are you asking me to marry you?”

She laughs, she laughs and laughs. She cries and shakes, she sniffles and she laughs and laughs and laughs.

The Prudence and Equanimity of Jack Broadus

Jack pulled every swatch of blue and yellow and laid them out to examine on the six-foot-long table in Buttergreen's Hardware. It was not enough that Minor Blue was such an exceptional shade, because next to Jolly Jolly Yellow, it turned a nauseating green like phlegm. Especially in bright light. Jack was flummoxed. He spread his swatches wider; he rearranged them—lightest to darkest, darkest to lightest.

Del Musik, watching from the nails and screws, pursed his lips in disapproval. The mess was outrageous. He pulled his Book from his satchel and made a note. Finally, Mrs. Buttergreen herself came to help.

Del marched over. "I say there, Clara, believe me when I say, this boy can do more damage than it seems, small as he is. Believe me. I know. You'd better shoo him on out of here before he turns the whole place upside down." He puffed out his chest and glowered.

Mrs. Buttergreen threw him a look of tolerant disdain and clucked her tongue. Turning back to Jack she said, "Honey, it's best to look at them in natural sunlight. Let's take them outside."

Jack looked back from Mr. Musik to the hundred strips of paper and sighed. Mrs. Buttergreen shook her head. "This is what we do, we take them out and lay them on the sidewalk and we eliminate."

She took the blues, he took the yellows. At the end of the next hour, he was down to three of each.

"You say it's for that old house back 'round the Old Rose Road?"

Jack nodded his head without a word.

"I do not believe there has been a mortal inhabitant of that place in . . . I don't remember, in at least . . ." She turned to the door and waved her finger trying to recall. "I will have to ask Mr. Buttergreen."

Del, who still hadn't selected nary a nail or a screw, but who nonetheless had come out to the sidewalk to watch them, interjected. "Certainly there hasn't been anybody living there for years. Only a lunatic could live there. It's outrageous!"

"I like these." Jack handed Mrs. Buttergreen two long swatches. His ignoring of Mr. Musik was practiced and perfect.

"Oh, honey, I was thinking that all the while. You read my mind, but I wanted you to choose from your own heart. It's important to choose from your own heart." She took his swatches and walked back to the store. At the door, Mrs. Buttergreen turned back and with tight lips and raised eyebrows she said, "Del, why don't you go on home now. There must be something you need to do."

Del opened his mouth indignantly and closed it again in a huff. "Well!" He removed his Book from his satchel and he made another note.

Inside, Mrs. Buttergreen handed the cards to Aubrey the Poet. "He would like Crushed Dahlia and Perfect Summer." She turned back to Jack. "Honey, how much you need? It's not for the house now, right? We can mix it for exterior, but I might recommend something . . . ," she raised her eyebrows and peered over her glasses, "more durable."

"It's for a sailboat in the garden." Jack smiled with pride in a job he had not yet completed, but which he would do better than anything he had ever done. "I need a gallon of both in semigloss." He considered that when he is done with the sailboat, he will paint the rocker on the porch, and he will repaint the mailbox post. Looking around, he asked Mrs. Buttergreen, "Do you have any pretty mailboxes?" And they do. He chose a yellow mailbox and added it to the order. He looked at his bundles and knew he could not carry all of it. Anyway, he needed to go home and get money for the mailbox. This would be his housewarming gift.

"Mrs. Buttergreen, could you hold all this? I need to go home and get a wagon."

Mrs. Buttergreen shook her head and tsked him like a silly thing. "Honey, why don't you just let us deliver it out there for you?"

"Oh no, Mrs. Buttergreen, I want to take it all out myself. She's in no rush. I'll come back in an hour or so."

"Honey, that's ridiculous. It's a couple miles back to your place, and then back and a couple miles out there, on foot? Aubrey the Poet can take you home, and then take you out there."

"I'm coming back, Mrs. Buttergreen. I'll take care of it. But thanks a whole lot." And he escaped out the door before she started up again. How could he explain the need to arrive at Gita's home, a little bit sweaty, with everything required to do a good job. The need to paint her mailbox post blue and attach her yellow mailbox, a job she had not even requested. He ran home hearing his own voice shyly tell her, "*I hope you like the mailbox, I thought it went right with the house.*" He could see her, so pleased, with her eyebrows all up with delight. He ran a little faster and soon he was home digging his money jar out of a hole in the ground he had marked with painted rocks laid out like X marks the spot.

When he arrived, he looked much the way he had wanted to look: a little sweaty, his hair matted and golden, his T-shirt stuck to his body, his jeans stretched out loose and ripped from wear and tear. He looked as manly as a twelve-year-old boy could look, and when he reached the turnoff from the Old Rose Road, he took a deep breath and then let free and raced on the honeysuckle wind. He ran the road in six seconds.

He parked his wagon, mounted the steps in one bound, and knocked heavily on the door. It was silent and he wondered if perhaps Gita had gone out. Then he wondered if he should simply get started, or if he should put everything up on the porch and come back tomorrow. Perhaps she had some instruction, some way she wanted it done. Did she want it blue outside and yellow inside? Vice versa? He sat on the porch step and thought about this for a while. She had said no rush. He did not want to displease her by acting rashly. This was the first time in his life he had ever stopped to think anything through—actually the second; the first was his choice of Crushed Dahlia and Perfect Summer. Then behind him, he heard the door squeal open, and he turned with his heavily beating heart and his shining, happy face.

But it was not just Gita. Standing there together in the doorway were Gita and Mr. Jones. Somehow, with only his twelve-year-old eyes, he could see they stood too close. Somehow, he knew what they had been up to. He knew it very much. Jack bit his lip and looked down at his wagon full of paint and his stupid yellow mailbox. It sat there in his Radio Flyer like a child's discarded mackintosh. He wanted to cry.

But then Gita, whose hair was blown about in a disheveled mane that smelled like honeysuckle and something else, came out on the porch in her bare feet and looked down into the wagon and began to jump up and down. "Oh, Jack! You brought a mailbox! Oh, Jack, please, please tell me that mailbox is for me!! I love it, Jack, a yellow mailbox!" She jumped up and down and Jack looked up at her and her eyebrows were arched with delight. He smiled at her shyly and felt his own thrill from her contagious jumping.

"Oh, Chris, look! Look what Jack has brought, Chris! A yellow mailbox! He has brought us a yellow mailbox!"

Jack turned around and faced Mr. Jones, whom he had known all his life, and the two met eyes like men. It was a moment that grew Jack Broadus.

Chris ran his fingers through his hair and stepped out onto the porch. Jack looked down and saw that he too was barefoot and when he looked back up he saw again that Chris was standing very close to Gita, looking down into the wagon.

Jack, sitting on the porch, looking up at them, ran one hand over his face and then cocked his head to the side and said to Chris, "I brought the tools to put it in for her, if you want me to."

Chris looked down at Jack, whose face was all of a sudden as grown as any man he had ever seen, and he nodded and said, "Jack, that's a fine-looking mailbox, and I would very much appreciate it if you could put that in for us. I didn't bring any tools with me."

Jack stood up and walked down the steps. Taking a deep breath, he steadied himself and walked back the way he came. Chris watched him until he saw the falter in his step from the honeysuckle wind that never before could touch him; the boy's first heartbreak. Chris came down the steps, caught up and said, "It's easier when one man holds the box and the other screws it in."

Jack flushed a little bit, and while he screwed in the yellow mailbox he thought things through for the third time in his life.

Laying Bare

Mrs. Buttergreen came anyway. She arrived to find them putting up the yellow mailbox from her shop. *I am an accomplice*; she reddened. Before her eyes, Chris Jones, with his chest pressed into a woman's shoulder. When the woman looked up to express some thought, smiling with a flashy grin, her face was so close to his that surely he felt her exhaled breath along his jawbone. Their bodily comfort crimped Mrs. Buttergreen's lips.

"Chris."
"Mrs. Buttergreen."
She turned a cold stare on the too-close woman.
"This is Gita Nair. She just bought the cottage."
"Clearly."

In her hand she holds a calla lily plucked from the shelf above her sink. It is splayed out and wilting from the heat, from the squeezing of an offended Mrs. Buttergreen. She leaves, forgetting to give her offering. She leaves having said only two words.

Chris turned to Gita and put his hand on her cheek. "It will all happen now," he whispered to her.

"Yes," she replied.

He took a deep breath and bowed his head. "I will go to Innisfree. . . . It might take . . ." His voice faded away. He kissed her on the forehead and then nodded to Jack. "Jack. Would you mind taking Gita to your house for the night? I don't want her here alone . . . in case anyone . . . comes by."

Jack nodded with his eyes wide. He took a step in closer to Gita. She reached out to Chris and squeezed his fingers. Chris pulled her in close to his huge chest and hugged her so hard she could not hear what he said, but she heard the deep and slow beating of his heart and she was not afraid.

From the Book of Injustices

AUGUST 21, 1999 (C)

They walk up the street, the Turkish odalisque and the boy from next door. She looking forward, he with his small head bent to the ground. She has been gone some two days and yet here she returns, leading the child wordlessly. I am greatly afeared.

Liking What You See

When it was almost October but still warm, George took Veena to the Inner Harbor because she had not been there since she was a child and so it seemed like a fun and convenient outing, considering their limitations, all the lying and sneaking about. He prepared for this like he one day prepared for his honeymoon, calling ahead, elaborate itinerary, alternate plans, and little chance for failure. It was their first date, because though they had been together many times, it was always in his apartment, for he could not bear to be near her and not be by themselves. At any moment, he wanted the freedom to take her in his arms, remove all her clothing and all of his and make love to her for hours and hours. He had waited his whole life to feel this way, and he needed a month and a half to indulge in the intensity of his emotions before he was willing to share Veena with the world. They went to the Inner Harbor with George's front pocket full of cross-tabulated phone numbers, places of interest, and times of arrival, plans A through E.

On the day they went to the Inner Harbor for their first date, Veena wore a blue dress that swirled around her knees and flared out with any breeze. George thought she had such wonderful knees that when the wind picked up, he automatically looked down and became aroused.

"We should have just stayed home," he whispered into her ear.

"Don't be silly, you silly." Veena grinned back. She squeezed his hand and kissed him on his cheek. She looked so stunning that he was sometimes left speechless.

"George, do you think that kiosk will have water?"

George begins to answer, but when he looks her way her hair catches reflected light off the water and gleams, her teeth sparkle, her skin glows; he stands there staring with his mouth open. She understands that this is love. She pulls him to the kiosk and buys a bottle of water. She pours it down his gullet, and the cold water revives him.

"Yes," he answers.

After lunch, the two wander hand in hand in the busy harbor throng and George checks his watch and is pleased to discover they are right on schedule and he loves her all the more, for it seems they travel well together with a similar sense of time. Neither she nor he dawdled in the shower, or arrived late, and they seemed to have very compatible ideas of what was urgent and compelling. He smiles to himself because these are even more reasons to count his blessings for having found this amazing girl. It is almost time to head to the science museum and he is beginning to lead her in that direction when Veena stops and points.

"Ooh, look, George, palmistry!"

George is pulled back by her anchored stance. He turns around and laughs because surely she is joking, but no, she is not. She bounces up and down and when she does not hear any response, she looks at him and stands still. Her pretty eyebrows rise with the question and innocently she asks, "What?"

"Palmistry?"

"I've never done it, have you?" She is completely serious.

"No but I did a Ouija board in the fifth, no maybe sixth grade. At a friend's birthday party."

"Ooh, Ouija boards. Scary. I've never done it. Too risky." She is completely serious. She shrugs and then begins to tug him. "Let's go see if we can get in! There might be a wait." She looks around surveying the options. "If there is a wait, we can just go in that shop for a while or something."

George blinks. He is flummoxed by her clear intentions. He hems. . . . "But it's time for the science museum."

She shakes her head and sucks her teeth with a smile. "Silly, we can't go to the *science museum* if there's a wait. We'd have to get our hands stamped and then walk all the way back here, and we'd have to be all concerned about the time to be sure we get back for our session."

"Session?"

"Well, whatever they call it. Our 'moment,' you know, our 'appointment.' "

"With the palmist in the kiosk at the Inner Harbor?"

"George? What?" She tugs him along.

Over the course of their lives, she told this story at family gatherings, at work parties, to friends and new neighbors over and over for the decades and decades of their marriage. When he died so many years later, she told it again, at the gathering in their home, for as she said, she learned all she needed to know about the man on that day. Not just from the miraculous compatibility of all the lines and mounts of their hands, but from the way he never mocked her faith in the unusual, never belittled her odd little whimsy, never shared his doubts as to the palmist's authenticity or ability to divine the truth. She laughed and said, "I was married for years before I saw the twinkle in his eye when I told the story and recognized it for what it was." When he was gone she pulled her voice in tight and whispered to them all, "In all our lives, he never stole a drop of my joy. Not a drop."

That day in the Inner Harbor when they left the palmists' kiosk, Veena was aglitter and assured, and they sat on a bench outside the science museum and he snuggled her as she held his hand against hers and noted her conic fingertips and his square ones, and their matching leads off the heart line to the Mount of Apollo.

"I'll never remember it all!" She lifted her eyebrows with magical thrill, and she smiled with delight as she took a small notebook from her purse to note down everything she remembered. She was very happy.

Many years later he would recall, "The palmist made her very happy."

"How about you?" they would ask.

He'd shrug and smile. "I liked what she said," he would answer simply.

Suddenly, there in front of the science museum, he had a thought. "I want to take your picture!" He leapt up and stood in front of her and when he pointed the camera she was looking at him with so much love he had to lower it to check if it was real, but when he raised it back to his eye, it was still there. Veena looked at him like he was a gift she never thought she would get, and couldn't believe was real. She looked at him like she couldn't bear the distance away he stood to take the picture. He vowed that day, looking through that lens, that he would live a very, very long life, and so he did. A woman passing by with her family saw the two of them; they were a vision. "Oh my," she said, "look at that."

Stopping her family, she tapped George on the shoulder and offered to photograph them together. George was very grateful and he handed her the camera and went to sit beside his beloved, but this lady was not accustomed to such complicated technology and fumbled a little bit. In the moments while she spoke out loud to herself, checking if she had the right button, fiddling with the telephoto, removing her fingers from the flash, George could not resist turning to Veena and pushing her cheek and her hair with his face and this is the picture the lady snapped first, accidentally. And then of course she took another, but in this first photograph George's forehead and his eyebrow are pressed against Veena's right cheek, his mouth is solemn and his eyes are closed. Veena's eyes are closed too, and her head is tilted to the left, to let him in deeper to her face. She is smiling the closed-mouth smile of the deeply adored; her shoulders are raised with joyful contentment, and it was this picture that Veena kept in a silver frame inside her nightstand drawer where her mother and her father might be less likely to find it. And it was the first picture of her, that he took himself, that stood in a matching silver frame beside George's bed, in plain view, the first thing he saw in the morning, the last thing he saw at night. These photographs were heartbreaking in their truth.

Her sisters, loving her so much, look at her photograph from time to time, and even Usha's eyes dampen when she returns it to the drawer in the nightstand, because such a picture should never be hidden away. And Veena looks at this photograph and longs for George. She knows she needs that forehead against her cheek all the time. All the time.

Necessary Lies

It was a cool morning the day that Veena looked strange and thus attracted the attention of her loving parents. Shanti kicked her under the breakfast table because she sat with a loopy face, but that made Veena startle. She cast shifty eyes, and dug down deeper into her bowl of Raisin Bran. Never really looking anyone in the face, the eldest daughter of Dr. Raman Nair rose from the table and grabbed her dish so fast she sloshed milk onto her wrist. She sucked her teeth at her clumsiness and took her dish to the sink.

As Veena gathered her things for work, she took a deep breath to strengthen her resolve and called over her shoulder, "I'm probably going to stay in town tonight, I have an early meeting in the morning and we want to go over the presentation before. If I come home, I'd have to leave here at four A.M. to get in on time." She readjusted her bags. "Well . . . okay then." Pulling her hair from under her briefcase strap, she headed for the door.

Her parents exchanged a look, and the few sisters who shared the table cringed. Dr. Raman Nair quickly called out, "Veena!" and the assembled girls sucked in their breath, fearing the end was near.

Veena Nair, whose heart was made of more honest stuff than she'd been using of late, and who hadn't the courage yet for her fight, stopped with her hand on the door, moments away from safety. She turned around and walked back into the kitchen. "Yes?" She wore a bright liar's smile. The effort of such forced eyebrow raising and teeth exposure gave her a headache.

"You are staying out again? Overnight? How much work is it that they are giving you now? Suddenly so many days you are working all hours?"

Veena shrugged and mumbled, "What can I do? It's my job?" She planted the smile back on her face.

Jaya shook her head, and raised her finger. "You know, I cannot sleep when you are gone like that? You know, if you are gone all hours late at night in D.C., I am so afraid all the time?" Jaya shook her head. "It is becoming too much."

There was birdcall outside. Veena, who knew the answer that would allow her to leave without worry, but to whom manipulation was so dishonorable, listened to it for a few moments. She wished she knew the songs of birds. Birdsong was the ken of innocent and honorable people. *One day I will learn birdsong.* For now she very sincerely said, "Oh, Mommy, I hate that you don't sleep when I have to come in late. I have been thinking that I ought to just look for an apartment in the city. I mean, it's an awful commute and I make plenty of money, and—"

Dr. Raman Nair stood straight up and pointed in the air. "You just don't worry about all that; your mother is just talking. She is just saying that we worry about you. If you were living there in the city all alone without a husband, do you think we would worry less?"

"I could live in Arlington."

"Worse!" Dr. Raman Nair decried.

Veena lifted her eyebrows up high. "But if I moved, you wouldn't know I was out, at least Mommy could sleep." She felt a little nauseated because she meant every word, and it was therefore even more nauseating, using true feelings to angle for freedom.

A bird trilled outside the window, *Veena's gonna trick you, Veena's gonna trick you.* Veena told it to shut up. *Shut up, bird. I can't fight about this yet. When it is time to fight about this, I will fight about this. Right now I am telling lies, leave me alone.*

"Guys, I'm gonna be late, can we talk about this later? Today at lunch, I'll call around, do some research."

"You just go to work. No research. Don't worry about these things now, we will think together later. You just stay here. Don't call around. Just, just come home when you are finished work tomorrow. Come right home." Dr. Raman Nair sighed and sat back down. "And be careful," he added. Veena walked away.

"And be good!" Jaya called out, as she always did. Be good. Veena heard it before the door closed. She closed her eyes and counted the steps to her car. As she arranged her belongings in the trunk, the bird alighted on a nearby tree and teased at her, *Be good, be good, ha ha ha ha, be good.* Veena glared at it and it shivered and hopped to a higher branch. *Yes, you'd better stay clear, bird, I am going to be good. Very soon. Just give me a minute. I am going to be good.*

Inside, Dr. Raman Nair and his wife finished their tea with deep, quiet, concerned sips. Shanti lingered, eating her cereal, reading the box.

"It is too much," Jaya worried. "Too much work."

"She is very busy."

"Yes, she might be very busy, but we can all become very busy when there is only that." Jaya shook her head in a continual anxious motion. "She never talks anymore to us."

Shanti, never lifting her eyes off the ingredients list, listened very carefully, caught every word.

Her mother continued, "She is becoming clumsy, she has never been clumsy." She looked at the wet stain on the cloth. "Spilling her milk?" Jaya rose from the table and cleared the newspaper and leftover dishes. Her husband sat silently thinking, his face dark and worried. "She is so tired, she is always blurry faced and sitting like a waking dream. I am worried, all these late nights." Jaya ran the water in the sink and turned to Dr. Raman Nair. "If it goes much further like this, she will become angry. She will be lonely. Like Gita." Jaya's brow furrowed and she drew in her mouth.

"She cannot be lonely, she is here with us," Dr. Raman Nair pointed out with loud certainty.

Jaya exhaled a pshaw. "Do you think your wondrous company can match a husband of her own? A family? She is getting too old to be alone with only us."

Shanti pulled the box in close to hide her face. Her father was nodding and making the sounds of agreement.

"It is true. It is true. She is too old for us to be so carefree with matters."

"It has never gone well," Jaya said quietly. "It has never gone well thus far." She put up the dishes. "We should have written their horoscopes."

"It is unnecessary here, Jaya, don't say stupid things now."

"We should have written their horoscopes," Jaya said louder. She pointed and shook her finger. "It can be done, even from here. It can be done. I should have insisted."

"Do you think the *jolsyen* there can write a horoscope calculating the stars from here? It is lunacy. Idiocy." Dr. Raman Nair stood up. "And furthermore, it is superstitious and unnecessary." He pointed right back at his wife. "I don't want my daughters married off into lunatic, idiotic, superstitious families!" He sat back down.

"And, kind sir, what then when the boy is very good and they want to see a horoscope? What then? What then, kind sir?" Jaya put her hands on her hips and leaned forward with grave seriousness. "Some things are just customs. Is there something wrong with customs? Can you say the family is idiotic simply because they observe the common customs?" She gave a firm nod.

"No, I cannot say that. However, I want my daughters married into families of understanding natures. Any family that would exclude my daughters from consideration because they did not have a horoscope, any family that would know Veena and fail to see her worth for lack of horoscope . . ." Dr. Raman Nair stood up again. "Any family that would not understand that she was born in a country where these things are not easily obtained, *that* family is idiotic. I do not want my daughters married into that family." He sat back down and had another thought. Turning, he continued, "In fact, Jaya, I think it will be easier to root out the truly idiotic families this way. If we had horoscopes for our girls, we would not be able to use it as a . . . litmus test of idiocy!"

"You just sit with grand pronouncements." Jaya furiously wiped the counters. Facing her husband again, she waved a dirty paper towel and raised her voice. "We must get cracking, kind sir. We must get cracking on this business." Shanti sank down deeper behind her cereal box and absorbed the whole thing. Her mother muttered to herself, "I should have insisted. I just should have insisted."

❧

Later that night, after a full day of work and a long drive to Baltimore, Veena let herself into George's apartment and made him a wonderful dinner. She lit the table with tiny candles and when he arrived, exhausted and grimy from his day, she stood at the table and smiled her honest smile. "I have made you dinner, but it is something that will keep, if you would like to change first." She came forward holding a small plate with a quarter of a sandwich. "I thought you might do better to have a tiny bite, though. Even if you want to shower first. But there is real dinner too." She kissed him gently on the mouth. "You choose."

To be greeted like this? George encircles her with his long arms and rests his tired eyes against her shoulder. He nearly falls asleep, so happy and content is he against her enormous, supple and comfortable body. She holds the sandwich in her hand behind his back and breathes in the scent of hard work on his manly body. She is quiet and understanding of his fatigue. He is grateful for her silence.

"I need to take a bath."

"Yes, you do," she replies.

George can hear the smile in her voice. "Come bathe with me?"

"If you eat just a tiny bite."

George eats the quarter of a sandwich from her hand, and is much revived. She is very good for him, he thinks, as he prepares the bath.

Veena lowered herself into the tub inch by inch. If she were to slip, George might rise out of the tub like a surfer in a tsunami, and this possible danger made his naked love looming above him like a zeppelin even more exciting.

"How can you be sitting in there like that? Aren't your balls boiling?"

"I don't think they are. Come check." George reached up and tugged a little on a stray lock that was hanging down by her hip. It was not yet wet. The thought of drenching it made George close his eyes. He let go and ran his wet fingers down her leg, leaving pretty droplets. Staring into one of these, he saw her skin magnified. Magnified, she was so much more exquisite. He imagined a giant water droplet that could cover her from head to toe, one that could momentarily encase her. How dazzling it would be to see her that large. His heart beat so hard he held his chest.

"It's going to take me ten minutes to get into this tub if you don't turn on some cold water. You must be part vampire."

"Vampires like hot water?" George moved himself to the other side of the tub so as to stay warm, and reached out to turn on the cold water. He opened the drain to let some of the hot water out, mindful of overflow. Once, he made the tub too perfect too fast. Veena entered quickly and the overflow glugged with dangerous overwhelm. George had seen a mortified embarrassment flood her precious face, and silently vowed to always make the tub too hot for the rest of his life.

"Don't make it too cold, though." Veena rested her hand on George's head and dug into his hair with her nails, stroking through the thickness. Her eyes filled with tears. Every time she stroked his hair, her eyes filled with tears. It was like peeling an onion. It was like watching a wedding. He wrapped his arm around her sequoia thigh and rested his cheek there. Holding his shoulder, she lowered herself and turned off the cold water. He had made the tub perfect. He made everything perfect.

She was facing him on the faucet side, though he had intended to sit there. George always took the faucet side because he loved her. He always made the tub too hot for her, so that he was able to get in first and take the faucet side. Veena leaned forward so he could feel her breasts. Right then, it was all she had to offer for denying him the faucet side. George took her breasts in his hands and wondered what could be better in his life. Just as he was thinking this, Veena remembered that she had one more thing to offer in return for having taken the faucet side and leaving him the better end. She needed to check if his balls were boiling.

"You asked me to check if your balls were boiling." Veena scooted in closer and proceeded to inspect them thoroughly. George, who now had an even better handle on her breasts, reevaluated and again wondered what could be better in his life. George lowered his head in thanks.

Strategically, Veena inhaled and George's head was resting on her left breast. Again, he reevaluated and wondered what could be better in his life.

Into his ear, Veena whispered, "I wrote you a poem."

"You wrote me a poem? I didn't know you wrote poems. How come you never told me that you wrote poems?"

"This is the first poem that I ever wrote." Veena had removed her hands from George's balls and had them in his hair. Through all the tears pooled in her eyes, George's face was magnified. Magnified, he was so much more perfect. She imagined being momentarily encased in an enormous tear and how breathtaking his face would be so large. "I don't remember how it goes exactly. I have to read it." Veena blinked. Her tears rolled down her face.

"Should we get out to read it?"

"It will keep."

"I love you."

"I know."

Stepping Away

Innisfree sat perched beside the water looking hand placed like a miniature in a pretty little scene. Chris walked the long pond road and stopped to look, but he was unable to really get into it. Unwilling, perhaps. He walked on without sure thoughts, without a word in mind. He had nothing to offer his wife in exchange for his betrayals except this house, and it had always meant much more to him anyway. This was for sure. So then, what was his penance, except his misspent life? And really, what did she get out of that either? It was an empty walk down the long pond road, one thought fading away as fast as the next one appeared. All of it hazy. There was nothing of any substance at all to consider, not even a firm plan of action.

He appeared in the door and from Jeri's absorbed studying of her files at the kitchen table, he knew that at least he had gotten to her before anyone else. That was a relief, for his shame was in knowing the embarrassments she would endure through his bold stepping away. He was also deeply shamed to know she would feel not good enough, when she was very good. He thought it as loud as he could, *You are very, very good.* Still, she would look at her thin, overtanned skin, and stand naked before the mirror scrutinizing her boyish figure. She would hold a small mirror in her hand and use it to see her back, and she would feel that she drove him away with the winding humps of her spine. She would feel she drove him away with her barrenness.

Jeri felt him staring, as quiet as the air. She turned and saw resolve on his face that she had seen only once before, when he determined to settle here and build a home on the shores of Quiet Pond.

Fear radiated from her stomach to all points of her body, and she began to shake, for there is a dark-shadowed difference between the hopeful resolve to begin a new life, and the unbendable resolve to end an old one. She held tight to the table and bent low with panic. She hadn't imagined the end would feel this way. In the years that followed she admitted that, even after she knew the truth of his infidelities, she did not believe he had it in him to leave and she never thought her marriage would end. They had suffered too much together; she thought it was a life's glue, that much suffering. Just as an equal share of happiness would be a life's glue. At that awful moment, she wasn't prepared to see such an unyielding determination to go.

Chris himself had been unable to consider this moment, this very moment, in all these many years of dreaming. He hadn't considered how much easier it might have been if she had screamed at him and thrown him out, if she packed her things and left, if she cursed his name loud before God. He hadn't considered that the worst possible thing to face would be the terrible knowledge that he had broken her heart.

Chris knelt beside her and held her trembling shoulders and yet she knew in his grasp of her that he would not even spend the night. It was all ending right now. Right now.

"Jeri." His voice cracked, and he couldn't stop tears from flowing for he was holding her shoulders so tightly in his hands, and he had not held her in a very long time. *She is so small.*

"Jeri," he said again. He leaned in closer to her face and then suddenly she let go a little sound, like an "ooh," and slowly raised her head and stared at Chris with her eyes wide with horror. Her mouth was locked in a terrible black circle that brought him true fear, and then she raised her hand to her mouth, for in his comforting of her, in his making good, and taking care, in his leaning in close and holding her steady, she could smell the honeysuckle on his hair and in his clothing. She raised her hand to her mouth. Her eyes suddenly stung with tears. They flew forward and landed on his cheeks and it seemed to her that the salty water of her pain made his skin come alive with the stench of faithlessness.

She whispered with a twisted face, "No, not . . . it is her . . . '*I want to lie under you, pressed with the weight of your kisses;/Your arms long like branches twined with mine,/Brown like branches*'—it's her. It's her." Jeri pushed her fists into his chest and yet could not beat him for they had shared a life of great disappointment.

She wailed and his blood raced and rushed in concert with the sound of her miserable humiliation. These few minutes before the inevitable acceptance of reality were long and terrible to endure. Chris did not remove his hands from her shoulders, though she fought him and screamed to let her go. She did not beat him with her tiny fists. They had endured greater tragedy in their lives together than this.

When her body was still and calm, her face defeated, her head hung down, Chris rose from his knees and took a chair at the table. He rested his head in his hand, and closed his eyes. They sat this way until there was no longer any light in the kitchen. In the darkness, it was easier to endure when she whispered a crushed, "You once told me you would not leave. You said we would figure it out together." She looked up at him and in the moonlight through the window, he could faintly see the glistening of her cheeks.

"I did." Chris could not hold his hands still from reaching out and wiping her face dry. "I did say that." He pulled his hand back and looked at the table. "I am sorry."

Jeri's mouth trembled and she sounded very young and so alone. It was her sound, Chris recalled, when there was no discernible heartbeat on the sonogram, when she would say, "Please, look again."

"Is it because we never had a child? Because I cannot ever have a child?"

Chris kept his eyes on the table. "No," he whispered.

"If we had a child, you would never do this. You would never walk away from here."

"No, I would not." This he always knew was true.

"Then you are leaving because we do not have children."

Chris looked up and his face was hot with sadness and truth, wet with tears. "I am leaving because I have loved someone else, and . . ." His voice broke. "And because I love her still."

She nodded her head. They sat in the dark so long until Jeri put her head down on the table atop her crossed arms and perhaps she fell asleep. Chris watched the sky over the pond cloud over and then release the moon, until he too laid down his head and fell asleep.

In the morning, he packed his clothing, his books and his tools. He loaded his car and then he stood on the doorstep to say good-bye to his wife, who sat on the steps in whitewashed quiet and replied, "I will see you all the time. It is a very small town." He looked up to say good-bye again to his house, and she again faintly spoke, "You will be back, you have too many things left behind."

"Should I get it all out of here today?" he asked.

Jeri looked up at him and turned her head to the pond. "I don't care." She paused and looked back. "I might care later. But I don't care right now."

He stood at his car door for a long while, unsure of the proper protocol. Unsure of the proper amount of time to allow before stepping away.

"You might as well go. I'm sure she is waiting for you."

In this last there was the tiniest grudging sneer. In the "sure," in the "she," and most pronounced, in the "waiting." And it was just enough to feel certain it was now time to go. They had been *waiting* for a very long time.

"Good-bye, Jeri." Chris swallowed and when she did not look back, he got in the car. As he pulled away he saw she was signaling. He rolled down the window.

She stood up and crossed her arms over her tiny body. "Good-bye." They blinked at each other with nothing left to say and finally Jeri turned and went into the house, leaving Chris free to drive away, back down the long pond road.

Dhanya's Dress

Dhanya removed her pajamas in the dimly lit dorm room and stood naked with her back to the mirror. When she looked down at her dress, carefully laid across her rainbow bedcovers, she could, despite the darkness, see the cellulite at the top of her thighs. She squeezed her eyes tight and still she could see. She squeezed her ears and still she could hear. Of course, she was completely alone.

"Cellulite forms on women's bodies because their muscle fibers run horizontal to the bone, the opposite of men. Once it has formed, it is nearly impossible to get rid of." His lips slid sideways as he looked her up and down. "It is trapped fat," he had told her, "and once the fat gets there, it's really hopeless." *Really hopeless.* He demonstrated this with the absence of cellulite on his thigh and then with the ready presence of it on hers.

"See how you can actually feel the dimpling here? Right here, touch right here." That morning, his hair had smelled like apple pie, and when she told him that, he began a discussion that had ended here, with his fingers manipulating the cellulite on her thigh, and she without a pillow to hide her shamed face because he had thrown them all to the floor to make room for her in the bed. She wished that his hair had smelled like broiled chicken and broccoli.

He flipped her over like a pancake. "The creams are only temporary," he had said, demonstrating on the cellulite beneath her baggy behind.

Creams? she wondered. . . . *I didn't know there were creams for this.* She came from a house with one bottle of Jergens for all purposes.

Once, at his place, she had taken a shower and come out and asked for some lotion.

"For what?"

"To moisturize."

"To moisturize what?

Dhanya stood there wrapped in the RTW towel he had allotted her, in his sun-drenched room, feeling entirely too exposed, so confused that she really didn't know what to say . . . struggling with the right way of putting it; she finally settled on, "Me?"

Dr. Worthy sighed and shook his head. He led her back to the bathroom and showed her his stash of moisturizers that looked like a pharmacist's repository. He asked questions about her skin type, her T-zone, her body chemistry, her blood type, and her point in her monthly cycle, and this much attention to her varied corporeal hydration requirements made Dhanya blush so high that she inadvertently aroused him with her red, glowing cleavage and her nervous, trembling lips, and so she had to wait a full twenty minutes for him to finish with all that, shower again, and then apply the cocktail he had laid out for her body and then another similarly complicated assortment to her face. He told her that the amount that she had used for just one application to face and body probably cost him in the neighborhood of five dollars.

"Maybe ten dollars for the body." He winked, slapped her butt, and told her he'd put it on her bill. The next time she came over, she packed her Jergens in her bag, in case she really was running up a tab.

She sighed and wiped the tears that had somehow or other leaked down her face. She put on the pink strapless bra she had bought to go with her coral gown and got dressed with her back to the mirror. She slipped on her silver shoes with the coral-colored rhinestones across the toes. And she sighed again. *Embarrassing.*

She went back out to the nearly empty suite where most of the girls were out for the night and there stood beautiful, tiny Clara Ballerina in her flying-waffle pajamas, rubbing her yellow head and blinking with sleep. When she saw Dhanya, Clara gasped. Dhanya's face creased with worry. *My dress. Ridiculous.*

Clara walked over slowly and reached up to pull the band out of Dhanya's hair, which cascaded over her bare shoulder like a jet waterfall.

"I can't believe you made this dress."

Dhanya raised her eyes in a sad question. Clara's eyes teared up at the doubts written there.

"You look so beautiful, I can't even believe it. You even look beautiful in the dark."

"I only look beautiful in the dark." Dhanya smiled.

"Don't be stupid."

"I wish I had a choice."

Dinner at L'Eau

Dhanya worried over her hands. She had meant to be more regular in their care these last weeks since he had invited her to the party, but it was more than she could remember to do and so tiresome, as well. And here she sat, the morning of the party, and her hands were as they always were. *Hairy, chapped, red, rough.* She could hear him now.

"Dhanya, your nails?" His eyebrows arched.

I'm sorry, Dr. Worthy.

"Dhanya, if you were to use the products I so generously purchased for you, the slight hair growth at the knuckle, the chapping here, the redness, the roughness around the cuticle, all these would improve."

I'm sorry, Dr. Worthy.

He had ordered her a full hand-care line from Bazhescu and given her an exhaustive demonstration. He insisted that she do this routine regularly, and though she tried to remember, it was quite a process requiring prescrub, and perimoisture cellular rejuvenation, and postscrub lubrication and toning, and after-toning deep-hydrating masque and then a final process that required gloves that plugged in, and she was not accustomed to such detailed personal ministrations. He had also added these to her bill, he said, and she wasn't sure he was kidding because his winks were complicit, and yet she had nothing to do with the joke, so she was never sure of his motivation in winking, so she tried to use the stuff because it would be a shame to have to pay for the products, never having used them. In any event, that was nearly a month ago and she had endured the full process only three times and when he held her hands he always turned them over and back and then looked at her with his eyebrows raised. "The sign of a true lady is her nails." She thought about her own mother's yellow nails, stained with curry, and quickly figured that Indian ladies were, of course, measured on a different scale.

ꕥ

There was every reason to be unsettled. Dr. Russell Worthy looked at himself in the mirror and for the first time in his whole life, he did not see his own face. He saw Dhanya. It was only for a few seconds, but it was long enough to know. He shook his head and walked away from the mirror; he was absolutely falling in love with her. He absolutely wanted to see her tonight. He was absolutely watching the clock, counting the minutes, and even considering what he might wear that would complement what she had told him was "a sort of coral-colored dress . . . like a sunset." He absolutely remembered what all small and precious she said: "In my family, we all sing." He had caught her singing in the kitchen when she thought he was at work. Her voice sent a rush into his face. He had every reason to be unsettled. *What is happening to me?*

Dr. Russell Worthy came across to his peers as extraordinarily learned, deeply interested in others, pretty damned good-looking, and most important, "quite a catch." He was a much sought-after bachelor professor. The problem here was Dhanya. She was not his typical teenage lover, and he sensed in her the dangerous possibility that she had his number, but that she wasn't letting on. It made him nervous and he overdid his whole Worthy thing. Her silence seemed to bring out a need to upset her, and really, the only way to even know she was upset was to allow her to overdrink or smoke pot. Even drunk or stoned though, she might cry but she never begged or complained or asked for a thing. She was undoubtedly one of the brightest students he had ever had, and yet she allowed herself to remain here with him when he jiggled her fat, and parsed out lotion in squirts, citing its exorbitant cost and her immense size. Her willingness to tolerate this made him feel like her science experiment, and he had made it a mission to break her; he spent much of their time together prodding at her from different angles, watching and waiting for the tipping point. He was vaguely aware and hugely troubled that, despite his calculated meanness, he was nonetheless falling in love with her. This knowledge was, as he just noted, terribly unsettling.

That perfect October night, he waited in the faculty parking lot behind the chemistry building. The day's unsettling thoughts, this feeling that he might call "love" or something just as unnatural, had him distracted and uncomfortable in his clothing. He turned down his rear-view mirror, half afraid that it might be her looking back at him again. But still, he needed assurance of his own perfect, dark-haired, blue-eyed beauty. He needed to ground himself in himself before she arrived. Hesitantly, he looked up in the mirror and indeed it was him and he was every bit as handsome as he ever was and *she should feel very lucky to have my attention and my time.*

Smiling, he righted his mirror, but without his having time to prepare, he saw her walking gracefully down the steps, calm, assured, spectacular. Before he had the thought to rein himself in, his heart leapt into his head and left him unable to pump blood. *What is happening to me?*

Dhanya was walking without any expression on her face. She was not smiling, she was not angry, she was simply walking, with her mouth steadily set and her eyes focused directly at his. She certainly knew he saw her but there was not an expression of greeting or of pleasure. She didn't look as though the sight of him made anything leap inside her. This made him feel something like sadness, but he wasn't sure, because he didn't feel sadness much and he wasn't familiar with its manifestations, exactly. Dr. Russell Worthy quickly shook away the thought that she didn't care, and replaced it with the better thought that she was a little vapid.

Her dress was astonishing and in it she looked like dawn. As big as the sun, and just as brilliant. She reached the car and stood at the door, because it always vexed her. Dr. Worthy, knowing her issue, came around and opened it.

"You look lovely, Dhanya," he offered, as he stood at the door waiting for her to arrange herself inside. She had been pushing the thought of being inside this car out of her mind all day. She was too big for the

Triumph, and she was not yet drunk so there was no pretending it wasn't so. But tonight, somehow, she seemed to fit better. Perhaps it was the two days of eating only tomatoes from the hamburger bar and water chestnuts out of the can that had done it. She had noted that her dress looked better today than it had yesterday too. She considered the nutritional benefits of a tomato/water chestnuts diet, versus its potential for electrolyte imbalance. Considering her relative comfort in this Bond car, considering that her dress after two days of such eating made her sort of feel like a Bond girl in a Bond car, it sounded promising. Tonight, she thought, no bread.

When they arrived at L'Eau, there were enough people assembled to watch as they entered. It was the perfect time, and they were a stunning couple. Her indeterminate youth and her exceptional beauty took focus off her size, and Dr. Worthy knew that he was the most envied man in the room. This was as it should be. He had his hand on Dhanya's elbow and she very gently held a small purse before her in an elegant and yet innocent clutch that he found endearing. Despite himself, he drew her in closer and gave her a kiss on the temple. This was something he had never done. She looked up at him with her lips parted and her eyes wide with surprise. And then she smiled. In that smile, so perfect and white, Dr. Russell Worthy felt a small dizzy spin. Shocked at this reaction, he realized he had not seen her smile so large and free since the Transcend Christianity moment that brought them together. He tightened his brow and cleared his throat. It was a very unsettling feeling. This might have been the moment that changed him forever. But before he might bend down and kiss her again, there was a loud "RUSSELL!"

Turning, they saw an old woman striding powerfully toward them. "RUSSELL!" She looked like a buzzard but was dressed like a peacock. Dhanya, feeling a little happy, looked up at Dr. Worthy hoping for a complicit wink, a smile, a squeeze on the elbow, another kiss on the brow. Instead, he dropped her elbow and returned the large smile. "Edith Holmes. How good it is to see you."

And before Dhanya knew what had happened, Dr. Worthy and this Edith Holmes walked away, leaving her behind, without an introduction, without an explanation, and without even a promise to return. She looked left and right, her beautiful coral dress turning with her in an elaborate lift and spin. She was gorgeous, perfectly attired, a spectacle in her own right, and standing completely alone.

But in the bar, down a small flight of stairs, Mary Maggie O'Neill was watching. She was so vastly more cutthroat and cruel than Dr. Russell Worthy that she considered him a little weak and mealy. But he was hot and so, weak and mealy notwithstanding, she slept with him ferociously and frequently when they were at conferences, and she was perturbed when she called to set up their date for this conference dinner and he had replied that he was bringing someone else. *This must be her. His someone else.* She downed her drink and quickly climbed the stairs toward Dhanya. *If all goes as it surely will, I will have his mouth on my breasts before midnight.*

Standing with his back to the bar and facing out into the crowd, Dr. Russell Worthy tried to regain composure. He worked to draw himself inward to a more comfortable place, but he had no mantra and so nowhere to hide but behind Edith's golden epaulet and Dr. Holmes's hair.

Earlier, moments after he had left Dhanya's side with Edith Holmes, there had been a horrible moment of pulling in his chest. The shock of that sensation and all it stood for still had him reeling. As he descended the open steps toward the bar where all his colleagues were congregated, he had sensed a familiar presence to his left, and before he had fully turned to see, there swept past an unmistakable glissade topped with glittery butter-colored hair. And when he turned to be sure, indeed it was so. Gliding up the steps as he went down was Mary Maggie O'Neill, and even her swiveling backside looked angry.

Dr. Russell Worthy thought he could smell her dangerous smell, like carrion on the breath, and he had felt a pull in his heart he had never known before to rush to the rescue of a beloved. Without thinking, he broke his arm free and spun around to follow that cream-colored suit before it reached the sunset dress and in that moment, he was the best man he had ever been. If he had actually been able to race to Dhanya's side at that instant, he might have been saved from himself, and so then might Dhanya have been saved from him, because that was the magic moment. But Edith Holmes said no.

"Russell, don't you dare try to escape me, you know how Martin's been looking forward to this evening with you." Edith grabbed his arm again and spun him around. Russell craned his neck as he descended, but the courage to behave honorably was new to him, and not deeply rooted. His desire to intervene on Dhanya's behalf was ebbing with each step down. And justly, having seen himself as a better man for a split second, only to have reverted to his less noble persona just as quickly, he felt doubly embittered, and in grave need of buoying up with the weaknesses of others. He ordered a drink.

Dr. Martin Holmes, who looked like the world's ugliest dog except for gleaming white hair rippling in splendor down his back, was quietly holding court. Dr. Holmes's revolting tics and tremors were exactly what Dr. Russell Worthy needed to see. His martini arrived and he downed it at once.

Martin Holmes looked up and a broad grin spread over his face. The effect was that he might have something caught in his throat. "RUSSELL!" Martin Holmes gave his glass to his wife and began the slow extension of his palsied and trembling hand. He was smiling so widely that his tongue seemed to Russell to have expanded. He thought he could see the empty tooth holes in his mouth and he looked around quickly to see if any of the others were witnessing this disgusting spectacle, but they were all either looking raptly at Martin Holmes with nothing but love, or expectantly at Russell, the favorite, the chosen, the protégé. Russell felt his pulse rise again at the sure prospect of having to shake Dr. Holmes's hand, and having seen the insides of his mouth, he was even less inclined and in fact physically repulsed, for sometimes Dr. Holmes pulled him into an embrace. . . .

Cur, mangy mutt, mongrel, ugly-ugly man, put back your paw. "Dr. Holmes! It's so good to see you after so very long."

Dr. Holmes moved closer and instead of taking Russell's hand, which he had gingerly extended, he fell into his chest with a suppressed sigh. Quietly into his ear, Martin Holmes rasped, "Oh, son, it's been such a long time. My boy . . . my boy." Russell could feel wetness on his neck and he wasn't sure whether it was tears or saliva, and then he heard Dr. Holmes sniffle, and with horror he realized that the wetness might be mucus. The prospect of mucus on his neck brought Dr. Russell Worthy fully back to himself, and he released from his mind his five minutes of anxiety and the love it might bespeak, and endured the embrace. He said nothing in return, but closed his eyes for effect, and all those who watched had tears in their own eyes at the touching moment between teacher and student. When he broke from the arms of his disgusting mentor and looked up, he found himself reflected just as he wanted to see himself, in all the pairs of eyes that watched him. He began an insightful discussion about Dr. Holmes's recent paper rethinking "complex equality" à la Michael Walzer while the crowd looked on, mesmerized by his curly hair, his blue eyes, and his keen understandings. Thus entranced, no one noticed him dip the corner of his handkerchief in his vodka and scrub down the right side of his neck. He was again good, clean, and brilliant. Raising his eyes, Dr. Russell Worthy watched from between Edith Holmes's golden epaulet and her husband's Greek god hair. The framing was perfect and the two women above were highlighted in frieze like Hera and Io, and it made him feel like Zeus. He inhaled deeply and asked a passing waiter for another vodka martini. In keeping with the theme, he asked for an olive.

Upstairs, Mary Maggie O'Neill had cornered Dhanya. The child was as helpless as a baby impala.

"Hi, there," she cooed. Dhanya, young and still possessed of her deep instincts, startled and shied away. The woman smiled, thin and cool. "You're here with Russ, aren't you?" Her hair was the color of butter; her black eyebrows were plucked thin and high. She looked like a wicked cheerleader.

Dhanya did not make eye contact, but instead looked wildly about for Dr. Worthy. But he was nowhere to be seen. She dropped her head. On the floor, she counted the black diamonds in between the white diamonds and the tiny gold diamonds within. She focused on her breathing. She had a mantra for escaping, thank God, that her father had taught her (not for escaping but simply as a life skill). The key was to cleanse the mind of all thoughts, he said. But that was too hard, so he taught her to start with this, "Eight eights are sixty-four, multiply by seven. When you're done, carry one, and take away eleven. . . . Eight eights are sixty-four, multiply by seven. When you're done, carry one, and take away eleven. . . . Eight—"

"What?"

The chill of Mary Maggie's voice shattered the fragile peace. She looked up so fast she managed to catch Mary Maggie off guard and the expression she saw on this woman's face would have made her say "mercy" if only she were not too afraid to speak. She had never seen eyes this color; they were somewhere between blue and silver, and on the phantasmic end of the spectrum. They were so light that the pupils looked inked on. So quickly Dhanya might have thought she had imagined the whole thing if only she weren't still shaking, Mary Maggie's face changed to a gently quizzical extension of a deeply kind soul. "What?" she repeated.

Mary Maggie was as cold as marble and as inescapable as a tomb; she was a mausoleum of a woman. Dhanya just looked at her, empty-headed, stunned motionless, and completely silent.

"Oh . . . ?" Mary Maggie began, laying a cool hand on Dhanya's shoulder. "I'm sorry, I thought you said something. . . . I saw you come in with Russ and I just came over to say hi, but it looks like . . ." Here Mary Maggie made a strong show of looking about the room. She looked high and low, even rising on her toes and bending right and left. She lifted her free hand (the other was still on Dhanya's shoulder, which was now as frozen as meat) and put it to her forehead to see farther, as though she were in a parking lot looking for a lost car. ". . . like he's . . . disappeared. . . . Oh, don't worry, honey, we'll just wait for him. I'm sure he'll be back."

Dhanya hadn't said a word yet, and was still as shocked as she had been a few moments ago when this woman had appeared out of nowhere to say hello.

Mary Maggie continued, "You *are* here with Russell, aren't you?"

Dhanya, not knowing what to say, simply nodded. In her head she began again with "The King of Peru," and focused on her breathing. *Eight eights are sixty-four, multiply by seven. When you're done, carry one, and take away eleven. Eight eights are sixty-four, multi- . . .*

As the crowd formed and re-formed groups, and as people came and left, Dr. Worthy soon found that his righteous conviction in the wonder of himself was somewhat challenging to maintain while protected by only the minor phalanx of Dr. and Mrs. Holmes. The view was too clear. Between her left golden epaulet and her husband's Greek god hair, there was a battle playing out in the background and suddenly, the niggling doubt about his virtue and rectitude with regard to his emotional affairs came bubbling up again and it didn't feel good. He called for another drink and took the moment to capture the picture above. Dhanya's juxtaposition beside his arch nemesis made her vulnerability shockingly vivid.

Now, having regained them in his sights, he could feel that same weakness in his knees that he felt walking down the steps knowing that Mary Maggie, the dark lady, was headed for Dhanya. His Dhanya, who sometimes made him wish he could speak in Spanish, because it would sound so much more loving, if ever he should choose to speak lovingly.

"Russell?" Edith Holmes moved her frightening face to the left. She was so close he gasped.

"Oh, I'm sorry. I must have drifted off someplace. . . . Vodka . . . too much before dinner." Russell Worthy lifted his empty glass as proof.

Edith Holmes's eyes widened. "Oh, darling, you are right! Everyone down here must be completely soused; they've all been drinking on nothing but olives and lemon wedges! We need to go get started, don't we? I am sure everyone must have arrived by now; it's already six thirty! You, Russell, will sit with us. Though I did see Mary Maggie. Did you come alone, darling?"

Russell took another quick peek up above. Dhanya was standing with her head down and her hands clutching her purse to her chest. Her hair was long behind her back and the pose made her look like she was praying. "No, Edith, no, I brought someone with me."

He felt his blood drop into his stomach and his fingertips were cool. Drink was making the corners of his eyes crinkle and there was a heaviness in his face that made him afraid to take a step, like he may have compromised his depth perception. But all that being so, he was a great, great man. And his innocent young girl was in the hands of an eggless automaton with no hope of happiness and he was a great, great man. He was her knight in shining armor and he would lead her out of the dragon's lair and seat her on a golden throne strung with . . . flowers. He would love her and take care of her and she would never again have to be alone. He would be there.

"Edith, I have to go and find my date. I will find you upstairs at dinner. Dr. Holmes, I'll see you in a few minutes." And without another word, Russell placed his empty glass on the bar, took his last look from below at the two women and set off to the rescue.

Gaining poise with every step, he climbed up from the bar floor. He could hear the room abuzz with his name. Every pair of bisyllabic words sounded like "Russell Worthy," and he was emboldened by what appeared to be as cinematically aesthetic a path as was ever walked. There was nothing but heads, and backs of heads, and blurred faces engaged in a murmuring back noise, while all around the periphery he imagined each head was turned toward him, each mouth shaping his name in slow motion as he headed for the women in spotlight.

As he approached, he could hear Mary Maggie's voice and it reminded him of all the times he had heard it before. She had a quick-change voice that made people who cared nervous, but let Russell know he was with a kindred spirit. She was a comfort in that uncomfortable way because Russell knew that nothing he did would register for a moment as anything more or less than what it was, and nothing really mattered. Slapping Mary Maggie during an argument might elicit immediate intercourse or it might make her grab her purse to go get Chinese for dinner, saying, "I think we both need a little space." Twenty minutes later, she would arrive with a handprint on her cheek and a bag of lo mein. If she slapped him, he could rip off her clothes and take her on the floor, or he could hit her back. Either way, it was all the same. Mary Maggie was a woman with no notions of the way it should go except her way. She sounded like a Valkyrie. At this moment, she was speaking in a complicit, honeyed tone, and he heard, ". . . it was amazing, just spectacular. We were with the whole group, you know, all of us, not just me and Russ, I mean, we were together of course, but all of us were there. It was so much fun . . . so romantic. Have you ever been to Vancouver?"

Russell Worthy walked up in time to answer, "I don't believe you have, baby, have you?" He came between them and slid his arm around Dhanya's wide back, and like a harness, he held her up. She turned to him with a fourteen-year-old look, an eight-year-old look. Her eyelashes were glittering, and her mouth trembled at the corners. Her eyes were too huge for his mild drunk and his teetering emotional state. He was felled by the look on her face. He felt the seething desire to take

Mary Maggie's jaw in his hand and lift her off the ground. In his mind, he imagined raising her to his height and drawing her in so close that his shouting voice would send shock waves through her cheeks, *LEAVE HER ALONE.* Instead, he bent his head and kissed Dhanya's temple. Dhanya seemed startled by the gesture; it was so new. She raised her head and quietly, answered, "No, Dr. Worthy, I haven't." Russell crumpled.

In this simple reaction, Russell saw himself as he was for one pure moment. He felt suddenly choke-chested and despicable. In that instant, the urge to run was overwhelming, to return to the belly of the bar where he was what he thought he was instead of what Dhanya knew he was and what he was loath to admit he was. He was crawling through his skin.

If ever Mary Maggie felt happy, it was in moments like these. She was unendingly fortified by the failures of others. Watching these two was as satisfying a scene as she had ever witnessed. Dropping her chin and raising her brows, she asked in a disbelieving voice, "Russ . . . please don't tell me you make her call you *Dr. Worthy*?"

Russell Worthy glowered and audibly breathed, for he had nothing to say in response. He kneaded a roll of fat on Dhanya's back between his finger and thumb. He had fought the temptation to pinch her back since the first time he felt her in the moonlight. The fat was as inviting as molding clay, as bread dough, as stress balls, but now, confronted with his shame, he squeezed hard and dug in a nail. Dhanya, without as much as a sharp intake of breath, stood still. Russell, looking down at her beside him, could see her jaw clenching in the pulse at her temple. Her restraint made him so much more foolish and bad. *When you are hurt you should scream out, you stupid girl.* He pinched her so hard, it hurt his hand. Before his eyes and to his great satisfaction, Dhanya blinked slowly; a tear perched on her lashes glided down her cheek. Winning here infused him with a sense of dominion over the situation and he lowered his head with disdain. Shaking it from side to side, he chuckled.

"Mary Maggie." This he extended over several seconds. "It's so good to see you are inflicting yourself on the innocent as usual!" Russell Worthy lifted a piece of Dhanya's ice-black hair to his lips and kissed it. He smiled with only his lips and it made him gorgeous. When he dropped her hair, Dhanya collected the lot of it and threw it over the opposite shoulder. It cascaded and it made her equally gorgeous.

"Russell . . ." Mary Maggie was fighting irritation that these two were such a beautiful couple. Together, as she recalled, she and Russell had looked as dangerous as paired warheads. "I have no doubt that if she was innocent when you found her, she is innocent no more." Mary Maggie leaned into Dhanya and smiled a big supersweet smile and crinkled her nose. She laid a finger on Dhanya's cheek. "I bet you're having some fun. As I remember, Russell can be . . . how should I put this . . . exceptionally . . . solicitous."

Dhanya felt her chest grow hot. The blood there, combined with gaslight lamps on the wall and candles on the tables, made Dhanya seem almost the same sunset color as her dress. She seemed to be disappearing entirely.

"Here I am talking about Russell's special sexual talents and we haven't even been properly introduced!" She poked Russell in the chest. He narrowed his eyes and kneaded on the bruise he had raised on Dhanya's back. She winced and shied.

"I am Mary Maggie O'Neill. Russ and I did our docs together at Harvard." Dhanya smiled weakly and shook her extended hand.

Mary Maggie turned to Russell and exclaimed, "Oh, Russ, she is just so adorable!" Turning back to Dhanya, she simpered, "I used to be Russ's *you*!"

Russell Worthy said with affected calm, "Mary Maggie, this is my—" And here, in a move as dramatic as being caught in an act of deceit, as panicked as forgetting lines on stage, as humiliating as losing an erection, Dr. Russell Worthy stopped. He did not know what to say. His dive into the ridiculous again had him spinning, looking for egress. They had never had that conversation before. *She calls me Dr. Worthy.*

Mary Maggie's eyes narrowed with a view to checkmate. In all the time she had known Russell, she had never seen him with nothing. And the girl hadn't said a word yet. She was an easy kill. She had begun to anticipate his mouth on her breasts by midnight when, from this girl, a sensible answer.

"Hi, I'm Dhanya. I'm Dr. Worthy's girlfriend."

The Setups

Dr. Raman Nair sat in his office perusing the promising proposal of a promising doctoral student who had hair that grew almost entirely backward as though he was from a planet with strong winds. In his long association with the Chinese, it seemed to him that their hair, if it defied gravity, was far more likely to grow almost entirely up, and this particular phenomenon, be it tonsorial or genetic, always gave him pause. The boy's name was Ryan but he was Chinese, and when his parents, whom he had met on a few occasions, said his name, it sounded like "Lion." For this reason, Ryan's backward hair always seemed like a mane to Dr. Nair, and therefore got his extra attention. Sometimes he wondered if anyone else noticed.

He was deeply engaged in Ryan's project and he was actively jotting notes, thoughts and suggestions, which was his favorite thing to do, when his watch alarm went off signaling lunchtime. He put Ryan's papers aside and began the monumental production of rising from his desk, an enormous desk that resembled a small apartment complex. Dr. Raman Nair pushed back his chair as far as it would go, which was only about four inches, and turned to the right as far as he could go, which was only about twenty-three degrees, which put his right knee almost out from under his desk. He held the armrests and pushed himself up slightly, which allowed enough clearance for his thigh to shimmy out over the right armrest and to land on the floor. Once this was done, the left leg was easy; he just pushed the chair back a few more inches and stepped away. He got his lunch from the mini-fridge, and then squeezed himself between the desk and the wall. Then he took a deep breath and savored his freedom. He stopped at his window that faced down into the campus and took his deep breaths.

The key was to cleanse the mind of all thoughts. To wipe free the random firing in the brain, and to focus on the slowing of the heart. To slow the heart, one must slow the breathing; he self-ministered, relaxing his breath without counting, without rhymes. His eyes were closed and his dark eyelids pulsed slightly with his effort to quiet them; the purple skin undulated with the back and forth of his busy eyeballs until slowly they slowed . . . and slowed . . . and slowed. By the time Dr. Raman Nair's purple eyelids were still, his pulse could not be seen by the naked eye. His thick brown lips were slightly parted and his hands hung limply at his sides. The only notable movement was the rhythmic glinting of a huge, round, golden Ayyappan pendant marking the slight rise and fall of his enormous stomach.

When Dr. Nair opened his eyes a few minutes later, he felt as if he had just awakened from a quick nap. He turned to his desk to retrieve his lunch and before he reached the doorway, his phone rang. He sighed with the hunger of having gone thirteen minutes past the noon hour.

Putting down his lunch and picking up a pad and pencil, he answered the phone, "Hello, this is Nair."

"O? It's me." It was Jaya. She sounded like there was something.

"Mmm?"

"Gopi called, just now." Jaya was sounding like there was something.

"Is it all okay?" Dr. Nair sat atop his desk at the corner, where it was doubly fortified. Her call was for something and he did not want to be standing if it was bad.

"O, it's okay, it's okay, but you know that Thalissery P. C. Krishnan Nair? His father was that K. P. Nair who was at UC College?"

"The judge, P. C. Krishnan Nair?"

"Yes, yes, Gopi called just now and said that that P. C. Krishnan Nair is here now . . ." There was more.

"Yes, then?" Dr. Nair was sure there was more and he found he was slightly breathless and that he had to swallow.

"Yes, he is here now for six months. In New York." Her parsed dole was trying his patience.

"So?" Dr. Raman Nair did not want to think faster than his wife allowed, and he wasn't sure which way it would go. It could be that someone needed money, for all he knew. It could be that he had to drive to New York and pick someone up, or that P. C. Krishnan Nair was coming this side and though he barely knew him he would have to host him and take him all about Washington and show all the sights for a whole week. Perhaps he had died . . . while in the States. Perhaps he had to identify his dead body, ride in a hearse in New York, see to a cremation . . . who knew. Dr. Raman Nair was peaked and bristled. "So, then?"

"*Anh, anh.* Yes, so, Gopi called . . . and there is a boy."

This was the line. Not death, but a boy, Gopi called to say there was a boy. And of course, he had a girl, and the family of P. C. Krishnan Nair could only be good, for all he knew.

The room to the right upon entering the home of Dr. Raman Nair was set up for company and no one entered there except to vacuum, dust and entertain. This night, Dr. Raman Nair sat in here, in this dazzlingly furnished room, in his capacious Colombian armchair in the light of his glowing Taj Mahal inlaid stonework table and listened to the baseline hum of his sleeping house. The sound of appliances and central air at rest was not quiet, but it was prosperous, and he was so thankful for his place in this world, but the unsettling burning in his stomach was out of keeping with his usual state of satisfaction. This threatening instability was one he wanted to meditate away, but it simply wouldn't lift. His chest slightly throbbed, and he was unable to capture his maharaja complacency and the concomitant generosity of spirit that such a feeling of plenty could bring. His deepest instincts sensed a looming disaster and, though he had stood at windows all over his house to do his breathing, his purple eyelids fluttered and fluttered, and his pendant trembled with the tachycardic rhythms of a heart that waited for a firstborn child to return from disappearing into the night.

Just before dinnertime, he had come home, full of hope. This Thalissery P. C. Krishnan Nair had heard of his girls. That they were beautiful, that they were educated, that they were well behaved, and even that they were fat, and he was not fazed.

"Gopi said he asked if it was so that Veena was fat and he told him, Gopi told him, that she was fat anyway but very beautiful, and Gopi said that he said, 'That is okay, a little bit of fat makes a woman happy!' Gopi said that he told him, 'Oh, yes, they are all very happy,' and he also told him that Veena was sensible and calm and very graceful with a blessed kind of face."

"*Anh.*" Dr. Raman Nair swayed his head in acknowledgement, his beaming pride growing in his heart.

Jaya continued, "Anyway, he was very pleased. So he is coming this side on Saturday—tomorrow—and he is going to bring his son."

"His name again . . . ?" Dr. Raman Nair had forgotten this from lunch. He remembered some things: he was an orthopedic doctor already finished residency, finishing fellowship in Boston. He was thirty years old. Or thirty-one or -two. . . .

"Jayan." Jaya smiled. It seemed fated.

Dr. Raman Nair could see his own hope reflected in his wife's eyes that too were filled with both hope and certainty. It was the way that it had fallen in their laps, without all the strange circumstances of times past, when it had come from someone who didn't know them well. These were such honorable people. It wasn't like the others that he didn't know much about, who came to him from somebody's somebody . . . the boy with the owl face whose family roots were suspect, and the one from Chicago who had shown up in a T-shirt and jeans and had only talked to Usha, though he knew whom he was there to meet, or the one with the handlebar mustache who had taken Veena out and told her that the Puerto Rican girls in New York had "big bazoombas" but that they had nothing on her. A boy from this Thalissery P. C. Krishnan Nair family could not be bad. . . .

A quiet had seeped up around them, muting all but the essential, and the essential was quiet too. "Will she be happy?" Dr. Raman Nair asked his wife. They stood close together and spoke in low voices. He lowered his chin slightly, looking down at her sandaled feet. His love for his child made him whisper.

Jaya tilted her head to the side and lowered her neck to catch his eyes; she buoyed him up to her face. "One way or another," she touched her husband's wrist for a moment, "she will be happy."

That night the table was almost full. Only Dhanya was missing. And Gita, whom anyway they had talked to the other day, bubbling and giddy. Manoj had come to eat fish, and the feeling of abundance and family made the food taste good. Muthachan, with his teeth out, sat at the head of the table opposite his son, and ate with glee. His gum-smacking joy at each mouthful made them laugh and tease him like an infant; the girls got up from time to time to kiss his cheek and stroke his hair. They wiped dribbles off his lips and chin, and he screwed up his face and turned away from the napkin. He reemerged fresh faced with a wide-open smile, pink and fleshy, his tongue twisted to the right. Muthachan in a good mood was such a rare gem of a moment and they all felt the excellence in the air. Jaya stood to his right and removed all the bones as she always did, and though these days he usually screamed to his son that she was injecting poison into random morsels, on this evening, at this moment, Muthachan called her darling and told his son that he always said Jaya was much better than him and that she was marrying entirely beneath herself. Into this blessed sanctum, how could any news be received in any way but in the spirit in which it was offered, full of love and hope and auspicious thoughts and feelings?

Pushing back from the table to release his stomach, Dr. Raman Nair inhaled and exhaled. He was signaling his satisfaction and that he was done.

"Are you finished?" Jaya asked though she knew.

"Mmm . . ." Dr. Raman Nair closed his eyes. "Don't finish," he announced to his girls, who were beginning to make signs of doneness. The magnitude of the cleanup from a Friday meal when everyone was present was something that demanded evacuation of all uninvolved parties, also known as the men, and he wasn't quite finished with the requirements of the evening. The girls settled back down and started some other chitchat, drawing their fingers across their empty plates and absently licking. Muthachan was quiet. He was petting Jaya's hand as she put tiny bites of boneless tilapia into his plate. His hand was covered with a soft coating of smushed rice, and he was carefully transferring some of this wealth to his daughter-in-law's fingers, with such gentle affection that Jaya was a little choked up. It was like the way he used to be, but with fishy rice.

"Veenamol." Dr. Nair sat up. Veena looked up from her sisters and saw something in his eyes that made her stomach rise to her throat. Immediately, she tasted acid-soaked mango curry and the pepper from her fish and her abdomen felt ominously suspended over a brink, as if she were going to jump out of a plane. The second and a half between the moment her father spoke her name to the moment he spoke again was more full of portent than any other second and a half of her life thus far.

"Tomorrow, one Jayan Nair will come here to see you." Dr. Raman Nair opened his eyes to say this, and afterward had closed them again. Thus, he didn't notice that the color of the air had changed from golden to gray with the sharp intake of air by so many large-lunged girls. Only the chemical atmosphere remained.

Having sniffed the change in the smell that rose from the table, Jaya looked up from her fish and saw that the color of the air made all her girls' faces look ashen. She quickly interjected, "*Shye*, don't say it like that. He is not coming here to *see* her." This way made it sound so bad a thing, she thought, like a sale or a something, like some merchandise . . . like it doesn't sound nice. "No, no, he is not coming here to see you. He is coming here to *meet* you." This sounded much better. But somehow it was still gray, and there was a growing fug about the table.

All the sisters swallowed one collective swallow that made a noise, like the thunk of dropping a tennis ball into its canister, and Veena simply stared. Her lack of response made Jaya rightly nervous, but Dr. Nair took it as happy obedience, the way he liked to imagine the world should operate.

"Of course, of course he is coming to meet her . . . and to see her too, no?" Dr. Raman Nair laughed a little bit, a "humpha." "They will come for dinner, and we should have a good time of it, they are coming a long way. . . . Maybe we should bring samosas from Bombay Memories?" Dr. Raman Nair was beginning his big planning, because of the happy obedience. Veena was so still that Jaya swallowed a tiny swallow too; hers made no sound except in her own head, where it sounded like the hopeful drop of a penny in a wishing well.

"Veenu?" Jaya quietly asked. Veena broke her fixed gaze at her father with some effort and turned her head. Muthachan looked at her with his gums slammed shut and his lips pursed out. His eyes were like a baby's who has just had something wonderful taken away and his brows were drawn down tight. He held her mother's finger with desperate need, stroking his rice smush into the grooves at her knuckle. Veena noticed all this before she quietly lifted her eyes to her mother's face.

"Is it okay?" Jaya asked. Dr. Raman Nair looked at his wife with a questioning face. *Is what okay*, he wondered. *Samosas from Bombay Memories?* She was not looking at him, but at the girl, and when he looked at her, he no longer saw the happy obedience. His stomach lifted a little too, he felt his breath catch and his blood rise in his face.

What had happened next made him squirm to remember. He rose from his Colombian seat once more to look out the window. How could she have left like that? *How could she have done this to me?* His heart screamed and he thought of all the things that could happen out there, driving in a rage. Is she still driving in a rage? Did she go somewhere to sit down, to stop the car? Would she stop the car on the road? Would she pull into a parking lot? Would she stay with a friend? Where would she go? Dr. Nair listened in the quiet and his heart leapt each time a car moved in the distance, each time the light brightened on the street. It was two in the morning. When would she come home?

It couldn't have been any worse than it was without bloodshed. As Jaya waited for the answer to her question, the table pulsed with dread. Veena asked, "And what if it isn't?"

"What do you mean, 'isn't,' " Dr. Nair interjected.

"Isn't okay, I mean; what if it isn't okay?" Veena was raising her voice.

"What do you mean, 'isn't okay'?" Dr. Nair rejoined. He was a little confused. He didn't understand. This had caught him off guard and he was not one to put up with being caught off guard. He answered the telephone with a pad and pencil to avoid just this flustered feeling. His purple eyelids were as dark as eggplants and he was now risen up forward in his chair with both hands raised.

"I MEAN, what if it isn't okay for Jayan Nair to come here from wherever to *see me*?"

"*Meet* you, *meet* you." Jaya shot her husband a dark look.

"Meet you, see you, isn't the issue," Dr. Nair proclaimed.

"What I am saying is, *what will you do if it is not okay with me to be met or seen by Jayan Nair from wherever*?" Veena was still raising her voice.

There was a moment of nothing. The sisters were looking from their father to Veena and back. Shanti was rubbing at both her elbows, each in turn, as was her habit in times of tension, and even the cat clock on the wall looked left-right-left-right while his tail wagged opposite. If it had suddenly begun turning widdershins, there would only have been that much more proof that nothing that was true before applied now.

"He is a *doctor*!" Dr. Raman Nair said, for no reason other than that he didn't know what to say. Jaya nodded with her eyebrows up, for this must count for something. Muthachan was holding her finger so tightly that it hurt, but she didn't have the will to pull it free.

"Okay, what I am saying then is, *what will you do if it is not okay with me to be met or seen by DR. Jayan Nair*?"

"Oh nononono. We won't have any of that." Dr. Nair closed his eyes and shook his head slowly. His hands were up as if to let Veena know that the argument was over, that he had already made up his mind. "You don't have to do anything, you don't have to feel any obligation. Just meet. Just meet and see. You don't have to do anything, but they are coming tomorrow. This is a very good family, you know. This is a very good family and we know each other from long time back and they are coming here and you have no say in that at all. Just meet and see. You don't have to do anything. But they are coming here to see you and all of us, and you will have to just meet. Nothing has to happen from it, just meet and see. Just meet." Dr. Nair got up from the table and stood above them all. The girls were all looking from him to Veena, and Manoj was just staring at his plate. Veena looked at her father and her face grew darker.

"Well then, if they are coming here because they are such good friends from so long back, they don't need to have me here at all, do they? Because I WON'T BE HERE." Veena stood as well, and stared hard.

Dr. Raman Nair's entire face flushed eyelid purple. He looked like Hades.

"YOU WILL BE WHERE I TELL YOU TO BE." Dr Nair throttled the air in front of him. He was shaking with the unexpected turn of the night, of his news, of his sense of things. He could see moves ahead and he knew it would not turn out the way it should. He knew there was more. The thought of what might be coming enraged him. The prospect of his shame being witnessed by these strangers who would come tomorrow unless he told lies or, even worse, truths, was too much. Dr. Raman Nair bent forward and leaned on the table with both his clenched fists. He whispered a hissing threat that vibrated the gray air like sound waves off an explosion, "I will not allow you to shame me."

Veena threw her father a hateful look that stabbed him as deep as a poisoned arrow, which hurt so much more because she had never looked at him this way. She struggled to get free from the table that was phalanxed by two enormous sisters who couldn't scoot in far enough to let her pass. Her mother, afraid of what would happen if she left the table before they came to accord, yanked her finger free from Muthachan and squeezed her way to her daughter. She held her arm, trying to pull her back into the fold.

"*Mole*, *mole*, he is coming to see you and if you aren't here, what will we say, *mole*, you have to be here because he is coming to see you all the way from Boston to see you. Please *mole*, what will we say, you have to be here. You might like him, he sounds very nice and this is such a good family. His father is a judge!" Veena was shrugging her off like an irksome child, she swatted at her fingers as they clamped around her elbow.

Muthachan, who had held Jaya's finger like a lifeboat as the table rocked with anger, felt abandoned and afraid. He reached under the table for his stick and started pounding the floor. "I TOLD YOU THIS WOMAN WOULD ONLY BRING YOU PAIN AND SORROW, BUT YOU DIDN'T LISTEN TO ME AND YOU BROUGHT HER INTO OUR LIVES LIKE A PLAGUE OF WHORES!" Muthachan boomed, pointing his stick at his once beloved daughter-in-law, who had known it was only a matter of time. He raised his stick over his head and swatted at the air. Shanti, who sat closest, stood to reach the stick, but Muthachan pointed it at her menacingly. She backed up, but still Muthachan defended himself. He pounded the table with ferocious strength.

The dishes shattered with catastrophic crashes. The rice exploded into the air amid shards of blue porcelain, and the whole thing showered down on them like hail.

He turned to his son and accused, "YOU WANT ME TO DIE LIKE A LEPER WITHOUT MY FEET OR THE TIP OF MY NOSE AND I TELL YOU I WILL NOT. I WILL DIE A WHOLE MAN, BEFORE SHE SEES ME WASTED LIKE A LIVING CORPSE, EATING POISONED FISH FROM HER HANDS WHILE YOU WATCH AND LAUGH FROM THE OTHER SIDE OF THE TABLE? *I RAISED YOU.* AND NOW THAT I AM OLD AND I HAVE LOST MY FEET, YOU WILL LEAVE ME TO BE WATCHED OVER BY A VENOMOUS POISONER . . ." Here he paused and turned back to Jaya. Pointing his stick inches from her chest he hissed, "*Lucretia Borgia. . . .*" These last were squeezed out through Muthachan's rice-mush-coated lips. He seemed to be foaming at the mouth. Muthachan looked about the table menacingly; his enemies were everywhere and he knew not how to break free. Jaya made her move back toward her father-in-law and fought with him to remove the stick from his hands. He shouted an aggrieved "AAAAAAAAAAAAAAHH-HHH" before collapsing to his chair in defeat. Shanti took the stick and hid it between the refrigerator and the wall, where it went when Muthachan lost his mind.

In the ensuing moment of quiet, they all heard a car start and drive away, and then they noticed that Veena had escaped in the chaos. The room lost its air entirely. It looked like a day-after battlefield. They all sat back down, except for Jaya, who stood behind Muthachan picking rice from his silver white hair.

An hour later, Veena appeared at the door of her beloved with nothing but her keys in her hand and a tear-soaked face. The hair around her temples curled with humid uncertainty and profound awareness of what she had done. George stood on the threshold and held her face between his hands. She was too worn to cry now, and she was too much at his mercy. She was afraid and he smelled it on her breath that she let out in uneven, metallic puffs. She couldn't tell him what she had done for him, because sometimes the greatest love is not enough to do *all* the things, Veena knew. She could not ask him if she was enough, and so she stood there and looked. Air-colored moths flitted too near as they stared at one another wordlessly. George drew her inside without asking what brought her, because it really didn't matter as long as she was there.

He led her back to his Spartan room and took her down with him and they swam for hours in her hair and tears and his sweat and all the other pools they made with their love and when they came up for air, there was space for talk, but only the softest whispers could fit without scattering the bending arc of moonlight in which they lay.

Veena's whispers always rose from her soul. They were moving whispers, and this is why George bit back his tears when she turned on her side and faced him and whispered, "George . . . are we still in our falling-in-love time?"

He opened and closed his eyes in rhythm with his heartbeat, which he could feel in her fingertips on his chest. He brought his hands from behind his head and held her hand there, and she raised her leg over his. Thus wrapped, he felt more securely cocooned and so it seemed entirely plausible (which it was) and equally simple (which it wasn't) when he said, "We will be together forever, and our falling-in-love time will never end."

Veena, who knew so much, smiled into his shoulder. He felt her happiness there and the warmth of her spreading lips over his skin danced down his arm and through his neck. He was aquiver with her happiness and he turned to her and kissed her teeth in the dark.

Just Be Good

Veena returned home in the full morning light and when she turned the key in the lock, she could hear the exhale of relief from all corners of the house; her ears popped from the notable change in air pressure. No one asked her where she had been, for the sisters already knew, and neither parent wanted to know. Her grandfather was still sleeping. His night was spent living a wonderful life where he was able-bodied and virile, where the sun was hot on his skin and his teeth firmly rooted in his gums. When he awoke, as he did hourly and semihourly to his decrepitude and itches, he moaned softly in his sleep. It had been this kind of night for everyone, who remembered when, only a few weeks or days ago, everything had seemed so easy and pleasant, everyone so happy. When they startled back into the current situation, they all sighed for what might be about to happen that might shake them from their pretty perches, introduce dangerous, ill-omened, ill-fated, nastier portions of life. They sighed over the incessant march forward, out with the old, in with the new. They all felt it, a sea change.

She went upstairs without looking for anyone to talk to and washed up again, though she had washed up before, and she changed her clothing, which was the same in which she had left. Sisters came and sat on her bed and she did not ask how it had been, for she could see by their dropsied faces that no one had slept a wink.

"Let's get out of here for a while," she said.

"You just got home," they replied, for they were afraid.

"I need to go again, but I need to go with you." She looked out the window for her bird, but he was too ashamed of her to show his face. He wouldn't even tweet. "Let's go to Tyson's."

Shanti, the baby, went to her mother, who sat on the edge of her bed and watched the door. "Mommy, Chechi came home, and she wants to go to the mall with me and Mira Chechi." Shanti looked at the floor because her mother's timorous face made her wish they would all just stay home, crowd along her arms, and watch her cook. This was the way to erase all the pain and make things right. Shanti wondered how it would sound to her sisters if she suggested it.

"You tell her to come here," she said. Shanti looked up and blinked and did not move. The mother saw in her young child's rooted stance that it could not happen and that she could not bear to see her mother further hurt. She too could not bear to be further hurt. "Okay, you go shopping." Jaya looked away. Before the door closed, she added, "Be good."

"We will," Shanti answered. She vowed that whatever suggestions were made, she would make her sisters be good.

Veena, Mira and Shanti wandered up and down the mall quietly looking at clothing that was ten sizes too small on mannequins that were curiously alive. In one store window the models were actually alive and stood stiff like mannequins. Shanti wondered if there was a message in this.

The three girls silently entered the kaleidoscope store and wandered about. There was a grief to the moment, for no reason but fear. Nothing had happened yet but that it was apparent to all the sisters that this relationship was going nowhere but on and on and converging more and more on perfectly perfect. George was Veena's unbreakable bond, and if she didn't spend the rest of her life with him, she would be alone, and if she didn't spend the rest of her life alone, she would certainly spend the rest of her life aware that she was not with her other half. She would berate her wrong husband, she would find fault with his paunch, and his breath, and his simpering expression when he greeted guests at the door. Across time zones, she would wince when George nicked his face shaving; from the other end of the earth, she would cry like a twin if he ever died. There was no end to this thing. She needed courage because for Dr. Raman Nair, and certainly for CV Thomas and Elizabeth, this was never going to happen but over someone's dead body. Of course, they didn't know yet . . . the fear was purely speculative. But these girls, and George, they had all seen it before. It never went well.

So quietly as to be a near whisper, Shanti murmured . . . "Why did he have to be a Catholic?" She was holding a beautiful red kaleidoscope to her eye. Inside there were amber and blue stars and they made a little miracle of things all contained in the end of the tube. *I wish I could fit our whole lives into the end of a giant kaleidoscope, I would just turn it and turn it until Chechi and George fell together and then I would carefully put it back in the holder and everyone would just stay where they were.* Shanti replaced the kaleidoscope and picked up another.

"Because God is a mischief maker," Mira answered from nearby.

"Shhh! Don't talk about God!" Shanti replied a little indignantly. She was frightened by blasphemy. She knocked on the wooden case that held the fancy kaleidoscopes to ward off the evil spirits. "He is not a mischief maker."

"Certainly God is a mischief maker." Shanti trilled her tongue. Mira continued, "Veena has had hundreds of opportunities to fall in love with other people, and she has even been introduced to matches, but what does she do? She falls in love at first sight with a boy likely to cause Daddy to have a heart attack. And within four hours she is *irrevocably* in love for the first time in her life? And then to top it off, he feels the same way so there is nothing left to do but get married? *And* he is the right age, he is good-looking, he is a doctor, he is from a good family, he is kind, he doesn't smoke, he doesn't have a drinking problem, he went to Princeton *and* to Harvard *and* to Johns Hopkins? *He's from KERALA*. . . . BUT he is a Catholic?" Mira's one eye was closed and she was looking into a huge kaleidoscope that needed both her hands. "Note please, this Thalissery P. C. Krishnan Nair's son? Orthopedic surgeon, Kerala. Good family. George Thomas? Orthopedic surgeon, Kerala. Good family." She replaced it in its stand. "*Oh* yeah, God is a mischief maker. He enjoys this stuff." She grinned and tossed up her eyebrows.

Shanti knocked on wood and quietly trilled. "Well, shh anyway . . ."

Veena fingered the kaleidoscopes and listened in. Absently touching cold, pretty things that she had no interest in made her eyes transfix. She was awash in that weird sensation of having her eyeballs stuck while her mind desperately struggled to catch hold of something to free them from these shiny, colored tubes. She remembered George stuck on the sunset. . . . With a huge sigh she felt too fatigued to continue with things the way they were.

"I can't live without him," she said. Her mouth turned downward and she put her hands over her face and cried. Shanti and Mira could not remember seeing their *chechi* cry. Ever. Even in these last weeks their sister had been buoyed up by her falling-in-love time, and though they all knew where it would have to end, Veena had the shocking ability to put bad thoughts out of mind. She just smiled and looked at her Inner Harbor picture and when she was too troubled or pained or shamed, she went to sleep.

With charged focus and apprehension, her sisters bustled her out of the shop and back through the mall. The kiosks running along the center might have the solution to the problem at hand, in their marblesque basins of rising smoke, in their jars of scented potions, in their mini magic carpets, in their invisible ink pens. Shanti, following close behind, wished again. *I wish I could go to that kiosk and buy a box of Magic Pens. The box might feel warmer than normal, or it might vibrate or something. But I wouldn't notice. I would get home and take out some paper and write the invisible question, "What should Chechi do about her and George being in love?" And then suddenly, the answer would appear . . . in magenta. . . .*

They walked like women consoling women, through Hecht Company and out to the parking garage, down the stairs and out to the second level and into Veena's cobalt blue Audi. Mira took the keys and the driver's seat. Shanti got in the back. Veena was still standing outside leaning on the car and weeping. Mira put the key in the ignition and waited. She met Shanti's eyes in the rearview mirror and they felt the gravity of the moment. The catharsis. There were decisions being made outside, being written with tears on the body of the car. The answer would be revealed in a salty script and by the time they got home, Shanti thought, they would know what to do. She got out of the car and stood next to her sister, who had never been this way in her whole life. She stood there and tried faith. She tried to read the runes, the temporary etchings in tears, the rhythm of the sobs. She tried to divine the outcome of the most catastrophic event in her tenderly tended family life. She stood there, and her *chechi* sobbed hard so her chest rose and fell against the window, shaking the whole car.

In a few minutes, Veena stood straight again and gathered her breath. She wiped her face against her forearm and her hands. She looked at her sister and stroked her hair once, to calm her. She told her to get back in the car, and she got in herself. Mira started the car and Veena said, "Don't go home yet. We need to find Gitammai."

"What?" Mira didn't understand. From the backseat, Shanti sat forward and thrust her head between; she would not be left out of this decision.

"Just go toward Gitammai's house." Veena urgently put her hand on the gearshift, to no avail as she was not driving, and she fixed a hard look on her sister who sat immobile, looking at her like she was crazy.

"We don't even know where she lives."

"She lives in Quiet Pond!"

Mira looked at Veena. "Are you kidding?"

"She does."

"Which is . . . according to my last conversation with her, Chechi, somewhere near Criglersville. Do you know where Criglersville is? Does anyone who is not Criglersvillian know where Criglersville is? We don't even know her number."

"We'll get a map," Veena insisted. "We need to talk to her. She'll know what to do."

Mira sighed in exasperation, but put her hand on the gearshift, for it was not in the nature of any but Usha to defy their oldest sister, who was so wise and full of sense. Mira put the car in reverse but sat, unsure, her own deep instincts unwilling to make such bad matters so much worse.

From nowhere, Shanti, baby of them all, raised herself up between her sisters and pushed the gear back into park.

"What are you doing? Sit down, Shanti. We are going to Quiet Pond to find Gitammai."

"Okay," Shanti said quietly. "We can go to Quiet Pond to find Gitammai. But we are going home first." She was nearly whispering and her voice quavered slightly like slow breath through a whistle. "We can just go home and tell them we are going to see Gitammai and we can pack a bag and give her a call and get the directions and we can go there like—" She paused and stayed still, with her hand guarding the car in park, "like good girls." She breathed more regularly. "We don't have to be bad. We can just go home and go visit Gitammai like good girls."

When they got home, their mother was preparing for the visit of Thalissery P. C. Krishnan Nair and his son, for they had been invited and if there was nothing else to offer but dinner, then dinner should be exceptionally good, Jaya thought. The girls helped their mother in silence and nothing was said of the matter, for no one wanted to arouse Muthachan with hysterics before company. Later that evening, they all saw that Jayan Nair was a very nice and good man, and pleasant, and pleasantly shy, and yet not at all sheepish. An altogether very good catch. When later the two sat alone to talk as was the custom, Veena, recently aware that she did not have to be bad, said with great truthfulness and modesty, "I am very sorry, but I am not interested in pursuing this any further, you seem to be a wonderful person, but I am in love with another man and I have not yet told my parents and, because I would like to spare them any embarrassment, I wish you would not tell yours. I did not know my parents' intentions until just yesterday, or I would have told them not to waste your time with such a long trip. I am very sorry."

Dr. Jayan Nair smiled gently and said with a simple and quiet voice, "I wish you the greatest happiness in your life. My visit has not been a waste; your family has been most gracious. My family and I will see the sights tomorrow and it will be an altogether enjoyable trip." He laughed a little. "And I will never tell your secret."

That evening, when the family drove away, his father asked him, "What did you think?" And Jayan answered, "Mm." Which left them nothing to say, and so the matter dropped without anyone's being any wiser, so discerning a man was Dr. Jayan Nair.

And a bit later than that, Veena, phalanxed by her sisters, stood before her parents and said, "Tomorrow, we would like to go see Gitammai for the day." Dr. Raman Nair and Jaya just looked at each other and neither had the strength for questions or answers. He looked in his book and wrote down Gita's telephone number while his wife turned away and went upstairs.

Veena made the call with a soft, needy voice that her *ammai* heard on the other end with great worry. When she hung up the phone and turned around, Dr. Raman Nair asked only, "Will you be home tomorrow itself?"

Veena answered, "Yes, we will leave early and return in the evening." And she and her father looked at one another blankly, for they both knew that soon something was going to break free, but neither had the strength for questions or answers. Then she and her sisters went to bed without talking. Under her covers, Veena felt the prickle of understanding. An epiphany coming on. *I don't have to be bad. I can just speak and behave like . . . a good girl. I can just be good.* Freed by the thought, Veena slept peacefully dreaming she was beside her beloved.

Wonderful Secrets

When the girls turned onto Main Street, Quiet Pond, their hearts soared the way they had upon their first sight of Main Street, Disney World, years before. Mira opened her window in wonder, and their directions to Gitammai's house fluttered out like birds set free.

"Oh, wow," Shanti whispered from the back.

"Don't worry. We can just ask someone."

"Not that. The street is so . . ."

"I know."

They parked the cobalt Audi along the curb and got out. They stretched their arms and their backs and looked around with lazy smiles from a long drive and two hours of relative peace. Mira put her arms over her head and breathed in deep. Across the street at Mo' Joe, three ladies in workout pants and visors put their cups down and noted that when these girls tossed their heads and looked about, their hair refracted the sunlight. They had only seen this show from one other head of hair in all their lives. When these girls smiled, their teeth were so white the ladies had to close their eyes. They had only seen one such mouth full of teeth in all their lives.

"They sort of look like . . . ," one whispered aloud.

"But they are so big and she is so small."

Leaning in tight, the one they called Mimi cooed, "Have you noticed? She's not so small anymore."

The ladies raised their eyebrows and pursed their lips. Lifting their coffees, they sat back to watch.

"It smells like donuts," Shanti said, looking around.

"It does smell like donuts," Veena agreed. They walked down the street and as they walked, the smell grew richer and closer and then Shanti put her hand on Mira's arm. "Oooo." They turned and exhaled in wonder.

CERISES ET SURPRISES. A baroque slab, spirals of lavender and green, like frosting, winking cherries to dot the "i's." Shanti, the baby, reached out a finger and scooped at the sign. Sheepishly, she turned back. "It's just paint."

Through the clean, broad window, an undisturbed tableau of art and food. The girls stood with their mouths agog. Inside were three flour-dusty women with the same chiseled mount of a nose and the same broad plank of a brow, the same eyebrows that grew like crooked fingers over their flickering hazel eyes, identical faces of different generations. They looked up in synchrony from their enormous bowls and paddles like oars; Veena, Mira and Shanti staring in the window had blocked all the light and the baker women worried that they had missed word of this morning's scheduled eclipse.

In the middle one's eyes, something like recognition, a twitching of the fingers on her lump of leavened dough. Had they noticed the middle baker woman, none of the daughters of Dr. Raman Nair would have recognized her expression of mistrust. Instead, they saw the youngest baker woman and the older baker woman, who smiled and signaled them in. They entered breathing shallow and surprised. Air hazy with suspended flour; dusty brick floors, towering ovens that pumped with heat; wide, arched oven doors. On bright days, they worked by the light of the window, nothing more. The older baker lady said, "Cakes baked by the pure light of day are lighter, sweeter, and less likely to produce crumbs." When it rained, she turned on the lights and made mostly cookies. To these three out-of-town girls, she said, "Hello, there, welcome to Cerises et Surprises. Please take your time and look around." She pointed to a case.

Veena, Mira and Shanti walked over respectfully mum, for the case was illuminated by what seemed to be only the resplendence of the confections themselves, too numerous to count, too varied to remember, too extraordinary to mark with ordinary names. Though this was imprecisely how they were labeled, "Cakes," "Cookies," "Pies," "Other."

Wiping her hands on her white apron, the older baker lady came over and said, "Hi, there. Welcome to Quiet Pond! I'm Augustine."

Veena smiled. "Hi, thank you. You have a delightful bakery." She looked back at the case appreciatively and then back again. "I'm Veena and these are my sisters."

Mira and Shanti both smiled and scrunched their noses with delight. Mira echoed, "A *really* delightful bakery."

"Really . . . wow," Shanti added. She leaned on Mira's shoulder, which was her shy habit sometimes when she interjected without being spoken to.

Augustine came closer and looked in the case with them. "As you can see, we tend not to bother with label cards. Sometimes we just make what we fancy on a day, and it depends on the light, and whether Lila has dance class in the morning, so I just put them where they go, and of course, we know what they are, so . . ." Augustine felt her daughter behind her and looked over her shoulder. "Patty? What's wrong, honey?" The middle baker lady held her bowl under her arm, her fingers still, and watched with straight lips.

"Oh, nothing, nothing. I thought, well, it seems like you girls look sort of familiar and I was wondering if you had been here before?"

Veena spoke up. "No, no we haven't been here before, but our aunt moved here a few months ago. She lives in a house on Old Rose Road." She looked from Patty to Augustine and continued, "Actually, we lost our directions and we really wandered in here hoping that you might know how we could find her place." Veena looked back at Patty. "Some people sometimes say we look something alike. Which is kind of crazy because . . . well, you'd never mistake her for one of us, because she's really, really slim." Veena shrugged and smiled. "Her name is Gita Nair." She looked back at Augustine and then back at Patty, whose brow seemed knit, displeased. Veena wondered if Gitammai had been surly or cross with these people. She had sounded so happy on the phone.

"Oh, Gita. Gita. You're family of Gita who lives in the cottage covered in roses!" Augustine with her round, happy face turned to her daughter and repeated with a large smile, "Patty, these are Gita's nieces." She turned back and said, "Your aunt is just a lovely girl. She's here all the time these days, you know. Once a week at least." Turning back to Patty she asked, "Wouldn't you say, Patty, once a week at least, wouldn't you say?"

Patty nodded her head without a smile. "Yes, these days, yes, once a week."

"Not so slim anymore," she laughed, throwing back her head, "you wait till you see her, just absolutely radiant." Augustine patted Veena on the shoulder. "Well, let me draw you a little map, its just as simple as can be, you just go right up to the end of this street and you'll see this old stone house, small like, it used to be a post office, and the road will start to go up, but before it does that, before it rises up, you just turn off, where there is no real road, but it's a mite like a road." She handed them a napkin map that Mira put safely in her bag, and then she continued, "It sounds a little vague, but it isn't. You really can't miss it." Augustine then bustled to the back of the case and began to pack a box.

"She absolutely craves these chocolate raspberry tarts." She put three or four into a box and poked her head back over the top. "She says it's something about the sweet and the tart together." Laughing, she dipped back under and gathered a few radio bars and sugar cookies. She closed up that box and started another. "Now what can I get for you girls? It's on the house, a welcome to town from Cerises et Surprises. Now, I already packed some radio bars for Chris, those have always been his favorites, even from before."

Veena, Mira and Shanti looked at each other without understanding. Complicit in their eyes was the possibility that people in small towns were like this. They had never lived in a small town. Shanti's look had an added, *can I get a cupcake?* Veena said aloud, "Oh, silly girl, my sister clearly would like something. Well, clearly all of us would like something, but you know, we really shouldn't." She scrunched up her face with a mock longing.

"Honey, let me tell you what. You need to live your life, every single moment of your life. Every single moment. There is not a single joy worth denying yourself, in my most humble opinion. When I was just carrying my girl Patty, I lost my husband. Well, he died, I mean. And when I got over the pain of that, I decided that there was not a single joy not worth grabbing while you could. You never know what might happen. Denying yourself joy will make you tired and old and miserable." Augustine turned to Shanti and asked, "So then, honey, what can I get for you?"

Shanti, taking one look at her sister, who was not looking at her but at Augustine, turned back and with a broad grin said, "A strawberry cupcake. But *this* sister likes chocolate best and *this* sister likes white." She smiled and then she giggled and put her head in Mira's shoulder.

Augustine packed the box and said, "That's right. That's right. Speak your mind, it's not every day you walk into a bakery and get offered cupcakes, and so when it happens, take it up. Take it up." As though she knew what Veena was here for, she turned to her and repeated, handing her the box, "When the joy is offered to you, take it up."

They walked to the door where Lila, the youngest baker lady, kneaded without looking up but to smile her good-bye, and Patty, the middle baker lady, frowned slightly and said, "Good-bye." Veena wondered again about the conduct of her *ammai* here in this wonderful town.

Standing at the door, Augustine called after them, "Now you send them my love and tell Gita to come by here whenever she really feels she wants something bad."

Veena, Mira, and Shanti nodded and smiled and when they were up out of sight looked at each other with complete confusion. "What was she talking about?"

"Who is *them*?"

If you take the road right past the old stone post office, and just before it begins to rise, bear slightly left, a smaller path becomes clear, though it might be made for lighter transport, bicycles, wagons, pushcarts. The brush and low trees grew inward, and Veena thought it prudent to stop and walk the rest of the way.

"Are you sure this is the road?"
"I think so, see the mailbox?"

There, marking the drive up to the cottage covered in roses, a mailbox in sunshine yellow sitting atop a bright blue post. It had been moved to the more main road at the request of the old postman who never expected to deliver here again. When last he had this stop, the trees were not so dense; it had been an easier entry. Chris left the old, rotten post where it was and bought another, and Jack painted it blue, just as he promised he would. Gita rewarded him with her slim fingers in his hair and her grateful smile. He forgave her for loving another man.

The three sisters walked through the woods, down the long drive to the cottage covered in roses, holding their bundle of sweets and breathing in the strong smell of honeysuckle that made them light-headed and weepy.

Shanti pined in her young heart for something magic that would let them plan a wedding like in the movies with everyone happy, and singing songs and dancing the hora. *Do Catholics dance the hora? I hope so, it's a good, round dance.* Then suddenly, when it seemed entirely possible that everything would work out, another gust of honeysuckle blew from the opposite side and she remembered when Usha cut her hand on the glass and she and Dhanya had to go to the neighbor's house because her parents were gone to the emergency room and so they went to Mass. They accidentally ate crackers that were the body of Christ. *I think that people who like to eat the body of Christ don't dance round and round together.* She felt a pitching sadness that swept through her legs at the loss of the hora.

Gita, who sat one porch step beneath her beloved so she could lean back against his comfortable chest, heard their not-so-quiet footsteps and looked up at Chris. He stood first, and pulled her up; she gathered her sweater over her shoulders and together they walked to meet the girls, whom he had seen before, in the airport years ago, at her graduation years later, and not since.

"They have grown," Gita described.

And so they had. Hair longer and thicker, womanly eyebrows of dramatic lines, even on the baby one. The baby one was rounder, taller too. They were graceful in the gliding way of ships and hot-air balloons. Veena came through the woods without dropping a tear in her own behalf. Gita saw a steely glint in her eye, and knew that all Veena needed was one sure blessing from her family. For whatever it was she was up to.

The three girls stop short at the sight of their *ammai*, who is not alone but alongside a startlingly handsome man who holds her around her shoulder with ease. They stand there like they own the place. Then, beyond that, Gitammai is wrapped in a cardigan that drapes her shoulders to keep her warm in the November woods, and which exposes, through its light blue bouclé, a large mound of middle and swollen breasts. The three nieces see this first, for their *ammai* is a slight slip of a lady, with protruding pelvis and all parts proportionate; they cannot help but stare. Their mouths open and suddenly, everything is in perspective. Things that have never made any sense make perfect sense, and they look up from her body to her face and it glows with a wonderful secret. Veena sees the perfect contentment there, and knows that all Gitammai needs is one sure blessing from her family for whatever she's been up to. Her hair is thicker, and blacker, and sleeker. The man leans down, so far down, and kisses it, without even realizing his public display of affection. The honeysuckle blows and all the girls rush forward and throw their arms around her with joyful abandon.

He had made them a comfortable cabin of delight. The ruthlessly aggressive roses he trimmed back and chained back and bent to his will. With brute force he shouted them down and he trained them to climb on only their allotted structures. He broke them to submission without chemical aid for within weeks of Gita's arrival they found she would have a baby before the summer came. He rebuilt the porch, the roses stripped from the rotted rails and tied with rope and chain to the ground. Jack returned home, night after night, bleeding and scraped, and Penelope, his mother, found that in the last days of summer, he had become something of a man. Gita palmed his head and made him lemonade, but Chris paid him well for his help. There were not many people he would let into their little circle in those earliest days.

He built the porch with his own two hands. He sanded it; he stained it with his own two hands. He built three arbors with his own two hands, he carved them, inserted their curled initials in secret spaces with the gentle touch of his own two hands. When he was done, he pulled those angry roses from their shackles and tied them to their arbors and to the new porch rails. He was merciless with the scofflaws; the roses learned respect. When he was done, he built her a new rocker and Jack painted it yellow and blue, just as he planned, and Gita rewarded him with stories told in the new porch swing while they watched her rocker dry. Chris gave him a new football and they tossed it in the yard.

Inside their home, he removed the damage, he replaced the boards, he filled the chinks and thereby subdued the unrelenting flow of honeysuckle that limited his power to think and work for so often did they flow into one another to make love, and make love and make love.

"Our baby was made the day you found me here."

"Yes. I'm sure that is true."

He leveled the floor, he rewired the house, he fixed the plumbing, he painted the walls, he moved their bedroom into the greenhouse and he built them a kitchen table and painted it orange because she thought that would be pretty.

"Orange?"

"It would be so pretty. And wouldn't it be so pretty if there were one red wall?"

"One red wall?"

"Yes. That one." She pointed. He painted it red. . . .

For who cared what color the table was, or the wall, so long as she was there every morning and every evening, and every time he came home from work. He no longer traveled. He fixed the crown and the ancient damper of the old fireplace and in the evenings, the reflection of firelight from their one red wall made the whole house glow with warmth and hearth and home to anyone who might see the window from outside.

Sometimes Jeri took the walk around the long pond road and through the town by cover of twilight. She went down Main Street hidden behind her long cardigan and her nondescript shape. Is it a man or a woman, an adult or a child? No one looked up in the early evening hour when she went past the old stone post office and down the road to just before it began to rise, and then off to the road that wasn't really a road, and past the garish, ridiculous spectacle of a mailbox and down the drive that swirled with a maddening honeysuckle wind that made her head beat with anguish, and which, over and over, brought her to her knees under cover of straggly bushes feeling the all-body ache of another stripping of her womb, another morning awakening with the loss of that delicious hope, another miserable packing away of foolishly purchased tiny shoes, or the lamb, or the *Goodnight Moon*. On her first stealthy visit, she had covered her biley vomit with leaves and left in shame, unable to go any farther.

But over time, she grew accustomed to it. How could she remain there in his Innisfree when she had seen them together at the hardware store, buying something like ten thousand pieces of wood without the slightest hint of shame. And there she was, overflowing her limits, bursting at the seams, already so full with their child. He kissed her every time he passed by empty-handed. She smiled and clapped her hands; she bounced with every new piece of wood he loaded. Jeri read her lips, she was calling him Hercules. He laughed in a new way. He flexed his muscles and she feigned a swoon, then he looked around with rising color. She was making him a giant fool. He was so handsome and happy. Standing across the street looking through the grocery window, Jeri's emptiness was painted on her tight, drawn face. She looked around and the entire market was staring at her in pity. Del Musik sidled up beside her and weaseled in her ear, "Disgraceful." That was the night she made her way to the cottage in the dark and vomited in the woods.

But sometimes she closed in. And sometimes there was the glowing red of home and the smell of a crackling fire. On those nights, she stood there until fear of the dark woods overcame her crushing and shameful curiosity. Like a doe, she walked back through to Old Rose Road, huge-eyed and skittish of being seen in her nighttime creeping.

On a night shrouded in mist, Jeri walked in quiet sadness to the cottage covered in roses because two ladies had stopped by with a basket of muffins for they thought she might need a little company what with what they were hearing that the girl was having twins. She tried to find peace in the mist over the water, but it only reminded her of all she had lost and all she would never have. She missed him more than she knew she had loved him. She thought, if only it were hers to do over again, she would make a better go of it, better decisions. She would have been more aware of his suffering. She made her way to the cottage because there was no peace in her heart, and no stillness in her body. She thought to take a walk, and before she was aware of it, she was there, on that heartbreak drive, in sight of the fire-glowing window. But this time, in the fog, she held her hand out against something that seemed to stand in her way. Holding it, she felt first and then she saw that it was a carved wooden sign, hanging from a post midway up the drive. Peering closer in the dark, she waited for a cloud to pass and there it was illuminated.

SECRET ROSE

This was something Jeri did not understand, and feared understanding. She did no research for many months, but when finally she risked a perusal of text, her pride raised its head against the affront. She cleaved with this Yeats as she never had with the first, with his miserable "Lake Isle of Innisfree," and she read it again and again in his most treasured room, with wide beams and broad glass, which somehow no longer mattered to him, after mattering more than anything else. She held this poem in her hands until it grew wet with sweat and tears, and then she copied and wet it again, and soon under such savage scrutiny, the insults within piled like a heap of garbage in her tired arms.

Wept the barrows of his dead; . . . [of course, all the dead babies]
. . . *dreaming king who flung* . . . *sorrow away, and* . . . *dwelt among* . . . *him who sold tillage, and house, and goods* [a mocking of her livelihood]
And sought through lands and islands numberless years,
Until he found with laughter and with tears,
A woman, of so shining loveliness, . . . [She groaned at the reference to his happiness.]
Surely thine hour has come, thy great wind blows,
Far off, most secret, and inviolate Rose?

It was perhaps this final blasphemy that stung her greatest. "Inviolate Rose." Inviolate? Secret, obviously yes. Inviolate? If Gita Nair was not the opposite of inviolate, there was very little to the meaning of the word.

Jeri gained strength every day from the memory of his house marker swinging on its post. She gained strength every day. Until the morning she drove to town and went straight to Silas, who sat in an armchair outside his shop with swooping hair that shone like white silk, who said he went to school in the hills a hundred years ago, who bragged of having whittled the face of Teddy Roosevelt somewhere in the Cumberland Plateau, Silas who sat in his armchair waiting for someone to ask him to carve something. Jeri pulled out her note and handed it to Silas. "I want you to make me a sign."

Silas looked at the paper and nodded.

"You may design it the way you think best, but it should look strong, and honorable, and sure of itself."

"The sign should look sure of itself?"

"Yes, as it swings on its post, it should look certain."

"Certain and sure of itself."

"Yes." Jeri came back in two weeks and her sign was perfect, in bold, black capitals on a broad white plaque. INVIOLATE. Free of embellishment.

She replaced INNISFREE with her new sign and after that she was newly free, and she resumed her journey.

Yet and still, when she heard the creaking of her sign on a windy night, she knew, if she had it to do again, she would take much better care of him, and she would have recognized his suffering. She would have tended to him as she knew he had tended to her, following her around, waiting patiently outside locked bathroom doors.

Nieces gathered in tight around the small, orange table. Their astonishment over Gitammai's secret made them breathe deep and slow. Her lack of shame, fear, embarrassment, or even explanation made her pulse like some kind of superhero. How was she so unafraid, unmarried, bulging with child, in a bungalow in the woods? Mira wryly thought, *We are afraid to open the windows.*

Gita looked up from the stove and lingered on their bemused gazes. For the full number of minutes that the milk boiled and the tea steeped in the pot, Gita stared at her nieces and they stared back. Imagine, in the looks, no reproach, no accusation, no questioning of morality, of sanity, of viability of the plan . . . then also, in the look, no resentment, no defensiveness, no eagerness to share the story, the situation, the specifics of the plan. Imagine a look flooded in acceptance.

She went to the door and called out, "Would you like tea?" From somewhere far away he answered, "Yes." She returned to the kitchen and brought the tray to the table. As she poured the cups she said to them, "Work backward from here." Then she turned to bring napkins and small plates.

It was a startling request. Shanti crinkled her brow, but no one was looking at her, and the quiet was so deep, she was unwilling to break it to ask, *what do you mean by that?* Instead, she pondered it on her own, and it came out in a muddled logic like this: *Work backward from here :: Start with the tea and then eat your cupcake. If you eat your cupcake along with your tea, or before your tea, your cupcake will be delicious, but your tea will not be sweet. If you drink your tea before you have your cupcake, they both will be deli-*

cious and sweet. If you must drink your tea before you eat your cupcake, you must have something else to go with your cupcake. Otherwise you will be thirsty. Gitammai is suggesting that you go get a glass of milk. She rose from the table and went to the refrigerator.

"What do you want, *mol*?" Gita asked.

"Milk."

"There are glasses in the cabinet to the left."

"Bring me some too," both the sisters called in chorus. In the heavy quiet of the cottage covered in roses, all three nieces had pursued a similar logic. It was easier than asking, *what do you mean by that?*

Gita sucked her teeth and laughed. "What? You said you wanted tea, all of you?"

There are many questions that must be left unasked, and perhaps forever unanswered in the tacit acceptance of such momentous changes of fortune. Sometimes the failure to communicate clearly will impact even the drinking of a simple cup of tea. When she gave her admonition, Gita had not been referring to the tea. It took Gita and her nieces several hours of silent staring to speak meaningfully. And when they finally did, it went something like this:

Gitammai, we came here because I have a problem. I am in love. He is a Catholic. He is perfect in every other way.

"Work backward from here. I could have been happy many years ago and instead, I chose fitful and sporadic joy and then . . . the opposite. Nothing permanent can come from it. Do you want to be with him forever?"

"Yes."

"Then have faith. Your father and your mother will not turn their backs on you."

"What if they do?"

"They will not."

"Are you sure?"

"Veena." Here Gita reaches out her hand, she touches her niece gently on the cheek and then through her hair. She smiles full of certainty and says, "Look at me." She smiles wider and her eyes are twinkling with mother-love, "Look at me. Your father and mother will not turn their backs on *me* and look at me . . ." She looks down at her pretty belly peeking from the blue bouclé and smiles back up again, "They will not turn their backs on *me*, and they would never turn their backs on *you*."

Veena looks unsure. Her brow is knit, she wrings her napkin, she bites her lip.

"Never." Gita says with certainty.

Working backward from where she is, she has never been more certain of anything in her life.

A Funny Feeling

Dhanya had a funny feeling in the tips of her fingers and she shook them out and squeezed and unsqueezed her hands. The funny feeling then slipped into her neck and down her spine. Turning herself left and right, she noticed that the funny feeling was still in her fingertips. It was spreading. She stomped her feet and clapped her hands and no one even looked up. Clemons had turned into a fraternity house of a library. Pizza boxes and Coke cans. She felt a flash of irritation over this travesty of a library. No peace. In Alderman, there was peace way back in the stacks, but it was hard to get up and move around. Cramped back there. The physics library was always quiet, but the stupid video was on reserve in the media center at Clemons so here she was watching this miserable movie in Arabic with funny feelings running all up and down her body. *Who cares*, she thought, standing up to jump blood back into her funny-feeling feet. Across from her cubicle, a line of boys missed the sensitive camerawork of Aguirre, Wrath of God's descent of the Andes, for Dhanya was entirely outrageous to behold while jumping up and down. She looked up and caught them staring, their mouths open. A blush exploded from her heart in all directions; her funny-feeling fingertips were now hot and red. *What is wrong with you, you look like a dancing hippo. Sit down.* Dhanya sat down.

Bab al-Hadid. Babal Hadeeed. Bab el-Hadid . . . Hanouma, for the love of Allah, leave him alone, he's like mentally retarded or something. She really didn't understand. As she watched Kenaoui muttering about in his hut sticking up pictures, she felt a greater shame over not understanding his helplessness, his pictures on the wall, his obsessions, his misinterpretations. Marginal understanding through cinematography and universal themes of the human existence, like watching Malayalam films . . . *I should have watched this when it was assigned. I should have gone to class more often. I should have learned some Arabic.*

Once, a month or so ago, she had tried to regain focus. She rose at 5:30 A.M. from the damp sheets and cool, hairless embrace of Dr. Russell Worthy, showered and tried to force-feed herself a quarter cup of Grape-Nuts, but it never agreed with her morning supplements. Dr. Worthy laid them out with a pharmacist's precision. She believed aloe was the culprit. It sent her to the bathroom a hundred times a day. If he was up, she waited until she was back on Grounds to take it. Embarrassing. But then it might be the guarana, the dandelion, the ma huang (that had her singing in the rain and swinging from lampposts), the chitosan, the pyruvate, or maybe the Saint-John's-wort. One of them was absolutely affecting her ability to eat Grape-Nuts. But he bought the Grape-Nuts "*for you*" he said, so she always tried to eat them. If he woke to find her at the counter dosing herself, he would clench his jaw at the sight of her so obedient, remove her night clothing in a feral rip, bend her forward over the whole collection of supplements—which would topple from the swing of her enormous, pendulous breasts—and amid the dramatic clatter of bottles and pills, he would take her from behind. She was as silent as a cat when she awoke.

But one morning a while back, she tried to regain focus. She tried to go to Arabic. But when she got to class on time and set up her things, she found she was terribly lost and didn't even know where to begin to ask questions. But on yerba mate and ma huang, courage could be drawn from the dust on a windowsill, from the nose hairs that emerged and disappeared with every breath of Dr. Zaid, or from the simple need to know. Dr. Zaid peered over his half-moon glasses and with nothing but disdain said, "Miss whoever you are, you have missed nearly every class for several months. I will not take up the time of diligent students to answer your elementary questions. Come see me after class."

. . . Dhanya had heard this before.

She didn't show her face in there again. But she had the syllabus. *I know how to be a diligent student. All by myself.* But she didn't know Arabic. *Perhaps,* she thought, *the exam will cover larger themes of the world condition from Arabic perspectives, but no actual Arabic.*

To yerba mate and ma huang, if one adds the guarana, the dandelion, the chitosan, the pyruvate, the Saint-John's-wort, and then *also* includes cascara and chromium, well, not only can courage be drawn from the minute dilation of pupils as shadows cross the eye, but also it becomes possible to have faith in theories that are actually daffy, ludicrous, cracked and completely absurd.

Having thus derived the most likely focus of Zaid's Arabic final exam, Dhanya turned off her movie and hurried to the bathroom. She was having a funny feeling in her stomach.

Earlier that morning, Gita awoke with a funny feeling. She closed her eyes and convinced herself it was that she must conclude her story today after so many months, and the ugliness of it had seeped into her spirit. And so it was that while her husband was gone, with her babies for company, Gita continued where she had left off with a funny feeling that she knew was about Dhanya, but which helped her write her terrible conclusion.

The Cursed Life of Sreemathi Omanakumari

A Terrible Conclusion

By the time he followed the trail back to the house of Omanakumari, Parameshwaran Namboodiri was slick and furious. There was not a soul to behold, but the trail was sure, and he climbed the steps like he owned the place bellowing at the top of his lungs, "BOY! BOY! Where is my nephew with that girl!?"

As he entered, he noted the smell of foul sickness and a shallow whimpering that disturbed even the pinched soul of Parameshwaran Namboodiri. As he followed the sound, he saw the hallway lined with more children. They were brothers and sisters that he hadn't even known existed. Their eyes were large and haunted. The younger ones huddled at the knees of older ones and cried. Parameshwaran Namboodiri felt a just fear as he walked down this hallway toward the whimpering sound. Before he reached the source, the father of the girl emerged from one room and told him to go away. His face was chalky and his lips were cracked. Parameshwaran Namboodiri, who noticed nothing, saw that his hair had gone white and wondered for a moment if this was a grandfather of whom he knew nothing as well.

But his sense of entitlement was greater than his shock and he was affronted by the father's crazy look and irrational request. "What do you mean? Go? We were on our way home and the girl disappeared. You have an unruly girl and you tell me to go?" He pushed his way past the father and entered a room that was black with death.

But she was not dead. On a blood-soaked bed and stinking of all manner of bodily effluent writhed Omanakumari, legs spread, pushing forth a screaming baby without uttering a sound, so weak was she. The newborn girl shrieked and writhed. She turned back to grab hold of her brother's foot and pull him out with her, but they removed her too fast and though she bent and strained, she could not tell them to go in and get him fast, and she could not keep hold of him though they had held hands through all the worst of it.

Parameshwaran Namboodiri rushed forward and looked over Narayanikutty's shoulder. She held the baby close and wiped her mouth and her eyes and tended to her newness. As patiently as he could, Parameshwaran Namboodiri stood still, watching and waiting, and when he finally saw, he gasped, and turned to Omanakumari. Kneeling down next to her, he put his face close and shouted, "It's the girl! Where is my son?" Anandan Nambiar, who had entered the room, put his hand on the old man's neck and threw him down. "You go now." Turning back toward his child, he watched her struggle to stay alive and he held her shoulder.

From the floor, Parameshwaran Namboodiri turned around and, like a cockroach, he scurried out of reach. "I will not go without my son." He squatted in a corner an arm's length from the father, and within striking distance of the girl.

Omanakumari stayed her father's hand, and whispered her last words, "Don't worry Achan, I am taking his son with me, and you can keep my daughter in my place." Hearing this, Parameshwaran Namboodiri rose in a wild frenzy and pushed the father away with surprising strength. "You are not dying until you give me my son. You have him there. You just had the girl, you can have the boy. Then you can go. You leave my son and then you can go!" Seeing her close her eyes, he reached for her shoulders and began to shake her, and in this act, he loosed from her blouse five small, green castor beans, which slid free and spilled out to the floor. Feeling them roll across her chest, Omanakumari looked up at her oppressor and smiled a weak and satisfied smile.

Parameshwaran Namboodiri stared down at them, blinking slowly. Narayanikutty and Anandan Nambiar also looked at these seeds and felt a cold horror pass from the roots of their hair through their toes. The old man bent down and picked one up and looked at it. . . .

"*Aavanakku . . .*"

Quietly and without any warning, Omanakumari began to whimper again and she spread her legs and contracted without any will. As still as a dead bird, another baby emerged. As he came without any fanfare in his mother's last living minutes, no one was even there to catch him, so focused were they on the seeds scattered across the floor. One look at this baby boy's blue skin and they knew he was dead. His sister, the only one who watched, immediately began a keening that chilled the heart.

Seeing this dead boy, rolled up like an opossum, dead from her hatred of him, Parameshwaran Namboodiri blanched and grew weak. If it was possible that hitherto he might have been saved, that was the moment he became an irretrievable soul.

With more hatred than one man ever had in his blood, Parameshwaran Namboodiri looked down on Omanakumari, who was sputtering her last breath. She was beyond hope, even her parents knew, and they looked at the seeds on the floor and were empty. Parameshwaran Namboodiri, unfazed by the screaming of the baby girl, knelt down to the ear of Omanakumari and asked her, "Omanakumari, are you going to die now?"

She said nothing and choked on her vomit and pain. He waited patiently for her coughing to subside and for her to open her eyes to meet his. When he was sure of her attention, he put his hand on her forehead and spoke in a chantlike cadence to make his words go straight to God, "Omanakumari, on your last breath, I curse you forever."

The girl's eyelashes fluttered up at him. Removing his hand from her brow, he spoke. "If you had simply died and left the boy, it would be your own foolish decision." His breathing was so labored, he feared he might die himself before he managed to say his piece.

"I loved you, Omanakumari. But now, you have done a terrible thing. You have deliberately taken my son from me, and for this I curse you and because your sin is so great, it will rest on your family forever." Calming himself, he took his towel and wiped his body and his face.

Omanakumari could barely understand him, and her parents listened with astonishment as he continued. His voice grew more and more powerful as he uttered shocking elaborations to his curse, which, if it had landed on the head of Omanakumari alone would have been limited to her few remaining moments, which were already cursed.

Booming like thunder and singing like a priest, Parameshwaran Namboodiri laid his hand back on her brow and pronounced, "On your head, one girl in every generation of your line will be cursed. On your head and those that follow you. Evermore."

Omanakumari's eyes fluttered like insect wings. They buzzed with helplessness. She looked at her only daughter who shrieked so lonely in her own mother's arms. She looked back at Parameshwaran Namboodiri and with barely a breath left, she uttered, "Please."

Parameshwaran Namboodiri stood up, stared at her for a moment and spat in her face. He turned and walked away.

With nothing left to do, Narayanikutty put the baby down on her daughter's chest and wiped her face clean. The baby grew quiet and squirmed an inch or two, until she was lying on her mother's neck. There, she caught hold of a stray lock of her mother's hair and tangled herself tight so as not to be left behind, but Omanakumari died anyway and when the baby began to keen again, they knew she was gone.

Gita could not help but weep and so she sat for several moments crying for her lost Omanakumari and for the baby girl that was left alone. She rubbed her swollen belly and imagined what kind of horror would give her the courage to take the life of her unborn children. But still . . . her funny feeling was still there. She looked up and took a whiff of honeysuckle. Just being pregnant had infused her with the instincts of mothers, and she knew something was not right. With Dhanya. She looked at the clock. It was 6 P.M. and she thought she would try Dhanya one more time before Chris came home from work. She was getting quite familiar with the wafer-light voice of Clara Ballerina, who apologetically called her Gitammai when whispering that Dhanya was again not home.

This time:

"Hi, Clara. It's Dhanya's aunt, Gita."

"Oh . . . Hi, Gitammai."

"How are you?"

"I'm fine, I'm just studying . . . that's about it."

"How do your finals look?"

"I think I'll do all right. Nervous about Chem."

"I was nervous about everything, so that's good you're only nervous about Chem."

". . . Yes, you're right, I should . . . look at it that way."

"Well, is Dhanya around? Has she come in yet?"

"Um . . . not yet . . ."

"Hmmm. Do you know if she got my messages?"

"Um . . . I'm not really exactly sure . . ."

"Well . . . okay then. Clara, if you could just let her know I called. I wanted to talk to her about driving her home for the break, for her birthday. When her sisters were here, I wanted to come get her then. But she—"

"Okay . . . I'll tell her you called. I'll tell her . . ."

"Clara?"

"Yes, Gitammai?"

"Is everything okay?"

"Okay, then. Bye, Gitammai!"

Gita hung up and stared at the receiver while the light dimmed and darkened the room. When Chris came through the door and dropped his bag to the side, she did not even turn her head. He took off his coat as he approached her and used these moments to run through what might be wrong. When he put his hand on her shoulder she turned up and with no preamble said, "I have a funny feeling about Dhanya. I wonder if we ought to go down there."

"What kind of a funny feeling?"

"The kind my brother should have had when I went to school."

Squeezing her shoulders and rubbing between her scapula, Chris paused a moment in thought and then finally replied, "Then it might all turn out in the end, right?"

He treaded carefully in his teasing. Sinking to his knees, he was looking up at her with gratitude, with respect, and his earnest face made her tread with equal care in her response.

Stroking his face with her small hand, she too paused before answering, "I would have liked someone to talk to. It was not the easiest journey to this cottage covered in roses." He gave her the look that wondered if he stole her life.

"Chris, I have never wanted, in all my life, I have never wanted any other life than the one we have in this home, than we will have with these babies. Never. In all my life." He lays his head against her broad belly and the four of them feel thankful for the not-so-easy journey traveled outright.

As the light dims and darkens the room, George stares at the phone and steels his broad shoulders against what he already knows will be an intolerable silence on the other end; his father, careful, polite, ashamed to admit that as forward-thinking as he might be . . . this? His mother, he sees her, simply unable to speak.

He picks up the phone and dials the number. If his mother answers he will chat a moment and then ask for his father. If his father answers, he will tell him. Just tell him outright. Then they will sit there with nothing more to say, but they will sit there.

CV Thomas answers the phone and is overjoyed at the sound of his son's voice. Baby George. "AH-ha! AH-ha! It is you! It is a long time, two weeks? Three weeks?! AH-ha! You are calling! What is going on there? What is the weather?"

"Oh, it's cold, but you know, not like home. Not like there." A good place to start. The weather. "What's it doing there?"

"Oh, my son, Oh, my son. Here? Already a foot of snow and it isn't even official winter. Already a foot of snow. Let me see." George can hear his father, standing, moving to the window, opening the curtain, gasping in wonder as though he didn't already know. "Already a foot of snow! Can you imagine?"

"I can imagine." George takes a deep breath; he steadies his breathing. Waits a moment too long. A funny feeling swells in the gut of CV Thomas. A sense of hesitation in his son. A parent's clarion call.

"*Mon*, what is wrong?" CV Thomas has returned to his chair. This boy, silent and austere, but never afraid, was afraid. CV is already sitting; he anticipates the worst.

Hehasbeenkickedoutofschoolhehasfailedoutofschoohehasfailedhisboardexam-hehaslosthispositionhehas. . . .

George, eyes closed, looking for words. He opens them and there sits Veena in her silver frame. Outright, he says, "Dad, I have met a girl and I want to marry her."

His father, silent. This was beyond the reach of his imagination. He redirects his thinking.

Sheispregnantsheisdivorcedshehaschildrenfromherpreviousrelation-shipsshehasHIV . . . gonorrheasyphilischlamydiagenitalwartsherpes. . . . Sheis astrippersheisonwelfareshehasacriminalpastsheisanillegalaliensheislookingfor-agreencard. . . . Shehascongenitaldefects. . . . Sheisblinddeafmutedeaf-mutesheisadwarfshehascrossedeyes. . . . Shehasmentalillness . . . schizophrenia biploardisordermanicdepression. . . . Herparentsarehillbilliesrednecksracistsher parentsaredivorced. . . . SheisaMuslimsheisa

"She is from Kerala . . ."

A pause in the flow.

"Her name is Veena Nair."

A longer pause in the flow.

"Veena Nair?"

"Yes." George sits back and takes a deep breath. "Veena Nair."

She is a Nair.

And then they sat there, with nothing more to say, but they sat there.

The light grew dim in the living room of Dr. CV Thomas who could see that outside another foot of snow had fallen on Rochester, Minnesota.

Dhanya's Birthday

On the eve of her birthday, Dr. Russell Worthy took Dhanya to dinner at the new sushi place in town and presented her with a brass bookmark shaped like a clown's head. It was the clown's extended tongue that was to lap over the page and the clown's distended jaw that held the page from behind. . . . He did, however, pay for dinner with no mention of her tab, but then . . . Dhanya no longer ate. In the morning, when she returned home, she tried the bookmark on New York Amanda's economics textbook, which lay out on the couch, but the weight of the clown's hat seemed to tip him forward. Regardless of how many pages she pushed between his tongue and jaw, again and again, he fell to the floor. Dhanya was a little ashamed of the gift. Then she was ashamed of herself for feeling that way. Often, she was in that boat.

She showered and changed her clothes and considered what of her many neglected subjects to tackle the entire semester of today. *Even his class, if it weren't for him, I would be failing. Perhaps he will fail me too. . . .*

Clara Ballerina came in from breakfast and found Dhanya in the room, where she rarely was anymore, on her bed surrounded with papers, open notebooks with no notes, open textbooks for every subject all around, piled and piled in teetering piles. In the middle of this show of brilliance or insanity slept Dhanya, head lolled back against the windowsill, mouth open, hair swept gracefully over one shoulder. On her knee an ugly brass bookmark of a laughing gargoyle.

Clara knit her brow and turned in her lips and then she shut the door behind her at the sound of other people coming and going. Dhanya was a sad sight, best left for the truly devoted. Clara was truly devoted. She picked up the phone right then and took it out in the busy suite. Tucking into a quiet corner, she called for help.

In the cottage covered in yellow roses, Gita turned to Chris and announced, "December eleventh. It is Dhanya's birthday. Perhaps we should just go today and wait at her dorm until she comes home."

"What if she has plans? She might not even be in town."

"If she isn't in town, we have done no harm in trying. She doesn't return my calls. I don't want to—"

When the phone rang, on cue, they both stared at it for a moment, because of course, still, still after all this, Gita had to answer the phone, reminding them that there was another trip to make together, news to break . . . lots of news.

On the other end, Clara Ballerina. "Hi, Gitammai." A tremor in her voice that makes the babies stop their playing and quiet down. Gita holds them with the palm of her hand, strokes the one's hair, the other's feet, they hold her hand tight with their tiny, powerful kisses.

"Clara? What is wrong?"

"Um . . ." She hesitates that moment too long. . . .

In her hesitation Gita's eyes flood with tears and it is perhaps the effect of impending motherhood, for she has never before felt such worry for her nieces as she suddenly feels all the time. Veena on the telephone asking to visit, Dhanya's failure to ever be home, to ever return a call. Gita forgets to be concerned for herself, forgets that she has difficult news to break, forgets that her brother will not understand, will be angry, will shout, will point at the ceiling, will glower at Chris. She forgets. When did she stop thinking about herself? She doesn't know she used to be different. She only knows that something is terribly wrong with Dhanya and today is her eighteenth birthday.

"Um . . . I think you should come down here now, if you can," Clara says in a halting whisper.

"Clara, please tell me." Gita has to sit down, her blood has fled from her extremities and her babies have huddled in a ball. Chris watches with a grim face. Gita's voice comes out in a croak, she clears her throat and is momentarily deafened by her pulse in her ears. She tries again. "Clara, please tell me that Dhanya is okay. Is she okay? Is she hurt?"

Clara pauses and sinks her head against the dingy dorm wall. What to say? *She vomits, she doesn't eat, when she eats she spends an hour in the bathroom, she faints on the floor and her hair falls out, her palms are always pouring sweat, her teeth ache, her heart flutters, she sometimes shakes in her seat, she never goes to class, she smells like metal, she runs without eating, she runs without drinking, she has lost so much weight that she needs to make new clothes, she cannot make new clothes because her hands shake and she cannot pay attention, she falls asleep in the middle of the day, she paces the floor in the middle of the night, I think she is having unprotected sex, I am not sure she is using birth control. . . . She is so sad. . . . She is so sad.*

"Please come here if you can. We are in Lile. On Alderman Road. She is here now. She's asleep. Gitammai, please come here if you can." Clara hangs up before there can be any more questions. The suite has quieted somewhat. What friends remain stand in a bunch and stare at Clara and she stares back.

"What?" they ask, afraid.

"I called for help." Clara holds the phone in her hand and sits outside their door. Today, Dhanya will not leave without Clara Tarakova clinging to her leg, fluttering like a kite tail. Turning her head to the wooden door behind her, she takes a deep breath and imagines herself with greater mass, for should Dhanya choose to leave, weight loss or no, her own slight body blockade would be no match. Clara braces her hands against the jamb and hopes that Dhanya sleeps hard and that Gitammai arrives soon.

Just before dawn was too late to rouse everyone with Suprabhatam in honor of Dhanya's birthday, so late was the sunrise in mid-December. In winter, when the chanting blessings filled the house, everyone moved too slow, lingered longer in their beds with their eyes focused on the dark ceiling, or the slight gray at the edge of the shade. When the preprogrammed ten loops were complete, they found themselves unbathed, unfed, unbrushed, unpacked, racing, racing, racing out the door. But it had been many years of trial and error. By her eighteenth year, Dr. Raman Nair knew exactly when to begin Dhanya's birthday Suprabhatam to be met with the greatest warmth and appreciation. Rising at precisely 5:30 A.M., he went to the stereo and in a moment took his first deep breath to that wondrous syllable.

Om.

Taking one more deep breath, Dr. Raman Nair proceeded to his *puja* room. It was cold in the living room, it was colder in his office; and when he opened the *puja* room door, the frigid air blasted his face with a slap; he squinted in surprise. He considered for one moment getting the space heater and setting it up in the tiny closet, but then thought better of it. Praying through his discomfort might give him needed guidance for the difficult days ahead. He closed his eyes and prostrated himself before Unnikrishnan, who despite his near nakedness in the freezing *puja* room, looked as jolly as ever. . . . The cold was making it difficult to focus. Dr. Raman Nair found himself considering that if he were a real *bhakti* Hindu, he would always keep a small space heater in this room. After all, these were gods accustomed to a warmer climate. He opened his eyes and noticed the carpet had small pencil shavings ground in; he would have to tell someone to come vacuum in here. Noting this bit of untended dust, Dr. Raman Nair, still prostrate, turned his head and saw the undersides of the tables and the baseboards were all dusty as well. Sitting up to take better stock, he counted that every picture frame was speckled and thick with dust, and that the light fixture above had dead insects inside. *I should pray more often.*

Shuddering against the relentless chill, Dr. Raman Nair prostrated himself again, but it was colder against the floor, so he sat up and crossed his legs, but the cold made them cramp and he had to stand back up. *It is Dhanya's birthday. You just stand here and pray for her and just stop your fussing and shivering.* He gave a strong shake to his whole body and took a deep breath. Outside his office, like birdsong from afar, came the faint cadence of Suprabhatam. Dr. Raman Nair tried again.

Om. Dear Lord thank you for your continued care over my child, Dhanya, please grant her another year's blessings. Watch over her as you have always watched over her. Please keep her safe at school, please grant her your blessings for her upcoming exams, please give her your blessings as she is far from home and not under our watchful eyes. Please care for her in her absence from home, in her studies, in her health, in her life and welfare.

Om.

Om.

There was however, in each resonating om that filled his body and his mouth and echoed out from his faithful heart, a niggling nag that quivered his purple eyelids and kept him from the deeply meditative state to which he aspired when praying. It was . . . that she never called back, and he hadn't talked to her in a very long time. And she never came home, not even once, no plans to do so. Not even for her birthday.

But with the catastrophes of recent days, who had time to linger over that worry? Somewhere in the house Veena, perhaps still asleep, was learning to do without the blessings of the Suprabhatam. Teaching herself a new set of songs, morose hymns with funereal melodies. She might be memorizing some doctrines, some unquestionable Catholic catechisms. Surely, once she left here she would never hear it again, the Suprabhatam. The thought, in this cold, with the drafts blowing in from unseen vents, became too much for Dr. Raman Nair. He blew out the flame in the *vilakku* and closed the *puja* room doors. All was still in the house, despite the ongoing blessings of "Good Morning" ringing forth. *No reason for them to get up now . . . Dhanya isn't even here.* He climbed the stairs and walked back down the hallway to his room, where buried under a mountain of covers he found his tiny wife, Jaya, crying quietly into a wad of tissues she clutched in her hands. In this private moment, he pulled her in close and she shook and sobbed against his chest.

On December 11, George's mother, Elizabeth, alerted emergency crews to her location trapped in a tremendous snowdrift on the side of Route 52. In the calm gained from true danger she clearly shouted into her car phone, "WE ARE SOMEWHERE NEAR ZUMBROTA!" Theresa, quieter as the years passed, gently fingered the window where she could actually see the difference between each of one trillion snowflakes that were silently enveloping their car.

When emergency crews had pulled mother and child from the darkness in which they huddled, and ushered them to safety in the local Zumbrota fire station, they shook their heads and scolded, "What were you *doing* out there in this storm?" Expecting silence or shame, they were puzzled when the woman crossed her brow and said, "We were coming home from church."

"Don't you have a church closer to home?"

"Of course."

"Then why were you on the road from Minneapolis in the storm?"

"It is the St. Jude Church . . . hopeless cases."

They looked at her blankly.

"Desperate ones . . . and, it wasn't storming when we left!" She stared all around. "Obviously!"

"But didn't you know there was a storm *on the way*? This is Minnesota, in Minnesota you have to watch the weather."

"I knew the storm was coming, it just wasn't here yet. It was very important that we get to church."

"You could have *stayed in Minneapolis*!" From the woman's buried Lincoln Navigator, from her daughter's thick gloves and boots, from her own perfect teeth and pompous demeanor, these men, trained to gather information in a glance, knew an unplanned hotel stay was a financially reasonable alternative to death by asphyxiation and exposure.

Elizabeth looked at them with wide-eyed disbelief. "Stayed in Minneapolis? Overnight?" She shook her head and exhaled with exasperation. "It was very important that we get home today itself. My husband is there alone."

Taking a look at the disengaged lady holding her mother's sleeve, the men relented somewhat in their chastisement; perhaps the husband too was slow. Perhaps he was her desperate, hopeless case. . . . Ernest Ansel, with his face like a kindly pot roast, gently patted the woman on the shoulder, shaking his head. It was his duty as a public servant to educate as well as to protect. "How long have you lived here, ma'am? There is *nothing* more important than heeding the weather in a Minnesota winter."

Elizabeth looked up at the paunchy red man with the North Country accent, lowering her jaw and raising her eyebrows. "I have lived in Minnesota for thirty-four years." With an arch look she deepened her voice and continued gravely, "And Minnesota winter or no, there is *much* that is more important than the weather."

Chris parked illegally in the small Lile lot and threw on his hazards in case they needed to shuttle Dhanya to safety. Gita shot out of the car holding her belly and her back, but moving quickly, staring up at the three-tiered building, unsure even where the girl could be found. *I never even took her address.* She was glum and ashamed in the bright light of her neglect. How quickly things had changed.

On the top floor to the left, a row of three girls stood sentinel, watching for the arrival of Gitammai, and there was no doubt as to who this beautiful woman below was. Pregnant, and thus fuller in the hip and bosom, she was a healthy/happy copy of anorexic/bulimic Dhanya. They waved and called out, "Gitammai? Gitammai? Up here!"

Chris held her by the elbow, for here in front they were excavating the sidewalk and the cracks were wide and deep enough to swallow a leg. "Walk carefully," he whispered.

The stairwell had the smell of old concrete and accidental pissing. Gita lurched in her throat and thought that she might vomit. She backed out into the open air and took a few clean breaths. "Can you smell that?" she asked. "What?" he answered. She swallowed hard and gulped down an enormous lungful and holding her breath she raced up the steps. At the top of the stairs, the girls held her shoulders and took her to the railing overlooking the courtyard to breathe deep because she was drenched with sweat, not from the running, but from the fear of what awaited inside.

Chris urged her forward. This was not a time to stand by sweating and worrying. He hadn't been so afraid for the welfare of another in many months, yet he was aware that, more often than not, he had felt this way. *Once more into the breach, dear friends, once more.* It did strike him that life is spent thus.

"Go. Now," he whispered in his quiet way that rumbled low and sure. He held her hand and she looked up at him, swallowed hard again and together they entered the suite.

Inside, Clara sat where she had sat for the last hour and minutes, waiting with her hands pressed firmly against the doorjamb. When she saw Gita she gasped and checked behind her, afraid that somehow Dhanya had escaped out the window and returned through the door. *Ha ha, you thought you could stop me, tiny girl.* But then, behind this woman, a handsome stranger with a gentle face, and a hand on her back, and a mouth that held quiet. This was *NOT* Dr. Worthy and so, this was not Dhanya.

"Clara?"

Clara began to cry and she came burbling up from the floor and collapsed against Gita's body, her hands raising up from her sides, from the release of pressure against the jamb. "Gitammai!"

Gita held on tight. In her back, Chris felt her heartbeat crashing against his hand. Again, he whispered, "Go. Now."

Clara opened the door and it creaked on its hinge. The room was dark with the shade low and the lights off. Dhanya was as Clara had left her, but her piles had toppled and her gargoyle was clutched in her hand. Gita sniffed sharply; the room had a strange metallic smell, an acrid burn. Gita felt her stomach rise in her throat again.

"Can you smell that?" she asked.

"Yes," Clara answered. "It's the smell of her."

Gita swallowed hard and went to the bed. Outside, Chris leaned against one dingy dorm wall and stared at another. Waiting.

Gita leaned forward and pulled the shade cord. When daylight entered, gray and filtered from the balcony overhang outside, the sight of Dhanya emerged from shadow and then Gita moaned.

From outside, Chris heard anguish and his heart flooded his fingers with blood. The sound was as though she had fallen into a hole, and the force with which he pushed in the room sent the door crashing into the wall. It bounced back and beat him lightly against his wide, strong shoulder.

Gita, clearing the bed of the useless flotsam and jetsam of a semester gone by, pushed in on her knees, throwing things aside, working her way to her niece, who despite all the chaos did not rouse herself from her sleep. Gita called her again and again and finally, with a drowsy slurp Dhanya awoke and Gita took a breath of foul air. *She is not yet dead.*

Dhanya's eyes were heavy and she tried to keep them open with the strength of her powerfully long eyebrows, which, of late, had begun to fall out. Gita held the girl ferociously in her arms and the babies inside kicked and pushed. *Too tight*, they said, *too tight.*

Chris stood in the light of the threshold and was overcome. He closed his eyes, *Those years when I left her alone at school, was she bereft like this? Were her eyes circled with black rings, were her lips swollen and parched, was she hidden inside a gray sweatshirt like a bruise, was she longing for someone to hold her like she is held at this momen? Did I leave my Gita like this when she was only eighteen years old?*

Dhanya had nothing to say; she sat, stupefied and squeezed, and it was the shaking, the shaking, the tormented shaking and then the wailing that finally let loose a torrent of pent-up tears into the knotty white sweater of her own *ammai*, from whom she could not escape, who would not leave, as she keened, "Until I understand, until I understand, and even when I understand, I will not leave without you." And so, the story came out one hushed word at a time, in halting phrases, in bits and pieces. Dhanya left out what she could. Clara filled in what she could.

"I . . . tried to control what I eat. I started to exercise."

"He gives her a lot of weight-loss drugs and tells her she's fat. He told her lots of girls only eat once a day. He told her lots of models use throwing up to control their weight. He told her it's called 'caloric restriction by emesis.' "

"He . . . is a very respected professor."

"He is a liar. He told her she was going to get to join a group. There was no group. There never was a group." Clara burst into sobs. She turned to Chris, whom she didn't know. "That's how he tricked her. There was no group."

"He loves me."

"Sometimes he pinches her and leaves," Clara gasps for breath, "big, purple welts on her body."

Gita looks up at the sound of . . . outrage. Chris has beaten his palms once against the doorjamb and he stands looking down heaving in and out, in and out. His silence has never been so . . . savage. She would be afraid if her faith in him were not so complete.

When he looks up again he looks to Dhanya instead of to Gita and Gita watches him looking and she knows exactly what he sees. In fact, she sees it too.

"Chris," she whispers. She tilts her head and gives that look. *I am my beloved's and he is mine. You have never wronged me in word or deed. This is something not at all the same.*

He looks back at Dhanya and sees her broken as Gita had never been. Angry, afraid, lonely and sad, but never broken (except, she said, when she left him until she came back) and suddenly these two, girl and woman, are as different as day and night.

He draws to his full height and when he takes his deepest breath, he fills in the doorway and sends a shiver down Dhanya's spine, for though she does not know him at all, she knows he is about to defend her honor, and how she knows this she does not know either.

Chris turns to Gita and speaks in a voice hoarse from suppressed rage. "I will be back when I am done." She nods and draws Dhanya down into her shoulder where she can kiss her temple and stroke the hair that comes out in tufts and long, loose strands.

A Disappointing Finish

In the quiet building, Chris's footsteps echoed, but who would have expected such an angry man to come to Randall Hall in the middle of the day? If Russell Worthy had been paying attention, he might have heard something in that steady footfall and deliberate breathing to make him twitch a nostril, dart his head back and forth, crawl under his desk and wait for the threat to pass. If he had been listening, he might have jumped out of the window, but he was not listening.

Chris found him standing at his desk, listening to jazz instead and packing a briefcase. He stood in the doorway long enough to see Russell Worthy throw back his head a few times and shimmy a private shimmy.

This was the tragic hour when Chris realized for how small a person, how pitiful a person, Dhanya had been shed of her youth and her absolute faith in humanity. Russell Worthy . . . was less than he had expected. How to kill a man who was not like a man, but more of a whining fop? How to kill a man in cold blood who was not worth the malice aforethought? His fall should come from public ostracizing for an ignoble nature, from pointed failure to be included, from overt neglect to find him worthwhile company. He would wear a black eye and a broken nose like a mark of superior intellect, of a more refined character; he would tell the story in ways that mocked the girl and all she had thrown away to love him. His unexpected worthlessness made Chris's anger turn to pure disgust. He groaned and shook his head.

Chris left without drawing blood, for there would be no resolution through the deserved violence nor compensation for lost innocence. The justice would never be done. But then, neither would Dr. Russell Worthy ever again use his choosing gesture on unsuspecting students in the hallowed halls of the University of Virginia.

"Drugs and alcohol, Russ? To a seventeen-year-old student, Russ?"

"Absolutely not."

"You suggested bulimia, Russ? *Suggested* bulimia?"

"Absolutely not."

"She is on academic probation, Russ. . . . She came here, you know . . . an Echols scholar, Russ. . . . She arrived with a 4.6 GPA . . . Russ?"

Silence.

"Russ, you know, you know . . . we are going to have to let you go, you know this . . ."

"Sir, I have tenure . . ."

"Russ, you have committed statutory rape. If they press charges, Russ, you won't be able to work—anywhere—in academia. . . . Russ, they could sue UVA . . ."

The final shame was, of course, in packing up his office without a secured position at a better university. . . . His lies drew snickers and smirks. He twitched and pretended not to notice.

A Better Birthday Present

When Chris came back, the girls were out in the common room of the suite petting on Dhanya, and then petting on Gita, and then petting her pretty tummy, which poked out hard and round. With so much attention, the twins put on quite a show, rolling around like dolphins. The girls, so young and amazed by what might lie in their own futures, patted her belly and the babies came up to their hands as though they were offering sweets. One and then the other in swimming circles.

Chris opened the door, which sighed a hydraulic sigh, and watched the scene. It seemed that all was well in the room, and for this much tenderness in a desperate time, he was very grateful. The girls all looked up at him and caught their breath; his return signaled the return of ugly matters needing to be faced, and he watched as Gita too wrinkled in her brow and pulled tight her lips. How quickly things could change.

He cleared his throat and smiled without his teeth and it made him look tired and somewhat forlorn. Gita stood up, held him around the middle, and sunk her cheek into his chest. The frank gesture of love tilted Dhanya's head and made her blink. Her own quietness. Had she failed to ask the questions, to demand the answers that might bring true love? Was she just cursed? *I am probably just cursed.*

He cleared his throat again and mindfully pushed Gita's hair aside from her temple and leaned down to kiss her there. When he removed his hand from her hair, it fell forward and covered his kiss. Quietly, he said, "Let's go in the room for a moment." And Gita went forward and took Dhanya by the hand and the three of them went back in the room and sat down together.

Inside, Chris asked questions in his quiet and gentle way and Dhanya answered in her quiet and meek way. They had not been introduced. Chris never even realized it, so little was this about him, and Dhanya knew who he was, now that she had seen those babies' elbows . . . knees . . . feet . . . hands. . . . They must get their size from him. . . .

And finally, "Dhanya, do you think you should take your exams?"

Silence.

"Any exams?"

A breath to indicate words to come . . . "History . . . I am ready for . . . his . . ."

Chris looked up at Gita and whispered, "Pack her up, we will take her home."

Up flew Dhanya's head, and the room began to close in on her; she stood and it suddenly seemed that there was no way out, that the room was made of solid concrete and buried underground. She felt the lack of air, the tingling in her fingers, she was unable to breathe. Her head spun this way and that, and she thought if she paced, she might calm down. Her breathing became too shallow to sustain her and she fell down, tripped, just tripped. But down she stayed and she closed up and hid under the floppy gray arms of her sweatshirt.

Chris raised her to her feet and sat her back down and Gita said, "*Molu*, it will be okay. I will stand next to you. Everyone will be there next to you." She stroked Dhanya's hair until she began to breathe normally. "Dhanyamol . . . today is your birthday. I brought you a present." Dhanya looked up at her *ammai* and Gita's tears rolled down her face in tiny rills, because the child looked so young and yet so empty of hope. "Would you like your present?" Dhanya nodded and looked over to her side where sat her clown bookmark, laughing hideously at the whole grotesque spectacle. Chris followed her gaze and saw the thing lying there beside her and momentarily, his anger swelled anew. Unable to stop himself, he leaned forward from his chair and plucked the clown from the bedspread. He held it out in his palm for Gita to see. Gita looked at it and then up at Dhanya with a question in her face.

Dhanya just sat there with nothing to say; she lowered her head in shame.

Gita exhaled through her nose and wiped the tears from her face with the back of her hand. Standing, she put on a smile and clapped twice to erase the bookmark. "Well. Enough of that. Let me get you your birthday present!" With spare movement, Chris carefully placed the bookmark on her desk beside him as Dhanya followed Gita with her eyes.

From her handbag, Gita drew out a small box wrapped in silky paper and overflowing with curly ribbon. She held it in her open palms and sat beside Dhanya, whose heart was squeezing and squeezing with the effort not to cry.

Excited and happy, Gita clapped again. "The paper is Japanese! I bought it for your present!" Dhanya gasped like a child, "It's beautiful."

Inside, there was a small box, and inside the small box was a beautiful silver locket in the shape of a heart and when you opened it, it unfolded and then unfolded again for four pictures. And engraved on the front were her initials, "DN." And Dhanya said, "Ooo, I forgot!" Because she had forgotten that Ammai bought all her sisters engraved lockets for their eighteenth birthdays and now it was her turn.

"Yours is special. It is the only one that has four spaces for pictures. I found it in Quiet Pond."

Dhanya stared at her very special locket that was so much like the ones her sisters had received before her and like her sister would receive after her, and she remembered for the first time in a very long time that, no matter what, she belonged to people who loved her very much.

They Have Come

Gita called before they left Charlottesville, which gave the four daughters in the home of Dr. Raman Nair time to bake a cake upon which Veena crafted a princess in a hoop skirt with a parasol in her hand. Veena always made Dhanya a princess cake.

Gita had said, "We have to stop by home first, to pick up some clothes." She did not mention whom she meant by "we." Veena, who was boldly committed to just being good, heard the news that Gitammai was bringing Dhanya home for her birthday and in response to Dr. Raman Nair's jubilant orchestration of a big birthday *sadhya* promptly announced, "I am going to call George to join the party!"

"WHAT?!" Dr. Raman Nair had bellowed.

Veena smiled very happily and said, "I want him to be with us." She was not being manipulative, but it did seem like a good time to bring him home, because there would be other things to distract her father when Gitammai walked in with her married American lover, and their children conceived out of wedlock busting through the spaces between her buttons.

While the phone rang on George's end, she looked over her shoulder at her father and didn't even notice his purple glower when she added with a happy smile, "I'll see if he can bring Manoj Chettan!"

George heard the joy in her voice when she said, "I am making her a princess cake. This time, she's going to have a hoop skirt and a parasol!" So instead of saying anything that started with ". . . um . . . ," (to indicate that he was sick to his stomach over the imminent verbal thrashing he would receive from the eloquent and loud Dr. Raman Nair), he swallowed hard and said, "How do you make a hoop skirt and a parasol on a cake?"

Dr. Raman Nair twisted his lips to the side and pulled his eyebrows together as his daughter's face lit up as she explained how she would bake a cake in a bowl and turn it over on top of a sheet cake . . . and she would frost it . . . and then she'd use a. . . .

He will listen to all this? He snorted through his nose and left the room. Jaya, listening from the hall, anxiously grabbed his forearm as he passed. "Is he coming?"

"Perhaps she will keep him on the phone explaining about the spun sugar and the evening will come and go." He continued to his office and decided to send up another prayer.

This time, the *puja* room was not as cold, but the gods were frowning, for sure. Even jolly Unnikrishnan seemed poised to throw his ball of butter smack in his face. Dr. Raman Nair shook his head. *It is not my fault.*

Again, he prostrated himself and closed his eyes. At least now, Gita was happy and Dhanya was coming home. Only this one to worry him like crazy. He opened his eyes. There, ground into the carpet—again, still?—were the pencil shavings he had seen this morning! Dr. Raman Nair stood up and boomed, "DIDN'T I SAY TO VACUUM THIS *PUJA* ROOM TODAY! IT IS ALREADY . . . ALMOST EVENING AND THERE THE PENCIL SHAVINGS SIT!"

The four daughters of Dr. Raman Nair and his tiny wife, Jaya, all jumped where they were and Veena quickly whispered in the phone that she had to go. George, who could hear Dr. Raman Nair all the way from his Spartan Baltimore apartment, really couldn't quite absorb that he too *had to go.* Never before and never since was anyone more grateful than George when he ascertained that Manoj was not on call and not scheduled in the morning. He almost cried with relief when Manoj said he'd come along.

"Thank you."

"You are welcome. George?"

"Yeah?"

"It is going to be very bad."

"Yeah."

"THEY ARE FURTHER GROUND IN. THEY ARE DEEPER IN THE WEAVE. THIS MORNING, I COULD SEE THEM FLOATING ATOP THE FIBERS, BUT NOW, I SEE VERY FEW. BUT IF YOU PART THE FIBERS . . ." Here Dr. Raman Nair got down on his knees to demonstrate for his daughters and his wife who crowded above his head in the tiny doorway, blocked by his enormous behind and their own enormous . . . ness. "THERE, THERE YOU SEE? CAN YOU SEE? CAN YOU SEE?"

Of course they could not, but they all nodded with very serious faces. Veena, toward the back, slowly left for the kitchen, for she wanted to put the cake in to bake and have time to freshen up, this still being her falling-in-love time.

"WHY ARE YOU ALL STANDING HERE LIKE YOU ARE UNABLE TO UNDERSTAND? GO AND GET THE VACUUM AND VACUUM IT. NO RESPECT?"

Jaya put her hand on his chest and said, "You calm down, you calm down and stop shouting. You will have a heart attack and if you wake up Achan do you want to see the results?"

Dr. Raman Nair put on a very sarcastic face, and said in a wheedling mock that he rarely used, "Well then, madam, can you please explain to me what is so complicated about vacuuming this floor? So many girls in the house and still the floor should be impacted like an ear with pencil shavings?"

Usha, who was bound to respond to such a tone of voice, declared, "Impacted like an ear with pencil shavings? That is about as mixed a metaphor as I have ever heard."

He slowly turned to Usha. "What was that?" He bent forward in an angry display of oversmiling and ridiculing postures. "Kind miss, what was that?" The remaining girls were somewhat taken aback at their father's rudeness and stood still trying to understand how much pain it was, making him speak to them this way. "Mixed metaphor? Is it now that my English is not good enough? Is my turn of phrase now embarrassing, am I a fool to you now? You mock my speech, you defy my requests, you backtalk me in front of others?" His voice raised up an octave and he waved his head back and forth talking like a girl, " 'Impacted like an ear with pencil shavings? Mixed metaphors, Daddy, mixed metaphors.' " Even Usha closed her mouth and was silent.

"O," Jaya whispered. "O. Come on. Let us go. Let them clean up."

Dr. Raman Nair gave a loud humph. Just a moment ago, his sister had called and told him she was bringing his daughter home from college for her birthday, and he had been so happy. He sighed and his wife put her hand on his arm for one moment. *How quickly things can change.*

In their room, Jaya sat down on the bed and waited while Dr. Raman Nair paced back and forth and back and forth, staring at the floor unable to regain the fragile happiness he had embraced with such . . . GRATITUDE, JAYA, GRATITUDE . . . before that girl blithely and insensitively decided to invite her wayward vices into the house.

She watched him pace and when he finally stood still she said very blankly, "You cannot behave badly to him." She looked down at the floor and back up at him. "Regardless of how you feel."

"Humph. I can behave how I believe."

". . . he is the child of a friend of a friend."

"THAT is the thing too. It is good to be friends. It is all good to be friends. We all have them for friends. It is balanced very delicately. They are for friendship, not for marriage."

Of course this was true. But still. Here it was. "You cannot treat him badly."

"I WILL NOT BE A HYPOCRITE!"

She shook her head back and forth. "You cannot behave badly to him."

Silence . . .

Jaya's expression turned misty and Dr. Raman Nair knew she might have given up hope when she admitted . . . "He was a very nice boy . . . right?"

Silence . . .

Downstairs they could hear the vacuum roar into action, and Dr. Raman Nair was somewhat comforted by what he believed was the crackle of all those ground-in pencil shavings whirring up the hose, and what it suggested about their obedience: the daughters' *and* the pencil shavings'. He managed a small smile. Then, behind him in the hall, he heard someone pound up the stairs and into the bathroom; he heard the shower start. It would be Veena, making herself more irresistible for this man she wanted to marry. He sighed and deflated like a sad balloon. He sat down on the bed beside his wife, and she rose up several inches before teetering sideways into his arm, where she stayed until she could delay cooking no longer.

George and Manoj arrived first, and Veena was not sure if that was good or bad. She spied them from her bedroom window, and she ran down the stairs with her fresh black hair waving behind her like the sea, or a flag, or a dark curtain on a windy day. She could not hold back her smile. Her father, standing in the opening of his red-carpeted maharaja room, knew from the way she flew, and from the way she had never shone brighter, that there would be nothing he could do to dissuade her, too complete was the love for this boy. He plotted instead to watch for chinks in this George Thomas, for the times he would fail to love her as completely as she loved him. *These I will list in an offhand way, no directly, directly. I will just plainly tell her the times that I saw him fail her, and then she will see that there might be greater . . .*

She threw open the door and before her father's eyes, became even more resplendent than she had been sailing down the stairs. She reached out her hands and Dr. Raman Nair saw one dark hand, fine in musculature, and each long finger wrap between each of the ten fingers of his firstborn girl. When she turned around, her smile was so wide and yet, her eyes were also so wide. And then she pulled him into the house without the least shame. And Dr. Raman Nair thought, in spite of himself . . . well, he just wouldn't think anything just yet.

At the table, Veena was showing off her princess cake and George really was admiring it with the glow of their falling-in-love time. (When he turned fifty years old, Veena made him a cake in the shape of the Roman Coliseum with rubble made from hand-dyed wafer crumble, and columns whose Doric, Ionic, and Corinthian caps she had carved from fondant icing dyed an unappetizing and entirely authentic shade of ancient. With it, she gave him his gift of tickets for a two-week Roman vacation. When he spoke to the guests, he wept. He said, "I'm sorry. I'm sorry. But, was there ever a man as lucky as me? I am the luckiest, happiest man in the world. Look at the cake my wife made for me." Their falling-in-love time never ended.)

Dr. Raman Nair and Manoj entered and the room fell into a frightened hush, with Veena trailing off on, "I spun the sugar right on the . . ." George, who had been facing the other way, felt the hairs on his arm raise like a rabbit, and he turned and found Dr. Raman Nair staring at him, grim, purple, and breathing through his nose. Jaya, in the kitchen, sent him thoughts through the air, *Don't treat him badly, but don't give in, don't say anything rude, but don't make him think we are pleased, don't be like a bully, but don't be like a turnover, don't talk too loud, but don't be too quiet. . . . Make him feel it would be best if he himself decided it was not a good idea.*

George, with his humble, handsome face, stood looking at Dr. Raman Nair with his eyebrows up.

When he blinks he does so quickly and gets it over with. Dr. Raman Nair found himself touched by the boy's unwillingness to appear inattentive. *Hmph . . . I am just grasping at straws, looking for anything to make this bearable. He blinks and gets it over with. What am I thinking about?* He inhaled and exhaled like a snore and rubbed his hand over his face like a tired schoolmaster. Without a word, he paced toward George like a sheriff, slowlike and bold, but as he approached, Veena slid out from behind and stepped between them. She put her hand up and stopped him dead in his tracks.

Dr. Raman Nair's heart, which was calmed somewhat by the boy's infrequent blinking and the respect it indicated, began to beat like a war drum. He raised his hand to the air and shouted, "WHAT DO YOU

THINK I WILL DO? WHAT DO YOU THINK I AM? WHAT DO YOU THINK I WILL DO THAT YOU HAVE TO STAND WITH YOUR ARM OUT LIKE A CROSSING GUARD DIRECTING TRAFFIC?"

Dr. Nair's fist shook over her head while he sputtered and pointed and tried to find the words and then when he was just about to pound his fist emphatically into his palm, which was his common gesture, George slid out from behind and stepped in between them. Again, Dr. Raman Nair was stopped dead, hand in midair.

"WHAT IS THIS? WHAT IS THIS HAPPENING HERE? YOU TWO, SNEAKING AROUND LIKE ROBBERS IN THE NIGHT AND YOU ARE GOING TO STAND THERE AND PROTECT EACH OTHER? FROM ME???!!!" He looked up at Jaya, horrified in the kitchen, and put on another show of wheedling smiles and with his head rocking side to side to mock them, he continued, "See, Jaya? It is *I* they need protection from? The one stands to protect the boy from my handshake and the other stands to protect my daughter from my . . ." Here he again grew enraged and he leaned forward and asked with a bellow, "WHAT WERE YOU GOING TO PROTECT HER FROM? FROM MY FIST? DID YOU HAVE SOME IMPRESSION THAT I BEAT MY CHILDREN? HAVE YOU NOTICED HER WITH BRUISES ON THE DAYS AND NIGHTS SHE HAS SPENT WITH YOU?"

The two stood together, Veena on tiptoe, peeking out over George's shoulder, George aware of her hot breath on his back. With her curled-up fingers, she clenched some of his shirt and stroked it.

"YES, DON'T THINK WE ARE FOOLS, DON'T THINK WE ARE FOOLS."

Jaya came out of the kitchen, put a plate with *moork* and another with *vada* on the table and stood silently beside her husband. *No, don't think we are fools, we trusted you because you are our child and we have never had reason to mistrust you. We did not trust you because we are fools. Know this.* In spite of it all, Jaya found herself touched by the fraction of a degree's decline in the angle at which the boy held his chin, and by the way he closed his eyes for several seconds and opened them with a look of terrible despair and shame. *Hmph. Good. So he feels ashamed. He should feel ashamed. Calm down.*

"Hmph," Jaya said aloud and she returned to the kitchen to shake off this feeling that the boy was very sweet and *paavam.*

Now they looked like this: Veena, down off her toes, but still behind George, who stood like a penitent before the Lord; Mira, Usha and Shanti standing by the table looking back and forth between the lovers and their father, who breathed in and out, in and out, in and out with his face pulled into a tight, angry scrunch. Behind the girls, their mother washed dishes that she just as easily could have loaded in the dishwasher, but then what would she do with her discomfort and hopelessness? And then Manoj, who sat at the table and ate *moork* and *vada* because what else was there to do?

When the barking began, loud and regular as church bells, they were too absorbed in their personal doom to even notice; but of course, Muthachan noticed.

As the great Taj Mahal, smelling someone old and someone new, lunged at the garage door with joy and hospitality, Muthachan staggered in from his room with his arms held over his head waving his stick and shrieking.

"THEY HAVE COME, THEY HAVE COME, THEY HAVE COME, AAAAAAAAAAA." And of course, they had.

Outside, Chris opened the car door and held out his hand for Dhanya. She looked up and her face crumpled in fear and shame. "Come on," he said. Hearing the dog, he smiled. "I think someone already knows you have come home."

Dhanya stood outside the car and listened to her dog. *Now they all know I am home.* She thought to just take her bag from the trunk and mosey on down the road, get a job someplace, disappear like milk-carton youth, all of it preferable to facing up to her failings. . . . Yet, the thundering boom of the great Taj Mahal, his cartoonish attempt to burst through the garage leaving a Great Dane shape in the door, his unconditional love and acceptance when everyone else might look at her sidelong, or thrash her within an inch of her life . . . it gave her the willingness to go inside. She could not walk away leaving him wondering where she had gone, wandering in and out of rooms, searching, searching and pining with sadness, wondering, wasn't she just today outside the garage door? She went to the trunk, but Chris had already grabbed everything and was waiting beside Gitammai. He too looked a little queasy and for the first time, Dhanya stopped to consider what Gitammai and he would face when they entered the home of Dr. Raman Nair. And then, for the first time, she considered her father and mother. *They will not know which way to turn. . . .*

Gita came forward and put an arm through hers. "Shall we go, then?"

"Through the front door though. Taj is in there." Dhanya points to the garage and Gita looks at the garage too. Linked arm in arm with their heads so close together, Chris is again momentarily startled at the sight of them. Chris takes a swallow that looks like a fist down his gullet and Gita extends her arm. "Shall we lock arms all together?" she asks with a laugh.

He bends for the luggage, and remarks, "We'll arrive like Dorothy, the Tin Man and the Cowardly Lion."

"I'll be Scarecrow," Dhanya says. She shrugs her shoulders. "He's the one that needed the brain."

"Stop such remarks," Gitammai says firmly, and off they go.

Inside, the chaos had begun. Muthachan, immediately alerted to the coming of someone, or the going of someone, by that harbinger of comings, goings, plunder, disaster and wicked intention that was the tremendous bark of Taj Mahal, was now standing amid them all swinging his stick and shouting this time, "BE ON THE ALERT, THEY COME, THEY COME, DIVIDE INTO REGIMENTS, BUT REMAIN TIGHT." He leapt atop a kitchen chair and raised both arthritic shoulders beyond their natural range of motion.

When Muthachan turned warrior, he was infused with the strength of Bhima. The doorbell rang. He shrieked with his stick held high, "*UALALAULAULAULA!*"

Outside, Chris heard the yell and instinctively pulled the girls away from the door. Dhanya put her face in her hands. Gita took a long breath and rubbed her belly protectively. From under his immense arms, the girls explained.

"It is my father."
"My grandfather."
"It is his battle cry."
"His battle cry?"
"It has nothing to do with us."
"It's the dog."
"He battles the dog?"
"No."
"But when he barks."
"It makes Muthachan excited."
"Oh."

Would they have heard the doorbell? Taj Mahal leaped and lurched against the garage door, and when he fell back down, he yelped each time his skidding paws lost their footing, again and again. Over and over. BANGsshhhhyelp. BANGshhhhyelp. And through it all, a raucous barking like Armageddon.

They rang the bell once more.

"UALALAULAULAULA. WE WILL MEET AT THE RIGHT SIDE OF GOD. HE WHO CRIES GOD IS TRUTH IS EVER HAPPY. THEY HAVE ARRIVED, THEY HAVE COME, THE TIME IS NOW TO TAKE ARMS AND STAND TOGETHER."

There would be no way but to knock him down, and even then, Dr. Raman Nair knew that at the end of the battle, the rain of blows might end his own life and his father would be spilled on the floor like a thousand broken matchsticks. *What difference anyway for either of us? Dead, alive.* Dr. Raman Nair, not prone to fits of fatalism, took a deep breath and rushed forward to grab the stick. Oh, but Muthachan was too spry this evening!

Like a puma from the treetops, Muthachan leapt right over the extended arms of his son, right past the second line of waiting daughters, and straight for the door. "AAAAAAAAAAAAA," he shrieked and when the doorbell rang the third time, he was ready. He flung open the door and stood on the threshold brandishing his stick, his white hair waving madly, his face covered with silver stubble, his mouth white with a furious foam.

Outside, Chris was still huddling Gita and Dhanya in his arms, unable to absorb that this was apparently normal and unthreatening behavior. When the door opened to the old man wielding what seemed to be a club, Chris pushed the girls to either side of him, stepped forward in one stride and, without a second thought, plucked it from his hand. On cue, Shanti gently moved Muthachan to the side, sidled out, grabbed the stick from Chris, and returned to the house where she quickly deposited it between the refrigerator and the wall where it went when Muthachan lost his mind. And then they all stood there looking one to the other, to the other, to the other, to the other. . . .

Muthachan began to weep in a quiet, muffled, baby-boy way, and his hair that had just the moment before stood high with electricity hung too long over his eyes and around his ears. Chris watched the old man grow smaller and smaller and he felt very sad for having shamed him before his children and grandchildren. *Was there any other way?* Jaya saw in this unknown face rare compassion, and in spite of herself she liked him very much.

In the stunned stillness that followed, Dhanya inched forward without notice and held her grandfather around his tiny shoulders. "Did you miss me?" she asked, gently walking him back into the house.

"*Molu*? Do you know my daughter, Gita? She is very much like you."

"I think I know her," Dhanya whispered into his hand. "I think I know her."

"Gitu?" Dr. Raman Nair looked at his sister's face and body so changed and he called her name with a question, because, perhaps this girl was not she?

"Chetta," Gita answered.

They stood and stared at each other and then Chris stepped back a pace or two and put his arm gently around Gita's shoulder and led her closer, where they stood and stared some more. Dr. Raman Nair's eyes finally stung so raw he felt shame at being seen in such humiliation. *It has, all in all, failed.* He turned and went inside the house. Not knowing what else to do, they all filed in behind him, with Chris and Gita bringing up the rear. Shanti held back and in her delicate and precious way, whispered to them both, "Don't worry, put the bags down. Everything will be all right." And so Chris put the bags down and took the hand she held out to him and the child led him into this home he had considered a thousand times, over the years and years and years he had longed to belong in Gita's real life.

In Muthachan's room, Dhanya removed his shiny black shoes and his long black socks and laid him back into his bed.

"*Molu*? Do you know if my foot is loose?" he asked in a tiny pleading voice.

Dhanya squeezed both his feet tight, and swiveled them on the ankles. "This one is nice and tight . . . and this one . . . good . . . good. Nice and tight."

"Thank you, *mole*." Muthachan patted the bed as though it were the top of her head, her back, her shoulder. A gesture of appreciation.

Dhanya went to his sink and wet a washcloth with hot water. She brought it back and washed Muthachan's face and neck, so he would rest peacefully. When his breathing became regular, she sat down at the foot of his bed and worked on the courage to face them all.

When she rose, she caught sight of a figure near the sink. She turned and held out her hand. "Ammai, come with me." But it was only her reflection in a mirror, distorted by distance and too little food. She was, for the very first time, shocked at how different she appeared, in Ammai's little top, Ammai's little pants, from the girl who left here big and happy. She went closer to the mirror and realized that big and happy was much prettier than little and miserable. Even beautiful, beautiful Gitammai was prettier now that she was happy. And she was bigger too. She sighed and made to leave. As she turned the knob, Muthachan moaned a little moan and slapped his gums. Dhanya stood still and watched him until he settled himself to sleep, and like a tired mother, she tiptoed from the room.

In the living room, everyone sat at odd angles, staring at the floor or at blank patches of wall, fingering the arms of the sofas with concentrated focus that was, nonetheless, completely absent of consciousness. Jaya, in the kitchen, stirred a pot on a cold stove, and Manoj braided and unbraided the carpet fringe with the dexterous fingers of his right hand. George sat beside Veena who, weary from her father's sadness, leaned her head on his shoulder. Without thinking, George reached over and held her hand. When Dr. Raman Nair took a deep breath that pulled the air from everyone's lungs, and looked up, there they were. Sitting like this. He exhaled and dropped his head back to the random patterns in the carpet that Manoj continued to worry with his fingers. Manoj looked up from his seat at the carpet's edge. *How quickly things can change.* All these months, he had worried about his role in the deception, letting his own cousin-sister lie to her father. It was tacit approval. All this time worrying that it would break his *ammavan*'s heart when he found it out. *But now, Gita Kunjuamma? Coming home pregnant?* He looked back down at the fringe, and continued to braid.

Dhanya entered the scene with her hair pulled over her shoulder, braiding and unbraiding it like carpet fringe, and truly, even just these few hours away from the depleting power of Dr. Russell Worthy had her looking a little healthier. And shame and fear made her appear modest and well behaved. When Dr. Raman Nair felt her presence and raised his eyes, he smiled a wide and happy grin, putting all his troubles behind him, for here was a girl who also belonged to him and this one at least was modest and well behaved.

"AAH-ha, my *chakarakutty*, the birthday girl!" He stood up and pulled her close to breathe her hair like a kiss. "Happy birthday, *chakaramolu*! You missed your Suprabhatam this morning! I played it, only you did not hear!" He moved her away from him by her shoulders to see her better, and slowly his smile faded and his eyes grew misty with the dangerous portent of her failure to meet his eye, or to return his smile, by the tremble in her bones and the strange metallic smell that rose from her sweat, and by her size, so much diminished she was as shocking as a shrunken sun.

The room was not the boisterous clamor of good wishes that might be expected on her birthday, but something altogether quieter, for who could mistake the grievous pallor of disgrace. Disgrace? Jaya came forward with a dripping spoon in her hand and her mouth open in a question. "Dhanyamol?" she asked, running her hand up and down the girl's arm, which quivered and was now not so much bigger than her own.

Veena, with the blood slipping from her head, stood up from George's side. The other sisters came forward too, and suddenly Dhanya was surrounded by her family in a circle of concern that made her woozy, as she had lost the habit of eating. Before leaving the cottage covered in roses, Gita had forced her to eat an apple and a piece of bread. She ate the apple, but the bread she had tucked into her pants and crumbled behind her like Gretel walking into the woods; it was a hard habit to break. One apple in so many hours did not agree with the morning cocktail of supplements that she had ingested before leaving Dr. Russell Worthy's house. In the center of the circle of heat and breath and hair as dark as a void, Dhanya felt herself disappearing; her knees buckled and she wilted to the floor.

"What is wrong?" Jaya crouched down and moaned, rocking back and forth, holding Dhanya's head against her breast. "*Molu, molu, Dhanyamole? Enthupati, molu, enthupati?*"

"Nothing, Mommy. Nothing," she whispered. She felt her saliva grow thick in her mouth and looked about for somewhere to turn, someplace to spit. There was no empty space, sisters everywhere. Stroking her arms, stroking her cheek, loosening her buttons, pulling back her hair, keening, calling, crying. She opened her eyes wide for a moment, turned her head to the side, and leaked a trail of bile onto her mother's knee. And then she was out cold.

Gita, from outside the circle, looked to Chris with brimming eyes and he lowered his face into his hands and sat down on a chair. George and Manoj, the surgeons, crowded along the perimeter, unable to break in, unsure what was happening, the hairs on their arms standing up and shivering, their long experience with trauma telling them, without even seeing her face, that as bad as this might be, she was not presently at risk of death.

Finally, as Jaya became desperate and began to shake the child, Gita came forward and laid a hand on her brother's shoulder. He turned and saw her, bursting from the middle and glowing like a torch, and his tears fell openly down his face. He saw in her calm sadness that she had the answer they all needed. "What has happened to my girl?" The quiet anguish in his voice brought the room to silence as though a sudden deafness had befallen them all. They looked at each other to see if lips were still moving and heads were still thrown back and if it was only they who could no longer hear it. But then he gasped in baffled fear and asked again, "Gitu, what has happened to my girl?"

Gita looked over her shoulder at Chris, who rose in response. Though he had never met her brother, the great and powerful Dr. Raman Nair, he held him gently by the arm and helped him to rise from the floor, where he kneeled beside his wife. He led him to the sofa and helped him to sit and Dr. Raman Nair looked up at this tall and powerful stranger who had come with his sister, and saw a rare kindness and fortitude, and he felt safer for having him there, whoever he was, for he himself was very weak. *I am very weak, and whatever needs to be done, I do not know if I can do it.* For the first time in his life, Dr. Raman Nair did not know if he could do whatever needed to be done.

He looked back at his daughter lying on the floor in the arms of her mother and then back at Chris and again he asked, "What has happened to my girl?"

Chris in his low voice answered, "Nothing from which she will not recover." And he smiled so gently and so small that Dr. Raman Nair believed him and felt ready to hear what had happened, and quiet enough to listen very hard for as long as it took for the story to be told. The next hours were almost the quietest and saddest of Dr. Raman Nair's life.

Rites of Passage

Veena opened the door carefully and peered through the crack to see if Muthachan was sleeping or awake. Inside, he was standing at the window looking out on the front yard, and when he heard the door open, he turned to her and smiled a smile she only vaguely remembered from years before, on the veranda of his home in Kerala.

"*Mole?* Come sit here, Muthachan has mango."

"Is it sweet?"

"It is so sweet, it is dripping sugar onto the plate."

"Can we give it to Mira too?"

"No, Mira is too small. It is only for big girls. Come sit and we will eat it together."

Veena saw his lucidity; she smiled in return. "Muthachan?"

"Yes, Veenumol?"

"I came to say good-bye." Veena sat on the bed. He turned from the window and tilted his head to understand, or to hear her better.

"Good-bye? Where are you going?"

"To meet my mother- and father-in-law." As she said this, a small sweat raised on the bridge of her nose. Muthachan, his eyes so used to seeing things invisible to others, noticed.

"Hmmm." He came and sat beside her and put his hand on her thigh. There was a long silence. Muthachan, tapping her leg, continued looking out the window. In the quiet, Veena imagined stony silences and grim mouths, a frigid reception in a Minnesota January.

"Touch their feet," he finally said in a bold voice, full and certain.

"What?"

"Touch their feet. When you arrive, first thing, touch their feet."

"Really?"

Muthachan tilted his head to the ceiling and lifted his hand from her leg to scratch his itchy stubble. "When your mother came first time to our house, she had no parents. She had no parents and she was a very serious person." Muthachan looked back at Veena to be sure she was listening. "When your Gauri Ammai saw her picture she said, 'She has no parents.' It was that evident from the look on her face. And I was very scared, because my son was a very powerful person and she had a . . . forlorn look. But she came inside our home and she bent to the floor and she touched your grandmother's feet. And then she stood up, came to me and touched my feet as well. And I knew that she would always be strong enough to bend like a willow tree, and that she would never break. Even with a powerful husband like my son."

Veena looked at her grandfather, whose face had become taut with thinking and presence. He was so handsome, and he looked like Gitammai. "Right now, Muthachan, you look like Gitammai."

He smiled at her and said, "No. Gitu looks like Ammukutty. Did you ever see my Ammukutty? She was a very pretty girl. Did you ever see my Ammukutty?" And in this question, Veena saw Muthachan's face slacken to a safer place where her grandmother still looked like Gitammai, and still came in the morning to give him tea on the veranda, especially at this time of year when it was so pleasant outside, and a little chilly in the mornings.

She gave him a kiss on the cheek and laid him back on his bed and before he closed his eyes she assured him that she would touch their feet.

On Christmas Eve, George had come to the home of Dr. Raman Nair unannounced, for they all thought he had gone home for Christmas. Veena almost fell off the stepladder where she was standing to hang mistletoe, although there was no one she really, really wanted to kiss if he was not there. *I will kiss my father one hundred times instead.* When she stumbled off the stepladder, he was standing beneath her, as he always was, and he shouldered her fall, as he always would. She held the mistletoe over his head, and planted one on his mouth, in front of everyone. It was quite a scene.

After dinner, he managed to get Dr. Raman Nair alone while the girls cleaned up and this is what he said in one breathless, nearly hiccupped, trembling sputter which was actually endearing to Dr. Raman Nair, who was learning to come to terms with things.

"Uncle, I am very much in love with Veena and, sheshesheshe is very much in love with me, at least I think so, I mean, I know so, but I mean, I don't want you to think I am speaking for her, but I am speaking for her in that sense that I am asking you for her, I mean, not that I am asking you for her, but that I am very much in love with her and she is very much . . . I mean, I would like very much to marry her." And here he took a breath, but this was not the way he had practiced, because he knew that there were issues, and he meant to deal with them in his speech, but he had forgotten, so quickly he resumed, "I know, I am Catholic and she is Hindu, but I want you to know that I would never ask her to convert for me, just as she would never ask such a thing, I mean, I know you can't just, but what I mean is that we have talked a lot about this, and I would never make her do anything, I will never make her do anything that she does not want to do and certainly not something like that. And I know that my family also has concerns like your family does, but I promise you that I will always take care of her and I will always love her and take care of her and I will take care of you and everyone, and I will always take care of her . . . and you." And here George stopped. He thought that was about all he had to say.

Dr. Raman Nair sighed and rubbed his hand over his face. He knew it was only a matter of time. And he was learning to come to terms with things. It was not the way he had always imagined it. But what was . . .

So he took a deep breath and called loudly for his wife and she came hurrying with a dish towel and a look of concern. When she saw the two of them standing in the office, she stopped and looked back and forth between them.

"He wants to marry our girl."

Jaya rested her eyes on her husband and sighed a little sigh. It was not the way she had always imagined it . . . but what was. She lay her dishcloth down on the desk and stood beside her husband. And together but one at a time, they raised both their hands and touched him gently on the head. A tacit blessing. *Please God, look after these two children who have embarked upon a rarely traveled road. Bless them with your care.*

Two weeks later, George and Veena entered the home of Dr. CV Thomas and his wife, Elizabeth. It was snowing, and the wind blew in heavy gusts. They opened their door with faces fearful and serious and the young ones bustled in bundled with only eyes showing between the wrappings of their scarves. In her thick coat, Veena appeared as enormous as a planet, and with her hair tucked away and heavy gloves, it was hard to imagine that she was a living, breathing person whom their handsome and perfect son wanted to marry. They were stunned to silence by her size, which only heightened their reservations about the viability of this doomed match.

But CV and Elizabeth were polite people with good manners. "Come, take off your coats." They removed their boots and moved away from the door into the living room where it was warmer. George undid his layers, Veena removed hers, and Elizabeth took things one by one, and by the time she had gotten down to her pretty white sweater and tailored pants, she looked positively normal sized, and both CV and Elizabeth were somewhat relieved. Elizabeth quickly took her son's things too, and put them out of sight and when she returned, George said, "Mom, Dad, I would like you to meet Veena Nair."

And before they had a chance to shake hands, Veena went first to his father and then to his mother and bent to the ground and touched their feet. And without a second thought, their instincts took over and one after the other, they touched their hands to her beautiful head of hair and blessed her, without having intended to succumb so easily. As Elizabeth touched the girl's head, the tears rolled down from her eyes, and she couldn't tell if it was from sadness, disappointment or the surprise of finding something very loveable in her son's future wife.

Months passed in the flurry of buying and planning and fitting and selecting that accompanies rites of passage. And Dhanya came home from school on weekends this semester, because her sister was getting married and every weekend, there was something wonderful to do, and in this way, Dhanya slowly became happier, and less ashamed, and she began to eat. Some weekends, Clara came along, because all girls love to plan a wedding. At night, sometimes the three of them, Shanti, Clara and, quiet in the corner bed, Dhanya, would lie in the dark and wonder what it would be like to get married, and whom they might marry, and would he be as wonderful to them as George was to Veena Chechi and sometimes, from quiet in the corner, Dhanya too would whisper a thought, like, "I would like to get married in the fall." And like this the months passed in a wonderful whirlwind for all five daughters of Dr. Raman Nair, and for his baby sister too.

In April, Chris and Gita went up the steps of the courthouse with only Penelope, Jack and Kate in attendance. The big wedding was two weeks away and it did not seem necessary to them to make a grand production of their own unorthodox event. "My brother would faint with unease," Gita knew. Also, Veena was floating on air, and she should have no interference with all things wedding.

"Certainly not another wedding!"

"And I am not waiting one more day than I must," Chris whispered in her hair.

"Besides," Gita said, "I look ridiculous!"

"You look spectacular."

"In the true sense of the word."

"A beautiful one. You are a beautiful one." By now, Chris could only hold her from behind, and his son and his daughter pushed his hands away with headbutts and kicks. "They are already jealous." He smiled.

That evening, they had dinner at Penelope's house, and Gita called her brother and told him she was married. He sternly said, "Good, it is better that way." Inside, he believed this, and she heard so in his voice. After a pause he added in a gruff voice, "Gitu, you come here by at least Thursday to stay. Both of you." He cleared his throat. "Manoj needs help to get the *kalyanamandapam* and take it to the place, and then also to do some other small, small things. George will be doing so many other things."

"We will be there." Gita closed her eyes and lowered her chin in thanks. "I will call Chechi and see what all she needs that week. Maybe I will come early and Chris can come by Thursday."

"You just drive together." He cleared his throat. "Too close to drive so far alone." He was quiet for a while and then, "Hmph. Are you okay then?"

"I am feeling fine."

"Hmph. Okay then. I will see you in a week or two."

From his basement lookout post, where Del Musik sat spying through their open windows, it was so outrageous he could not manage to write anything down.

One hour before dawn Dr. Raman Nair and his wife woke, but she stayed in bed and stared at the ceiling, praying without knowing she was doing so. He walked down the steps of his house as quietly as he could with his immense size and aching knees, and with a long, deep breath he hit play.

Om.

He made a slow walk to the *puja* room and opened the door, where Unnikrishnan and the rest greeted him with cheery or placid faces. They didn't seem at all worried, so . . . perhaps. . . . He prostrated himself and without the slightest hesitation or distraction, he prayed for the well-being of his child and of her husband. He prayed that they would find solace in each other's presence and love. He prayed that they would be true to each other and that they would be granted blessings equal to their nature. He prayed that they would be blessed with children and that these children would be raised with understanding and open-minded guidance. He prayed for their health and happiness. He prayed they would always seek comfort and care in their families because their families loved them very much.

Om.

When he emerged, the house was beginning to stir. He came into the foyer and looked up, and at the top of the stairs his firstborn daughter stood rubbing her loose hair and smiling at him. At that moment, he could see every moment of her whole life like a slow-moving film inside his mind.

Upstairs out of the noise and bustle below, Jaya wrapped Gita tight in a sari that Veena had bought her as an offering to her elders. It was a pale pink color that made Gita feel pretty in these days of mythic size. The black line down her middle made her self-conscious of baring her belly in front of others, as silly as that might have been.

"Please, Chechi, please, tomorrow, put my sari on upstairs? I am so big and blackened."

"Athuenthina? *Why do that? No one cares? My stomach is like a highway map of America, with these enormous girls I grew. And it hangs in loose, loose drips.*"

"Please, Chechi, please?"

"O, such a production. Okay, okay. Just give it to me now to iron the sari and blouse. You look like you are going to have those babies last week. Look how he kicks you so hard he leaves inside-out footprints. That is the boy, only a boy will kick so hard."

"Then you should see the girl. She puts her whole face up and you can see her nose and her lips."

"Don't have them until after the wedding."

"Did you hear that? Ammai said you cannot come until after the wedding."

"Ha! She looked at me."

"I told you."

"Ha!"

It was an all-day affair. A morning ceremony, brief and unintelligible, but replete with the magic of sacraments conducted before fire, joining them once. Round and round they went. Seven times? Eight times? It didn't matter; when George tied the *thali* around Veena's neck and they exchanged those hand-tied garlands, it was real, they were married, and so they were less afraid later in the afternoon, when Father Michael, whom Veena and George had found through the grapevine of unorthodox brethren who wanted to marry in the Catholic Church without conversion of one party or the other, asked, "Does anyone here know of any reason that these two should not be united in Holy Matrimony?" Because it didn't matter who spoke up, they were already married, and if the *pujari* had asked the question, no one would have understood anyway because he was speaking in Tamil.

And so it was done. In the morning, Veena wore a red sari threaded in gold. It was as heavy a silk as Jaya had ever felt. When she was done with her dressing and she emerged from the room, everyone said, "Ooooooo," and nothing more. In the afternoon she changed to a cream sari threaded in gold, and when she came down the aisle, she sparkled and shimmered like a star. George forgot she was already his wife. His heart thudded and his eyes brimmed. And so it was done. They were married. And perhaps it was the power of two wedding ceremonies in one day, performed before a multitude of gods, each attended by the same hundreds of friends and loved ones who first gathered *here*, and then got in their cars and shuttled *there*, and in each place of worship prayed doubly hard for this odd couple; perhaps it was all these blessings squared that gave their marriage extra-special benediction, because it was a very happy union that was filled with abundant love. And on the day they were married twice, the party lasted until the wee hours of the morning for everyone except Chris and Gita.

As the dance floor twirled with Indian girls in beautiful colors and all their American friends who wished they had thought to wear something a little less black, Gita sat with her head back on the deep chest of her husband. She was feeling less normal than she had felt even in her recent discomforts, and of course, she was due in only two weeks, and she was so big by now that when she extended her arms before her, she could not reach the end of herself.

"Chris, I think perhaps we should head back home."

"Home? Or home home?"

"Home home."

His heart began a more pronounced thumping; she could feel against her cheek. "It is not contractions, I don't think. Nothing hurts. I just have a strange feeling that I don't know."

Chris got to his feet and helped her up. From across the room, Shanti saw them rise and she raced forward with a smile on her face. "What?" she asked.

"Nothing, *molu*. But I think we need to go back to Quiet Pond. I feel strange."

"Do you think you should go now? It's so far. Maybe you need to stay here in the house."

"It will be better to just go. It's only two hours and my doctor is there. I am not in any great pain. I just think it is best to be safe."

Shanti ran off and returned quickly with her mother.

"Is it now?" Jaya asked with concern.

"No, Chechi, no. I just feel somewhat tired and I think . . ."

"Stay at our place."

"Chechi, I think it might be coming soon. In the next few days. I should go home."

"Mmm. Mmm . . ." Jaya's face piqued with concern. *Should I come along? Should I let her go? Should I make her stay?*

"I'll take her home," Chris said decisively. "When we get there, we will call you and let you know we have arrived safely. Everything will be fine."

Gita turned to Shanti and said, "Will you tell Daddy I am fine?"

Shanti wrinkled her brow and nodded. It seemed too long until Ammai would be safe at home in Quiet Pond.

When they called from the cottage covered in yellow roses, Gita could hear the thumping rhythm of a party still going strong.

"Chechi?" Gita said.
"*Gita*?" Jaya shouted.
"*Chechi*?" Gita shouted back. "*It is me. We are here!*"
"*Gita? Is it you? Are you there?*"
"*Yes!! Yes!!! It is me!! We are here!!!*"
"*Is everything okay?*"
"*Everything is okay.*"
"*Okay, call me tomorrow in the morning, I can't hear properly.*"
"*I will call you tomorrow.*"
"*What??*"
"*Bye!!*"
"*Okay. Bye.*"

And perhaps it was the effort of shouting so loud after such an uncomfortable trip home that pushed the twins into action, but by the time they called Jaya in the morning, it was Chris and not Gita on the line. And what he said rang out in ecstatic echoes around the home of Dr. Raman Nair, where some of his girls were still asleep.

In his low lava voice, Chris announced, "Gita is asleep, the babies have come. They are fine, she is fine. The babies have come."

And in the background he heard it come back again and again, fainter and closer. He lowered his tired face into his hand and listened to them chant, "The BABIES have come! The BABIES have come! The BABIES have come!" Quietly, he breathed the first happy sigh of fatherhood.

Oh, what beautiful babies they were. Each the color of the other and both the color of sunset, dark pink and gold, bright with shine. When they slept in a naked summer bundle, one could never tell where Krishan ended and Kiran began. Around their middles, they each wore a golden chain tied by their only *ammavan*, Dr. Raman Nair, who had gone to the Vietnamese jewelers and selected each 22-carat *aranyanam* himself.

"One should be stronger like a cord, and the other should be delicate. With a more . . . filigreed pattern."

"Filigreed pattern will bend and then it will scratch her, remember that useless one you bought for Shanti? She wore it only one week, and then I switched it to Mira's, or one of the other ones."

"You! Eddi, you just be quiet, always making difficult comments."

"Aha, kind sir, will it be you there to wake up in the night when the filigreed pattern disturbs her sleep? No, never you. Always me. You buy filigreed pattern and then someone else suffers the consequences. No filigree!"

And in the end, on the twenty-eighth-day ceremony, with the whole family, Penelope and her children in attendance, Dr. Raman Nair tied a sparkling cord around Kiran's bare waist that was not filigreed, and not like a cord, but twisted in a slim braid. He felt it marked her as the girl. And for Krishan, he bought a flat chain thick like a belt, and as soon as it was attached around his waist, he peed in a long arc that missed them all, but drew resounding laughter and applause. "HA! See that! He likes it!" Dr. Raman Nair beamed with the baby in his lap. And then he leaned down and whispered their names in their ears.

Shhhh.

Your name is Kiran.

Shhhh.

Your name is Krishan.

And Krishan they all called Kris, and Gita knew even her brother would not wrinkle when he heard it called, because his name was actually Krishan. She had always said that Chris was her favorite name. . . .

Those twins were happy in the night, playing with each other in the cozy space between their parents, and fighting for their mother's breasts, which she had taken to just leaving exposed for them to find on their own, *Please God, let me sleep for only twenty minutes, just twenty minutes is all I ask.* And when morning finally came, those babies were quite tired. They nestled down to sleep, hunkered over each other such that the only way to see who was who was by the chains around their waists, one a delicate braid and one a thick belt. But though the babies rested peacefully in the morning, Gita was unable to relax her vigilance. Just as she felt herself go deeply down, a panic, and with her eyes closed, she would reach out to make sure they were still there, a braid and a belt, ingrained in her tactile knowledge, a braid and a belt, and finding them, she would calm her worries. But again, as she felt herself go deep, she would reach out to check, a braid and a belt. Again and again. She began to make silly mistakes like pouring milk into the skillet to make scrambled eggs, and drinking the beaten yolks instead.

But it couldn't happen for long, with Chris always watching over her. One morning before she fell into her relax, panic, check, relax, panic, check pattern of sleep, he whispered, "I am taking the twins for a walk."

"But it is four A.M.!"

"They don't know it is four A.M. You are to sleep until you no longer feel like sleeping."

"But it is chilly, still."

"I will bundle them up, and they will be perfectly fine."

"But when will you return?"

"In time."

"What if they don't take the bottle?"

"Then I will bring them home to nurse."

"Do you think it is okay?"

"Yes."

"Okay." She looked up at him with so much gratitude that he blushed and kissed her forehead. *How quickly things can change.*

He gathered up Kiran and put her in a pink tuft with arms; he gathered up Kris and put him in a blue tuft with arms. So tired were they from the night of frolicking that there was no risk of waking them; they slumped into the double stroller like tiny sacks of basmati rice. Four hours later, when Gita came out onto the porch to check for their return, she found them, perhaps twenty yards from the house. Chris, laid back in the hammock, with two bundles, pink and blue, clutched to his chest like . . . festive sacks of basmati rice. She laughed and went inside to find the camera and she took something like fifty pictures from different angles. For the last, she balanced the camera on a stump and used the timer, so she could stand behind her family and be captured with them in happy repose. It was a photograph Chris kept for his whole life.

July was so hot there was no relief in being still. Jack and Kate traveled the long pond road looking up at the sky, for every now and then a small droplet would fall, striking them on the nose or cheek.

"It's too hot to stay home and do nothing," Jack said to no one in particular. It might have been foolish to have come so far on foot. But the only breeze was the one you made yourself by walking into the stagnant air. And even that breeze was so hot.

The rain began to fall in solid sheets that pelted the children and lay them flat against the slipping mud. When lightning struck the pond in furious white flashes, they felt the hairs on their arms rise up and quiver. They huddled together in a mass, searching for safety. Far in the distance, but closer than any other shelter, INVIOLATE swung on its post, like a screen door in a hurricane. White, black, bold and not at all inviting, but they still ran toward it, while the lightning whipped the pond behind them.

Inside, Jeri quietly made a noonday meal and listened to the storm outside. She found great comfort in her home on stormy days, for Chris had built it with a solid hand. When she heard the pounding of so many feet on the porch and of so many hands on the door, she dropped her fork and bit her tongue. She threw back her chair and ran for the door, for what could it be in her quiet, lonely life that would bring so many people here? She had no one at all.

The children, scared beyond their excellent manners, spilled into the house with no concern for the wood floors or their dripping, muddy clothes. They wriggled and slithered, tripping over each other, struggling to close the door behind them, but still someone's leg or another one's arm was sticking out through the doorway. Keeping—them—from—shutting—out—that—storm. When finally all errant limbs were bent and pulled from the entrance, Jack slammed the door and they both lay in a heap, gasping, gasping, heaving. Catching their breath.

Jeri, who never had a chance to help them in, immediately began to strip them of their wet shoes and socks; she brought towels and T-shirts and shorts. After she sent them to the bathroom to change, she called Penelope to say the children were safe at Innisfree and she would bring them home when the storm was over. Innisfree . . . as boldly as her sign swung in the battering storm, still she never called her home Inviolate. *If only freedom from sorrow were as simple as changing a name. . . .*

They sat together and ate chicken-salad sandwiches and watched the storm through the window overlooking the pond. There was no sound except the thunder and lightning and finally, a flash, and the lights went out. The house became even quieter. So quiet, the children felt the question before she even opened her mouth.

Still looking over the pond, Jeri asked them, "Have you seen the babies?"

They shared a grave look and did not know how to answer.

Jeri turned to them, and she had a peaceful sadness on her face. Sadness and peace, all at once. Kate replied, "Yes."

"How are they? Chris . . . all of them?" she asked and looked out on the pond. "What do they look like, the babies? Him or her?"

Kate put a hand on Mrs. Jones's shoulder. "They don't look like him or her. They are fine. All of them are fine."

"They don't look like him or her?"

"They are really pretty babies, but they don't look like him or her. To me, anyway."

Jeri looked over at Jack. He looked back at her and finally answered, "They are more like her than like him."

He paused, looking out on the lake, and finished, "Kiran looks just like her and Kris looks like both of them."

"What are their names?" Jeri tilted her face and concentrated.

Kate answered very somberly, "The girl's name is Kiran. It is Sanskrit. It means 'ray,' like of light, and the boy's name is Krishan which is like Lord Krishna, but they call him Kris like Chris. But with a 'K.' "

Jeri sat with her brows knit. The mention and discussion brought back a stack of loose lists, in every drawer, behind any cabinet door, under her pillow, wafted down from her desk. "He always wanted to name a baby Chris. He never out and said so, but he always did. I used to . . ." Jeri looked down at her knees. ". . . make lists." She chuckled softly. "We had a son named Jack. Did you know that?" She finished, "He died in the hospital, before we could bring him home."

They were quiet for the rest of the storm, watching it fade to rain and then brighten to a sunny afternoon. As Jeri drove them home up the long pond road, Kate looked back at the house and shouted, "Look, look!"

Jeri stopped the car and they all looked. A full rainbow arced over Quiet Pond and at its end Innisfree glowed like a pot of gold.

There was now a daily routine for the family of Chris Jones. In the morning, Gita rose at dawn after nursing the twins; she readied herself, and wrote for three hours. When her babies awoke she nursed them in the rocker on her front porch. On mornings when Chris could work from home, they ate on the porch as well, with the babies playing with their own and each other's fingers and toes on a blanket at the foot of the table. Those were the days at once peaceful and vibrant in their cottage covered in roses, far from the road and town. At 10 A.M. Gita plopped her children into a wide double stroller, kissed her husband good-bye, and took a walk that lasted hours. Every day, the three of them visited her best friend—truly her only friend—Penelope Broadus, and her lovely children, who watched for them from the garden, and then ran to greet them with swimmy, swimmy baby talk warm as melted goo. They sat on the front lawn in the bright sunshine, shading the babies in their shadows. On their way home, Gita, Krishan and Kiran stopped at the farmers' market. They went home, and she cooked dinner, and they ate it the way they ate breakfast. Outside, all together, peacefully, vibrantly, altogether. The best days of their lives. Bathe the babies, nurse the babies, put them to sleep, write some more, nurse the babies and sleep blissfully in the arms of her beloved. *These are the happiest days of my life.* Everyone in the cottage covered in roses was thinking this thought.

Shushed in the garden with the plants over his head, Jack approached his net box like an Indian would his traps. The butterflies flew in as though the box held the nectar of the gods. When he quietly closed the door, there were twenty butterflies fanning the air with their slow, slow wings.

He brought the box into the sunshine and lay down on his stomach with a sketch pad and a palette of oil pastels. By the time the noon sun was directly overhead, he had finished his drawing, and he signed it with "JB," which was his new way.

Kate watched through the screen door, and when the trap was safely shut, she quietly came out and lay on her stomach in the grass opposite Jack. "Can I draw them now?" she asked.

Jack passed over his pad and colors and climbed up on the step to sit and watch the sky. High clouds, hazy heat. He was trying to keep still. It was so hot, he wondered if there might be any respite. His mind turned to inventing a solution. He was inspired by immense discomfort. "Hey, hand me the book for a sec." Kate handed it up. Jack reached for a pen and made some notes, a drawing. He held his hands up around his skull and jotted down some approximate measures. He ripped out his page and handed back the book.

Standing abruptly, he announced, "I'm going into town. I want to check on something at Buttergreen's. I'll be back." Jack brushed off his jeans and walked away. Kate heard the gears in his head; she wondered what the rest of the day would hold. She turned her concentration to the slightest shift of pigment from indigo to purple. She rubbed the line in between his markings and smiled. She had shaded perfectly. A first. *Maybe it is a lucky day!*

Inside the net box, the butterflies began to switch twigs. In the flutter, they bumped and pushed, but when they landed they were serene, their wings opening and closing, slowly, slowly.

In the front, there was a shout of happy greeting. She looked up; it would be the twins with their naked thighs and socks on their feet. Standing, Kate thought to take the net box, because when they switched twigs the butterflies were marvelous to see.

From inside his basement lookout post, Del Musik watched with increasing indignation. It was happening every day. This one, with her bastard children born out of wedlock, prancing over, pushing them in a double-wide buggy.

"She nurses them on the front lawn," he growled at Euphoni.

"Under a blanket. And they were not born out of wedlock."

"You fail, as always, to see the point."

From the Book of Injustices

JULY 12, 2000

Unbelievable. Today she came to the house with a dish of some kind of desserts. She calls them "sweets"! She said she came to thank Euphoni for the gift!! For the gift? I came as close as I ever have to fully thrashing that woman. It is lucky she was not home. I dumped them in the trash and the whole house smelled of it. I had to remove the garbage and when I went outside to throw it out, they were laughing with their heads thrown back and their long necks exposed. They thought I ate it and that they got me. They thought I would not be able to resist, and they are surely expecting to hear soon that I have become violently ill. I am watching them through the window, and I am on to their trickery.

Del Musik has made a full-time job of watching through the windows. He has convinced himself that any moment those babies will have grown, and in their entitlement and laziness, they will rob him blind in his sleep. He has changed the locks; he has added dead bolts, here in a town where no one remembers where their house keys ever were. When he sees Gita on the street, he crosses to the other side. Gita doesn't even notice because while she walks, she sings to her babies in Malayalam and notices the color of the trees, the air, the shop signs around her.

JULY 14, 2000

Today I saw that jezebel in the open market. She was asking for strange peppers and she smelled like burned oil. She began to sing some songs in Arabic. I think someone should notify the authorities.

Euphoni has noticed that these days he forgets the name of the thing you use to wash yourself in the bath. It is white and shaped like . . . this.

It smells good, and when you use it you are clean. Soap? What are you saying woman? What are you talking to me about soap for? He sometimes wanders away in the middle of a rant. She has found him crying in the hallway upstairs. While she was at the market, he snipped the phone cords. He thinks she is plotting against him.

The babies slept curled together like puppies, and by the time Kate got to the front yard, it seemed that the butterflies too had drifted off to sleep with their wings in slim prayer.

"What do you have there?" Gita asked.

"It's Jack's butterfly trap. He draws them and he counts the variety of lepidoptera at different times of the year." Kate turned the box slowly and the butterflies did not awaken. "You should see. There are . . . maybe . . . six different kinds in this sampling alone."

"Wait until they open their wings." Penelope took the sketchbook from her daughter and proudly showed off their work.

From the Book of Injustices

JULY 15, 2000

They have set up camp in the yard yet again, but this time they have implements. . . . I cannot believe the introduction of this threat to our community. The half-breed children growing and socializing around here, the threat of future miscegenation . . . They have a box . . . and a book of . . . instructions. . . .

In town, Jack stares with minute focus at a shelf of small water bottles. In his basket he carries his designs, a set of plastic sheets, a small hose head, and his own baseball cap. It seems possible that he can attach specifically designed fan blades to the top of his cap and devise a hand pump to spray water that would then allow him to walk in a misty rain all day long. He does not even notice the passage of time.

The babies awaken in the curly adorable way of mammalian infants. First one, then the other, pushy pushy, rolly rolly, but only back and forth because the twins have not yet learned to flip over. They are only two months old. They are so fat it is almost indecent. When people see them with their skin the color of bright sunsets and their hair as black and shiny as rings of onyx, they exclaim in wonder and clamor to take them from their mommy, to shower them with kissy kissy, *boojjie, booojie*. Gita always obliges because they are so *wujubujubooju*, who wouldn't want to snuggle them to pieces?

The babies are enraptured with the fluttering wings of the butterflies trapped in the net box. There is the full spectrum of color inside; the babies kick their heels and stare wide-eyed. Perhaps they see nothing, perhaps they see it all.

When the show is over, they all go inside, for Gita would like to wash up the babies before they go shopping. They leave the butterflies outside where it is bright and sunny. It is bad enough to be trapped in a net box; let it at least be kept outside.

Del Musik watches them enter the house, and he knows the time is now or never. Their fate rests on his trembling, narrowed shoulders. He fears he may not be up to the challenge, but when he takes one last look between the blinds, he knows there is no limit to his power today. He takes the stairs two at a time and bolts past Euphoni who shouts after him, "What is WRONG?!"

"I AM A PATRIOT AND I WILL NOT FAIL." He slams the door and shoots across to Penelope's yard, where he takes only the quickest peek at her door before he grabs the box and the instructions, and races back to his driveway. Del Musik has never been so focused as he is at this moment of need. He sends up a prayer and throws open the door of his 1969 Plymouth Swinger that sits at the ready, key in ignition. In all his paranoia, he has forgotten that his beloved car sits at the ready, key in ignition, just as it always has since 1969. Today, he is most grateful for the presence of keys. He throws the net box into the passenger seat and tears out of the driveway. He has to beat her into town. He has to beat her into town.

Gita, Krishan and Kiran kiss Auntie Penelope good-bye and proceed into town at a brisk clip, for they have lingered longer than usual and it is almost time for Daddy to come home.

Del Musik has gotten lost. He sits on the side of Weathervane Drive pouting and scared. *Where am I . . . where am I?* When he looks at the box, he sees the slow beating of butterfly wings, but they look like paper and wires. He hears a gentle ticking in his mind. The rhythm of the wings takes on a cadence of counting . . . counting down. The device is elegant in its simplicity. A wooden frame nailed together without even a mitered corner. Fine, clear netting to hold the guts of the machine. Del Musik feels his panic rising, but also his courage. He starts the car again and with a rebel yell, he guns his engine. "GOD WILL RIGHT MY COURSE. TO TOWN! TO TOWN!" They reach town at almost the same moment.

Jack, his face lit with his new project, has exited Buttergreen's with wild energy. He runs with his packages before him, he can barely see the road, but in the very slight breeze, he smells Gita's most lovely scent. He looks up on instinct and grins. He speeds his pace. Gita sees him and smiles. From so far away, he can see the brilliant flash of her teeth and it only makes him run faster. She waves, and looks to cross the street to greet him.

Jack runs with superhuman speed and calls out, "GITA! LOOK WHAT I'M GONNA MAKE!" But she cannot hear him, and anyway, by now, she is standing in the middle of the road. She stops where she is and calls back, "What?" Of course, it is a small town, and the roads are very safe to pause on. . . .

Up over the hill into town, Del Musik is driving like a maniac because the butterflies have begun to flutter madly. In the buzz of their wings, he believes he is about to die, but he doesn't care. *If I manage to get to the authorities, they will know about the goings-on here in town. If I die first . . .* He pushes the net box hard away; he is afraid. But it is too late, it is too late, he has set it off. An arm on the box comes loose and the butterflies escape their cage; in their fright and freedom they flap and flutter against his face, his neck, his arms. He is enveloped in their furious effort to get out.

"AAAAAAAAA!" Del Musik lets go of the wheel and steps harder on the gas as he stands up in his seat; he tries to escape the car himself, but he is locked in. He does not remember how to get out.

In the middle of the road, Gita hears the car and turns her head to the right. Her eyes widen and she begins to run, but there is, in the middle of the road, a hole only a few inches wide and a few inches deep, but it is enough to catch her foot and she slips. Holding the handle of her double stroller, she turns to the right again and sees the car is only a foot away. It is so large in her eyes she can only see the grille and nothing else. She lets go of her babies with a tremendous push and falls. Jack has long ago dropped his bags; he reaches out as she pushes and he pulls the stroller out of the road. The babies are lifted off the ground by his bionic force. He sets them down on the sidewalk as the town comes running forward, screaming, crying, calling on their phones, 9-1-1, 9-1-1. It is too late. It is too late to pull her forward as he had the babies. It is too late. Maybe she didn't even see that Jack had saved her children. She might have gone thinking they were going too.

He cannot lift her head onto his lap, because it is crushed. There is nothing to lift. Looking down, he sees her bloody foot trapped in a hole in the road. Jack sits in a puddle of blood. When Penelope arrives screaming and clawing through the screaming and crying crowd, she finds him rocking back and forth wrenched tight with sobs. There is nothing to do but pray.

Chris, who had nothing, and then had something, and then had everything, sometimes sat on the porch of his home long after the moon was risen high in the sky. He did not put his babies down, even when the nights were chilly. Instead, he wrapped them in bundles and strapped them close to his chest. How long would it take them to drink from a bottle with satisfaction? They lost a little weight. The doctor said sometimes it happened in a traumatic transition from the breast.

After the beginning, when they were there all the time, the family of Dr. Raman Nair came in waves, never all at once, for it overwhelmed Chris into silence and they wanted him to talk and to cry. Sometimes he took his babies and walked in circles outside. Even Jaya Nair, who knew everything, knew nothing about this. She watched from the window and worried her fingernails. Dr. Raman Nair had let Chris bury her, though it was not the custom. He feared the man might die if there was no place to visit her where she had been laid intact. He himself was so sad; there was no more fight in him. From the time his sister died, Dr. Raman Nair was a changed man. Gentle in speech and gesture, accepting of all things, full of appreciation for the simple existence of everything that managed to remain alive.

Though they tried never to leave him alone, Chris was an alone man, but for his greatest love. He sat on the porch step every night, wrapped in his twins, looking out into the woods, breathing the honeysuckle and unable to weep.

On the evening in August when the moon was full, he sat on the porch as he always did. The moonlight was so bright he could see the leaves and sticks of the forest floor. Through the woods he saw something move, upright and graceful. He mentioned to his sleeping babies snuggled hot to his chest, "A deer is coming, do you want to see?"

Into the clearing, someone was walking, nondescript, a child or an adult, a man or a woman, he could not tell in the silver night. It stopped and stood still.

"Chris?" It was Jeri, wrapped in a sweater against the night chill.

Chris stood up and leaned forward, unsure. "Jeri?"

He hugged the babies strapped to his chest. "Jeri." He sat down. "Did you walk all this way?" He patted his hand on the step and she sat beside him.

Side by side, they stared out into the woods. There was nothing to say that they did not already know.

Acknowledgments

This book is the result of so many tears and so much prayer, sometimes I felt I might drown in them and then rise straight to heaven. I doubt if I would have had the courage to do it on my own. To that end, I would like to thank Tom Nash, who read every word ten thousand times and always told the truth, even when I was a real pain, first for his friendship and assistance, and second for letting me use his lovely poem "Sandlot" for this novel; and Dee Schneidman, who read and cheered and read and cheered. My gratitude to you both is deep and forever; I will do anything for either of you, always. I would like to thank my whole family, who always indulge me because I am *precious and delicate*, but especially my mother, Chandramathi, for her unfailing support of this endeavor and for saying these priceless words: "It is a beautiful book." When you said that, I thought maybe it might be okay; and my husband, Brett, who took care of me while I pursued this dream—thank you, I could not have managed without you. I would like to thank Sally Wofford-Girand, who read my eight-hundred-page manuscript and took me on anyway; and Karyn Marcus, whose editorial vision was perfect. I am a lucky girl to have been found by such keenly sensitive women. And finally, I am enormously grateful to all my friends who read this book three-hole punched in a binder, stuffed in a folder, stapled, paper clipped, or piled in a loose, tatty stack. You will never know how I hung on your words of praise. Thank you.